CW00547925

WHY READERS
YOU THINK YOU KNOW ....

'**Impressive** debut'

'Beautifully paced. It settles you in so you think you know what's happening, then **it turns the world upside down**, again and again.'

'Crafted to perfection. **A very clever book.'**

'**A real page turner**, I defy you to put it down.'

'The **best** new-thriller **writer** of this millennium.'

'A solid, **exciting story**, full of twists, turns and misdirections'

'It completely **subverted my expectations'**

'**Fast-paced,** exciting'

'It is scintillating - **and a joy to read.** Why aren't all books as well written as this?'

'The words flow effortlessly across your eyes – **a real delight'**

'Brilliant. I loved it. **Best read for ages.'**

TO JO
Carry on being BRILLIANT

YOU THINK YOU KNOW SOMEONE

With best wishes,
ENJOY !

Holman
J B

J.B. HOLMAN

SO
15

SO15 Books

First published in Great Britain by SO15 Books
Copyright © 2019 J.B. Holman

This e-book edition 2019

1

J. B. Holman asserts the moral right to
be identified as the author of this work.

A catalogue record for this book
is available from the British Library.

ISBN: 9781916064508 (PB b-format)

This novel is entirely a work of fiction.

The names, characters, and incidents portrayed in it are the work of author's imagination. Any resemblance to actual persons, living or dead, events or localities is entirely coincidental.

For more information visit www.so15books.co.uk

In memory of Helena

(She's not dead. I just haven't seen her for a while)

CHAPTER ZERO

D arkness had fallen. The rain was light, the breeze negligible. He lay on the roof, fifteen storeys up, motionless. Intent. Focused on the back door of London's top five-star hotel, just visible between the tall buildings, 1,247 metres away.

He aimed and he waited.

The door opened, the security light clicked on, the target was illuminated. He squinted through the telescope; sniper and gun became one.

The Prime Minister had avoided the front door - no time for demonstrators or photo-journalists tonight. He strode out onto the wide marble step and stood vulnerable to the night.

Sheltering from the drizzle, he waited for the car door to be opened and breathed in the fresh cold air.

Target locked, aim secured, the highly trained finger pressed firmly against the precision-engineered trigger. Two bullets cracked through the air.

Job done.

∼

Two years earlier, in a small provincial town, Julie Connor sat alone on her sofa and cried. Her book fell limp in her hands, tears blurred the words. She felt the hurt.

'Why do you do that?' she said quietly to the men in her book.

'Why?' she said to the men in her life.

Her sighs filled the emptiness. She read on, sobbing raw emotion across Thomas Hardy's penultimate page. *Tess of the d'Urbervilles* had been a bad choice. She rested her eyes remorsefully on the unrepentant words, as ever, a reluctant victim, before flicking to the final page. *'I'm through with men.'* Her thoughts mingled with her reading. *'I don't need you, any of you, not now, not ever. Not again.'* Hardy's final words flowed hesitantly across her eyes. Heartbreak flowed unceasingly across her mind.

She looked up; her gaze resting on his picture. He was smiling. She was not.

It was quiet, deathly quiet.

The flat felt uncommonly silent, eerily empty. She wondered if empty was better than hurt. She rubbed her bruises, nursed her cuts and winced. Her eyes slid down the last page, cautiously, slowly, delaying the inevitable end. That had too often been her habit: cautiously and slowly delaying the inevitable end. She read on until there were no more words to read.

Her exhalation was as deep as her sorrow as she closed the book as gently as she would the lid of a coffin. She placed *Tess* carefully on the floor beside her, dropped her head in her hands and wept.

'I can do this,' she said, with all the conviction she wished she had. 'I can do this.'

'Can't I?'

BRIGHTON LANES

'I'm Peter Jones'

'And I'm Amanda May Hewitt.'

'We will be presenting News Today at the top of the hour. Stay with us to hear the latest on the Prime Minister shooting – we have new developments.'

'Brexit – negotiations continue as we look at a profile of the Deputy Prime Minister as leader of the country.'

'And how, what your grandparents did in World War II affects this year's population census.'

'All that and much more'

'Join us in fifteen minutes.'

The television in the Ploughman's Bar on Saltash Street spoke quietly, as students shared earnest conversation about the way the world should be, elderly tourists dithered over crumpled maps in dog-eared guide books and the locals hunkered down at their favoured tables in their favourite corners and let the world spin by.

Half a mile away, Sam Stone stood in the shadows of a disused doorway, watching the world wind its way through the bustling historic Brighton Lanes. Passers-by twisted and turned down the cobbled paths, past trendy cafés that emitted smells of coffee and all things organic, and past bars that exuded jazz and bearded men. This was the centre of Brighton's old town.

Brighton Lanes was bohemian - a haven from the world outside, a place to lose yourself in creative shops and quaint coffee corners, designer jewellery and contemporary art, alternative therapies, independent boutiques, buskers, bric-a-brac, burlesque, embroidery and bars. It was night, but the darkness was dazed by a rainbow of mellow lights from shop windows, candle-lit tables and street performers. He stood in the doorway and watched. It was time.

Slipping his six foot four frame into the gentle flow of passing people, he melded in, unobtrusive, unobserved - just as he had been trained.

He walked and watched. He liked Brighton. It was eclectic. Young couples on first dates snuggling past pairs of senior citizens holding hands as they strolled through the night air. Men walked along hand in hand, women kissed each other romantically in the corners of bars. It was a world of mixed cultures, mixed race, mixed ages, and a mix of a myriad proclivities mingling harmoniously in a microcosm of a perfect Britain. This is what he'd fought for.

This is what his friends had died for - the right to have a country of simplicity and peace, where old mixed with young, straight with gay, affluence with alternative, money with mad-eyed moon-shadow dream catchers: all safe, happy, harmonious. And that is how he needed to keep it.

He was no longer Special Forces, not even military, but his values lived on. Justice was what mattered more than anything. Anyone who threatened that was an enemy of the State and, by definition, an enemy of his.

He made his way along alleys, through twisting twittens and cut through cobbled cat-creeps, across the uneven paving of eighteenth-century pavements. He stuck to the dark side of the street.

A posse of laughing students passed him by; two boys, three girls, two with too much make-up and one with glasses. One boy was five foot ten, the other six foot, but harmless, all intent on enjoying the night. The lane split ahead of him. At the end of the left fork, two policemen stood talking. Two policemen so close together was a rare sight in Brighton. He took the right fork, passed a man with a well-trimmed moustache and a lady dressed in Chanel and a hurry. He weaved his way past a pub that overspilled its walls with happy cackling customers; he smelt Benson and

Hedges Light and a menthol brand he didn't recognise. He took a left down Lovett's Lane and a right up Market Meddles, the crowds thinning now as he headed for the main road and the edge of the Lanes.

He spun round, ahead of him he saw the silhouette of an armed policeman, gun clearly visible, a sight never seen in Brighton.

He retraced his steps. Tonight was not a night for fronting out an officer of the law. He kept his profile low, as he sloped his way up the slopes of Moran's Rise towards the top of the Lanes. He passed Finnegan's Whiskey World and took a left down Little Lane. There was no one now. Ten seconds later, he emerged onto the main road.

He stopped on the corner, leant against the wall as if checking his phone and peered nonchalantly to his right and left. To his left, there was a police car fifty yards down the road, the occupants pre-occupied by a bevy of mini-skirts filled with smiles and bosoms. To his right, nothing but darkness, street lights and parked cars.

He put his phone in his pocket ready to cross the road, but froze into the darkness as he heard the clicking clacking of high heeled shoes to his left. A lady had come from nowhere and was walking up the road towards him. He snuck back into the shadows, waited and watched. She was elegant and tall, statuesque as she strode towards his place of hiding. Her blonde hair, a wig maybe, glinted as it swayed in the reflection of shop lights. Green ruffled dress, false nails on long fingers gripping a large holdall bag; stockings, high heels and confidence strutted past him as she walked on up the hill towards the darkness, round the corner and out of sight. He checked again. He was alone.

He crossed the road, invisible to the world, left the Lanes and lightly sprang up the long steps that headed to the south end of Saltash Street.

He could see his Vauxhall Astra, but hesitated: the lights of the Ploughman's Bar beckoned him in. He needed a drink, another drink; not to calm his nerves, but to steel them. He took a stool at the end of the bar.

'Now it's time to join Peter Jones and Amanda May Hewitt in the Newsroom.' As the familiar theme tune played, he caught the barman's eye.

'Whiskey, a double. That one, the Finnegan's. And a beer, please mate.'

'Tonight's top story. The London sniper and the shooting dead of . . .'

'And can you change the channel, mate? I think we're all sick of the

Prime Minister story. They don't know anything and haven't got anything new to say.'

'No,' piped up one of the students, 'they say there are new developments. We want to listen.' Sam Stone let it pass, shook his head and sipped the head off his beer.

'We heard an hour ago that the police have the name of a man they want to interview in connection with yesterday's shooting. An inside source said they know the identity of the suspect, but are not in a position to release it to the public. However, the focus of the search has turned to Brighton, where they believe the suspect is in hiding. The public are asked to be cautious and not to approach anyone suspicious, but to come forward if they have any information.'

'See!' said the student as he turned to speak to the man at the end of the bar. 'I told you there were new developments.' But, all he saw was a solitary bar stool, an undrunk beer and an empty whiskey glass.

The man had gone.

Sam Stone turned the key in the ignition, put the Vauxhall Astra into gear and gently pressed the throttle. His foot was steady, but his head was light. The whiskey, on top of the earlier ones, told him that driving was not a good idea. He took a left at the top of the road, drove another hundred yards, caught a glimpse, stopped by the kerb just before Five Ways Circus and smiled.

The blonde with the green ruffled dress and the confident stride was walking down the other side of the road, less sure-footed now. He waited and watched as she approached, hobbling, heel broken. He turned to look. Her whole gait had changed. Hip-swinging had been abandoned for a clunky clumping sexless stomp. Was it shadow of the night or was that mud up the length of her dress? Was she alright? The tall one-shoed figure drew closer. The walk was solid, the walk was unmistakable - the walk was a man. She was a he and he was struggling in a single high heel. *Brighton, god bless you.*

She approached a lamp post and leant on it, took off her blonde wig and stashed it in the holdall she was carrying. She had definitely fallen - or been pushed. Even Brighton had bigots. She stomped on, up to Five Ways

Circus, ignored the sarcastic wolf whistles from the pub opposite and crossed the road, temporarily out of sight.

A man, mean faced, muscular and tattooed, put down his drink on the pavement and nudged the reprobate next to him. Nods of covert hostility and the malice of shared glances indicated immoral intention. Sam read the situation, stood behind his open car door and looked directly at the roughage of men. His six foot four was a warning of caution.

A short sharp whistle summoned a third man with similar tattoos and short, shaven hair. He looked across the road, saw the transvestite stumbling in a dress, then turned to see Sam standing by his car. He caught Sam's eye, almost deliberately. His face said, 'Not your business, back down.' Sam stood there. He was a warning; a warning that was being ignored.

The transvestite came into view across the Circus. She hadn't turned left, as Sam thought she might, nor had she gone straight, along North Brighton Road. She was heading for the fifth way, the alley, the lane. It was Raper's Hide, a wide cobbled walkway, a spur that had grown north out of the Lanes, but there were no shops, no bars, no cafés, no anything. It was bordered on one side by the bleak black back of a big hotel and on the other by the hill and the tall walls of various warehouses and council storage buildings. It was wide enough for a horse and cart and lit by the original gas lights. It slowly swung its way round through twists and curves to duck down under the North Brighton Road and eventually to join the top end of the Lanes. It was a shortcut to nowhere and made little or no sense as a route to anywhere. The transvestite entered blindly to be enveloped by the gas-lit darkness.

The third man ducked into a pub-side alleyway and emerged a moment later with a shaft of wood. He joined the other two, heading with increasing hostility across the road. They looked around, straight at the Astra. A taunting, single digit was raised to Sam in defiance, before they dived headlong into the darkness. Sam's whiskey head gave him a spin. He made a long slow blink and sat back into the Astra.

Leave it, he said to himself. *Walk away. Keep a low profile, keep out of trouble, especially tonight.* But he couldn't. He knew it was a bad decision; *Fuck it! Not on my watch.* It was the look the guy had given him, it was the finger; he was hooked into it. He clicked the engine into life, drove across Five Ways Circus, heading for the darkness of Raper's Hide, but pillars prevented vehicular access. He yanked the car up on the kerb, leapt out and ran into the dimly lit alley.

There was no one.

Then he heard it, the sounds of menace. He ran full tilt ahead of him, down the alley, past the dim streetlights, past the railings high to his left, past the smell of hotel detritus to the right and round the first bend. It was about to kick off. The three guys, heavy, menacing and muscular formed a semi-circle of aggression in a stance of impending attack. The transvestite wasn't running away, she was running towards them, arms flailing. A whack of the stick just missed her, a warning of what was to come. She tripped over her own heel and slithered across the cobbles.

'We're taking you down, Lady-boy,' said one. Two fists and a fence post approached the petrified transvestite who was scrabbling to her feet. It was now or never. The guys were tough, they were serious. Sam sensed the danger.

'Hello darling,' he shouted, raised to his full six foot four. 'Are these men friends of yours?'

'Fuck off, mate! Not your business,' spat one of them.

'Yes, it is.'

'Your choice,' said the man with the pickaxe handle, as he swung it violently at Sam's head.

Sam was fast and agile. He grabbed the wooden shaft, moved into the attack and the man was down. Two punches later, he was out. Sam advanced on the two threats remaining. Fists flew. Sam's knuckles connected hard and fast on the face of one, as the fist of the other caught Sam's lip. Blood spattered the nearby wall. Sam went in hard. More punches added to the mess of blood and teeth that teetered backwards in front of him. A body blow and a final punch and the second man went down.

The third stood and faced him. A knife, glinting in the half-light was thrust hard towards Sam's abdomen. Sam's instincts kicked in, martial arts took over. The knife flew free, the man's arm snapped, his body flew through the air, then landed crumpled and broken against the wall. He groaned, slipped down and moaned, motionless.

Sam span round to check for threat. There was none. He had won.

'You don't mess, with the SAS!' he said, more to himself than anyone else. He turned to the quaking victim, 'You alright?'

'Umm. I . . . you . . . er . . .'

'Get your bag. We gotta go. Where you heading?'

'The station. London.'

'I'll give you a lift.' She just stood there. 'Come. Quick. Get your bag. We've got to get out of here before these gay-bashing bastards wake up.'

'Yes, sorry,' she said, retuning into reality. 'I'm with you.' She turned her back on Sam, disappearing round the corner, to emerge twenty seconds later with her bag. Sam was walking away, towards the car, looking for the knife. He found it, picked it up and kept on walking. When he turned, he saw the transvestite way back, standing by the motionless bodies. She saw her saviour look back and she spat on her assailants.

'Coming,' she said, as she hurriedly hobbled awkwardly, heel broken, in apparent shock. Sam waited. The two of them faced each other, but before either could speak, a voice broke out above them.

'I saw what you did.' It was the benign and croaking voice of an elderly, dog-walking lady. Her face peered over the railings twelve feet above them and the head of a Scottish Terrier peered out by her feet.

'Scruffy! Get back here, I don't want you to fall,' she commanded. 'You were very brave. If you need a witness, just ask. I live round the corner, 64 Primrose Hill Road. I'm always in, except twice a day out with Scruffy and church on Sunday, asking for forgiveness. People like that don't deserve forgiveness. If anyone asks, I'll tell them.'

'Er yes, thank you madam, very kind. Thank you,' and she was gone.

'Come on,' said Sam, 'get in the car.'

'Do you mind if I sit in the back? I really need to lie down.'

'Whatever!' he said, in a loud whisper. 'Just get in the fucking car!'

And that was it; in that one second, as she stepped into the back seat, their mutual fate was sealed.

Once clear of the danger zone, Sam exhaled deeply, threw the knife on the car floor and swore under his breath.

'Jesus! That was a bit hairy. Hairier than a badger's arse in winter.'

'Oh my god. Yes it was, it was.' The voice in the back was flustered, still in apparent panic. It was sounds more than words.

'Bastards like that, they should be locked up and have their testicles put where their spectacles should be.'

'You were very brave . . . like that lady said.'

'Yes, I've been thinking about her . . .'

'You saved me. I can't thank you enough.' They drove, in darkness, two strangers in the night. 'Thank you. You're an angel.'

Sam reflected on his last twenty-four hours and shook his head.

'Yes, I am,' he said at last, adding almost silently under his breath, 'an angel of death.'

2

FLY BOY

In Whitehall, deep in the building across the way from No 10, rooms were dark, corridors were quiet, desks were empty and phones were silent. This was the home of the Special Security Service, the Prime Minister's own protection and anti-terrorist force, and for the last twenty-four hours the building had been in embarrassment and turmoil. But now, at four minutes to eleven, only the Ops Room in the basement had life in it; and a single room on the fourth floor.

This was the Sceptre Room. It had long heavy drapes, tired wood panelling and high Westminster windows overlooking St James' Park. Three men had arrived. Two chatted. The other, a dishevelled man in his fifties, sat in dower gloom at the far end of the table. His name was Brekkenfield, Head of Operations. He was not on form; he closed his eyes to the puerile banality.

'No, said the old lady, you don't spell it W-O-O-M or W-H-U-M, you spell it W–O–M-B,' prattled Jai McReady, Head of IT and Encryption. 'And then one of the African boys turns to her and says: Madame, I doubt you've ever heard a hippo fart, let alone know how to spell it!'

He burst into self-generated laughter. Brekkenfield shook his head in disapproval and muttered '*Inappropriate*', under his breath. Hoy, the intended target of McReady's story, smiled politely.

Hoy was Head of Investigations and still in his thirties; neat hair, good suit, no tie. Investigations was a small but prestigious department, and for him it was an invaluable two-year secondment in his fast track career in Special Branch. He'd done six years with the Met, two with the FBI, one in close protection and five more working his way up the ranks of OS-12. He'd been with SSS for just seven months and the Commander liked him.

Brekkenfield, the curmudgeon, didn't like anyone. Operations was the largest and most powerful department within SSS. He had a history of controlling it with passion and a titanium fist, but tonight he was in mourning and just wanted to be in bed. He sat, detached from the younger two men. His skin was pale and flaccid, his jowls drooped and his spark had gone; that's what three weeks in hospital would do even to the fittest of men. He had come out that morning under strict medical instructions to take a full month off.

The door opened. In strode the Commander. Tall, slim and gristly, a man of bone, muscle and discipline. Though in his early sixties, he was happier in fatigues than a suit and in Hereford or the Highlands than Westminster and Whitehall. His preference would be a bivouac in Iraq or a dugout in the Falklands rather than an office in London, but this was his duty and he would do it to the best of his abilities. His name was Storrington. He looked around the table.

'Where's Flyboy?'

'Parking his jet, probably,' said Jai, the jocular computer geek, 'where every-one can see it. He thinks he's so sophisticated. And what's with the whole hand-shaking thing? We're not French.'

Commander Storrington ignored the prattle, stood by the window and looked out, not for the missing man but at the night-shrouded world he was beholden to protect.

They sat waiting for Nickolas Morgan-Tenby. He'd been an RAF fast jet pilot many years before. He was not born double-barrelled, he added the hyphen himself; an affectation adopted by him and neglected by others. Big Ben struck eleven, the door opened. Tenby smiled and entered.

'Not late, am I?' He shook hands round the table.

'*Bonjour*,' said Jai, to be met by the disapproving eyes of Storrington.

'We lost our man yesterday and I want the killer. No smiles, no jokes, no leave and no excuses until I get him. Understood? Now, Brekkenfield, how are you?'

'Alive and present, sir.'

Storrington scanned the room and surveyed his senior team, now sat sombre around a board table, as large as it was old. Brekkenfield was Navy and hard as nails; Tenby was Air Force and had achieved through charm; Storrington was Army through to the core; Hoy was constabulary and Jai was nothing, just a civvie-street technician. He needed them to work as a team.

'This is a crisis. We need action and we need results. The police say it was ISIS. Do we agree?'

'No, sir. It was not ISIS,' said Hoy, as Head of Investigations.

'Then what led the police to think it was?'

'That would be me, sir,' said Hoy. 'I told them it was Al Akbar J'zecr, a known threat. They'll get him. Good for public confidence.'

'But it wasn't him?'

'No, sir.'

'Are you sure?'

'Yes, sir.'

'So we're back at square one. We need to know who did this.'

'I *do* know who did it,' continued Hoy.

'You know?'

'Yes, sir.'

'Who?'

'Eduard Foxx. That's with a u and a double x.'

'Edward Fox?'

'Yes, sir, Eduard Foxx. Of course, that's not his real name. That's just the name he goes under.'

'Why do I know that name?' Hoy looked firmly at Tenby.

'Because he works for us . . . for me. He's one of my tacticians in the Tactical Planning Department,' said Tenby reluctantly. 'He's one of my agents.'

'Jesus Christ, man! What's the matter with you? We've got one of our own running rogue with a sniper rifle?'

'We have the rifle,' said Hoy.

'Do we have the man?'

'No, sir,' said Brekkenfield from the gloom of his table end. 'Two of our agents staked out his flat. One saw him enter the building, the other saw him enter his flat.'

'Why didn't they grab him?'

'Because we didn't want two dead agents. He killed eight prison guards when he was tied up in an Azerbaijani prison, and four policemen in Georgia - while sedated on drugs.'

'So send in a team.'

'We did, sir. We stormed his flat. It only has one door in and the same door out, but when we got there he was gone; cup of tea still steaming.'

'How?'

'Vanished into thin air.'

'Really?' It wasn't a question that needed an answer. 'What's his real name?'

'Dunno, sir.'

'He works for us?'

'Yes, sir,' replied Brekkenfield.

'Then look in his HR file!'

'Did that,' chimed in Hoy.

'And?'

'Nothing.'

'What do you mean, *nothing*?'

'There's nothing in it It's wiped, gone, empty, clean. Nothing.'

Storrington threw a look at Jai the joker in the pack and asked him, 'What about the Security Database, it has to be on that?'

'No, he wiped that too,' confessed Jai, no longer feeling the humour in life.

'I thought that was impossible.'

'So did we, sir. My team encrypted all the files and made access impossible.'

'So it *is* impossible?'

'Apparently not.'

'Back-up?'

'Unfortunately not.'

Storrington gave a long withering look at the rapidly diminishing computer man. 'So we have no computer records of any sort about Foxx; he's wiped them all?'

'Yes, sir.'

'And no one in the whole building knows his real name?'

'No, sir.'

'So we lost him?'

'Maybe. Maybe not,' continued Hoy. 'A transport bobby thinks he saw him boarding a train for Brighton. Well, he thinks he saw him, but well, you see . . .'

'No, I don't see. He's gone. Find him. And when you do, kill him. . . . and do it fast, before any more innocent people get hurt. Meeting closed. Reconvene tomorrow 17.00 hours.

Brekkenfield, thank you. Stay home. We'll keep you informed.

Hoy, in my office ten minutes.

Jai, clear your desk. Do it now. Security will escort you out.

You're fired.'

Hoy sat in a darkened room, gazing through the night as he waited for his phone to connect. It rang. A sleepy voice answered.

'Sorry, love, did I wake you?'

'You know you did,' said a soft female voice, 'but as Karl Marx said, *It's alright I had to get up to answer the phone anyway.*'

'Karl Marx?'

'Maybe it was Groucho Marx, and on the subject of grouchy, why are you phoning me not cuddling me?'

'It's just a Stevie Wonder call.'

'What?'

'I just called to say I love you.'

'You must be feeling guilty. What brought that on, my little Inspector Clouseau?'

'I just had a meeting with the team and I looked round the room and felt lucky. Jai just got fired! *Bing-bang-bosh* and out of the door.'

'Well, he always was a prat. What did he do?'

'Long story, but the point is, Jai has no wife; Brekkenfield, who was looking half-dead poor guy, has a wife but separate lives; same house, but a thousand miles apart. The boss, well you know about his wife, and Tenby, he has a wife and she is lovely and all that, and a looker, but is as dim as a duck with no head; and I have you. You're beautiful, loving, funny and smart. I'm a lucky guy.

'What do you mean she is *lovely and all that*? So you think she is *a looker*?' she said in mock jealousy, ignoring the Stevie Wonder of his call.

'Clearly not up to your standards, but most men would consider she had a certain aesthetic appeal. Y'know if you like slim hips, long legs and a full set of curves,' he said, teasing back. 'But that's Tenby all over. It's all about appearance with him. He's a superior son of a bitch. Gets a dumb wife, so he looks smarter. Last week, she asked him why they had to choose a new pope when the old one dies . . . why doesn't his son take over! Then she thought the black smoke and the white smoke were from burning the old pope. Thing is, he tells these stories about her with pride, like he likes it. More than that, he tells them in front of her. Bad form.'

'I don't know what she sees in him. He's a man of hidden shallows - paunchy, rude and twice her age.'

'Money; inherited just short of forty million. Oh, gotta go,' said Hoy abruptly as his phone vibrated. 'The boss is after me. We've got an incident in Brighton and . . . I'll see you later.'

'You *do* know the last train to London left over an hour ago, don't you?' said Sam.

'I'll wait for the milk train in the morning. I'm fine.'

'Really? Because you look like a seventy-year-old scrotum after a ball-slapping party. When did you last sleep – or are you on drugs?'

'No drugs, sir, but no sleep either.'

Sam took the main route to the station. There was a roadblock ahead. The police were checking cars. The dazed passenger watched from the back seat. Sam took a right and weaved his way through backstreets towards the station. Again, he saw blue lights ahead and avoided them.

'You don't like police then?' The driver didn't reply. He took a left to find another route. He circled the centre of Brighton – more police. There was no way to the station that was not impeded by the boys in blue. He turned and headed for his flat - five miles away in Hove.

What to do with his passenger? He should never have rescued her. They both felt the awkwardness. They were both thinking: *What now?*

They drove. They talked.

'Where did you learn to fight like that?'

'In the forces.'

'Are you still serving?'

'No, but I loved it. I was happier than a boy touching his first vagina.'

'So, why did you leave?'

'Me and Her Majesty's Government fell out over two bottles of Irish whiskey, one asshole of a colonel and the best punch I've ever thrown. I miss it, but I don't regret teaching that arrogant bastard a lesson.'

'Look, I am going up to London in the morning,' he said, as he stopped the car outside his flat. 'Tell you what, let's go up now. How does that sound?' It wasn't a choice.

'No, really, I couldn't ask you to do that. Just drop me at the station. I'll be fine.'

Sam's tone changed. His whole countenance transformed from Samaritan to Samurai. This was not a discussion.

'Don't argue. You've seen what happens to people who argue with me.'

Then he smiled. It was a joke . . .

Probably.

3

THE ASTRA

The car was quiet, dark and cold. It smelt of earth and kitbags, but for now it was the cocoon that kept her safe. How had this happened to her?

Yesterday life had worked. But, last night had been a nightmare. The club had been OK, she'd gone there because she didn't have anywhere else to go, but it hadn't ended well. She'd arrived alone and should've left alone. Mistake. Never trust a man with a head full of coke. And the alley – she hadn't expected that, nor a guy to turn up out of nowhere and save her, then offer her a lift all the way to London. But he was hardly a hero - there was something not right about him, too anxious, conflicted, danger-ous; and whiskey on his breath, but she was hardly in a position to argue.

She lay on the back seat of the car, head on bag, knees tucked up, dress pulled over cold shoeless feet, waiting obediently outside her saviour's flat, wondering. Time slid by, sleep evaded her. She leant forward and flicked on the radio.

Easy listening slipped uneasily into her ears.

'This is 99.2 BBC Brighton Rock. Thank you for listening. More of your soft rock favourites after the news. Now over to Paddy McCarthy in the BBC Sussex newsroom.'

'Two men are dead and one is in a serious condition after a senseless and violent attack in a backstreet in Brighton. Police reports indicate that *the three men had been drinking in a nearby pub and were walking towards Brighton's old town when they were savagely attacked in Raper's Hide just under North Brighton Road. Cause of death is as yet unknown. Police are looking for a black or dark blue Vauxhall Astra and appealing for witnesses.*

We will keep you up to date on this breaking story as we have it.'

'Oh my god!' she said out loud. She grabbed her bag and got out of the car.

'Get back in!' said an approaching voice that was six foot four tall.

'No. I'm fine. I've changed my mind. I'll walk. Thank you.'

'Get – in – the – car.' The voice was cold and steely and not to be disobeyed. 'Now!'

Her saviour closed the door firmly behind her and got into the driver's seat. There was a click as he engaged the child lock. The passenger was now a prisoner. 'Just for your safety,' he said as he started the engine and pulled away. 'You've been listening to the radio. So you heard the news then?'

'No,' she lied and crumbled, 'I mean yes. Yes I did. I heard it. They're dead. Those men are dead. You . . .'

'Me? What makes you think I killed them? No, we're in the clear, but we'd better leave Brighton for a while. Keep cool. We're a team now. Get some sleep. Everything will be fine.'

'But they're dead. I mean . . . that's bad. Really bad.'

'But not my bad, not my problem. They're scum; gay-bashing thugs. They deserved to die.'

There was silence from the back of the car – a long, heavy silence. She lay in thought. She lay in darkness. She lay at the mercy of a man called Sam, a good Samaritan, trapped by his kindness; too tired to run, too dire to stay. What to do?

'You wanted to see me?' said Hoy, to the towering figure of Commander Storrington.

'Eduard Foxx: is he mad, in the pay of the Russians, converted to ISIS?'

'None of those. I asked around. He's an oddball, a one man operation, but not mad, not a communist and not easily swayed. According to everyone, he seems to be a stand-up guy.'

'For an assassin.'

'No, what I mean is everyone says he's principled, a straight arrow. Is in the job because he signed up to the cause, believes in Britain and what it stands for.

He's not a sheep, definitely not a follower. If he did it, and I'm sure he did, then it was because he believed it was right. The PM pissed off a lot of people, y'know, especially in the Security Community. His Brexit stance will leave us wide open. We'll be outside Europol with no access to their intelligence, while opening up our military intelligence to them through the Defence Deal. Even I think it's madness. The first role of a Prime Minister is defence of the realm. Palmer let us down. I guess Foxx sees him as an evil in our midst and felt he had to take action. If someone had shot Hitler in 1938, the world would have been a better place.'

'Are you saying Palmer is like Hitler?'

'No, not Hitler, but . . . but I know that you share that view. You spoke about it at a closed meeting last week, and discussed it with two of the Chiefs afterwards, confidentially. The PM's strategy is seen as bad for the security of this country, Foxx was hired to safeguard the security of this country – and in his mind, that's exactly what he did.'

'How do you know my views? How do you know what I said at closed meetings and who I met afterwards?'

'I am an investigator, sir.' Storrington was expressionless.

'Tomorrow, I want you to take me to the building where the shots were taken and run me through all the evidence.'

'Yes, sir.' Hoy turned to leave.

'Did he really go to Brighton, or is that another line you fed to the police?' Hoy turned back.

'It's our best guess. The Ops Room gave the heads up to the East Sussex Police, so they put a hundred coppers out on the street looking for someone unknown. That's why I buzzed them the name of Al Akbar J'zeer. At least they have a face to focus on, which left us clear to send in three of our own guys to find Foxx. They messaged me; they had a sighting but needed to lure him in. He was in Brighton Lanes, but it was way too public to take him down. They've got to trap him, get him somewhere they can deal with him without collateral damage. But I haven't heard from them since.'

'Do you think he will kill again?'

'Yes, if he has to.'

'Then find him. I want him. Dead. The police can get Akbar, but I want Foxx put down. Permanently.'

'It will be done.' Hoy turned and reached the door before Storrington spoke again.

'You know I value loyalty. What about Tenby? Is he a member of the pack?'

'Why are you asking me?'

'You're an investigator.'

'Tenby's not a dog, so he doesn't live in a pack; he's a snake.'

'Evil?'

'No, a snake's not evil, it's just a snake. It does what it does. And handy if you have rats; but Tenby is loyal to one thing and one thing only: and that's him.'

'Is he after my job?'

'Is Beyoncé a virgin?'

'Who's Beyoncé?'

'Of course he's after your job. We're all after your job, but him more than most. It's his life's mission.'

'So he'd stab me in the back?'

'Negative. He wouldn't stab anyone in the back. He would get someone *else* to stab you in the back. Your danger is if Tenby gets too close to the Deputy Prime Minister. If the DPM takes over as PM and appoints a new head of his Special Security Service, that's when the snake will strike. My advice: Keep Tenby and the DPM as far apart as possible.

'So, he's not loyal?'

'He has the most beautiful wife I've ever seen. She's a cracker; kind, gentle, loving, generous, thoughtful, affectionate and very good to look at.'

'Your point is?'

'If he can't be loyal to her, there's no chance he'll be loyal to you.'

Their phones buzzed.

'Holy fuck!' Hoy spoke first. 'Yes, he's definitely in Brighton. Or was. He's killed the three guys we sent to get him. Well, two of them, one's in

Intensive Care. Holy shit! The local LEOs will be all over it. They mustn't make a connection.'

'Who did you send? Brekkenfield's guys or your own?'

'Neither. They're freelance. Ex-coppers. No obvious links to the Department.'

'Good.'

'Not really. Three men are down.'

'That's the least of our worries. Find this turbulent bastard and rid me of him. I will give a thousand ducats to anyone who can bring me his head on a plate.'

~

The Astra drove through the night, its occupants drifting slowly further apart. The driver was troubled, he took side roads, a circuitous but cautious route, until they were clear of Brighton and Hove. The passenger said nothing as she tried to understand what was really about to happen. It was late. They joined the deserted A23 and headed north for London. Conversation had long since fallen into a difficult, tense silence. The only sounds were the road and the radio. The music died away.

'This is a special news bulletin on the latest in the Brighton Mass Murders. It's been confirmed that the dead men were policemen. Their names have not been released. A spokesman said it was a senseless attack on the three innocent victims while off duty. It's not known why they were in Brighton, but it has been confirmed that they are not with the East Sussex Constabulary. We will give you more details when we have them, but for now it's back to Soft Rock after Midnight.'

'They were coppers. You killed . . . I mean we . . . Oh god!'

Shock was not concealed on the driver's face. His thoughts raced. What should he do? He bluffed confidence and feigned self-defence.

'It doesn't matter what they did for a job, they were homophobic violent vigilantes. They got what was coming. Which would you prefer: it was you or them on the slab? What's done is done. Brighton's behind us. Everything's going to be fine.'

His eyes were visible from the backseat in the dark of the rear-view mirror: they didn't say everything would be fine, they said that the biggest trouble was yet to come.

'Why did policemen do that? I mean, why attack me?' It wasn't so much a question, more an escape of emotion.

'You wouldn't believe what some people do. There was this chick in East London, got raped in a park and left for dead. She pulls her knickers up, hobbles towards the nearest person for help and says she's been raped. He thinks *Hell yeah*, takes her back in the bushes and rapes her again. People, eh?'

'Why are you telling me that story? Am I the girl?'

'Relax. You're too jumpy by half.'

'Too jumpy? Just how jumpy should I be? They're dead. They were policemen. We were seen. The old lady.'

'She'll be tucked up in bed now and won't know nothing about it 'til morning. Are you saying we ought to go and see her? Sort her out?'

'What? You want to kill her too?'

'No witnesses. That's what a professional would do.'

'OMG, are you a professional?' said the witness in the back of the car.

'No. I'm just messing with you. I told you, they were alive when I left 'em. Beaten up, but not dead. It's just, I don't want to explain that to the police. Keep cool. Everything's gonna be fine.'

He clicked the indicators and slipped off left, leaving the road that headed straight for London.

'What're you doing? Why did you turn off?'

'Just taking minor roads, y'know, just in case. What's your problem?'

'Well, coming this way, to get to London . . . it's not normal.'

'Sorry mate, right back at you. What is normal after you've just beaten up three guys and they wind up dead?'

The driver had a problem; and that problem was the passenger. He should never have picked her up. They drove through the night, both realising in synchronicity what had to happen next. Conversation turned to silence. There was nothing more to say.

The phone rang as the nose of the personalised Jaguar F type swept passed the electric gates and up the tree-lined drive towards a sumptuous six-bedroom white stucco mansion.

'Morgan-Tenby? This is Storrington.'

'And what can I do for my esteemed leader at this time of night? Have there been any developments?'

'I've been thinking about the fallout. Sensitive situation. Needs kid gloves. Single message. Single line of communication. I will handle the politicos, so you can stand down on any meeting with the DPM.'

'I can handle the DPM. Actually Richard and I are getting on really . . .'

'No. Stand down. Think about it. Foxx was your man. I should suspend you. I don't want your face in front of the DPM. No communication at all with Richard Buchanan. Got it?'

'I hear you loud and clear, chief.' The last word was lightly laced with sarcasm.

The car pulled up outside the columned doorway. He clicked off the engine and checked the time. It was after midnight. Too late to call, so he sent a text:

Hi Richard. Wife and I are looking forward to dinner tmrw night. Will turn up at your mews at 8.00.KR Nicki

No sooner had he reached the door, than his phoned buzzed the reply, *Perfect*

⁓

The A roads turned to B roads, and the B roads turned out to be devoid of houses, villages, street lights or habitation. The pace got slower. The driver seemed preoccupied, indecisive, reluctant, wrestling with what to do next - or maybe just how to do it.

The passenger sat in the darkness of the back seat. What to do? For the moment, she had no choice but to sit and wait for whatever was going to happen.

Remove all witnesses, echoed in her mind. Could she really believe she was in danger? *You wouldn't believe what some people will do.* Did she believe anything that had happened to her in the last day or so? She sat in discomfort, mental and physical, and let herself be distracted by the immediate tensions of a suspender belt that was biting into her. She moved to release it.

'Don't you dare,' came a stern voice from the front. He seemed to see through the dark with eyes in the back of his head 'You're not changing in my car.'

'Sorry, I was just . . .'

'We'll stop somewhere up here, so you can change, then I'm going to drop you at Gatwick. There are trains twenty-four hours a day. I need to get back to Brighton. There's something I have to do.'

A jolt of adrenaline shot across her heart. Distant dread became immediate threat. *Remove all witnesses.* This was it. 'No, I'm fine. I can change in Gatwick. Really.'

'Yeah sure, a guy in a dress at the scene of a triple police murder goes to Gatwick Airport that's full of coppers to get changed. Nah, you do what I say. I'll stop up here somewhere.'

'No, I'm good. Don't stop. Drop me at Gatwick.' The request was ignored. The car drove on into the darkness.

'Shut up!' said the driver with increasing tension in his voice. 'Everything's going to be fine.'

They were the last words they would say to each other. She felt the car slow and take a left. The road was narrow, the hedges high. She watched the driver looking for a place to stop. The car drove slower, as her heart beat faster. Her eyes closed as she weighed up her options. She didn't have any.

She saw the driver lean forward to pick something up from the footwell floor and put it on the passenger seat. It was the knife. It was in grabbing distance. She leant forward, planned her move, but the driver looked round. She sat back, waited for a minute, then leant forward again to seize her chance. But before she could grab it, the driver slid his hand onto the passenger seat, picked up the knife and put it in the glove box. A hundred yards later the car turned.

They had left the road and joined a farm track. It was slow, deadly slow; and dark around the beam of the headlights. A clump of trees appeared in a barely visible silhouette some distance ahead. The driver turned off the headlights and drove between open fields lit only by the moon. They were no more than a few yards from the end of their journey. The driver watched in his mirror and saw weakness, a defenceless vacuum; he saw helpless panic dig deep.

～

Storrington had walked home. At full march, it took but moments. He cold-showered, as he always did, laid out his clothes for the morning and stood clad only in boxers in his stark, dark bedroom.

The floor was bare wooden boards, ill-fitting and rough-hewn. The bed, wooden framed and old, was a man's bed. The two cushions were not. The bedside table to the left was draped in Liberty print and an ornate clock. The hands had stopped. The bedside table on the right was bare except for the photograph. His gaze rested on the far side of the empty, desolate mattress. He turned to the picture of his wife on the bedside table, said *goodnight* and laid out his bedroll on the floor. He knelt, murmured to himself and settled silently on his bedroll.

He lay there for fifteen minutes, waiting for the anguish to subside, but the torment wouldn't stop. Sleep avoided him. He rose slowly and drifted to the window.

'I love you, Pookey,' he whispered almost silently, letting his breath leave heavy condensation on the glass, 'like I never loved anybody. And I always will.' He turned to the bedside table and picked up the picture of his wife. 'I'm sorry for what I've done. I know you would have disapproved, but it's something I needed to do. And it's not over. I need to see it to the end. I have to.'

Remorse turned to anguish, anguish to anger and anger to rage. He laid the picture gently on the bed, face down, spun on his heels and strode purposefully to the opposite corner of the room. He threw an almighty punch at the boxer's speedbag that hung from the ceiling. As it rebounded, the face etched on it was just visible in the half light of London darkness. He punched again. For a five full minutes he punched. Then he stopped. He held the target still and stared at it with venom.

'Foxx, I am going to find you. And I'm going to kill you.'

The night felt darker, sense and civilisation had slipped ever further away, as she found herself alone in the night, in the back of a car, with no lights, as it bumped over the potholes of a deserted barren farm track in the middle of an isolated nocturnal nowhere.

Her heart beat louder. Trust in the driver had long since faded. Silence prevailed.

Had the driver just killed three people? If he had, he didn't seem to care. Had he taken them out with his bare hands? Was he going back to Brighton, pre-meditated, to kill an innocent old lady? He had spoken of silencing all witnesses, then claimed it was a joke. He was a kidnapper, but was he a cold-blooded killer? He was ex-special forces, a fighter, dishonourably discharged, drunk, deadly.

She sat and felt the fear, as the Astra slowed by a dark deep woodland. The car rolled over the final bump and came to a harrowing, heart-thumping halt. She watched the driver click open the glove box.

Her heart almost burst her eardrums. She tried the door handle, no escape. She tried the electric windows, no movement. She tried not to think about what was about to happen, but she knew only too well what had to happen. No choice. No way out. No way at all. She braced herself and took a breath; a deep, deep breath. This was it.

4

TEA AND SYMPATHY

It took but a second. The battle was on, like landing a defiant devil fish intent on her destruction. In the dark, her action was deft. The stocking she had slipped off her leg looped around the neck of the man with murderous intent. She pulled. She twisted it round an upright of the headrest, leant against the passenger door, keeping low to avoid the flailing hands of the driver, and pulled. She pulled harder. The nylon squeezed, the pressure increased. She pulled. Panic, choking, squealed screams, violent resistance, adrenaline, fear . . . until at last it was over.

It was as gruesome as it was devastating. Pure horror. But better it being the other guy on the slab. She pulled more and pulled longer. The driver was still, but she wanted to be sure, like her life depended on it. When she was certain, she loosened the grip. Nothing. She loosened it more. Still nothing. She let go. The driver slumped forwards, head on steering wheel, limp, depleted . . . safe.

She leant forward, unclicked the child lock, scrambled out of the far side, opened the front passenger door, entered the glove box and grabbed the knife; but left the torch that lay next to it. The light in the car shone on the collapsed and deflated body of her hitherto protector and potential assailant. All threat had gone.

Two minutes later, the body had been dragged into the woodland. Where should she dump it? She ran back to the car to grab the torch. It was only a moment, but when she returned, there was nothing, no body;

nothing but darkness. Fear grabbed every part of her. She swirled round. Darkness surrounded her.

The thin pencil beam of the torch light flicked in all directions looking for the danger. She searched for the threat. She spun round 360 degrees, then backed up to the car. Her heart missed a beat until at last the torchlight settled on the body, still and motionless, just where she'd left it. Darkness had disorientated her.

There was a quarry, a small lime quarry in the midst of the woodland, a pit thirty feet across and twelve feet deep, with rocks, building material, corrugated iron sheeting, bottles and random refuse at the bottom, now engulfed in brambles, nettles and nature's reclamation. She dragged, positioned, then slid the body over the edge. It fell, landing hard, head hitting rock and body slithering down the iron sheets to a halt, half bound in brambles amidst the tin cans and empty booze bottles.

'Yes, SAS, don't mess with a man in a dress!' she said, not feeling even half as brave as her words suggested.

She hurried back to the car. She didn't feel the bravado. Had she just been a hero or a villain? She didn't feel like a hero. She felt regret and remorse. What had she done? She asked herself over and over: what had she done? The answer was simple.

Survived.

~

Storrington woke with a start. He sat bolt upright. He felt like his world had just changed. Something was different. He could feel it, but couldn't see it or touch it.

He chided himself. It was his mind playing tricks on him. Nothing had changed, it was still the same; the man would die. He would make it happen by his own hand.

As he sat there in his bedroom and the darkness, a decision formed. He would not trust the police, nor Operations. He would build his own team to hunt and kill the enemy within. Eduard Foxx was the target. He was a danger; a danger to Storrington. Storrington needed to see him dead. It was the only safe and sensible course of action. Storrington lay back and let thoughts fill the vacuum that sleep had left behind. He thought about Prime Minister Palmer, about his irresponsible Defence

Strategy and how it had to be stopped. But he thought about his own responsibility to serve and protect the Prime Minister. He felt guilty. He thought about Eduard Foxx, what he would do to him and rationalised that it was for the good of the State, not just for his own self-interest. It was for the best, the right thing to do.

But the guilt would not go away.

~

The torchlight jittered as the hand holding it shook.

She checked the body one more time, then started the car. She needed to get away. She drove for twenty minutes, then stopped. She changed. She removed her make-up, took off her nail varnish and exchanged her dress for trousers and shirt, slipped into her man-shoes, then put everything in the bag, torch and knife included. She had just become a he.

He tilted the driver's seat back a few degrees and drove on. Narrow lanes turned into wider lanes until the B roads reverted to A roads and he headed for a place of beauty and calm.

The Cotswold Hills were sparsely populated and a long way from Brighton and London. He just needed to get away.

Allowing irony to take control, he headed for a cluster of villages called the Slaughters. He slipped slowly and quietly into the sleeping hamlet of Upper Slaughter, crossed the ford almost silently, headed towards St Peter's Church until he found a quiet nook to park and to sleep.

But sleep eluded him.

It was too cold. He needed to conserve petrol, so the engine was off. He shivered until the early hours, but it was no good. He got up and headed for the nearest town: Cheltenham. He parked in the suburbs, left the car, picked up his bag and walked.

It was early. It was Saturday and still quiet. He walked past the grandiose architecture of Cheltenham's fine and noble terraced facades, past the pillars and the white urban fronts, the Victorian and Edwardian railings and took a left, then a right, two more lefts and a right again. The architecture was less grand now. A café on the corner was opening its doors.

He bought a takeaway coffee, walked a further two hundred yards and took a seat on a bench in a small park surrounding a war memorial that listed so many people who had perished for the good of their country.

He sat, drank and stared in a semi-somnolent state at passers-by, at first occasional, but gradually more frequent as the hands of his watch moved their way silently round the dial.

He was opposite Berkeley Heights, a large, stylish block of comfortable flats. People came and went; some in running gear, some in a hurry, some more leisurely. The sky was blue and it was set to be a fine day, but his attention was consumed on the thoughts within.

Where to go? What to do? He was cold and tired. He'd been up all the previous night in a club with a coke head. He'd wandered the streets of Brighton by day, waiting to meet a friend in the evening; a friend that owed him money and had been safeguarding his important things, but the friend had not been a friend at all. They argued and he left. He had broken his heel, fallen, bruised his hip, been attacked by three maniacs in a dark alley, been saved only to be kidnapped in a locked car, driven to the middle of nowhere and been the victim of murderous intent. He had just strangled a man, dumped his body and made a run for it. Human kindness was in short supply.

He needed tea and sympathy.

He needed a bed.

And a bath.

He needed a place to stay and think, to recuperate and plan. He needed to sleep. But most of all he needed help; he needed someone to help him. The door of the flats opened. Out walked a woman, a young woman, no a middle-aged woman. She walked slowly and softly, shoulders at a slight Saturday morning stoop. He read her countenance. She was the one.

He caught the briefest glimpse of her face; it was soft and kindly if somewhat vacant and preoccupied.

He read her character as she walked. Was it science, was it intuition or was it just wishful thinking? He saw her as soft and submissive, caring and responsible, a proper person, not a mother, but an established person, a person of morals, maybe someone who saw helping as the right thing to do. Above all he saw kindness. He might have been wrong about everything else, but he definitely saw the vulnerability of kindness. Yes, it was her help he needed.

He stood and followed. She entered the Tesco Metro mini-market, unremarkable, unnoticeable, almost invisible, and picked up a trolley. He did the same.

He caught glimpses of her as she shopped in a world of her own.

She had dressed in a hurry, like she didn't care. She clearly had no one to impress. The quality of her clothes was good enough, but it looked like she had thrown them up in the air and stood underneath or been in an explosion in some upmarket charity shop. The effect was frumpy. She was mid-thirties, but her clothes said over forty.

She picked up eggs, bread, cheese, Lea & Perrins and tomatoes. She paused by confectionery, touched a box of mixed Lindt delights, but let it go and walked on. Over-priced drinking yoghurt, a small box of tissues, a small tin of tuna and three 'meals for one'. She rolled her trolley on and round the corner to the wine section. She stood and studied, before picking up a bottle of Merlot and placing it in the trolley, then picking up a second bottle, hovering it above her trolley and replacing it on the shelf.

'Is that a good one?' he asked innocently from behind her.

'You're asking the wrong person. I'm no wine buff, but I've had it before and I like it.'

'I'll take one,' he said, as he placed a bottle in his almost empty trolley. 'It should come in half bottles,' he added 'for when drinking alone.' He paused and reflected on his words. 'That sounds bad, doesn't it?'

She smiled.

'I have no difficulty finishing a whole bottle,' she said in light humour. 'Once it's opened, it would be rude not to.' Realising her thoughts had escaped uncensored, she added, 'Not that I'm an alcoholic.'

'No,' he said reassuringly, 'you don't look like one. It's hard this shopping for one.'

'Yes,' she said, 'it takes a bit of skill, but you get the knack of it.'

'D'you know if they do chicken pieces here or is it just whole chickens?'

'No, they usually have pieces. Next aisle over, about half way down.'

'Thanks,' and he trundled off in a determined chicken hunt.

She hardly gave him a second thought. It was a mindless supermarket exchange of pleasantries; no thought, no motivation, just automatic pilot. Somewhere in her subconscious, she registered that he was a man, gentle, un-threatening, had an unkempt charm about him and was OK looking. But a man was certainly not what she was looking for, so she shopped on.

They passed in the detergent aisle, smiled pleasantly, almost awkwardly as trolley sides rubbed lightly and said nothing. A radio was playing quietly in the store. Music gave way to news.

The Prime Minister will make his first public appearance tomorrow after the unsuccessful assassination attempt on his life on Thursday.

The Prime Minister said he was glad to be alive, but expressed deep sorrow at the death of one of his advisers, who was shot by a stray bullet in the incident. 'It's a tragic loss of life,' said the Prime Minister. 'He was a bright, well-educated, promising young man.'

The man has been named today as Colin Lewis. He was a civil servant, unmarried and 29 years old. His family are deeply shocked. The funeral will be a private family affair.

The Prime Minister's appearance tomorrow will be at the Bodleian in Oxford, where he will hold a formal lunch, before addressing the Oxford Union. The Bodleian is currently hosting the European Table Tennis Championship, a sport in which the Prime Minister is known to excel.

The popularity rating of the Prime Minister has gone up seventeen points since the shooting, but he still faces strong opposition in Parliament over his Brexit negotiations.

In other stories, the . . .

The news moved onto international issues as he made his way around the store. He bought chicken pieces, burgers and oven chips, baked beans and a packet of sausages; as well as the box of Lindt that she had left behind, then with careful timing joined the checkout queue immediately behind her.

'I'm not stalking you,' he said in jest.

She smiled and said nothing. She finished packing her shopping.

'£54.28 please. Card or cash?' asked the robotic lady at the checkout.

'Card,' she said, as she swung her bag round from her back and dug inside for her purse. It took a while. 'Hang on. It's in here somewhere.' Her hands got more frantic, the top of her chest just below her neck started to redden and she smiled a wan humourless smile at the face of indifference of Mrs Checkout.

'I'm sure I put it in here. It's always here.' A final search proved fruitless. 'I can't find it, sorry. Can I leave my trolley here and nip back home? I must've left it there, but I can't think how.'

'Excuse me,' said the almost charming, slightly awkward man behind her. 'May I be of assistance?' He turned his head to speak to Mrs Checkout. 'Please add that to my shopping. I'll pay for it all.'

'No. No, really,' said the fully embarrassed shopper in front of him. 'I can't let you do that. It's alright, I only live round the corner.'

'Well, I live in Berkeley Heights,' he said. 'It's a block of flats in Jurors' Road about two minutes from here. You can drop in £54.28 next time you're passing.' He indicated to Mrs Checkout to start ringing it up.

'You live in Berkeley Heights? Me too!'

'No!' said the good Samaritan in apparent surprise. 'Which floor are you on?'

'Number nine, on the second floor. Where are you?'

'Top Floor. Haven't been there long.'

'It's really kind of you. I feel so foolish. I was sure I had my purse with me. I will pay you back. In full.'

'With interest,' he added, a glint in his eye. 'Have coffee with me.'

'I don't know about that,' she said defensively.

He looked instantly downcast.

'Alright then. It would be a pleasure.'

With shopping stowed and Tesco's paid, they walked together towards Berkeley Heights.

'Let me take that,' he said, taking her two lightly filled bags to add to his own and the bag on his back.

'No, you're already laden down.'

'It's fine,' he said, 'and now you can link arms.' She hesitated for a moment, then slipped her arm through the crook of his elbow. What harm could it do? And he had been a real gentleman. 'Linking arms is OK is it? I mean you're not married or have a boyfriend or fiancé hidden away somewhere?'

'No. No men in my life right now. Too much trouble.'

'Sounds about right. You work around here?'

'Yes, I'm a civil servant.'

'Sounds exciting,' he said with a smile.

'It has its moments. School pencils won't buy themselves, y'know!'

And that strain of conversation came to a gentle halt. They walked a few steps in silence.

'My name's Conner, by the way,' he said.

'You're kidding! I don't believe it. Mine too.'

'Now you're winding me up!' he replied. 'That would be way too spooky, and for a start Conner is a boy's name and it's Irish – and you don't look like you're either!'

'No, it's my surname. Julie Connor.'

'Well, that *is* a coincidence. Obviously Fate. I'm pleased to meet you, Julie Connor.'

'Likewise.'

They turned together, still arm in arm, up the eight steps of Berkeley Heights to the large glass double front door of the well-kept, upper-middle-class block.

'Have you got keys?' he asked. 'My arms are full. Or have you lost them as well?'

'No,' she said, in light scolding indignation. 'I don't lose everything.' She reached her keys out of her pocket and opened the front door wide. He was a charmer and made her feel good.

She couldn't say she had a crush on him, not by any means, but he'd made a good start. She might meet him for coffee sometime in the week and take it from there. Maybe.

She unlocked the door and caught his eye.

His face lit up when he smiled; she liked that. He was alright, for a man. He was polite, inoffensive, thoughtful and not bad looking. Yes, maybe, just maybe she might have coffee with him. No harm in talking. She would take it step by step. He stepped towards the now open front door.

'So, is Conner your first name or last name?' she asked, as she invited him through the door and into her life.

'It's just a nickname,' he said, nonchalantly. 'My real name is Eduard, Eduard Foxx.'

5

THE GAG ORDER

'Then come in, Mr Fox. I'm on the second floor. But you know that. Stairs or lift?'

'Stairs every time.' They chatted until they reached the door of Number 9.

'This is me. Thank you so much. You've been more than kind.' She opened the door, stood on the threshold and held out her hand for the bags.

'No, it's OK. Let me drop them inside for you.'

'No, I'm fine,' she said, as she took the bags. She turned and placed them on the floor. 'I'll find my purse and drop the money up to you.'

'If you like,' he said. 'I'm really not that bothered about the money, but coffee, now that's a definite.'

'I always pay my debts, but yes, we will fix up for a coffee sometime. Let me check my busy social calendar.'

'How about now?' he said, making a move to follow her in.

'No. Not really a good time. Flat's a mess. But we'll make it soon.'

'I don't mind the mess. Just five minutes.'

'Edward, no. I really appreciate your help, but no. Pushy doesn't work for me.'

'Well, I need some help from you. I just need five minutes.'

'Goodbye Edward,' and she closed the door . . . until it met his foot blocking the way.

'Please move your foot. This is not right. You're beginning to . . .'

His foot remained.

'Edward! Move your foot. I'm not joking. Move it or I'll call the police, I have them on speed dial.' She had the phone in her hand.

'OK. Sorry,' he said, moving his foot. 'I just needed . . .' She pushed the door, waiting to hear the reassuring click of safety as the lock clicked into the latch. She let out a small sigh of relief.

But the door was still a millimetre from closed. He kicked it open. It slammed into her forehead and knocked her backwards. He entered, dropped his bags, she regained her balance but he pushed her away. He slammed the door with his foot and slapped her face hard, and again, and a third time. She reeled, shocked. He shoved her back forcefully, she stumbled, she fell to the floor.

'Don't you dare scream or I'll kill you.' He looked at her with hard meaningful eyes. She started to scream. He dived forwards, picked her up by the throat, stifling the scream and pinned her against the corridor wall, her feet off the ground, his hand now tighter on her windpipe. 'Don't – scream.'

A knife appeared from nowhere and was held jagged under her jaw, the tip firm against her skin.

'One push and this goes through your mouth and up into your brain. You will die slowly and in agony. When I say: *Don't scream*, I mean it. I don't want to kill you. I have other uses for you. But if I have to I will and I won't give it a second thought. D'you understand?' She did her best to nod. 'OK then,' he said and let her slip down the wall until her feet touched the ground. He loosened his grip on her neck, as fear gripped her face. 'Don't scream.'

Agitation seized her, she looked round for an escape, a weapon, an explanation. But all she saw was panic. He could see it in her eyes. She was going to scream; she couldn't help it. He let go and stood back, still holding the knife as a visible threat.

'Take your coat off.' Distracted, she obeyed.

'Now strip. Take off your top and your trousers.' She stopped and paused. Thoughts rushed through her head. It took but a millisecond. Reality clicked in. She had clarity of his intention.

'No,' she said. 'Kill me if you want to. But no. I'm not doing that.'

'Undress,' he said insistently.

'No,' she said defiantly and put her arms in female defence position across the front of her chest.

'OK, please yourself.' He put the knife in his back pocket, grabbed her and dragged her across the floor. He kicked doors open until he found the bathroom and bundled her upright into the tub.

'Stand there and don't move.' He turned on the shower, cold tap only. The frozen water poured ferocious upon her still clothed body. She whimpered, let out a high-pitched gasp, but she didn't scream. The water seeped through her clothes. 'Stay there,' he said and took out the knife. She saw it in his hand on the other side of the shower curtain and felt the cold water bite deep through her skin and into her bones. She saw the knife come closer. Adrenaline consumed her.

'You know the film, don't you?'

She nodded.

'What's it called?'

'*Psycho*,' she said almost inaudibly, as the shiver of cold and fear mingled into paralysis.

'Exactly. Misbehave, fight back and I will go psycho, no holding back. You will be in pieces. I will cut you up. Stand still.' She stood, for a full five minutes, maybe ten. She was pale, shivering, cold to the core, all energy to scream had gone, the panic subsided, her will diminished. She just felt cold.

That was the plan.

He turned off the water and hauled her sopping, cold, dripping, subdued body out of the bath, dragged her on her heels through the elegant, single woman's flat and dropped her on the wooden floor in the hall. String from his bag tied her wrists to the radiator pipe. She was cold; too cold to panic, too cold to scream, too cold to fight, but he wanted to be sure.

'Just one sound. Just one and . . .' He didn't need to finish the sentence. She nodded. 'I can gag you if you want. Have you ever been gagged?' She nodded. 'Gags hurt. You can't swallow, they make your face ache. Make a sound and I will gag you.'

He left her in shock and began getting the lay of the land, room by room. He picked up her iPad and laptop before disappearing into the bedroom. She wriggled. She struggled, but that just made her wrists hurt. She was cold, so cold. Her spasms of shivering became uncontrollable.

She could scarcely breathe, but she didn't scream. She had no idea what was happening, but she knew one thing: *Edward was in control.*

She heard the barely audible sound of the radio, playing in her neighbour's flat.

The Prime Minister will speak tomorrow at . . .

The Housing Benefits Bill has come under heated debate . . .

In the Brighton double murder case, the third victim is out of surgery, but is still reported to be in a critical condition. The perpetrator is thought to be a local transvestite. The police are looking for a man in a green ruffled dress, wearing a blonde wig. The police are asking anyone who knows of his whereabouts to come forward, but warn that this man is highly dangerous and should not be approached.

The weather will be bright and sunny . . .

It went in one ear and out of the other. Her only aim was to avoid being a victim on tomorrow's news.

She lay, tiny on the floor, as shock turned to anger. Violation, invasion, injustice, the need to kill him to make it fair; her mind filled with thoughts that wouldn't help her. The minutes became longer, the cold unbearable, the air-conditioning vent above cut through her like an Arctic storm. She would fight him. She struggled to get free. The futility and the tightly bound string both hurt. She fought harder, pulled harder. It just hurt more. She stopped tugging. She stopped fighting. She cried.

An hour passed, maybe more. Calm returned. *I'm not dead.* She was determined to stay that way. *I am frightened.* She knew that was unhelpful, so told herself it would be OK. *He's not a burglar.* She reframed the situation, as her counsellor had taught her. *He's a man. He's come into my life, he will hurt me, take what he wants and leave. I know what that feels like and I can handle it. I won't fight him, I'll play him. He can take my things, he can defile my body, but he cannot take 'me'.* She would keep her own self safe. She would be kind, compliant . . . and then kill him. But for now, she would obey. Julie knew what to do. Julie was back in control.

'I'm sorry,' she said quietly. She increased the volume. 'I'm sorry.' He came out of the bedroom.

'Cold enough?' he asked. No reply. 'If you'd taken your clothes off when I asked, you would be warmer now. Lesson 1: do as I say, without question, always. I live here now. With you. Get used to it.' He cut the string with his knife. 'Stand up.'

He discarded the knife and stood six feet away looking at her standing, sodden, sad, still dripping, still shivering, slumped in her clothes, wet, weak, still frumpy, but now fragile. He spoke quietly, 'Come here.'

She moved a step forwards.

'Closer.' There was no knife, no fists, just his eyes and his voice. She moved another step closer.

'Undress,' he commanded in a whisper.

She looked into his eyes. There was power. She knew she had to comply. She wanted to comply. She was cold. He was strong.

His eyes were blue, deep blue. They were calm. They gave her no choice. She would strip for those eyes and to keep her own self safe.

She unbuttoned her top, slipped it off and let it fall to the wooden floor. She was wearing a camisole underneath. He wanted more. She unbuttoned her trousers and lowered the zip slowly, not seductively but reluctantly; he indicated to continue. She lowered her trousers and added them to the soggy pile.

She looked at him as if to say, '*Enough?*' It wasn't. A single finger indicated it was time to take off the camisole. Its clammy wetness stuck to her body. She wriggled out of it to reveal a thin flimsy cotton bra. She dropped the camisole and faced him. That commanding finger told her to turn around.

She stood with her back to him. He looked. She was slim, very slim from the waist up. She was size eight at the most, maybe a six above the hips, but an Italianate ten below. Her underwear was not expecting visitors today, that was for sure. Her waist was so slim he could almost wrap his hands around it. Her knickers were all covering and her bra was just a pair of loose cotton pockets with little to cover.

'Turn,' he commanded quietly. She turned back. She looked him in the eye and slowly, of her own volition, knelt in front of him, then bowed her head. She was playing him. He left her there, walked away to return moments later with a towel in his hand. She was still kneeling. *I can do this*, she repeated to herself. *I can do this, can't I?*

'Stand up.' She obeyed. She knew she had to strip. She stood in front of him. He looked; trim tummy, strong thighs, small breasts; very small breasts. The bra was a child's and even so was unfilled. It was a region of some personal sensitivity. She looked at him and proceeded. She chose knickers rather than bra and put her thumbs under the elastic of the waistband, ready for the reluctant reveal. But before she could pull them down, he passed her the towel and guided her into the bedroom. *Of course, the bedroom*, she thought to herself. She was even almost ready for the inevitable.

'Dry yourself and take your underwear off.' She managed this with her back to him to reveal nothing of her modesty. 'Put on dry underwear.' *That*, she had not expected. She tied the towel around her waist, and with her back to him, put on a bra, a more structured, more ornate bra; then she fished around for a suitable pair of knickers, which she put on. 'Give me the towel and brush your hair.' She stood, in matching underwear, bent over and brushed the shower out of her shoulder-length hair. She turned her back to him.

Interesting, he thought. *Out of a full knicker-drawer, she chose a pair with a triangular see-through panel at the front that only covered a diagonal half of her buttocks at the back.*

'Lie on the bed,' he commanded gently.

'Which way up do you want me?' There was a long pause.

'Lie on your back.' She complied. There were cable ties already attached to the metal frame at the bottom of her bed. He put another round her leg and pulled it tight. It bit into her.

'Ow!' she complained. He did the same for the other leg and produced two more cable ties for her wrists. 'They hurt,' she said. 'Why don't you use handcuffs?'

'I don't have any.'

'I do. Top drawer; next to Big Boy Blue and the Pink Tickler.'

He slid open the drawer and there indeed was a set of handcuffs exactly where she said. He tested them to ensure that they locked properly. The key lay next to them. He handcuffed her to the ornate but feminine metalwork of the bedhead, then lay a blanket across her, left the room and returned a moment later with a cup of coffee.

'I told you we would have coffee together. Drink this.' His voice was without humour and without warmth.

'What, with handcuffs on?'

He released the handcuffs and sat with her as she drank. No words were spoken, but somehow the mood had silently changed - not a lot but perceptibly. The threat level had reduced.

After a long silence, she took the last sip of her hot coffee and started to feel warmer under the thick blanket.

'So,' she said slowly, 'you don't like raping cold girls.'

'The temperature is immaterial,' he replied. He took her empty coffee cup and placed it carefully on the bedside table. He gently rubbed her forehead where the door had bruised it using the soft tip of his fingers, then followed through with a caress that swept softly across the side of her head and tenderly down the back of her soft, showered hair.

He gently bunched her hair together, pony-tail fashion, and held it firmly, but not aggressively. He pulled it down, tilting her face upwards. Their eyes met. It was the first time he'd looked at her face. She was not as plain as she portrayed herself. Her eyes were glistening bright aquamarine, her nose was cute, rounded and small and her complexion was porcelain. She had a triangular mark on her lower cheek and a scarred crease on the right-hand side of her lower lip, the result of a long-gone trauma, but her lips had a distinct appeal. He looked into her eyes and saw an inner resilience, a potential stubbornness but a submissiveness, a compliance, a desire for adherence to the rules.

She looked into his murky impenetrable eyes. He was handsome, almost pretty . . . and fit. There was something happening in his head, but she didn't know what it was. This was home invasion and he was clearly a rapist, but he didn't seem like one. She was angry that he had hoodwinked her; he was a conner for sure. She wanted to feel outraged, to feel hatred; but in a way she felt it wasn't real, it wasn't a real threat. Maybe she was just too scared. Maybe a rapist in her mind, was out of control; this man was very much in control. She admired control, usually; but assured herself she would learn to hate this man.

He looked at this frightened submissive woman, this woman who obeyed him when he said not to scream, who chose to kneel at his feet, who said she had been gagged before, chose alluring underwear, owned handcuffs, and had bought a bed with an iron frame perfect for bondage. But according to her Facebook, her last boyfriend had been two years before, his picture was still on the mantelpiece. Her look was quiet and self-effacing, her embarrassment came easy, whether in a supermarket queue or when hiding her breast size. Her frame was small; she was five foot three, if that. He wished he'd met her under different circumstances.

He would have liked that. They held each other's gaze for a full ten seconds.

He spoke and the moment passed. It was almost a whisper, but it was enough. The threat returned.

'I need your help, your full and complete assistance. All I want is . . . everything.' She swallowed at the thought. 'We can do this nicely, with kindness and we'll both get through it. Or you can fight me, in which case, it will be rough on you. *I* will be rough on you. I don't want to hurt you, I don't want to maim you and I don't want to kill you, but if you force my hand, I will destroy you and everything you care about. I need to stay here for a while, with you. It's complicated.'

'Will you beat me?'

'Will I beat you at what?'

'No, will you beat me, if I'm a naughty girl?'

'This is not a sex game. This is real. Get it into your head. This is real.'

'I know. That's what makes it so intense.'

A look of resigned exasperation flowed across his face.

'Hands,' he commanded. She duly offered them up to the handcuffs. He might be a rapist and a pervert, but she could play him at his own game. He wouldn't really kill her.

'More coffee?' he asked. He was too kind to be a killer.

'Yes, please. There's cake in the tin if you want it . . . seeing as you live here,' she said with the faintest trace of sarcasm.

He entered the kitchen and flicked on the old transistor radio that stood on the window sill by the kettle. He opened the kitchen window, just a crack. It was an old Secret Service habit, in case he needed to leave rapidly. He grabbed some mugs and set them down on the work surface.

Noise from the kitchen was the signal. She slipped her hands out of her own well-known handcuffs, leant forward and tugged at the cable ties. There was no way they would break. Maybe the knife was in his bag, which was now on the floor by the door. She carefully but painfully manoeuvred her legs and slid the cable ties down the leg of the bed until she was lying face-down on the floor, ankles bound tightly to the bed, hands free to grab at the bag. It was out of reach. She stretched. She tugged. The bag fell on its side. A green ruffled dress and a blonde wig fell out.

She gasped. *Brighton! He was a killer. He was the Brighton Killer. He would kill her.*

Oh my god! He had told her his name, she had seen his face.

She was as good as dead.

She needed that knife.

She pulled the bag closer and shook it. A sheaf of typed paper held together by a single treasury tag slipped out dishevelled. Then slowly, as if in slow motion, a pistol slid across the paper. Her eyes lit up. She grabbed it. He was a dead man.

But she still needed that knife. She pulled the sheaf of papers out of the way, but a word caught her eye. She tried to ignore it, the knife was more important, but she had to look. *Holy Moses!*

Her brain made sense of what her eyes could not believe. She flicked pages. She flicked back. She had to be sure. It had maps, charts, instructions, angles of trajectory, wind compensation. It was a report; a fanatically accurate report on what had happened two days previously in London.

'Oh Christ!' she said almost silently. It was not a report. It was a plan, a minutely detailed plan of the Prime Minister's assassination. It was exact. Everything. How he had used social media to build crowds at the front of the building; where the PM would emerge at the back; and where foul-intentioned Mr Fox had to be to get the best shot. There was a diagram: a big X marked the spot, right over the heart of the Prime Minster - in fact two, it was to be a 'double tap', two bullets, just to make sure. The Firing-spot where the gun was placed was marked with an F. All the Optics were described in detail: the focus, distance, wind factors; there were four columns of interdependent 'Optic factors'.

He was for real, a real hit man. A killer hired to shoot the Prime Minister.

But he had failed, he'd killed the wrong man. Despite all his planning, he had missed and hit an innocent bystander. And now he was on the run, here, taking refuge in her flat. She flicked to the next page. It was headed SECOND SHOT and dated to show when it would happen. It involved poison. The THIRD SHOT was dated for later the same week, and involved shooting or breaking the neck.

She flicked. There were ten or more precise instructions on how to kill the leader of the United Kingdom: dates, places, methods. He was not on the run, he was biding his time. He had not finished yet. He was going to see the job through . . . and he wanted her help.

No, never. That's never going to happen.

She jumped. He was standing in the door. He had left the kitchen unheard and was watching her. She pointed the gun straight at him.

'You killed those men in Brighton.' She shook the blonde wig at him. 'And I've seen your plans. You're the failed assassin.' She was feeling braver now.

'So it would appear,' he said, with cool and unperturbed indifference, despite the fact that a gun was pointing at his head and he was seconds from death. He took a step forwards.

'Stop! Take one more step and I will shoot.' He knelt slowly and, despite her caution not to, slipped his fingertips into the side pocket of the holdall and gracefully pulled out a box.

'Bullets,' he said. 'You need them to make your threat credible.'

'Give me those bullets or I will shoot you.'

'You haven't thought this through, have you?'

His face said he had won. Her face said she knew it. It was over. He spoke softly. 'Give me the gun.' She handed it to him. He took it. He clicked open the cartridge and looked.

'Sorry, my mistake. It was loaded.'

'You're one mega mind-fuck,' she said with genuine venom.

'Thank you. Now get back on the bed. It's time to hurt you.' Fear returned.

She tried, but it was not possible from her face-down, ankle-bound position. He watched her struggle. She scrambled, turned and contorted but she could not obey his command, she could not get back up on the bed. She got as far as sitting on the floor at the end of the bed, knees up, feet flat on the floor. The ankle ties had got twisted and were digging in. The pain was evident. Progress had halted.

'I should leave you there,' he said, crouching by the side of the bed, knife being put to positive use. He slit the first cable tie and looked down on her. She was so small and almost sobbing; he was so large, towering over her, even in his half-crouched position. He was in control, she was nothing more than his lapdog.

He slit the second cable tie and as he did, she sprang at him like a stretched bungee straight into his chest. He fell backwards, saving himself only by standing unsteadily more upright. She surged on like a high-speed rugby scrum, forcing him back, over-balancing him, adding momentum to his loss of control. The knife fell from his hand as she slammed him unbalanced and unready against the window. It wasn't fastened. The pane flew open, his body flew out. His head, his shoulders, his back, teetered thirty feet above the ground, toppling backwards. His legs kicked as she kept on pushing.

Gravity was on her side. But luck was on his.

He grabbed the window frame with his hands, drew up his knees and kicked blindly into the room. It caught her ribs, she fell backwards. He pulled himself up, she grabbed the knife, he leapt from the window sill. She thrust and missed. He grabbed her hand and twisted; the knife fell. She was in trouble.

He raised his fist, looked at her face and brought his knuckles down hard. She screamed as she hit the floor. She lay there for a second or two, waiting for the knife or a kicking, or to be dragged by her hair before having her face reshaped by the persistent pummelling of a ferocious, heartless fist.

She lay there. Her cheek stung, but there was no blood. She stayed on the floor and relived her last standing moments. The hard clenched fist that rained down on her had opened just before it made contact. It was not a punch, it was a slap; a girlie slap, not even a very hard girlie slap; it stung but it did no damage. She had fallen through the shock of expectation, not through the force of the blow. Now she was confused.

'Stand up.' His voice was serious and the command absolute. She stood, stared at him and waited for the fearsome retribution. A gun was held straight-armed against her temple.

'Time to die . . .' he said, as he cocked the gun. Anxiety stabbed hard at her heart.

'Die . . . or obey. Your choice. But you make it now. Die or obey?'

'Obey.' Her voice was weak and querulous as the fight within her died. Her frustration of failure hid frightened behind her eyes. She was beaten, really beaten, and at his mercy.

She wanted to say '*Die*' and hoped he would make it quick; but she was too scared. She repeated, even more quietly, as much to herself as to him, 'Obey.'

'Strip.'

She stared into his hard resolute eyes. They were different. They'd stopped playing. They had lost their emotion. They demanded compliance. She unclipped her bra for him and let it fall. She stared at the gun, and bending, removed her remaining undergarment, dropped it to the floor, stood up and looked back at the gun. She was exposed and vulnerable; and momentarily aware she hadn't shaved her legs. She dared not look at his eyes. It was awkward, embarrassing, humiliating, suppressing. She feared what he would do next.

But he was not a pervert, he was a pragmatist. Naked people are easier to control.

'Stand by that wall. Face it.' She obeyed, she had no choice, not anymore. 'Hands on your head. Spread-eagle. If you move, I will slash your back to pieces.' She stood, compliant and defeated.

He repacked the contents of the holdall, closed and secured the window, slipped the ankle ties up on the bed, ready for use. Then he stopped; and looked. He examined her standing motionless and obedient. Slim fingers knitted together at the back of her head, long hazel hair down to her shoulder blades, a slim smooth back, rounded Latin buttocks and legs many inches too short to be a supermodel. She thought herself plain. She was not. She lacked nothing in beauty, only in confidence. Now her visual torture would begin.

'Turn.' She stood, back to the wall, hands still on head, breasts flattened even more by the position she had no choice but to hold. He stared. It was not lust, it was punishment. She blushed, and squirmed a thousand internal embarrassments, as his eyes seized on her sensitivities.

'Lie on the bed.' He watched her move, slowly and dutifully. 'No, on your back.' She obeyed. 'Spread-eagle. Spread your legs.' More embarrassment. He used new cable ties to secure her ankles and her immodesty. He looped the handcuffs round the metalwork of the bedhead and stared into her eyes.

'Put them on.'

'But you know I can slip out of them.'

'Yes. But I know you won't.' She clipped herself in and felt his eyes check each limb in turn. She lay obedient, subservient and silent. He knelt on the bed and straddled her body, a knee each side, sitting lightly on her pelvis, his eyes on hers, his knife resting between her flattened breasts. He was a killer, she was defenceless. Fear gripped deeper.

'You should be dead. Your body should be on the floor, bleeding out as your heart pumps its last beats, sighing your last regrets, shedding a final tear as everything goes hazy then black. But you're not. Why d'you suppose that is?'

Silence was her petrified reply.

'Because I need you. I need your help - fully and willingly. I have a plan. It needs to succeed and you are key to its success.' She wanted to say nothing, but could not stop herself.

'I've seen your plan; you'd better kill me, because I'm not helping.'

'Alec is sweet.'

'Who's Alec?'

'You know Alec. Adrian and Miranda's kid. What is he now? Two? Three? You went to school with Miranda, didn't you? She would never get over the death of her child, if anything happened to Alec? And Barbara, your mum? She's at home with Barney her ugly dog. Steve is watching her - outside her house right now. He's my accomplice. Her fingers will be removed, a digit at a time. One finger every time you foul up. Shall I go on? Daisy, Helen, Matt, Sindy, Lisa . . . definitely Lisa. She's special isn't she? You have her picture on your mantelpiece – you and her together.

I know all your friends. I raided your Facebook and your address book, the one you keep in the top drawer in the lounge. I will devastate everyone you care about, one by one in ways you cannot even contemplate, unless you do everything, and I mean absolutely everything, I want. I have a plan and you are instrumental in it. You have no choice. My plan must not fail. Do you understand me? Speak!'

'Yes. I understand you.'

'What do you understand?'

'I have to help you. I know there's a plan to kill the Prime Minister after the first attempt failed. And you need my help.'

'D'you know when his death is scheduled for?'

'No.'

'Tomorrow.

Will you help me?'

It took a long time to come, but it came; slowly, reluctantly, almost imperceptibly, but it was there and it was all that was needed.

A nod.

Welcome to today's Fiery Phone-In. We want to hear your views.

The Prime Minister dodged a bullet, but is still in the firing line to get a good deal from Europe. His negotiations have been described as 'a farce' so far. The Leader of the Opposition described him as 'a stubborn, muddle-minded, arrogant buffoon who's giving the Crown Jewels away and getting nothing in return.' Do you agree?

The new Census form: Do you know what your grandparents did during the war? The Census has always asked about ethnicity, but now it's asking about family history. Does the Government have the right to ask?

The Social Services Reform Bill will change the way the system works so that 'People who deserve more get more, and those that don't deserve anything, get nothing.' Who do you think deserves to get more?

The Brighton Murder. Killing policemen; d'you think we should bring back the death penalty?'

Call us now and tell us what you think. Let's go to our first caller . . .

6

SATURDAY MORNING

Richard Thomas Buchanan, the Deputy Prime Minister, was not enjoying the conversation. Bettie Slaker was as skilful as she was annoying.

They had known each other from school, but he had made it his successful duty to avoid her for over twenty-five years. University had been the escape from her demonic schoolgirl clutches and a career in Law had kept him in a different world. Had he not been lured into the immoral world of politics, then he would have avoided her still.

He was a politician of conscience; he wanted to make a difference, drive change, serve the people. She wanted a position of power and manipulation. He disliked the lies, half-truths and distortions. She thrived on them.

Bettie Slaker revelled in pushing his buttons and exercising her inestimable skills of exasperation to trigger a deputy-prime-ministerial explosion. It is what hostage negotiators called the *Theatre of Blood*. When she got the explosion, she'd won - for today, and would be a calmer force for good; until tomorrow . . . when she would need to generate her endorphins again by stirring up his adrenaline-cortisol mix.

His temperature was rising.

'Look, I know you wrote a series of brilliant speeches for the PM which won him the election, but let's not forget the other thing.'

'What other thing?'

'You got fired.' Her face denied that it had ever happened. 'He fired you for being patronising and condescending. Just saying: don't get fired twice.'

'I'm never condescending. You don't know what you're talking about. You've only been in politics five minutes.'

'I'm a lawyer. I got a degree in condescension. I spent fifteen years as a partner of a major law firm and patronised whomsoever I wanted. But I will *not* be patronised by you or anyone. I'm only with you because we have history.' His voice was agitated.

'Yes, we do. And because you like me.'

'Don't be ridiculous! Nobody likes you. And for the record, this is the last time we're meeting at your house, like it's some covert witches' coven. You will come to the local constituency party office or to my office in Westminster.'

'Will you send a car for me?'

'No, get a cab like anybody else.' He was shouting, but her reply was dismissive.

'Of course you'll get a car for me, if I ask.'

'I won't. I'm not your puppet.' He looked deep into her eyes and could hear them shout back at him, *Yes, actually that's exactly what you are.* 'I'm not,' he repeated.

'Then you won't be Prime Minister.'

'Right now, I don't want to be Prime Minister; or at least not the PM of a failing, ailing, out-dated, outmoded, imploding, dissolving Government that is rife with internecine struggles and as bereft of power as it is of original ideas. If I'm going to do it, I'm going to do it right, or rather when the time is right. I don't want it as a default option because the Government's in a mess.' He sat. She waited silently.

She was a game player and he was being played. The silence lingered.

'Alright, so what do you want me to do now?' he asked, as she flicked through her papers, too busy to give him an immediate answer.

Bettie had been in the shadows of politics for most of her adult life. She was a speech writer, lobbyist, strategist or any amoral role that required well-developed skills of manipulation, as long as she was not in the limelight. She was a consummate support act, the puller of strings; all she needed was a marionette.

He had been a respected and well paid lawyer. It had suited him: the job had rules, it gave him the guidance he needed. He was a conformist, albeit a highly charismatic one, with an adept mind, who argued a legal case well, but in the middle of his successful career at the Bar, he had been seized by conscience and the Liberal Party.

He'd won a seat the first time he stood as an MP. Four years later he was re-elected and became a *de facto* shadow minister. Two years later, he was elected leader of the Party and just over a year after that, he led the Liberals to the best election results they had seen for generations, which put them in coalition with the dilapidated, fragmented and humiliated Tory Party.

Then Bettie appeared.

She had turned the Tory fortunes round at the end of the campaign. They'd been lined up for certain and crushing defeat, but she urged them, through trickery and manipulation, to change strategy at the eleventh hour: a high risk manoeuvre that worked. She underpinned it with some of the greatest political speeches ever written and the Tories crawled over the line with more seats than any other party, just; but no overall majority in the House.

She bludgeoned the Tory and Liberal parties into partnership, an alliance which was inevitable in any case, but her contribution was to negotiate the terms of Richard Buchanan's appointment as DPM. In America, if anything happens to the President, the Vice President automatically takes office. Not so in the UK; until now. Bettie had ensured that this principle of succession was a fundamental element that had to be agreed if the Tories wanted Liberal support.

The Tories had no choice and the deal was done. The concept of a Liberal leading the Tory Party, for as long as it remained in coalition, had become a constitutional reality. She'd also brokered a deal with the three Welsh Nationalist Party MPs and the two Green Party members, either of which could swing the balance of power in any vote on any issue, to form the flimsiest, mismatched coalition in the history of the UK.

Buchanan had berated the Government for being bereft of ideas, but ironically original thought was not his strongest suit. He needed to be given an idea, then he could embellish it, develop it, refine it and hone it until he owned it. Then he could sell it. He was powerful, credible, empathetic and appealing; a superb mouthpiece and an ideal puppet for any manipulator to handle.

He appealed enormously to Bettie, both personally and professionally, even though she was as asexual as she was amoral. He would have been quite a catch for any woman, but had established himself as a confirmed bachelor; not gay, just insular. He told himself that he'd been turned off intimate relationships by his first and only real girlfriend, a demon-bitch-girl woman from hell that had ruled, ran and ruined his life from pre-pubescence to his pre-university teenage years.

Now here she was, making his political aspirations come true. He despised her and needed her in equal measure.

'When the PM is finished with Brexit, Britain will be finished with him,' Bettie continued. 'I labelled him the worst Prime Minister ever, and now everyone is saying it.'

'No,' argued Buchanan. 'The Prime Minister before him was the worst Prime Minster ever, the one that set up the referendum, simply because he was too weak to control his back benches. Then he lost the referendum and ran away into obscurity. He was the worst - he was Neville Chamberlain bad. They both allowed us to get trounced by Europe.'

'The country has spoken. Brexit is a reality.'

'Yes, because he was so goddam weak in the Middle East. He let it get out of control. If he'd had the balls to go in and sort it out, there wouldn't have been a million and a half refugees heading our way, which means Europe and the UK would not have had a massive illegal immigration problem, so all the bigoted xenophobes in the UK wouldn't have balloted their racist vote.

He created the worst possible environment, then unleashed the vote and expected to win. He was a fool that has irrevocably damaged the UK on the world stage. Then he does a runner and hands the baton of indecision to Palmer, who is a rigid, intransigent buffoon busy doing the worst deal possible with Europe, ruining future trade hopes, weakening our defences and doing nothing about the immigration problem.'

'Yes, and it would take a genius to get us all out of this mess and turn it around.'

'It certainly would.'

'Exactly. A genius strategist, planner and speech writer; and a credible, good looking, persuasive, upper-middle-class mouth piece to put it into action. This is a one-time offer. We can turn this around; you and me.

We can create strength from the remnants of weakness and seize victory from the jaws of defeat. We can take politics to a new level and take the country to new heights of success. Do you want to be Prime Minister of the strongest country in Europe and preside over the greatest period of growth and success this country has seen for decades? Are you in or are you out?'

'I'm in.'

'Then stop whingeing. We need to be clever and we need to be unorthodox. Be quiet and listen.'

Storrington was not at home, but he was feeling at home in his army fatigues, in a top secret army base, in a briefing room, in the middle of Salisbury Plain, looking at the highly trained operatives who would be the solution to his problem. The six men sitting in front of him exuded confidence. They were the right team.

They had been the wrong side of enemy lines in Iraq, Afghanistan, Syria and a dozen other countries where they shouldn't have been. They had rescued colleagues, blown up critical targets, extracted unwilling prisoners and executed enemies of the State. They trained hard, revelled in danger, lived for a challenge and dedicated themselves to serving the best interests of their country. All Black Ops. They broke the rules, broke the law and broke with convention, but they always got the job done.

'Some of you know each other, some don't. Introductions later. You'll be eating, sleeping, breathing and living together for the next week or the next year; however long it takes to complete your mission,' began Commander Storrington. 'Your social arrangements just got cancelled. Do any of you have anything more important to do than serve god and country?'

'No, sir,' said five voices in unison.

'No, sir,' said the sixth, 'only my kid's sixth birthday party next Saturday, so no, sir - nothing more important.'

'Then you'd better catch this bastard by Friday night.' The door opened. In walked man number seven, except she wasn't a man.

'You're late!'

She'd just flown in overnight from Syria. She'd been in hostile territory when she got the call and had run through a kill zone, stolen a motor-bike, driven under fire, and got a plane to Brize Norton. She'd run to the car, come straight to the Base and sprinted from Hut 233 where the driver dropped her.

'Yes, sir. Sorry, sir. Won't happen again, sir.' She sat at the end of the row of chairs and despite the chastisement looked confident, assured, but half the size of the smallest of her male colleagues.

'This is Maria de la Casa. She is your captain.'

There was nodding and acknowledgement.

'I have a job for you. If you don't want it, I will throw you back into whatever you were doing yesterday, no hard feelings. But I have chosen you personally because I have worked with you all and I trust you to get the job done. It's a job that sounds simple. I need you to capture and detain the would-be assassin of the PM of Great Britain and Northern Ireland. That's all. At ease. Speak freely. Ask any questions first. I'll fill in details afterwards.'

'Why us, sir? Why not the police?' asked Man Three.

'There are sensitive elements to it, and your methods may need to be *imaginative*, so I want to keep this in-house.'

'Do we know who he is, sir?' asked Captain de la Casa.

'His name is Eduard Foxx, or at least it is at the moment.'

'So, this is an anti-terrorist op. Is he a converted Jihadi?' responded Captain Maria.

'I heard it was a woman,' added Number Five.

'I can tell you he's not a woman, a Jehadi, nor a terrorist. He is one of us. He works for PM-SSS. That's why you're handling it. The police will no doubt find someone to pin it on. Al Akbar J'zeer is the current target; a hostile who needs to come off the street. But we need to find the real culprit. On the signal, you will go, capture him and bring him back. I want him in Safe House 421 in the Leicestershire countryside.'

'Will you question him?'

'Yes. I will ask him: are you Eduard Foxx? If he says *yes* or if I think the answer is *yes*, I will put a bullet through his head. Nothing else I need from him. When you grab him, don't kill him. No bodies on the street. I don't want the paperwork. Or the publicity. Is that clear?'

'Yes, sir.'

'Shoot him, maim him, injure him, break his limbs, break his back, just don't kill him. That's my job.' There was no shock in the team. This was just another day at the office. 'Don't let him speak. Not a word. Gag him and bag him. Have you got that?'

'Yes, sir.'

'What have you got to do?'

'Gag him and bag him, sir.'

'Correct. He must not speak. Speed is vital. Choppers will be standing by. Speed limits don't apply. Red lights don't apply. When we find him, get there and get it done. 421 is in a remote rural location. When I've finished with him, you will clean up, leave no evidence. Then name your assignment and you will get it. Understood?'

'Yes, sir,' said seven voices in unison.

'There is one more condition. It's an order. It will be obeyed without exception. You've been selected because you're the best. You have Black Ops experience. And you're tough. Foxx is half your size, but resourceful and fearless. Each one of you is a one-man army, but the order is this: do not tackle him alone. If you do, he will kill you.

I don't care if that offends you. It will take three of you to bring him down, and even then, you'll need to shoot him first. You are not authorised to take him individually. He's an ultimate danger. He just killed two top ops and put another in ICU. Don't be fooled by appearances. Any more questions?'

'How do you know it's him?'

'Because I do. And I'm confirming the evidence this afternoon.'

'Where is he now?'

'In the wind. Last seen in Brighton, so all we know now is, he's not in Brighton. We'll find him. Your job is to fetch him to me.'

'Do you think he'll make another attempt on the PM's life?'

'Yes. But I know how to stop it.'

'How's that, sir?'

'Kill him first.'

$\sim$

The door opened. She flicked the switch with her long seductive fingers and two dozen downlighters lit the lavish Poggenpohl kitchen. It was morning; she wasn't long out of bed, sweetly showered, hair brushed, make-up absent. She was beautiful; graceful, fluid, almost sylph-like in motion. Mrs Nickolas Tenby was everything her husband wanted.

She clicked on the coffee maker, flicked on the kettle and set the oven to heat. Her hands were fast and precise: jam from jar to dish, butter curled from slab to plate, milk decanted into jug, croissants and pastries on baking tray in the middle shelf, oranges juiced, table laid, fruit cut, cereal poured. Her actions were deft, swift and effortless. She knew what her man liked and how he liked it.

'Alexa,' she said, 'Morning Playlist 7.' She heard him coming down the stairs. She stopped, Flicked her hair, took an instant look in an almost concealed mirror, straightened her thin silk dressing gown, parted it a little more at the breasts and stood with her back to the door, silk draped sensuously over her buttocks, just as he liked it. The door opened, his eyes approved, she turned and smiled.

'You look beautiful,' he said, only slightly lasciviously.

'Thank you,' she said coyly, as she did every morning after his ritual and regular compliment. She brought him coffee, orange juice and a kiss. He gave his approval, his hand on her back sliding down to her thigh. She was his porcelain doll, his focus of adoration, a gentleness of curves and softness; and she never let him down, not once in eight years.

She returned to the other side of the kitchen. He watched her move. She bent to take out the croissants and place them on a plate. She was naked beneath the thin smooth silk, but she didn't flaunt; there was no overuse of hips nor brashness of stance, she was just her; good natured, smiling, affectionate, natural.

'Sweetie,' he said, with more than usual seriousness, 'I know you don't follow the news, but you know that someone shot at the Prime Minister on Thursday?'

'Yes, but they missed, didn't they?'

'Yes, my love, they did. They missed the Prime Minister, but they hit and killed someone who was with him; an innocent member of his team.'

'Yes. I know. I feel so sorry for him.'

'Well you know at the party a couple of weeks ago; Brekkenfield didn't come, so I invited one of his team? The young man, about your age. I think you took a shine to him. You spent all afternoon with him.' She looked quizzical. 'You know, the one I said you were chatting up but you were wasting your time because he was gay.'

'Yes, Colin. I remember, he was a real sweetie, a lovely boy; so shy. I took him for a walk in the Rose Garden and then spent most of the afternoon talking to him in the conservatory. He has a disabled brother in a home. Yes.' Realisation slowly dawned on her. 'It wasn't him was it?'

'Yes, my sweet,' he said, by now at her side, ready with a supportive hug, 'I'm afraid it was. It was him.'

'Oh.' She searched for what to say. 'Oh my god. That's a tragedy. Such a shame; such a nice guy. That's terrible.' He consoled her by squeezing her bottom. 'Are we going to the funeral?' she asked with genuine feeling.

'Yes, I thought we should.' A few slight tears, betrayed her emotion. She had spent the afternoon with him. He hadn't wanted to be at the party; he wasn't comfortable around people and she'd spent all her time chatting and laughing, prying and confiding, relaxing and entertaining the boy. She had known he was gay, she hadn't been flirting, she had just been kind. And now he was dead. She had a heart and it filled at that moment with a sadness for a fleeting friend.

'I'd like that.' She spoke quietly. 'He was a sweet boy. Can we do anything, y'know for his family?'

'I don't know him. I mean, I *didn't* know Colin very well at all. Not really our place. We'll just show up, pay our respects and be off.'

'But I would like to do something, if we can.'

'Yes, I know. You always do. It's just about showing our faces, that's all. I'll buy you a new dress.' Her thoughts were not on dresses, but on the bereaved and a desire to make their pain less unbearable.

'Are you doing eggs this morning, because I have to hurry?' The topic of conversation descended into the mundane until it was almost time for him to go.

'We're going to dinner with the DPM tonight,' he said through a mouthful of heavily buttered croissant. 'I need you to look your best.'

'When don't I?' It was a wounded, rhetorical question left unanswered. 'It's not easy being beautiful, y'know.'

'I need to build a closer friendship with Richard Buchanan, because in the current political climate there may be imminent accession and that results in reappointment of prime roles, so I want to position myself as . . . oh, never mind,' he said. 'Just be your wonderful self. We're going to his house. A mews.'

'I always do.'

'What?'

'Amuse.'

He chuckled.

'Yes, you do. Constantly,' he said and finished off his orange juice.

She smiled and asked,

'What's he like?'

'Rather too serious. A lawyer through and through. Very bright, but doesn't seem to enjoy life. I don't care for him much. He's passionate about doing the right thing, if only he knew what that was. But he's virtually running the country while the PM's handling Brexit, so it's worth getting him on-side. Your job is to smile and look sweet. He's not much of a lady's man, but if you can get him chatting about something that interests him, that would be good.'

She straddled his lap and started to tie his tie.

'D'you think he watches reality TV?'

'Doubt he even has a TV.'

'Celebrity gossip?'

'No, not really his thing, I wouldn't have thought.'

'Fashion?'

'No.'

'Then I'm out of options.' She kissed his forehead and dismounted.

'Actually, fashion is not a bad option. He has none.' He readjusted his own tie, leaving it askew. 'If you could give him some advice on his image without upsetting him, that would be good. He is a man in severe need of help and advice.'

'That's lovely, because I love giving help and advice. I'm sure we'll get on very well.'

'Let's hope.' She remounted his lap, side-saddle and re-tackled his tie. 'I'll be ready just after 6.00.'

'I'll be there at 5.00. I want to see Lesley. I've got a little present for her.' He sipped the last of his coffee and she followed him to the door, ready to hand him his briefcase.

'See you later,' he said, gave her a final squeeze and was gone. She stood at the open door, leg showing, hair tumbling and fingers waving.

She closed the door and hurried upstairs to change. She had only six hours to get ready. Today, as always, would be a busy day.

~

Brekkenfield was tired. He was standing by his bedside, awkwardly kicking off his slippers, about to remove his well-worn dressing gown, when the phone rang. He was his own carer. A strenuous expedition downstairs into his black-beamed Elizabethan front room and his 1950's kitchen to get toast and tea had proved exhausting. Now, back upstairs, everything ached as he regretted his dutiful trip to the office last night. He answered the phone.

'Hi Brekkenfield!' The voice was chirpy. 'How are you doing? You looked like you were on death's door last night. I just wanted to see if you're OK.' It was Hoy, his team colleague and maybe friend.

'Surviving. Aching. Still bloody sore, but not complaining. I'll be fine; just need a few weeks to get back up to snuff. Bad timing, huh? Any developments?'

'Have you heard about our guys in Brighton?'

'Yes. Bad that. It's been a bad week for Ops. I'm still reeling over Colin Lewis. Damn good chap and destined for better things. And the Chief liked him.'

'Affirmative.'

'He was the best Resource Manager I ever had - worked all hours. Then, when he wasn't working, he'd spend every waking hour in the Foxdale Home caring for his younger brother. And gave them most of his money, from what I hear, to stop the home from going under. He was a good guy. Dependable. We need more like him.'

Hoy had stopped listening a couple of sentences ago, but sensing a pause, continued with the conversation he wanted to have.

'So when did you come out of hospital?'

'Yesterday morning, about 11.00.'

'Which hospital were you in?'

'St Mary's. Why?' he said, irritably. 'Are you investigating me?'

'Sorry, it's just my way. I wanted to ask you something about the Chief. You know him better than I do. D'you think he's OK? These last few days seem to have shaken him.'

'Storrington? Yes, of course he's shaken. Who wants an assassination attempt on their watch?'

'Yes, I get that, but Storrington is usually very measured. Never overreacts, he's ice; so cool he could freeze hell; and yet he wants to have a man executed for an assassination which we know he planned, but don't know he implemented, and for a triple murder without any hard evidence. No trial; just a bullet. It just seems . . . odd. What if Foxx didn't do it?'

'You investigators think too much. The simple answer is usually the right one. If it walks like a duck and quacks like a duck, it's a fucking duck. He's a killer and he needs to be put down.'

'But you do think Storrington is acting differently?'

'Desperate times demand desperate actions.'

'So he's a desperate man right now?'

'God, you don't give up, do you! You're like a terrier. I didn't say he was desperate.'

'You didn't have to. There's something going on with him. I just want to make sure he's OK.'

'He's OK. He's always OK. He's Storrington. Solid, but don't ever forget, he has the weight of the PM sitting on his shoulders. He'd do anything for the safety of the country.'

'Yes. I'm sure he would.'

～

The Prime Minister sat in his office in Number 10 surrounded by an avalanche of Brexit papers. His wife sat in their family home in Kent. A solitary policemen stood outside her door.

Outside Number 10, a single, symbolic policemen stood, as his predecessors had done for decades, with a further eight inside, eight more in the garden, a dozen in the short length of Downing Street, thirty on local rooftops and more than two hundred within a half-mile radius – and over a thousand members of the Prime Minister's own Special Secret Service working on a Saturday to keep him safe.

But he wasn't.

Safe.

Neither he nor they knew that his death was scheduled for tomorrow, in Oxford.

Security around the Bodleian had been tightened, heightened, reappraised and heightened again. There would be more men with more guns than anyone had previously imagined.

But they wouldn't stop the person who would kill the Prime Minister tomorrow.

They wouldn't even dare shoot at the person who would kill the Prime Minster, because unbeknown to the Prime Minister and all his protectors, the person who had been designated to kill the Prime Minister tomorrow was the Prime Minister himself.

And a lowly unwitting civil servant.

7

BUYING PENCILS

'So Julie Connor, how long have you been a civil servant?'

She was lying under a duvet, bound and spread-eagled; not a position conducive to conversation, but his tone was incongruously warm and seductively pleasant, like the man she'd met in the supermarket.

'Just under fifteen years,' she replied, seeing conversation as part of her agreed obedience. 'I joined straight from university.' He removed the duvet. 'Manchester,' she added, as a rush of cool air flowed over her still naked body. He cut one of the cable ties and indicated with a look and a nod that she could slip her hands from the handcuffs.

'And you buy pencils? For schools?' He rubbed her released ankle, the red ring sore from the unforgiving edge of the plastic cable ties.

'And rubbers. I'm very versatile,' she added.

'I have no doubt you're very versatile where rubber is concerned. Is it an exciting job?' He massaged the length of her right arm, knowing it would be tingling with the pins and needles of handcuffed captivity.

'It has its moments.' There was a pause in conversation as he brought the life back to her other arm and she rolled over to take a more foetal and protective position.

'Would you like me to cut the other cable tie?'

'Yes. It hurts.'

'Then tell me the truth. The more you lie, the more you get hurt.' A thought flashed across her mind, about the men in her life. It had always been: *The more* they *lie, the more I get hurt.* 'Are you a civil servant?'

'Yes.'

'Correct. Do you buy pencils for schools?'

'No.'

'So, what do you do?'

'Typing, filing, emailing and organising, mostly. Not very exciting.'

'Correct. Except for the *not very exciting* part.' He sliced through the remaining tie that was cutting through her ankle and, without thinking, rubbed it caringly. 'You're not to leave the bed, do you understand?'

'Yes.'

'Are you pleased to be free of the ankle ties?'

'Yes, very pleased.

'Then hug me.' He sat on the bed and twisted round towards her. The request disorientated her. She hesitated. This man made no sense. He was a killer and she definitely did *not* want to hug him. She wanted to hate him. And probably did. But nor did she want to die, or be hit, or stabbed. Maybe this was the gentle start to rape. If that was his plan then she would not allow it. She would rather die. But she thought about her mother and little Alec and all her friends. She drew up her legs in self-sacrifice, twisted round, leant over and hugged him.

He had showered. He smelt good. He held her gently. At first her skin crept but after only a moment, with one of his hands on the small of her back, she felt bizarrely comforted. This didn't feel like rape. She pressed her fingers against him to pull him closer. It felt like seduction. His hand very slowly slid soothingly up the length of her spine to the back of her neck.

Then it changed.

He gripped her neck, gently at first, then firmer, too firm; not brutal, but controlling. He whispered quietly in her ear. 'Do not lie to me anymore,' and released his grip. She felt momentarily abandoned, then paused for permission or instruction, but in the absence of either, lay back, pulled the duvet around her and sat up in bed.

'Do you work in Cheltenham?'

'Yes.'

'Do you work for GCHQ?'

'No.'

'Let me ask you again. Answer honestly and you get fed. Lie to me and your mother loses a finger. Do you work for the top secret Government listening organisation, GCHQ?'

'No,' she said emphatically. 'I do not.'

He smiled.

'I guess that is technically true. Do you work in the GCHQ building?'

She paused, then answered, 'Yes.'

'Do you work for GCHQ-2?'

'What's that?' she said, displaying apparent ignorance.

'GCHQ-2 is an organisation so secret that over 98 per cent of people who work for GCHQ don't know it exists. So secret that even people who work for GCHQ-2 don't know who works for GCHQ-2, because everyone uses a code name. It's based in Newbury, but has representatives in GCHQ offices in Bude, Scarborough and, of course, the particularly senior ones in the Doughnut building in Cheltenham; the building in which you work. So I repeat, do you work for GCHQ-2?'

She said nothing. She was thinking.

'Well? Do you?'

'You're clearly well informed, so if I say yes, then you would know I was lying, because anyone who worked for such a secret organisation would clearly say no: *First rule of Fight Club: you do not talk about Fight Club; second rule of Fight Club: you do not talk about Fight Club.* I'm sure it's the same for GCHQ-2, so I have no comment. I'm going to have to pass on that one.'

He smiled. It was a good answer. He looked her straight in the eye.

'Hello, Serafina.' Her look confirmed she'd been caught bang to rights. 'I am,' and he emphasised the next two words slowly, 'Eduard Foxx.' A glimmer of realisation tilted her head and squinted her eyes in recollection. 'Foxxtails, Foxxy Lady, or most recently Foxxgloves.'

'Foxxgloves! You're Foxxgloves? Edward Fox? Eduard Foxx, single U, double X!'

'The very same. Pleased to meet you.'

'Jesus Christ, Foxxgloves! What the hell are you doing breaking into my flat treating me like a bondage master's plaything? We're on the same side. What's the matter with you? What's all this home invasion, raping, bullying, beating up, tying down? Are you mad? All you had to do was tell me who you are and ask for my help.'

'I tried that. You shut the door on me.'

'Yes, but why the violence, why the threat?'

'Sorry, no choice. You wouldn't even tell me you worked for 2 when you clearly knew I knew. You would never have told me if I'd been nice about it. And don't think it was a show. The threat was real; *is* real.'

'We're on the same side, you idiot. We're a team. We are on the *same* team.'

'Well, we used to be, but I'm not so sure now. Things change. And don't think we're friends or I'm any nicer just because we've worked on Operations together.'

'I never said you were nice. You killed sixteen people in an Azerbai-jani jail and eight policemen in Georgia; and gutted a live bear in Norway. No, I never said you were nice.'

'Yes. That's me.'

'You're smaller than I thought.'

'Thank you. And you're frumpier. And why Serafina? I've often wondered.'

'Serafina Pekkala. It comes from *Dark Materials*.'

'So you like Philip Pullman books?'

'No. They're really well written, but they hurt.'

'So why choose one of his characters as your code name?'

'Because it fits. He's an author who can't keep a relationship together. *Dark Materials* is a thousand-page litany cataloguing the destruction of every single relationship there is. Whether it's a young boy and girl in the same place but separated by parallel universes or angels that have been together for four thousand years, Pullman pulls them apart and destroys everything they ever had. It fits.'

'Relationships not your strong point?'

'Let's just say that you've broken into my house, beaten me up, tortured me with cold water, stripped me naked and threatened my life; which makes this one of my better relationships.'

'But why Serafina? She's a witch?'

'A good witch.'

'Still a witch.'

'So you don't think it suits me?'

'On the contrary, I think it suits you very well. She has strength of character, is kind, has a will of her own, is brave and . . .' he hesitated for a second, 'and she's beautiful.' Julie opened her mouth to refute at least the last point. 'No comment required,' he said closing her down. 'The point is, Serafina Pekkala, Queen of the Witches, Ruler of GCHQ-2 Cheltenham, I need your help. I need your help to carry out my plan.'

'I know you do, but I can't do that. You know I can't.'

'Again inaccurate. In fact, it's not so much that I need your help with the plan, to be honest: you *are* my plan. The plan is *you* and that's why I'm here.'

'Look you can try to seduce me with your charm or threaten me with your fists, but I took an oath and you're asking me to break it by threatening my friends and family.'

'Yes. That seems like a good synopsis of where we are – except the bit about asking you to break your oath.'

'Well, I don't think I can help you kill the PM without smashing my oath to pieces. Why do you want to kill him anyway? And why did you kill those people in Brighton?'

'I didn't.'

Her eyebrows conveyed all the disbelief she could muster. 'So the green dress and blonde wig - just coincidence?'

'No. I was in Brighton. I was wearing the wig and the green dress. And stilettos. I'd broken a heel so I headed down an alley looking for a place to change. They'd been tailing me and followed me, looking to the world like a bunch of gay-bashers. I figured they were Special Branch or Brekkenfield's Ops guys that had come to arrest me, but some good Samaritan, an ex-SAS guy, got involved. He came to help and what can I say, it got messy.'

'So *he* killed them?'

'Meh.'

'What does *meh* mean?'

'Maybe he did, maybe he didn't.'

'But you didn't?'

'No.'

Her face conveyed no element of believing him.

'But you did plan the assassination of the Prime Minister?'

'Yes.'

'So why are you trying to kill him?'

'I'm not.'

'And I'm supposed to believe that? Really? You say I have to tell you the truth, but you tell me the most horrendous lies and expect me to believe them. I've just been through your bag. You have a step by step instruction manual on how to kill him in twenty different ways.'

'Fourteen, actually.' He went to his bag and pulled out the document. 'Didn't read it very carefully, did you? You should always start with the front cover.' He threw it on the bed. 'The title is not *Assassin's Instruction Book*. What does it say?'

She read it aloud. 'It says *Risk Assessment*.'

'Yep, that's my job. Like they use top class hackers to test the security of IT systems, they asked me to look for cracks and loopholes in how they protect the PM. I wrote a *Risk Assessment* to help keep the PM safe, but the person who asked me for it wanted an Instruction Manual on how to kill him. Someone has taken my document and rather than plug the gaps in security, is using the gaps to wipe out our country's leader.'

'It didn't work very well first time.'

'No, interesting that.'

'So, you're saying you didn't do it?'

'That's right. I'm not the assassin. I'm a desk jockey, a planner, a tactician. I was just following instructions; instructions that I thought were approved and legitimate.'

She put her hand on his. 'I kinda like you, even though I shouldn't. You tell a great story and you tell it with sincerity and belief . . . but I don't believe a word of it. You're trained to be charming, but really you're evil.' She took her hand away.

'You think? There was no evil intent in writing it. The evil lies in the malice and the premeditated hostility of whoever wants to bring down the UK Government. That's the deep, dark, danger; and that's the evil that has to be destroyed. It's the person who asked for it, not the person who wrote it, who carries the guilt.'

'And do you know who that was?'

'Yes, I do.'

'Really? You know where the evil lies?'

'Yes, 100 per cent. No doubt.' He put the document back in his bag.

'So tell me, who asked you for it?'

'You did.'

8

ONE OUT OF SIX

'Put the gun exactly where it was. *Exactly*,' ordered Commander Storrington.

Hoy, Head of Investigations, set up the long-range rifle precisely as it had been when the police found it. He checked the photographs and confirmed the measurements.

'That's it, to a millimetre.'

They were on the rooftop of the fifteen storey building. Storrington looked with a detailed eye at the scene, imagining the sniper lying there, gun to shoulder, eye to scope, silent, waiting.

'Why d'you think he left the gun behind?'

'Who can say?' replied Hoy. 'Maybe he panicked or ran out of time, or lost the bag. It's not here and the police haven't found it yet, and without the bag he had no way of concealing the weapon. Or maybe it was part of his plan.'

'Yes. Maybe it was. Who signed it out? I assume it was kept in the Triple S Armoury?'

'Yes, it was. It was Foxx. It's his gun; no one else uses it. Every officer is issued with their own weapon. We've checked serial numbers. It's definitely his gun.'

'I'm not doubting it. But was it him that signed it out?'

'Yes, of course. It wouldn't be released to anyone else.'

'I know that! Did he sign? Did he sign for it? Do we have his signature?'

'Yes, sir. His gun, his signature. His fingerprints all over it. It was him.'

'Have you spoken to the QM who saw him sign?'

'No, sir.'

'Do it.'

'Yes, sir.' Keen to move the conversation on, Hoy continued, 'We also have his detailed plan. It was caught there on the grille of that air-conditioning unit.' He pointed to the exact spot. 'I guess the wind blew it and it got wedged. The hit was planned in the minutest detail. It's got Foxx's name all over it.' He pulled out two A4 plastic evidence wallets with a sheet of paper in each. The paper was torn and damaged; it had holes in it. Storrington examined it.

'It's typed,' snapped Storrington. 'It could have been typed by anyone.'

'No, it's got Foxx's name all over it.' Storrington looked disapproving. 'Literally. Look here.' He showed the diagram. 'He's labelled the Firing point as F, the Optics as O and the target with a double X – FOXX. It has got his name all over it. And here, on this sheet, if you look at the first letter of each paragraph it spells *Eduard*. And on this page, the first subtitle starts with an E and the second subtitle with an F. That's his thing: he puts his name all over it.'

'And he left it behind?' asked Storrington rhetorically as he stared at the distant hotel and the kill zone. 'What's the distance?'

'1247 metres.'

'Did we measure it?'

'No. That's what it says in his notes. And he doesn't make mistakes.'

Storrington's face turned. 'But he did, didn't he,' said the Commander emphatically. 'He did make a mistake. He missed. He hit the wrong person. He's not a god. He got it wrong. He failed.' Anger dug deep in his voice. A nerve was hurting, and Hoy had hurt it.

'Yes, sir,' said Hoy, feeling the taste of his own foot in his mouth.

'Take a look, sir,' he said, suggesting that Storrington should take up position lying in the sniper's hide. Storrington tacitly declined the offer. He observed the scene with care, needing to see what he might have missed at first glance. The roof was flat and concrete. His eyes examined its rough surface. There were two scratches on the floor; recent scratches, one about fifteen inches long and the other about ten inches long. The lines were not straight, but curved, like they were part of the radius of a large, mostly invisible circle. Storrington looked closer. There was a third scratch, about half way between the gun and the two curved scratches. It wasn't curved, it was just a zig-zagging mess. He said nothing. Hoy, believing he had not been heard, spoke again.

'Take a look through the scope, get the view that he had. See for yourself.'

Storrington was not in the habit of following orders from staff more junior than him, which was everyone, except the Prime Minister, but it seemed churlish or suspicious to refuse. He knelt, then he lay, moving naturally into position. The weapon melted into his hand like a baton to a conductor.

'Because, you used to be a sniper, didn't you, sir,' continued Hoy. 'You were top marksman five years running according to your military records and you had the record for the longest range kill in your time. Beaten now of course, but at the time you set a new benchmark.'

'You're well informed.'

'I'm an investigator, sir.'

'As you keep telling me.' Storrington, adjusted the sights and homed in on the now absent target. He swung his right leg to and fro as he focused, then his left, but not so much. Then he froze; and took the imaginary shot in his mind. Job done. He stood up.

'Interesting thing,' said Hoy, once Storrington was back at his full height, 'you see those marks on the concrete; the scratches? When you lay there, they fell directly under your toes. Even when you moved your feet. Metal toe caps, I'd say.'

Storrington glowered. Hoy felt it.

'I've seen enough,' said Storrington abruptly, turned and walked away.

'But I haven't shown you Foxx's cap. They found it in the stairwell.' His words fell on absent ears. Storrington had left. Hoy was alone on the roof. He lay down and peered through the scope. It was set up exactly on target, with compensation for wind factor as prescribed precisely in the document by Foxx.

It was a dead shot. And no mistake.

～

Serafina Pekkala, Senior Communications Officer in the Government's ultra-top secret GCHQ-2 sat in the bed, thinking. *What do I say, what do I not say, what do I believe, what is a trap?*

Eduard Foxx, secret agent, tactician and orchestrator of many assassinations sat staring at her. He was reading her face. *Are you guilty, are you part of a conspiracy, are you the leader of the conspiracy, or are you as innocent as you pretend to be?*

Serafina Pekkala, aka Julie Connor, needed to prove her innocence or she feared for her life. If Foxx didn't finish her, the State would condemn her and the Special Operations Department would lock her in some dark military dungeon and vanish her away forever.

She racked her brains. Had she sent the request for a Risk Assessment to Eduard 'Foxxgloves' Foxx? She'd certainly written to him recently, she remembered that; but she'd sent hundreds, if not thousands, of emails since then. She couldn't remember what the Eduard Foxx emails had said, even if she'd known at the time, which she probably didn't.

Eduard Foxx was in a jam. He'd been sitting at his desk two days previously working late, as normal, making the Prime Minister's country a safer place. He'd been tracking down and spying on bad people, as normal. This time it was Rafiq and his brother: two abhorrent, violent North London gangsters, who specialised in human trafficking, slave trading and child prostitution. His job was to stop them, this was normal. He'd finished work, gone home to his flat, in the dark. He'd put on his tea and flicked on the TV, as normal; and that is where normal ended.

The television had announced there'd been an assassination attempt on the PM in the exact place, at the exact time and in the exact manner that he had prescribed in his Risk Assessment. It had been a confidential document for only the very most senior eyes at the top of SSS. This was not good. Two and two added up badly in his brain.

For no reason, except inbuilt professional caution, he looked out of the window. A police raid was about to happen, except they were not police; they were SSS Operatives. They had big guns and one of them was pointing at his flat. He was in trouble; being hunted down to be shot as a well-framed assassin, to cover the tracks of whoever had ordered the document. He had to get out.

He had planned for such an escape, but had never expected it to happen. He would be in danger until he could find out who had set him up; and why - then prove it.

Serafina was the first link in the chain.

Serafina slowly let the reality of the situation dawn on her. If he was right, if Foxxgloves was telling the truth, then she was part of a conspiracy to murder the Prime Minister. If he was right, then she had indeed requested the Assassination Plan and forwarded it to the assassin. She was complicit in crimes against the State, just by doing her job. She started feeling the noose of the set-up tighten around her neck. She was in trouble and she needed Foxxgloves to get her out.

Unless he was the assassin.

Eduard Foxx sat there and waited. Silence fell hard on her ears. The words '*You did*' would not go away. She knew it was time to speak.

'I might have done. I might have requested the document from you. Oh god, what a mess!

Most of my job is sending communiqués to our agents in the field, for your lot and 5 and 6, and even Special Branch when they've embedded their people oversees, but that's not the part of my job that matters. Me and two other operatives are a forwarding station for emails from Top Officials and the whole of SSS to . . . well, to anyone really. If an email is so secret that it just *cannot* and *must not* be traced back to the sender, then it's sent to us. Y'know, if the PM were to order a hit on a Russian agent in Ukraine, or the Head of SSS wanted to negotiate with, say Syria or the Taliban, they would want more than plausible deniability; they would want absolute deniability. So, they send me an encrypted email and I create a totally separate untraceable hyper-route email address, re-encrypt it and send it on.'

'So who has access to this service?'

'Everyone in SSS in one way or another, plus some high-ranking politicians. That's about 1200 people.'

'And there are three of you who do this in GCHQ-2, so you get 400 people each?'

'Kind of, but it's not evenly split. I'm more senior.'

'So, you get what, about 100?'

'No, six.'

'Six hundred?'

'No, six. Just six people. I lead the team so I get just the top six people.

So if I sent you a request for a Risk Assessment, it would have originated from one of those six people.' She thought of the consequences of what she had just said. 'Jesus. That's bad, isn't it?' She swung around to put her feet on the ground. 'Can I get off the bed? I need my laptop.'

Nudity forgotten, she fetched her laptop and returned to the bed.

'OK. This is bad. This is very bad. You see, I can't access my emails from anywhere other than my work station in the office - not officially.' She closed her eyes in disbelief of what she was about to admit. 'So every week, I copy over my emails and keep them here in the flat on my laptop. I could go to prison for this.'

'Why do you do that?'

'Prudence, anxiety, insecurity. I don't know . . . in case this happens, I guess. Have you got the dates when I supposedly emailed you?' He handed her a piece of paper. She scrolled through her illegal email stash. 'Yes, yes, it's here. I did. I sent you the request. Oh my god!'

She read the email. 'You were asked what it would take to assassinate the PM, and you answered *a million pounds and a bit of imagination* . . . and . . . yes, here it is: you were asked to conduct a full risk assessment and to find holes in current security arrangements. Yes. But it wasn't from me. I was just forwarding it from someone else.'

'Who?'

'Wait, wait, I'm checking.

Yes, here it is. I've found it.'

'Who was it?' asked Foxx with a mix of urgency and impatience.

'Dominion 1431'

'And who is that?'

'No idea.'

'What do you mean, no idea?'

'I look after six top people and only six top people. They all have code names, chosen at random. I never get to know who any of them are. That's the point of it: credible anonymity and total deniability. I've no idea who Dominion 1431 is. And it can't even be traced by the IT department, even if they would, which they wouldn't. I would need to know who it was first, which terminal they sent it from and exactly when, before they could verify it. I really have no way of knowing who Dominion 1431 is.'

'But you know it was one of the six?'

'Yes.'

'And do you know who the six are?'

'Yes. I shouldn't, but I do.'

'You just don't know which one is which?'

'Correct.'

'OK, well that narrows the field. Who are the six?' She looked at him as if to say, *I can't tell you*. Then the reality of her plight, the danger she was in, the danger he would cause her family and the vulnerability of her nudity came flooding back to her. He read her face. He stood up, grabbed some sweat pants and a tee shirt from the back of a chair and threw them to her. She dressed. They looked at each other in silence. They were odd bedfellows, reluctant accomplices and an unwilling team, but the reality was they had to work together to get the answer. Words were superfluous. His eyes allowed her out of the room and onto the sofa in the lounge. She was in his eye line as he made coffee and grabbed the cake tin, two plates, two forks and the Lindt chocolates. He placed them on the coffee table and in a moment of recollection turned to his coat and took her purse out of his pocket.

'Sorry I had to take it in the supermarket, but I needed to know it was you for sure. And leave you with no money.' She didn't even acknowledge him. She was intent on her laptop. 'So, who are these six?'

'The first is the Prime Minister.' He showed genuine surprise for a split second that she was so closely connected to someone so senior. 'But I don't think it was him who ordered his own assassination.'

'I don't know,' said Foxx, in a light-hearted digression, 'with the way Brexit is going, suicide seems like a good option.'

'The second one is Richard Buchanan, Deputy Prime Minister,' she continued.

'Well, he stands in line to run the country if the Prime Minister does get shot, but it's bit out of fashion; we stopped doing that sort of thing in this country about 500 years ago.'

'But it is a motive.'

Yes, but unlikely. He doesn't have a military background, has only been in politics a few years and most of that in a party with almost no seats. He's only been leader of the Libs for a year or so and DPM for even less. It would be hard to get the contacts, to know his way around the system. And look at him. I just don't see it.'

'But a possible.'

'Yes, a possible. Who's next?'

'The Leadership Team of PM-SSS, so that's Storrington, the boss; Sir Morgan-Tenby who I guess is your boss and Head of Planning, Strategy and Tactics; Brekkenfield who runs Operations and someone who is Head of Investigations. He's a new guy; I don't know his name.'

'Can we make a guess at who it is based on their code name?'

'No. As I said, it's totally random. They don't choose them for that very reason. But frequency of use is a clue, maybe. Three of them are high volume, one is low volume, one almost never and one absolutely never. My guess is that the DPM is the never and the PM is almost never. Head of Investigations maybe the low volume, leaving Storrington, Morgan-Tenby and Head of Ops as the higher volume users. I don't know that, it's just a guess. It's impossible to tell who is who.'

'Is there anything in the style of writing?'

'I've not really looked but nothing jumps out. It's all very terse and to the point.'

'And the request that you got, was it from a high volume account or a low volume account?'

'High volume, definitely high volume.'

'So we have three prime suspects, and we're guessing they are Storrington, Tenby, he's not a *sir* by the way, and Brekkenfield, Head of Operations. All long term military guys and vetted to the hilt to get the job.'

'So who do you think it is? Pick one. Guess.' He was clearly reluctant. 'Play a wild card. Who?'

'Storrington. Tenby isn't smart enough and though Brekkenfield is well placed to find an assassin, he has dozens working for him, and logic points to him, I know him and I'd find it hard to believe. I say Storrington. What about you?'

'I don't know these guys, not really, but I say . . . errm,' she thought carefully, screwing up her eyebrows, 'I say Tenby.'

'Tenby? Why him?'

'He's an ambitious, self-centred, pole-climber by all accounts. I'm sure he spread rumours in the lower ranks that he'd been knighted. If he removed the PM, then there would be a new PM. Each new PM choses a new head of PM-SSS, or usually they do, so it would be his chance to get the top job.'

'To kill a world leader, just to get a hike in your pension contribution? A bit extreme.'

'OK, so why did you say Storrington?'

'He's a military man through and through and I think the hit was politically motivated. The PM is not popular with the Defence Community because they feel his Brexit strategy is weakening the nation. It would be tragic to kill a PM, especially one you've been hired to protect, but better that than leave the defence of your whole country exposed. I'd say it's more likely to be Storrington, than Tenby. I would put saving the nation above gaining a pay rise.' He looked at Julie 'Serafina' Connor for an agreement. He didn't get one.

'But thinking about it, it's even more likely to be the Head of Ops, despite the fact that you think Brekkenfield is a jolly good chap. He has the means and the motives. He would fight to protect the Defence capabilities of the country and has 100 hit men working for him. It's the simplest solution.'

'Or the Head of Investigations: neither of us know anything about him,' added Foxx.

'And the Prime Minister's popularity has rocketed since the shooting,' said Serafina.

'OK,' said Foxx. 'It's make-your-mind-up time. Who do you think it is? Write down who you think we need to go after and I will do the same.' He tore a sheet of paper in two and handed her half of it. She scribbled on the paper, hiding what she was writing with the other hand. He sat back, paper out of her sight lines and jotted down his answer.

He held the paper, like a trump card about to be played.

'OK, who should we go after? One – two - three' and on *three* they both played their hand, placing their papers face up on the table.

'Snap!' she exclaimed. 'At least we agree on something.'

They slowly high-fived. As their palms meet at the top, their fingers latched and they held hands. They were a team.

He looked at her and didn't believe she was innocent. She looked at him and doubted everything he'd said.

'We're a team,' she confirmed.

'Yes, we are,' he acknowledged. 'And at least we know who to go after.'

'Yes,' she said. 'All of them.'

9

THE FIVE O'CLOCK

'We've nailed him! Forensics don't lie. It was definitely Foxx,' said Hoy down the phone, while reading the analysis report on the blood and saliva traces collected from Raper's Hide.

'And what about the other guy: the bulldozer? Did we get him too?' asked Storrington.

'Sam Stone. Lives in Hove. Gathering details now. The Astra should check out to be his. Find the car, find the man. We'll get him.'

Storrington clicked off the line. Adrenaline of anticipation was running through his veins. He was a hunting dog straining at the leash at the smell of his prey. His blood was up. He faced Captain de la Casa and her team.

'We will have him by tonight. I need you all on your toes. When we go, we go hard and we go fast.'

'Yes, sir,' barked the hunting pack in unison.

'We have a lead on his accomplice. Get him and we get Foxx.' A helicopter landed. 'That's all. At ease.' Seven highly trained operatives relaxed their stance as the Commander left to board the chopper that was bound for the heliport four floors above his office and three floors above his five o'clock meeting.

Captain Maria de la Casa walked with him. If he'd had a favourite, it would have been her. She had served him well in the past, and was the closest thing he had to a daughter. He was proud of her, feared for her loss, but told himself it could never happen. She was too smart for that. And so far he'd been right.

'This one's important to you, isn't it, sir?' asked Captain Maria. There was a pause.

'They're all important, but make sure nothing screws this one up. In - extraction – out; and no mistakes.'

'Yes, sir. You have my word.' He looked her in the eye.

'You're right. This one matters. Do it for me.' He boarded the chopper and was away.

Lesley had been his secretary for nearly five years and knew Morgan-Tenby better than anyone, including his wife; or so she told herself.

She prided herself on being one step ahead, anticipating his every need. Her predecessor had taken quite the wrong approach. She had treated him as if *he* worked for *her*; Lesley was very clear about who was the boss. He was.

She was in her forties, elegant in a traditional style, and enormously capable. She was submissive to him, and actively superior to everyone else. She had perfected passive-aggression. Her desk was bigger than she needed, she sat in control right outside his office and had a team of minions to run around doing her bidding. She was the PA to the second most powerful man in the Service and she loved it. She would love it even more when he was Number One.

It was ten to five on Saturday afternoon. She'd just sent her boss to the Five o'Clock. Two of her almost-equals from the secretarial community hurried mischievously up to her desk.

'Is she coming, the Trophy Wife?'

'Yes, any minute now. Put it there,' she replied, with all the malice she could muster. 'On that table, she always sits there. I bet you she picks it up and reads it.' Her co-conspirator placed the comic on the table. It was a light weight, lightly glossy, pink covered publication aimed at girls of ten to fourteen.

'Though it might be a bit advanced for her!' They chuckled at her mental ineptitude and predictability.

'Why is she coming in at five, when she knows he's in a meeting until six?'

'Too much time on her hands.'

'I thought she had her own business to run?'

'Yeah, right,' said Lesley. 'I don't know for sure, but rumour has it that it's a modelling agency. She said she used to do a lot of modelling for money, of course for money, slutty or what? And now, with someone else's money, she has her own agency. I once asked her how many girls she has working for her. Guess. Guess how many?'

'I don't know – ten, twenty, more?'

'Four.' They laughed in a manner that aptly defined scoffing. 'Four! That's not an agency, that's a knitting circle! I bet all she does is get the girls around a table and gossip about which celebrity did what to whom? But the best bit is the name she gave it. Someone told her that to be at the front of directories you need to start your company name with an A or better still AAA. So she did that, but wait for it . . . she called it . . . *Triple A Portfolio*, starting with a T, not an A. Dumb or what?'

At that point the topic of their conversation walked in.

'Hello, Lesley,' she said breezily with a big smile. 'How are you today? Is Nicki ready?'

'Mr Morgan-Tenby is still engaged in a meeting, but please feel free to sit and wait.'

The three girls watched with care as Mrs Charlie Tenby gracefully and sweetly sat in her usual chair, put down her expensive designer bag, ensured her silk was hanging right and instinctively picked up the teenage magazine that was next to her on the low table. Lesley and her accomplices were all old enough to know better, but they made a deliberately poor job of concealing their sniggering.

Charlie was instantly aware of the cause of their mirth, but undeterred read on. What choice did she have?

The two conspirators departed. Charlie read silently as Lesley clicked through screens on her computer.

'You might like this, Mrs Morgan-Tenby,' said Lesley, feigning kindness as she looked at an image she had summoned up from the internet. 'Come and see.' Charlie walked over, tight silk concealing nothing of her perfectly toned form. Her movements were graceful, her voice was soft and delicate.

'Please call me Charlie,' she said, as she did every time she met Lesley. The screen had an image of a kitten in a handbag, with bows in its hair and large diamonds round its neck.

'Oh how cute it is,' said Charlie, disregarding the caption that read: *I am just a pussy, but the diamonds say I'm not so dumb.*

'Thought you might relate to it,' added Lesley, in case her point had been missed.

'Thank you. You're too kind. It's very cute. But I can't have a cat, I'm allergic. I get catatonic, I think that's what it's called. Oh by the way, I've got something for you.' She dug in her handbag and pulled out a vellum envelope. 'D'you remember a few weeks ago we talked about music and you listed your favourite musicians?'

'Yes, and you hadn't heard of any of them. I remember.'

'Well one of them was a saxophone player called David Sanborn. You said he was the best saxophonist alive today.' She looked for confirmation from Lesley.

'Yes. You said jazz had too many notes in it for your liking.'

'Well he's doing an intimate concert in a very exclusive nightclub. There's dinner to go with it, by a Michelin star chef, and I got you tickets; two tickets right at the front. Then I phoned and asked if you could get a back stage pass to meet him afterwards and, after a bit of chit-chat, they said yes. That's in here too. I hope you like it.' She handed her the vellum envelope.

'You don't want to go then? Not to your taste?'

'No. I got them for you.'

'OK, I'll take them then. If you don't want them.' The room went quiet. Charlie looked at her watch. Only 56 minutes before her husband was due to return.

'We've got it!' The young detective couldn't hide his excitement as he rushed into his boss's office. Hoy was picking up his files to leave for the Five o'Clock. 'We've got it: the registration plate of the Astra. It does belong to Sam Stone.'

'Great! Put out a BOLO on him.'

'A what?' The detective, unlike Hoy, had not spent two years in America with the FBI.

'A BOLO: Be On The Look Out.'

'That's a BOTLO.'

Hoy had no time to argue semantics. 'Get a message out to all police to be on the lookout for this car. Make it top priority. We need to find it fast.' The detective just stood there. 'Go on man, get on it.'

'I have, sir. I've already done that. I made it double top priority and added a crate of beer for good measure.'

'Really. You can do that now?' Realising it was just a turn of phrase, he added, 'What else do we know about Stone?'

'Lots. Ex-forces, highly trained, accomplished record, three years' SAS, chucked out for thumping a senior officer. Since then, off the radar a bit: a couple of drunk and disorderlies and right now has a warrant out for his arrest for whacking a traffic warden in Brighton over some stupid argument about . . . well, it's all in the file.' He handed over a thin cardboard fold file. 'I thought you might need it for your Five o'clock with the Chief.'

'Does Stone have any connection to Foxx?'

'None that we can see, but that doesn't mean he doesn't.'

Hoy gathered himself to leave. The detective's phone buzzed. He read the message.

'Hold on, sir.' The detective carried on reading, then looked up at his boss. 'Have you ever heard of a place called Upper Slaughter? It's in the Cotswolds. Well, some old bloke reported a suspicious car parked up overnight last night - the Astra. The registration matches. A local panda car went to check it out but by the time he got there it had gone. I'll get the locals to check the CCTV of all the petrol stations in the area. We're closing in.'

Storrington opened the Five o'Clock meeting.

'There are only two points on the agenda today. One: Foxx and his termination. Two: the Bodleian and keeping the PM alive tomorrow. OK. Item One: Foxx. Hoy, tell them what you've got.'

Hoy detailed his progress in the investigations and modestly rejected all praise like it didn't matter. Internally he absorbed it like it was oxygen to him. He looked at Storrington for a smile of approval. That was a step too far. He detailed the dossier on Stone, sticking closely to the evidence and avoiding speculation.

'Of course they're in league,' confirmed Tenby. 'This Stone guy and Foxx, in it together. No doubt.'

'There's no evidence to confirm that yet,' reasoned Hoy.

'Sometimes you don't need evidence, take it from me!' retorted Tenby, demonstrating his greater experience in matters of this kind. The debate rolled on until Storrington lost patience with conjecture. He cut to the chase.

'What's the nearest town to their last sighting?'

'Cheltenham,' confirmed Hoy.

'I can get an extraction team on standby, if you don't want to use the police,' offered Brekkenfield over the speaker-phone.

'We've got that covered,' said Storrington, unintentionally marginal-ising his ailing colleague whose role it was to recruit, train and deploy teams for exactly this purpose. 'As soon as we find him, he's finished.' That conversation was finished. He opened another file and continued. 'Now, onto Tactical Scenario Planning. Is the PM still vulnerable? Have we got Oxford sown up? We need the Bodleian to be tied down tighter than a barrel. I want to review the plans.'

'Up to you, sir, but . . .' The voice on the phone tailed off.

'But what?' demanded Storrington.

'We've got that covered.'

An hour later, Storrington started to believe him.

The DPM was home. The phone rang. It was Bettie.

'We need to meet. This evening at my place.'

'No can do,' said the DPM. 'I'm entertaining guests tonight.'

'Anyone interesting?'

'No one that concerns you.'

'Monday then.'

'Maybe. Tomorrow is better for me. Sunday, in my office. What's it about?'

'Your future.'

'I think my future is quite secure, thank you. I'm definitely the man everyone needs to know right now. I've had the PM tell me I'm indispensable, every Cabinet Minster sidling up to help me, more Civil Service mandarins than I can count wanting to do beauty parades and the PM-SSS all over me seeking my favour: Storrington, Hoy, Parker and Tenby all baying for my time. I seem to be the man of the moment.'

'Exactly. The man, but only *of the moment*. You need to turn opportunity into actuality.'

'So, what do you want to see me about?'

'The big reveal. I have all the numbers back. On Monday, I'll tell you how we will change history.'

'OK. Monday. I'll send a car.'

The conversation in the Five o'Clock had become heated, as senior meetings often did.

'Of course he'll make an attempt at the Bodleian. He was seen at Upper Slaughter. That's no more than 30 miles away. He left the South Coast not because he was running, but because he was heading for the PM's next public engagement,' reasoned Brekkenfield with all the passion his flagging body could muster.

'No way. He's on the run,' said Tenby, like it was a statement of the obvious. 'He failed, he fouled up and now he's trying to get away. It was last night the car was spotted. They could be in Scotland by now.'

'This is not some terrorist cell that took a pop and then decided to lay low; this is a hit man on a mission. A hit man trained by us. He has some reason for wanting the PM dead and that reason still stands. I fear he'll go ahead with his mission,' asserted Hoy, frustrated at the seeming naivety of his colleague.

'Then cancel it; cancel the Bodleian appearance,' said Brekkenfield, more through frustration than tactical necessity.

'Can't do that,' said Storrington.

'Yes, you can.'

'I can, but I won't. Our job is to protect the PM as he goes about his business - and that is what we will do.'

'Well, don't blame me if he's dead by tea time,' said Brekkenfield, as a parting salvo.

'Actually, I will.'

10

SATURDAY NIGHT

'The Prime Minister is going to die tomorrow, unless we're there to stop it,' said Foxx.

'That's a little hard to believe,' replied Julie. 'Half the army and all of the Secret Service will be there. He'll be untouchable; no one will get close.'

'They don't have to. Tomorrow the Prime Minister will end his own life.' Julie sighed in disbelief. 'He will. Poison,' asserted Foxx.

'What? You mean everyone at the lunch will be poisoned?'

'No, just him.'

'Just him? Really? No-one else? The assassin will pose as one of the highly vetted kitchen staff and lace the PM's antipasto with arsenic, with no one noticing and no chance of the wrong person getting the wrong plate? I don't believe it.'

'No. The assassin will be miles away. The trap is set. It's already done.'

'How?'

'You need four pieces of information. One: When the Koreans wanted to be rid of the leader's troublesome cousin, they persuaded some innocent girls to spray what was supposedly harmless water in his face as he approached the check-in desks at Singapore Airport. They were told it was for a reality prankster show and that his wife had set it all up. They were innocent, but it was deadly poison and he died. That's not what's going to happen here, not exactly. But they are using a patsy in the same way.

Two: The Bodleian is also hosting an international table-tennis tournament. The PM is a fanatical table-tennis player and won't miss the opportunity to show off his skills, especially against the French.

Three: The top table at lunch, the one that the PM and other special dignitaries are on, will have special champagne, a gift from the French Government. Only the top table have it and everyone sitting at the top table will drink it.

Finally: Watch these YouTube clips of the PM at public occasions.'

He showed her random news clips of the Prime Minister at public functions. In one, the PM put his hand in his pocket, then raised his hand to his mouth and coughed; then another of him putting his hand in his pocket, raising it up again and laughing; then at a speech with his hand casually in his pocket, then his hand in front of his mouth; another of him hand in pocket and then drinking from a bottle of water.

'You see?'

She didn't. 'Well, and this is a real secret - this is the most secret thing I will tell you. The reason he does that is because he's taking drugs; beta blockers to be precise.'

'So what's such a big deal about that? It's heart medicine, isn't it?'

'Yes and no. It's anti-anxiety medication, which in turn helps the heart. The PM gets so nervous at public occasions that he has to take beta blockers to calm his nerves. They are very small tablets, ten milligrams each, he has a special dispenser in his pocket. That's his secret. I mean, taking anti-anxiety meds, it's not the trait of a strong, forthright and gallant leader, is it? If the Press ever got hold of that, they would crucify him. It's a secret between him and his doctor.'

'How do you know then?'

'Research. I'm very thorough.'

'So? I still don't get how he's going to die.'

'Simple. He will play table-tennis. To give him maximum reach, he will remove his jacket, which will be eagerly grabbed by a civil servant, who is the patsy and will have been told, apparently by his wife through her supposedly high-ranking Civil Service messenger, that the PM has put the wrong dispenser in his pocket and it needs to be switched. They won't say what it's for, only that the PM needs it. The PM will then take the new artificial beta blockers, but they won't kill him. He'll go in to dinner and drink champagne with his colleagues at the top table. When the false beta blockers mix with the elements found only in champagne, they will react with each other and *boom*, his stomach will literally explode and *Goodnight PM*.'

'How do you know he'll take beta blockers?'

'First public appearance after being shot at, TV cameras everywhere and a big speech after the lunch? He'll need them for sure.'

'So, how do you know he will drink the champagne?'

'It would be a slight to the French Government if he didn't. They already don't like us and the PM is not going to want to inflame a diplomatic incident. Anyway, he likes champagne.'

'So tell him not to, or tell the police to tell him not to.'

'I will, as a last resort. But I want to intercept the dispenser switch first. And find out who set it up. That will give us a lead. If I can't do that, I will phone with an anonymous tip off and just hope they take it seriously. But I really don't want to publicise his need to take drugs. Not helpful right now.' Julie thought for a while, balanced it all up in her mind and spoke.

'So, I'm going to need a very big bowl, a lot of water, a gallon of soap and a really big pig.'

'What are you talking about?'

'Hogwash. It's all hogwash. The truth is, you want to go there to shoot him and you're going to implicate me in some devilish and devious way I haven't even thought of yet. I know I have to go along with it so you don't decapitate my family, I don't want to, but I can take all that. But you lying about it just pisses me off.'

'Look,' he said, 'it's all in here.' He threw the Risk Assessment document at her. She didn't even read it.

'Just because hogwash is written down, doesn't make it any more likely that it is going to happen.'

'You clearly don't know how Government works!' replied Foxx curtly.

And the conversation was over.

~

Darkness was falling. The Jag glistened under the carriage lights that hung strategically on the wall of the magnificently restored mews house. The policemen checked the credentials of Nickolas Morgan-Tenby and his wife. Moments later the DPM opened the door.

'And you must be Charlie. What a pleasure! I've heard so much about you. Do come in. Can I take your coat?' He was gracious and kind, in a well-rehearsed and over-polished manner. He ushered them both into his well-appointed living room and offered them drinks.

'Gin and tonic for me,' said Tenby with the confidence of an experienced *bon viveur*, 'and a pina colada for the wife, if you have it; otherwise any fruit juice will do. She's not a big drinker! More's the shame.' She smiled obediently.

'How do you like your G&T?'

'More G than T. It's more of a G with a splash.' This was the launch pad for an overlong diatribe on his wife's G&T creating ability. 'Every night I have a G&T, I mean *every* night for the last eight years. Nine times out of ten – perfect. But then, when you least expect it, *bam* - a concoction from hell. I'm sitting there in my study, I work every night, just checking emails, tidying up after the day . . . y'know how things are. And my little angel sits in the corner looking for all the world like a perfect pixie. I take a sip, and *Jesus Christ! What is this?*' He re-enacted the scene to avoid any confusion. Charlie smiled. It wasn't a great story; and she'd heard it before - many times - but she knew the pleasure it gave her husband to tell it and had practised her reaction to compliment his story perfectly.

'So what do you do, pour them away?'

'No, never. Waste good gin? Not likely! I repair it. Unless she puts . . . what was it you put in it the other day? . . . nutmeg wasn't it? I don't know where she gets these ideas, but it keeps romance alive doesn't it, babe?' She reached out and held his hand to show solidarity.

The DPM was finding this conversation awkward and difficult. He looked for some interesting diverting question to ask Mrs Tenby, but women were still mostly a mystery to him. A suitable question did not find his lips before Nickolas took out his buzzing phone and read it.

'Disaster!'

'What?' said the DPM, fearing for the life of the PM.

'I have a perfect G&T in my hand and I have to go back to the office. Now that really is a tragedy!'

'What?' she said softly. 'We have to leave now?' Charlie was more than aware of how rude that would be.

'No babes, only me.' He turned to the DPM. 'I have to head back to the office. It's bedlam since last Thursday, I'm sure you can imagine. All hands on deck. I'm gonna be hours at the office, maybe all night. The PM has a big gig in the morning and we're going over plans to keep him safe. He might still be under threat so we have to make sure he's well protected.' He took a gulp of well mixed G&T and put down the glass. 'Would it be alright if Charlie stayed? She can get a cab home, but I'm going to have to take a rain check on this one.'

No sooner had the DPM agreed, than the door shut and the Second-in-Command of the country's most powerful security agency had left the building.

Charlie and the DPM looked at each other, each feeling more embarrassed than the other and neither knowing what to say.

The DPM was good with people, but not with women; and Charlie was a very attractive woman, and someone else's wife, in his house and a stranger. He was not prepared for this. She sat there and looked awkward. She knew she should offer him some advice or talk about his fashion but didn't know how to get into it. He looked for a safe place to begin, a question that would help the conversation flow, a simple, trouble-free question to get this already awkward evening started.

'So Charlie,' he asked, 'which university did you go to?'

Tenby revved the engine, waited for it to settle and engaged drive. He slowly slipped the F Type along the cobbles of the mews, waiting for the phone to connect.

'Hello darling,' he said with boyish excitement. 'I got away from Charlie and the DPM. I was going to stay longer but I thought, *What the hell?* I'll be there in about twenty minutes.'

She spoke. He laughed. She spoke again, he replied.

'No, I can't wait either. Oh, and I have a present for you. Well, more for me actually,' he said with such lascivious intent he was almost dribbling. 'We're definitely going to ramp it up tonight. I have some new toys.

If anyone calls, you'll have to say you're tied up! Prepare to be invaded. The PM is gonna have to look after himself tonight.'

The evening wore on.

The DPM found Charlie easier to be with than he thought. She found giving him advice was even more fun than she had anticipated.

Nickolas Tenby found his mistress even more desirable when she was helplessly locked up in his new sex toy and he could haplessly display even more of his manly control - more fun than he could have imagined.

Storrington was mission ready. He was *not* having fun. He was thinking and had no intention of sleeping.

Hoy was studying countless files. The day was lengthening and showed no sign of ending. All he dreamed about as he worked, was sleeping.

Brekkenfield was already asleep; and needed it.

The Midnight News played to whoever listened.

There are reports that the Prime Minister will cancel his public appearance later today. Opposition members said: We are not saying that would make him a coward, but it's what we have come to expect from our invisible, insipid, indecisive leader. After what we've seen from him in the Brexit negotiations, running away seems to be what he is best at.

The PM redrafted the redrafted speech he was giving tomorrow and popped two more little wonders to keep himself calm.

Foxx tried to forget that he had just had two nights with negligible sleep, one in a club in Brighton and one in a cold Astra in a village square in the Cotswolds.

Julie felt her eyes get heavy. The shock of the day now wore wearily on her eye-lids. She had spent the morning in fear and the afternoon with her new unwanted running mate making legal use of Google and illegal use of simple computer hacking. She had studied hard, ten hours at the screen, and together they had built a weighty dossier on the six suspects. The day had left her drained and exhausted - but she would not sleep; not with him in her flat. Never.

She lay on the bed.

He sat beside her.

She was not going to sleep.

He caressed her hair and gave her head a slow and soothing Ayurvedic massage. She was not going to sleep, definitely not . . . and that was final.

She lay awake, eyes closed, thinking about how he had not raped her, not punched her, not stabbed her, and about how he'd brought her a blanket, Lindt chocolates, made her coffee, cooked her dinner and how his threats had turned effortlessly into affection. But she refused to sleep. Her mind slowed, her thoughts blurred, his gentle fingers soothed her scalp. Moments later her petulant resistance gave way to deep purring snores.

Her mind was still; his raced.

At four in the morning, Brekkenfield woke with a pain, took tablets and settled back down; Tenby finally let his willing and wicked victim go to sleep; Charlie got out of a cab and unlocked her front door knowing her husband would not be there; and Hoy rolled over and hugged his wife. Foxx waited until five, but could stay awake no longer.

'Julie. Wake up. I'm sorry. I need to sleep, so I have to lock you in the bathroom. No monkey business or you know the consequences. We need to be up by 8.00. I'll let you out then.' He set the alarm on his phone and took a pillow into the bathroom to make his prisoner more comfortable, then locked her up, took her bed, felt the warmth she had left and in moments was deep in sleep.

There was only one thing he'd missed.

As he'd taken the pillow into the bathroom, the nimble fingers of Julie had cancelled the alarm on his phone.

He slept.

Eight o'clock, nine o'clock, ten o'clock and still he slept. Julie heard the local clock strike midday. Foxx didn't. He slept on through.

The PM arrived at the Bodleian right on time. At 12.05, he stood at the ping-pong table, TV cameras rolling. He took off his jacket and handed it to a willing and ready civil servant.

The game was on.

Julie lay in the empty bath, hugged her pillow and smiled.

11

PING-PONG AND POISON

I t was 12.05 on Sunday. Commander Storrington stood unnoticed at the back of the Bodleian as the Prime Minister removed his jacket, ready for an international bout of table tennis. So far so good. It looked like nothing would go wrong today.

His phone blipped. *I have news.* It was Hoy. Storrington slipped out of public sight and called.

'What have you got?'

'The car! We've found the car. It's in Cheltenham.'

'Good man. Any sign of him?'

'Not yet, but we think he's still there. We've checked for stolen cars in the area. None were taken yesterday. We're using facial recognition on the CCTV from the railway station and the bus depot, but no sign of him. There's a good chance he's still there, in Cheltenham, somewhere. We've sent mug-shots to the local police. With a little bit of luck, we're gonna get him.'

Storrington ended the call and hit *Maria* on his speed dial.

'Get the boys to Cheltenham. Pronto.'

'Yes, sir!'

He returned to the field of play, where he saw the PM score the winning point against his French opponents. The crowd cheered with elation. *If only politics was as easy as ping-pong,* he thought to himself as he envisioned the victory as an empty allegory for how the Brexit negotiations should have been.

Now all he had to do was keep the PM alive. They went through to lunch, to the speeches and to the long-planned champagne toast.

'Jesus Christ!' permeated the door of the bathroom. 'For fuck's sake!' Foxx was frantic. The door was flung open. 'Have you seen what time it is? It's 1.35. We screwed it. The PM is dead. I know he is. Switch on the telly. Quick!' He paced the floor, restless, hyperactive, fidgety; like he was on cocaine, but worse. He was desolate, defeated, angry, unbelievably angry with himself. How could he be so stupid? '*BBC 24*! They'll cover it in detail.'

The television flashed on, Julie flicked to the right channel. He sat to watch, then stood and paced.

The Prime Minister seemed in good spirits when he arrived at the Bodleian in Oxford today. He waved to the crowds showing no concern for his security. Opposition back benchers had taunted him by saying he was invisible and would cancel the engagement. Despite evident protests from his security detail, the PM mingled with the crowds, shook hands and spoke to supporters and hecklers alike.

'Why aren't they saying he's dead? Come on, come on.' He urged at the large plasma screen in front of him.

The Bodleian is hosting part of the European Table Tennis Championship and the Prime Minister took no time in accepting a challenge from the French team.

'There! Look! I told you. He's taking off his jacket. And there – she's the patsy. She has no idea what she's about to do. Watch her. Damn, she's off-camera.' His agitation increased by the second. 'Why didn't you wake me?' he said accusingly at Julie. Her reply was a look that said, *because you locked me in the bathroom without a clock,* but she said nothing.

There was loud applause as the Prime Minister hit home the last shot and secured victory over the French team. The French team captain said: We were being easy on him, but he came back faster than we thought. He won square and fair.

'Look. There: jacket on, hand in pocket, wait for it . . . Damn! He took them,' screamed Foxx as the PM brushed a bit of imaginary fluff from his upper lip to conceal the act of self-medication. 'That's it, he's dead now. I can't watch.' He sat down, but kept his eyes intent on the screen.

For the first time Julie felt bad, very bad; anxiety and uncertainty kicked in. She had prevented Foxx from going to Oxford, she had prevented him from killing the PM. But what if she was wrong? What if Foxx really did want to save the Prime Minister and her actions had caused the assassin to be successful?

And here is the champagne toast. The champagne was a gift from the French Government.

Oh my god! The French are going to be blamed for killing him! thought Julie. *I've just started an international incident.* The Prime Minister raised his glass and drank. Foxx slapped his hands to his face. He really couldn't look, but nor could he stop himself.

'Twenty seconds,' he said. 'Twenty seconds and he'll be dead.' Those few seconds seemed like a lifetime. They watched the Prime Minister, they focused on his every move. He laughed and joked, then his eyes opened wide. He sat motionless, as if in intense thought, jerked his head to the side, eyes dead in line with the French Foreign Minister's and froze.

He froze for two dread seconds.

Then he stood, demanding attention. In his best school boy French, he proposed a toast to the French Table Tennis Team and thanked them for a fair and exciting game, then added a wish that the French Government in the Brexit negotiations should do *la même chose*; the same thing.

The audience laughed, the diners clapped and the French Minister smiled sardonically as the salt of victory was rubbed into his defeated ping-pong wounds. The PM was clearly enjoying the moment. The TV report cut to an hour and a half later as the Prime Minister left the building and addressed the assembly of reporters.

Foxx was stunned; motionless for the first time since he'd woken up - relieved, incredulous, confused.

'He's not dead,' he said quietly, more to himself than to his companion.

'No,' said an equally relieved Julie. 'He's not.'

~

Captain Maria de la Casa stood in a squad room at the back of Cheltenham police station facing the six men in her life. She spoke with authority.

'We wait. Foxx is in this town somewhere. We will find him. When we go, we get it right. No heroes, no loners, no mavericks. We keep it tight, keep to formation, by the book. The Chief wants him back alive, so I do too. But mostly I want you guys back alive, so if he gets tricky, put him down. I will take the rap; it's on me. If you have to put him down, don't think twice, just do it.'

'Yes, sir,' they said in a single voice. She smiled. She liked being referred to as *sir*, she insisted on it and never tired of it.

'Now, Number Two,' she addressed them by number not name. 'Special assignment for you. See if you can rustle up a decent cup of tea in this place. Take Four with you.'

'Yes captain, will do.'

$\approx$

The Prime Minister was feeling buoyant as he addressed an informal gathering of press and public outside the Bodlian. They had questions, he had answers. There were many exchanges but, like the ping-pong, he won. With game set and match in his pocket, he strode confidently to the car.

An abrupt microphone was thrust in his face accompanied by an abrasive volley of questions on the subject of a document that had been leaked about Housing Benefit Reforms. The Prime Minister skilfully defended its apparent extremist views.

'That document was one of the far-reaching proposals being considered by an internal think tank on improving the fairness and efficiency of the Housing Benefit system. Some of the content was more radical, but this Government is one that weighs up all the options before acting. Thank you, Thank you.'

He waved, smiled and got into the car.

'Get me that bloody document,' he said to his Private Secretary once safely away from the crowds. 'What the hell is it and who the hell wrote it?'

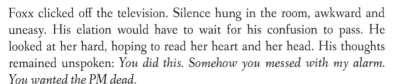

Foxx clicked off the television. Silence hung in the room, awkward and uneasy. His elation would have to wait for his confusion to pass. He looked at her hard, hoping to read her heart and her head. His thoughts remained unspoken: *You did this. Somehow you messed with my alarm. You wanted the PM dead.*

She looked at him, confirming her silent beliefs and strengthening her resolve. *No, the PM is not dead, for one reason and one reason only, because you were here with me, asleep, not in Oxford carrying out your plan. Round One to me.*

Julie's internal triumph was short-lived, as she felt the discomfort of the atmosphere cut through her. The silence hung motionless above her. She had to break it.

'I need to use my phone,' she said matter-of-factly. 'I need more information. Our dossier is speculation, all PR spin and internet gossip. I need to get some facts.'

'How?' said Foxx, his mind still very much on the events and non-events of the morning.

'I need to get hold of the SNGS and see what they know.'

'SNGS? Who are they?'

'It's a top secret organisation. You can only join by invitation. It has the best information in the whole of the Secret Service and is always right. It puts MI5 and MI6 in the shade.'

'I've never heard of it. And it's called SNGS?'

'Yes: the Secretarial Network for Gossip and Slander. I've worked a while in the Civil Service, so I know a few people who might be able to help. Some of us started together a long way back.'

'Like who?'

'Well, no one special, I suppose. I don't mix as much as I used to, but I do know the PM's Under-Secretary, and I'm godmother to the child of DPM's Assistant Private Secretary. I trained all the PA team for SSS and shared a flat with the Cabinet Secretary's daughter . . . oh yes, and I . . .'

'OK, I get the idea. Yes, you can use your phone, but stay in ear-shot. No text messages. I will check your phone after. Any mistakes and it will cost your mum and your friends dearly.'

Julie turned on her phone and through apparently casual conversation found out all she wanted to know.

'Morgan-Tenby. People say his name is only hyphenated because his mum wasn't sure who his dad was. Oh yes, a real slime bag. Kind of guy that likes his whisky older than his girlfriends. You know you can describe men by the sound you make in your head when you realise you are going to sleep with them; some are Oh! Oooh! Ah! Eh? Awwww! Or even Yay! He is a Yieeew! Just one big showboat. Pretty house, pretty car, pretty wife, pretty useless!'

'Storrington. One scary dude. You wouldn't mess with him. People say he can kill a man with no more than his thumb. I could believe that.'

'Foxx. I'd let him in my hen pen for sure. Good-looking guy, but a loner. Apparently killed 23 guards in an Azerbaijani prison, annihilated a whole police force in a town in Georgia, gutted a live bear in Norway and swam 50 kilometres from Kaliningrad to the Baltic Straits in winter.' 'Baltiysk Straits' corrected Julie in her mind. *'He's a legend. Our own Kent Clark.'* More corrections ran through Julie's mind.

Tenby. Yeah the story is, when he dies he wants his ashes turned to diamonds. Apparently you can put the carbon remains under high pressure and make diamonds. But the office tag line is that he is so soft that they could never make diamonds; pencil lead would the best he could manage. But even the lead in his pencil is too soft; that's why they call him 10-B!'

'Hoy. Too good to be true. He's a little darling. Always busy, like a manic beaver building a never-ending dam. Nice enough guy though. Thinks he's American. No, I didn't know he had four months off before he joined. I wonder what he was doing.'

Brekkenfield. He used to be such fun. Tough as old boots, but a good sense of humour. I have known him for twenty years. I blame his wife. He looks permanently miserable, poor guy. Good at his job though.'

She clicked off after her fifth call and handed her phone to Foxx. He checked it.

Previously, allowing the man in her life access to her phone, and having access to his, would have been a milestone in the relationship. This didn't feel like it.

'So what did you find out?' asked Foxx, putting down her personal phone next to his work phone. 'Just edited highlights, I don't need all the gossip.'

'OK,' said Julie, being as concise and organised as Serafina is known to be. 'Hoy is Head of Investigations; a swotty school boy and very much in the Commander's good books, but there's a four-month gap in his CV before he took this job. No one I spoke to knows why or knows where he was.

Brekkenfield is glummer than ever after being laid up in hospital for three weeks, St Mary's in Paddington, so that might put him in the clear.'

'Or be a well-crafted alibi,' he said. She nodded.

'Nickolas Tenby is twice the slime ball I ever thought he was, like a durian fruit - prickly on the outside and a real stinker on the inside. Self-promoting, two-faced. His wife is nice, but a bit dim and loose-lipped; sits in the office sometimes waiting for him, reading celebrity gossip maga-zines, trying to do the puzzles in the back. She likes puzzles. Bit of a trophy. He keeps her hidden away most of the time.'

'She's dim, but she likes puzzle books?'

'So they say, but remember these are puzzles in the back of trashy magazines. Hardly Mensa.' She continued with her summary. 'Stor-rington is interesting. He has had secret meetings with the Defence Chiefs. Laura, my friend, took the minutes. They're very unhappy, I mean *very unhappy* about the Defence Deal that the PM is doing with Europe. It leaves them hopelessly exposed and severely weakened. And, get this: he said to three of them in private sessions that he would '*sort it out.*' They asked him how, but he wouldn't say.'

'So you think he's our man, then?'

'Not really,' said Serafina. 'I know it looks that way at the moment, but no, I don't think he is.'

'But,' challenged Foxx, 'the evidence is good.'

'Yes, but it's not perfect,' she refuted.

'But it never is,' countered Foxx. 'I say Storrington is a definite possi-bility, but I'm suspicious about Hoy. We need to investigate the inves-tigator.'

'Oh!' she said. 'Stupid me. I know one of his assistants. She works closely with him. I'm sure I have her number.' She leant over, picked up her phone and turned it back on.

It took Foxx only seconds to notice. Alarm struck him like a lightning bolt. She had picked up his phone; not his burner phone, but his work phone. It was just lighting up.

'Jesus, woman!' he said, grabbing it. 'What are you trying to do? Get us shot?' He killed the phone and looked at her like she was an imbecile.

The implication of what she had just done sat on the periphery of her brain, then slowly and insidiously sunk in.

Storrington smiled, a brief, thin smile. The first for as long as he could remember.

12

HOME INVASION

'Progress?' demanded Commander Storrington, as he strode from the squad car across Jurors' Road to where Captain Maria Santiago Olivia de la Casa was standing waiting for him.

'We didn't get an exact trace. It was only on for a second, but that gave us a 200 metre radius. We've searched the houses, swept that block, Grand Rise, bottom to top. It's all geriatrics so I left the team in the van so as not to alarm the residents. That only leaves Berkeley Heights. The exits have been covered since the pandas got here. There's one front door and one service exit at the back. He's in there, Chief. He's in Berkeley Heights.'

'Time to bring him out. Get the van up to the service door. We want to keep this discreet.'

'OK, Chief.' She turned to address the team as they decanted from a SWAT mini-bus.

'Right, lads. This is it. This is Foxx's burrow. Remember what I said?' They nodded. 'OK, let's get it done.' They turned and the invasion began.

It took but moments to sweep the ground-floor flats. All the residents were in. They searched the rooms, the cupboards, under the beds. No sign of a Foxx. They moved up to the first floor: three residents were in; one door gave no reply. The concierge was summoned to bring the keys.

'One and Five, stay here. Watch that door. The rest of you with me.' Maria led her troops up to the second floor. She could almost feel Storrington's breath on the back of her neck. They moved silently as they approached the door to Flat 10. Storrington clicked his fingers and pointed at Number 9.

'He's in there,' he whispered to the captain.

'How d'you know?'

He pointed to the kick mark high up on the door, level with the lock. 'I just do.'

Six was about to knock on the door. Her hand signal stopped him. She turned to the policeman standing on the stairs and beckoned him up, battering ram in hand and signalled to bring One and Five into play.

'Formation,' she said quietly to the troops and counted down from three on her fingers.

One hit of the ram and the door flew open. A gas canister was thrown in. Maria and two men burst in after it.

'Clear!' she shouted as she left the hall. Two more men followed her in; two held position at the door. With military precision, they invaded the lounge, the kitchen, the bedroom.

'Clear!'

It was clear that Foxx and his accomplice were in the bathroom. She assembled her men in a new formation and gently tried the handle. It was locked. She had him like a rat in a trap. He was there for the taking; but was he armed? Did he have an automatic rifle pointed at the door? How was she to bring him out alive? Storrington arrived. She was working. She gave him a clear and decisive hand signal to leave. This was *her* operation. This was a military zone and he was not combat-ready. He left.

'Foxx, we know you're in there. We need you to come out with nothing more than your dick in your hand. Put down your weapons. You know how this works. Open the door gently and show us your hands and you live. Ignore me and you die in a storm of bullets. Let's not mess up this nice lady's flat.'

Silence.

'Is she in there with you?'

Silence.

'C'mon, Foxx. You know we don't do hostage negotiations. We've come for you and we're taking you. You have one minute to think this through and open the door.' At that moment she gave the order for the ram to smash open the door. It struck hard, the door shattered. The bomb detonated. She was thrown back by a god almighty white flash and an ear-numbing explosion that ripped out of the bathroom. Dazed, dizzy and deafened, the men were floored, but retrained their guns on the bathroom door, supported from behind by the two door guards. Slowly the smoke cleared, the haze evaporated. They could see into the bathroom. No one. Number Five went in, gun first. Nothing. Nobody. No pieces of body, no guns. Just the remnants of a rapidly made, home constructed, almost harmless, flash bomb.

'Clear!' he said. 'He's not in here. Foxx has fucked off.'

'Sorry, sir,' she said to Storrington, in the hall, her ears still ringing.

'You can't catch what isn't there. Get your guys out of here and into the transport.'

'What about the other flats? He could be there.'

'Leave it to the bobbies. The bird has flown.'

'Yes, sir.'

Storrington stepped slowly into the flat. He looked again at the kick on the door. Forced entry, but no damage to the lock. Civilians kick doors low down; the military kick doors up by the lock. He meandered through the flat, eyes alert. A pile of slightly damp clothes in the hall: female clothes; tidy flat, messy clothes. Two coffee cups in the lounge, one on a coaster, one not. A tiny length of plastic by the bed, the snip-pings of a cable tie, a blonde hair on the carpet. He looked round for a picture of the occupant. He found none, so checked her array of brushes on her dressing table. She wasn't blonde. He moved to the kitchen; dishes not washed but left to soak, an incongruous habit in a flat that had been kept immaculately before the invasion. And the kitchen window was open, just a crack, but enough. He peered into the bath-room and left. He waited with the team, until the police had checked the other flats, but he knew there was nothing to find. The fox was on the lam.

Foxx knew it was time to leave the second he saw the light on his phone. He knew the drill. A call from GCHQ tracking station to PM-SSS, a call from PM-SSS to the local police, a call to the nearest squad car and a short trip across town to the flats; maybe four minutes, maybe eight. They would assemble a SWAT team and prepare for extraction; maybe another twenty minutes. There was no time to waste.

He barked orders at Serafina Pekkala, a Secret Service employee who should have known better. She packed a hasty bag of essentials, while he went from room to room removing evidence. He had not expected to be leaving so soon. She had not expected to be leaving at all. Holiday wash bag, handbag, purse, enough underwear for goodness knows how long, as many changes of clothing as she could cram in, a warm jacket and, of course, her favourite trousers. She picked up Duncan's photograph to put in her bag, but replaced it where she found it. He could stay here and guard the flat. She kissed it, did the same with Lisa's picture next to it, and left them both where they belonged.

'Time to go,' he said, as he saw a panda car pull up by the war memorial across the road. 'Is there a back way out of here?'

'There's the bin door,' she said as they left her comfortable flat, closed the door and skipped down the stairs two at a time. They were leaving through the back exit in the basement as a fresh-faced young policeman peered through the glass front doors into the ground-floor lobby. He saw nothing unusual. He stood there and kept guard while his colleague took Grand Rise.

'Have you got a car?' asked Foxx.

'Yes, in the garages across the way, about 200 yards in that direction.' She pointed away from the police car.

'Good. Let's go.'

Once outside the back door, his whole countenance changed. He came into his own, he was on a mission; this was his element. He became lithe and alive, supple and effortless, as he glided at speed across the grass and up the walkway towards the garages. She clunkily trotted behind him, like a three-legged donkey. He had vitality, energy and awareness; he was in control of his world and in control of his surroundings. This was the first time she had seen him really be him.

In the supermarket he'd been acting, being a naïve, charming, but nervous singleton; in the flat he'd been a rampaging rapist, then a business negotiator bargaining for her help, then overly distressed at the fictional demise of the PM. Now he was being himself, she could feel it, see it, know it. It was hard not to be drawn in. *He is a killer*, she told herself, *he's a cold blooded murderer and an assassin; he's a bad man*. The first three descriptions reviled her, but the last, being a bad man, just multiplied the attraction.

Once at the garages, her unintentional donkey-ness continued. Her fingers fumbled with her keys. She was not used to this lifestyle. She tried the key twice. The garage wouldn't unlock.

'What's the problem?' he asked.

'Wrong key. This is my boyfriend's garage key.' She pointed at the garage next door.

'Is there a car in there?'

'Yes.'

'Do you have the keys?' She nodded. 'The car keys?' he confirmed. She nodded again.

'Even better! We'll take that.' She hauled up the door to reveal a sporty hatchback. It would be their base for the next few days. The car was dusty, the garage was damp. It had clearly not been used for a long time. Two hooks on the garage wall caught his eye. One had a crash helmet hanging on it, the other was empty.

'He left his skid-lid,' observed Foxx.

'No, he didn't. That one's mine.'

She got in the car, it started second time and she carefully reversed out. Foxx peered through the bushes to see increasing activity at the front of the flats. He checked his exit route. He walked down the short driveway that circled the back of the garages. It came out on to a small side road twenty yards from its junction with Jurors' Road in one direction and the oblivion of Cheltenham suburbia in the other. It was a good escape route, except for one thing; it was blocked by a police van full of six large, heavily armed men and one equally well-armed woman, all ready for action. He knew they would move when they were needed, so he strolled back to Julie. She had closed and locked the garage and was ready to go. He gave a sign to kill the engine. She looked back at him quizzically. He just turned and peered through the hedge. She scurried over.

A branch was edged to one side to allow her to observe the bustle of police activity in front of the previously quiet Berkeley Heights. She moved closer to him to get a better view. Police were coming and going, talking on radios and getting in and out of cars. He gave her a running explanation of what was happening and what they were thinking. He predicted their actions like it was a rerun of his favourite movie. She put her arm round his waist, only so that she could squeeze in closer for a better view, his arm fell across her shoulders, their heads pressed closer together. They watched. He described every action step by step. He was one step ahead, always . . . until the helicopter arrived. He hadn't expected that.

They heard it flying low overhead, but it didn't stop above the flats. Hovering would have been bad news, heat sensors would have found them in seconds, but it was not looking for them, it was coming down.

'They're landing on the school playing field,' said Julie. She had jogged across it often.

'I wonder who that is,' he said out loud. The activity stepped up a gear.

'You see her, the one in the full combat gear, walking towards the front door?' he continued. 'She's the boss of the SWAT team. I saw her in the van at the end of the lane here. But she's not SWAT, she's full-on military. This is a military operation, not a police operation.' They watched the woman stand with confidence as she took a commanding position over the assembled police presence. People came and people went.

'Who's that?' asked Julie, as she saw a tall slim man exit a squad car.

'Him? Well, he's a surprise for sure. He's the reason for the helicopter. We are in the presence of greatness. That is the Number One, Commander Storrington, Leader-in-Chief of the Prime Minister's Special Security Services. What the hell is he doing here? Why is he here, in person? That's very interesting.'

'What's happening now?'

'The captain's talking to the boss. They'll call the van round the corner in a minute. There it is. That means they're about to enter the building. They know we're in there, so we're safe out here. We're good to go.'

They were standing close together. She felt ragged, like her whole head had just gone through an emotional spin cycle. She had spent twenty-four hours being scared of Mr Eduard Foxx and now she was scared by all the guns, uniforms and military activity that had come to get him. She was small, but she felt the warmth of his body next to hers and it felt good. He was not like anyone she had ever met, and she was determined not to admire him. But he was in a different league; he had an air about him, a charisma; and, perversely enough, for a cold-blooded, callous, murderous assassin, being with him felt safe. She moved closer and stared at the guns that she feared one day would be aimed at her.

'Those six guys and their captain are his blood hounds and it's our blood they're after. They would shoot us as look at us. That, my dear Serafina, is what you've brought upon us.'

'I'm sorry. It was a genuine mistake. What do we do now?'

'Simple. He's invading your home, so we will invade his.'

13

THE WRONG TROUSERS

'Who owns the flat?' asked Storrington.

A policeman flipped through his notebook. 'A Miss Julie Connor, thirty-four, civil servant. Pays her council tax and keeps herself to herself. Never been on our radar, except two years ago, but that was nothing criminal.'

'Civil servant? Here in Cheltenham?'

'Yes, we assume so.' Storrington had what he wanted. The picture had fallen into place. He walked away, took out his phone and called his Head of Investigations.

'Julie Connor, thirty-four, civil servant. Find out what we've got on her and which department she works for. Check the Doughnut first. If she's GCHQ, I want to know. And her car registration, get me that too. On the double.' Hoy took down the details and hung up. There was a lot he needed to find out, but just one question that needed an answer: Julie Connor, friend or foe?

The M5 was not the quickest route to London, but it was the fastest way out of Cheltenham. Julie Connor was driving her boyfriend's car, slowly and steadily as instructed. Anxiety, remorse, insecurity and unwarranted guilt were all eating her from the inside out.

'So?' asked Foxx.

'So, what?' she asked him back, with no energy or real desire to know what he was talking about.

'The crash helmet?' She ignored the angst-ridden shot of adrenaline that pricked her heart.

'What about it?'

'That's what I'm asking. What about it? The crash helmet, the dusty car, his keys still in your handbag.' Her eyes welled up. Reality hit him. 'Oh, Julie, I'm so sorry. Clumsy of me. I'm really sorry. I have no tact.'

Julie stared at the road ahead. A tear slid down her cheek. 'It was a big flashy racing bike. It didn't suit him at all; he wasn't like that. He said he would get rid of it, so we took one last trip round the Cotswolds. It was my idea. I was on the back. It wasn't fair. I was thrown clear: cuts, scratches, bruises, a fracture and concussion. He slid right under the lorry.' Her face felt the pain of it still. 'And that was it. I should get rid of that bloody crash helmet, I don't know why I've kept it.

He was a good one; the only good one. All the others were even worse than you.' He ignored the implied, but justified insult. 'I'm still mad with him for dying. Why did he do that? Why leave me? Why? I still haven't forgiven him.' Speech faded to thought. The car was silent. Her hurt wouldn't go away. It was too much.

She pulled off the motorway and into the services. Her eyes looked at him and said 'You drive'.

The Commander and his captain stood very close, on the edge of Jurors' Road, a short distance away from the others. She looked up at his bony weather-beaten face.

'Do you think he saw us coming?' she asked.

'No,' he replied. 'He knew as soon as the phone went on that we'd be on to him.'

'Then why turn it on?'

'My guess is it was her. But was it a mistake . . . or a signal to us?'

'When you figure that out,' she said, 'let me know, so I know whether to shoot her or not.' There was a trace of bullish bravado in her voice born of the frustration of a failed raid.

'You'll get your chance soon enough. Your boys did well.'

'Mostly. A couple of them want to go it alone, see the target and chase it. But I have hammered formation into their heads a hundred times.'

Storrington looked at his watch. 'When this is over,' he said, 'I want to take you to tea. We have too much catching up to do.'

'Yes, sir!' said the lightly smiling captain.

Julie sat. Foxx drove. They were on the M4 now, heading for London. Foxx was talking, but Julie wasn't listening to the words outside her head, only the images that tormented her within.

She felt small, like so many times before: when she was ten and Archie, her stepdad, had made her feel insignificant; when she was with Terry, her first real boyfriend, and he'd made her feel stupid; or when she was with any of the next three poor choice, egocentric, unchivalrous, incompatible boyfriends, who just made her doubt she had any value at all.

Duncan had been different: he understood her, taught her to be herself. With Duncan she'd had a value; without him she had nothing. Men weren't like women. They had all diminished her, misread her, mistook her quietness for weakness. But in truth she had been weak, she had diminished herself and she had made a promise to Duncan that she would never do that again. And here she was sitting in the passenger seat of his car, hunched into her own self, subsumed by her self-inflicted sorrow, being no one, showing nothing, being invisible. She was wallowing in that all too familiar, self-subjugating, downtrodden, self-betraying miasma.

She felt so alone. She had sat in that passenger seat a hundred times with Duncan at the wheel, feeling safe, feeling loved. Now she looked over and saw the wrong man. It was not right: on so many levels, it was as wrong as it could be.

Her life was a mess, even before Eduard Foxx had barged into it. Depression dropped her head and she looked down at herself. What had she become? Scruffy top, moth eaten and baggy, over last Thursday's T-shirt. That was bad enough, but it was the trousers; they were the wrong trousers. Saggy, misshapen tracksuit bottoms, stained, unwashed, tramplike; they made her look fat. Foxx was right: she had become frumpy. She didn't feel special, she hadn't *been* special, not since Duncan died. She'd had offers from men, but she'd let them lapse in preference for a life of loneliness and self-pity.

She looked back at Foxx. He was enjoying the adventure. She wasn't. The feeling got worse. She knew that if she let him control the relationship, like all the Terrys and Tysons before him, it would not end well. *Julie for god's sake, be Julie! Get a grip. Be yourself. Be Serafina, be the Queen of the Witches.*

'Stop the car!' she yelled. 'Pull off at this junction.' He'd almost passed the exit. He swerved and took the slip road. It was the Newbury turn-off. She knew it well: Head Office of '2' was just down the road. She guided him round the roundabouts, along a short winding lane and into the car park of the Hilton Hotel, venue of many tedious management meetings. Today, it was a temporary sanctuary of familiar ground.

She said nothing, but grabbed a small vanity bag, a hairbrush, a blouse and the right pair of trousers from her roll bag, left the car and headed for the hotel. He made no effort to stop her; she knew the consequences. He got out of the car, locked it and sat on a bench in the sunshine by the door of the reception.

A change of clothes worked for Clark Kent and his Superwoman counterpart. One of Julie's earliest memories was of her dad, her real dad, wearing a suit. It had been a rare occasion for a metalworker, but he'd said it made him feel like a real man. She walked into the reception area and up to the desk. She knew the Duty Manager. A room was borrowed and the transformation began.

She brushed her hair and put on the lightest trace of make-up, but it was enough. She did her lippy, subtle but fresh, and shed her sloppy, ill-fitting scruff bags, like a butterfly emerging from a chrysalis. She changed her attire, her attitude and her approach. She held up her favourite trousers, looked at them, put them on, pulled them up and did the zip. They felt tight, good tight and she knew she was back. She knew that clothes didn't make you a different person, but they made her feel like herself, her real self, and that was all she wanted. Julie 'withering' Connors had entered that hotel, but Serafina Pekkala, Queen of the Witches came out.

He saw her as she approached. Same person, different attitude. She had purpose, a determination in her strut. She was the girl from the flat, but more so - a lot more so. Her movements were seductive, her demeanour more decisive, her desirability had increased tenfold. She walked past the bench where Eduard was sitting.

'Keys,' she said, holding out her hand, as she walked past. He handed them over.

As she walked in front of him, he kept his eyes on her. Both she and he were enjoying the trousers, differently but simultaneously. She looked good and that's all he could say. But he didn't: he didn't say anything, no comment was needed. She drove, with enthusiasm, back round the roundabouts and out onto the motorway.

'I've got a question for you, Mr Eduard Foxx.' Her tones were firm and decisive. 'If you're just a lowly desk jockey, what were you doing in Azerbaijan and Georgia?'

'I never said lowly.'

'Implied,' she replied. 'And the question still stands.' She forced herself to be strong.

'I used to be in Operations. That's how I know Brekkenfield. I did five years, almost all of it undercover on foreign soil. It had its moments, but my real talents lie in planning and tactics, so I transferred to a desk, trading my pistol for a laptop.'

'Hmmm,' she muttered, seemingly unconvinced. 'And why did you plant a - what did you call it? - a flash bomb, in my bathroom? I'm going to have to redecorate now. It seemed a bit pointless, like a teenager raising a rigid finger and sticking it to the man. Are you really a teenager in disguise, Mr Foxx?'

'It was a message. Storrington knew or would pretty quickly have found out that I'd been in the flat, so I left him a message.'

'And what was that message?'

'I could have killed you, but I didn't, because I'm not that type of guy.'

'A bit subtle if you ask me. You could have written a note.'

The conversation died, and dried into a period of lull, before she turned her mind to the next step of his plan. She thought back about the gathering police and military presence outside her flat.

'Why was Storrington there?' she asked.

'I don't know, but let's say for a minute that it *is* Storrington we're after, why send the heavies after us, when he knows we didn't do it?'

She gave no reply. It had become apparent that he was talking to himself.

'To silence us,' he continued. 'With us silenced, he's clear to carry on with the other assassination plans. He won't stop until he kills the PM and that means he won't stop until he finds us. I've also worked out why the hit on the PM didn't go ahead today,' he continued.

'Because you weren't there?' she retorted sharply.

'No, because Storrington's a gunsmith, not a poisoner. Hence, going for the first attempt – a sniper attack - but not the second, because he's not a chemist. But he'll definitely go for the third, because it gives him the choice of shooting or strangling. We have to be there to stop him.'

'So what is the third attempt?'

'Too simple to fail.' Foxx explained the intricate background and the exacting context. She was impressed by his insight.

'How could you know that? You're very well informed.'

'Thank you. It's my job to know more than other people.' Then he explained how the assassination would take place. She was shocked at its simplicity. 'It'll be like shooting fish in a barrel,' he said. 'For a man like Storrington, it's a gift.'

'So, Storrington,' asked Julie, thinking about their destination, 'how do you know where he lives?'

'I don't.'

'That's a bit of a flaw in your plan, isn't it, Mr *It's my job to know more than other people?*'

'I thought *you* knew. You were researching him.'

'No address on the internet. All I know is his wife died of cancer seven years ago, so I hope that means he lives alone, but I don't know where.' She paused in thought. 'D'you think Mrs Charlie 'loose-lipped' Tenby might know? Because I know where she lives.' He looked at her visibly impressed; not because she was clever, but because she thought of it first.

'Sounds like a plan. Let's go there now.'

'You know she lives with Mr Tenby, right? It's a Sunday evening, so he'll be home getting ready for work in the morning. And he is Second-in-Command in the country's top Security Service.'

'It's Sunday evening, SSS is on Red Alert. There will be a Security briefing this evening. He'll have to attend; he has no choice. If we're quick we can make it before he's home.'

He set the satnav. Next stop: Tenby Mansions.

THE ROSE GARDEN

Nickolas Tenby lay with his mistress and talked. He talked too much for a Security Head, but only to his wife, who feigned interest, and to his lover, who fawned with interest.

'But why does it matter?' she asked, more interested in him than the answer.

'Because I have £15 million invested in it, that's why it matters! That's what my shares in the company are worth. But this Brexit deal is going to finish me. The company is in a very niche defence market and we exclusively supply the European Community. That will go in an instant. Not only that, the UK Defence Budget will be rationalised to provide funds to boost the economy and pay the £100 billion EU divorce settlement. The Ministry of Defence will want mega discounts and they'll go for the big companies. We won't even get a look in. It will go from £15 million to 15 pence overnight. And it's a terrible Brexit deal anyway. I've talked to the DPM about it and he agrees, but his hands are tied. He's not running the negotiations.'

'So, sell the shares now.'

'Yeah, good idea, and get put away for fifteen years for insider trading. I can't do that, and even if I did sell that many shares, alarm bells would ring in the market and the shares would drop anyway.'

'So what are you going to do?'

'I don't know. I'll think of something. I've talked about it with Charlie . . .'

'Well, that was a waste of breath!' said the slightly jealous, very naked lady a little too abruptly. He rolled her over and gave her a quick slap on her behind.

'Don't be uncharitable. She's a good listener and has more common sense than you give her credit for. She runs the house, runs her own business, runs our domestic finances, runs the village charity committee . . .'

'And puts me through to you on the phone.'

'Yes,' he said, in her defence, 'she did, but she could see I was stressed, knew it was about work, so she thoughtfully phoned you and handed me the phone. We were in the study, but she set me up in the conservatory, because she knows I don't discuss work secrets with her. She brought me coffee and left us to it. It was a good thing to do.'

'Yes, except it was me! She called me . . . and I'm your mistress!'

'But she doesn't know that.'

'I know she doesn't, but she put us together. Now *that*, from a woman's perspective, is pretty dumb.'

'She's not dumb, she's just alternatively gifted. If you say she is again, I'll have to punish you.'

'She's dumb, she's dumb, she's dumb!' she said screaming like a defiant teenager, as he made a grab for her and the little leather whip that lay next to them.

~

'Hello, is Mr Morgan-Tenby in? I'm from his office.' Julie 'Serafina' Connor spoke clearly and formally into the electronic entry system as she stared at the initials N-M-T woven into the wrought iron gate.

Foxx had briefed her on the plan. They would get Storrington's address, Julie would keep the wife talking, while Foxx snooped around the house. That's why he had insisted on stopping at a DIY store on the way.

'I'm sorry but Nickolas is out at the moment. Can I help?' The electronically sweet voice was the loose-lipped lady known as Mrs Tenby.

'Yes, maybe you can. May we come in?'

The gates opened.

'Mr Hoy,' said the female voice on the phone. 'This is Mrs Hoy. I'm your wife. I don't know if you remember me, but I'm the person you cuddled up to after I went to sleep and left before I woke up this morning. We need to talk.'

'We are talking.'

'No, I mean, *we need to talk.* We had a plan. Remember? In Iran before you started with the Special Security Service? It was the reason you joined. We talked it through and we decided what you had to do. And now you must do it. We didn't spend four months putting plans in place for them to get away from us now. You're so close. Get it done.'

Mrs Hoy was a thoughtful, intelligent, ambitious woman, but also formidable when the mood took her. Her husband was besotted by her. She was the driver behind the plan. She had the aspiration and the inspiration then expected her husband to make it work.

Her respect for a man was in equal proportion to the strength of that man – and right now, her husband was wavering.

'It's probably a good thing your husband's not here,' bluffed Foxx. 'We've come to do a security sweep of the house. He said we were fussing and shouldn't come, but we only want to keep him safe.' He proved it by waving a meter that measured dampness in walls, complete with coloured lights and flicking dial that he'd just picked up in the DIY store.

'Let's not tell him, then! Our little secret,' she said. 'Come in.'

'Hi, I'm Julie,' said Julie forgetting to use a false name. Foxx threw her a look of lightly contemptuous despair.

'I'm Charlie, Nicki's wife. Would you like a cup of tea?'

'Yes, that would be lovely, if it's not too much trouble,' said Julie, as they crossed the capacious hall and were shown into the immaculate modern drawing room. 'It's a lovely house. I love the decor. Is that you or Mr Ten . . . Nicki's design?'

'Me, mostly, except that picture. That's his.' Julie ignored its vulgarity.

'You got interior designers in?' Julie asked.

'No. I did it myself.'

'You have a real eye for style, if I may say so.'

'Thank you. It's a far cry from where I grew up.' Julie's look asked the question. 'Lancaster,' continued Charlie. 'And not the nice part; a real rundown council estate - knife fights every night, alcoholics on every corner. Nothing like this.'

'Is that where your parents are from?'

'It's where my mum was from. My dad was from the Merchant Navy. I don't think she even knew his name. Just a meal ticket probably.'

'Rough start in life then?'

'I guess so. But life is what you make it. She had her own problems, hooked on what she called *Mummy's gin*, which was anything she could smoke, snort or inject, so she lived pretty much in her own world. But I got through.'

'Sounds like she didn't help much.'

'Well, she gave me a good name. Charlotte Penelope Clarke. She said if she gave me a posh name, I would end up in a posh place – and look, it worked!' She smiled.

'It certainly did,' said Julie, smiling back at a woman of her own age, who looked much younger. She might be physically and mentally light-weight, but Julie admired her positivity.

Foxx pulled a small book from his pocket.

'I heard from someone in the office,' he said, 'that you like doing puzzles, so I got you this.' He gave her a puzzle book that he'd picked up *en route*. Charlie looked at it, puzzled. She took it and flicked through the pages, a trace of confusion crossed her face. Foxx tried to allay her fears. 'It's intermediate, they didn't have basic, I hope it's OK.'

Julie's foot connected with Foxx's shin and her eyes tried to drill a hole in his head.

'It looks lovely,' said Charlie graciously and vacuously. 'Let me get you your tea,' and she left.

'What?' said Foxx, almost silently.

'You're an arse! Never tell a stupid person they're stupid, they don't like it!'

'But I only said . . .'

'You said she was stupid. We need to get her on side. Do try not to be . . .' she searched for the word. 'Well, just try not to be you!'

Foxx smiled. He liked watching his protégé grow in confidence.

'I like her,' said Julie. 'I think she and I could click. She seems happy to talk openly.'

'Yes. If a thought comes into her head, it comes out of her mouth.'

'Which is good for us,' whispered Julie, hearing Charlie returning. 'You go round the house waving your damp do-dah meter and I'll see what she knows.'

The door opened and Charlie entered holding a tray on one hand. She set it down on the hand-crafted coffee table and poured the tea.

'So you were glad to leave Lancaster then?'

'You could say that! I ran away.'

'Really? How old were you?'

'Fourteen.'

'That's very young to be on your own.'

'Oh I wasn't on my own. I was with a man; he was twice my age, he took me to live with him.' Julie tried very hard not to raise an eyebrow. 'In Guildford,' Charlie continued. 'It was really nice. I loved it.'

'And you carried on your schooling there?'

'Nah, I was done with school. But I did go to the university - the University of Surrey. It's in Guildford.' Foxx spluttered in his tea, but tried to conceal it as a cough. Julie looked at him as though he were an errant child.

'And what did you do at university?' she asked, turning back to Charlie.

'Waitressing.'

'I never knew there was a course in that,' said Foxx.

'No. I did waitressing. In the Reflectory. Breakfasts and lunches mostly. I was only fifteen.'

'Sounds like hard work,' said Julie, as Foxx mopped up the dribbles of tea.

Charlie stalled for a moment, maybe even thinking if she should say the next thing. 'It was very hard, because I used to work nights as well.'

'Waitressing?'

'No, not really. It was a club, called SOAPS.'

'And was there soap involved?' asked Foxx, determined to be crass.

'Yes, I suppose there was. I used to shower my clients before . . .' She paused again.

'Taking them to bed?' filled in Foxx.

'Yes,' she said. Julie fought hard to hide her shock. 'I used to have up to four clients a night; and I usually spent the whole night with the last one, then up in the morning and off to the Reflectory.' She lost none of her sweetness, as she spoke in a very honest, conversational manner. No wonder Nickolas Tenby kept her hidden away. She certainly had no filter between brain and mouth.

'Does Nicki know you did that?' asked Julie.

'No, I don't think he does. It's not a secret, it's just never come up in conversation.' *Tess of the D'Urbervilles* shot across Julie's mind: *always tell your man . . . before you get married!*

'If it does come up, maybe it would be better not to mention it to him,' advised Julie, already feeling slightly protective of a girl who was so simple Julie feared she might have brain damage.

'No, I couldn't do that. If he asked, I would tell him. I believe in total honesty. With everyone. I've never told a lie in the whole of my life.'

'Really?' asked Foxx.

'Yes,' she said. 'I may not be the smartest person in the world, but that doesn't stop me from being the most honest.'

'Well, if I am going to be honest,' said Julie, seeing an opportunity to get back on track, 'there is a way you can help me. After checking round this house, we've to go to Commander Storrington's house but, and this is all my fault, I've lost his address. I'm going to be in such trouble. I don't suppose you have it, do you?'

'Yes, I'm sure I do. We don't see much of him. He and Nicki don't really see eye to eye. Nicki thinks he's a bit stuffy and old-fashioned and he thinks Nicki is . . .' she was lost for words. '. . . is too lovely probably.'

'Yes, I'm sure that's what it is,' confirmed Julie.

'I'll just get it for you.' She stood up. Her clothes hung perfectly as she floated to the door, looking every inch a princess and in no way a retired prostitute. Foxx and Julie stared at each other.

'Did she just admit to being a hooker?' asked Julie.

'Like mother, like daughter,' confirmed Foxx.

'And her husband doesn't know!'

'Well, that's the kind of scandal you keep to yourself.'

'Oh my god, the SNGS would go wild for that.'

'Yes, the Press would too,' added Foxx, as he lost himself in a world of imagination with a teenage Mrs Tenby.

Julie picked up her phone and googled SOAPS club in Guildford, Surrey.

'And,' continued Foxx, 'she was underage! My god, three or four punters a night? She must have slept with half of Surrey!'

'Here it is,' said Julie, reading the entry on her phone.

'She's a wicked lady with a shady past,' said Foxx, almost in perverse admiration.

'You reckon, Sherlock?' said Julie, as she started to read about SOAPS club. 'It's an acronym, SOAPS, it stands for - are you ready? . . . Surrey Old Age Pensioner's Support club. She was a volunteer, she spent her evenings cooking and cleaning for old people and then helping the disabled ones to bed. She's not a sinner, she's a saint. You mustn't be too quick to judge.'

The saint returned.

'I've got it,' she said and handed Julie a slip of paper, with a beautifully handwritten address on it.

'Great, thanks.'

'So, you never tell a lie?' asked Foxx, with a gentle menace in his voice.

'No. Never.'

'How many men have you slept with?'

'Eduard!' exclaimed Julie in outraged and heartfelt disbelief. She turned to Charlie. 'I am so sorry, I don't know what's the matter with my colleague today. Really, I am so sorry. Please just ignore him.'

But she didn't. She looked at him gently and asked, 'How many men have I slept with? Hmm . . . do you want me to include my stepfather, who raped me repeatedly from the age of twelve?' A momentarily nonplussed Eduard had no reply. 'Including him, it totals . . . yes . . . a total of three. Not many for thirty-two years.'

'Eduard,' said Julie sternly, 'I think it's time you did a security sweep of the house.' She turned to Charlie. 'Is that OK?'

'Yes, please, help yourself, Eduard,' Eduard was looking at Julie wondering what had happened to their agreed false names gambit. 'It's kind you give up your Sunday to keep Nicki safe,' she said to Julie and turned to Eduard, 'I owe you a million thanks.'

'Yes. My pleasure,' said Foxx.

'You know the young man that was shot?' continued Charlie. 'I knew him. He came to a party here once. So sad. It was so unfair.'

'Yes. We should have kept him safer. We never expected it,' replied Foxx, getting up and fiddling with the pseudo-security meter.

'I was shocked,' she continued. 'That sort of thing should not be allowed to happen.'

'Well, we're working hard to make sure it doesn't happen again,' reassured Mr Foxx as he waved his hydrometer at each corner of the room and checked the dial.

'That's good,' she said, as Foxx left the room.

'Charlie, I am so sorry,' said Julie, once they were alone.

'What? That I've only slept with three men?'

'No, that my colleague is an idiot.'

'He's not an idiot, he's just a boy.'

'I think you'll find he's both.'

'But he likes you.'

'No. We're just work colleagues.'

'Maybe. But he still likes you. A lot. But you're not sure about him?'

'He's OK.'

'He's more than OK: he's hot,' said Charlie with teenage dorm-room excitement.

'Yes,' said Julie giving away an unintended smile. 'He is hot. But men and me haven't really been working out, so I'm taking a break.' And it became Julie's turn to be loose-lipped and alarmingly honest. She told herself it was part of the plan, part of getting close to a source, but the words flowed too naturally for that. The story unfolded, from Terry to Duncan, and ended badly as it always did. Charlie laid a reassuring hand on Julie's arm. A bond had started to form.

Foxx had scoped the house and spent time on the high target rooms: the study, the den and the master bedroom. He searched through drawers and convenient places for hiding notes or memory sticks. He tried to log on to computers, but the SSS firewall was too big even for him to climb, in the time available. Wiping his HR files had been easy because he was inside SSS, but logging into the Head of Planning's home PC proved impossible. He searched fast, carefully and to leave no trace. But the only thing he found was a list of names on the top of the desk. He took a picture of it and carried on his search.

By the time he got back to the drawing room, the girls had gone. The French doors were open and the garden was lit with a hundred hidden light bulbs. The girls sat deep in conversation on a bench by a fountain at the far end of the Rose Garden.

'And what about you?' asked Julie, feeling it was time to stop pouring her own heart out. 'Did you like Guildford? And living with a man twice your age?'

'Yes, he was my brother, or half-brother. He had a different dad . . . obviously! He was fun, but he made me study! I was in Guildford for three or four years, then moved to St Ives for three years, then lived in America for a year, near Boston.'

'Wow, how exciting. Were you working there?' Charlie nodded. 'What did you do?'

'Waitressing. Then I came back to London. I was only here for a couple of months when I met Nicki.'

'Where did you meet him?'

'I was at a big gala dinner at the Dorchester.'

'How posh! What were you doing there?'

'Waitressing.'

There was a certain predictability to Charlie's career history. 'He was all flirty and handsy, then didn't leave at the end. Long story short, I woke up here in the morning and have been here ever since.'

'What's it like being with Nicki?'

'It's good. He's a real control merchant, but he's only here a few nights a week and some weekends. I'm only with him for about twenty hours a week, so I do my best to make him happy. I always make myself look my best, wear the clothes he likes, let him ogle my bum, wave goodbye when he goes and meet him at the door when he comes home. He's a very simple man, a bit ass-phixiated, but it's not hard to make him feel good.'

'It doesn't bother you that he is a lot older than you?'

'No, he was a lot older than me when I married him. He gets a bit tense sometimes, that's all. Lately there was some report about something and he got totally uptight about it. The Antelope-Beaver report I called it. I can't remember what it was really called. But then I just gave him a . . . what can I say . . . special attention.'

They chatted for twenty minutes or more, until Charlie said,

'Your friend is waiting at the doors. I think he wants to go.' They'd enjoyed their unexpected deep dive into each other's lives, but Julie had not learned much of anything. Two minutes later they were all standing at the front door.

'Thank you, Mrs Tenby. You've been very kind,' said Foxx. Then as he left, he turned to Julie. 'I'll see you in a minute. I'll be in the car.' Julie was facing Charlie, not sure whether to kiss her or shake hands and settled on neither.

'Yes, thank you Charlie. It was very nice to meet you.'

'No, it was my pleasure. It was nice talking to you. I guess I don't have many . . .' She paused for a moment.

'Friends?' suggested Julie helpfully.

'I was going to say people to chat to, but I suppose you're right. I chat to the people at work, but not so much, and the only other people I see are Nicki's friends and he always wants me to be on my best behaviour, so it was nice chatting to you.'

'Who knows, maybe we'll meet again,' said Julie as she leant in an inch to kiss a cheek and thought better of it. 'Look after yourself.' She bent to pick up her bag. She leant, she picked and then it happened. Julie felt it, Charlie heard it. They caught each other's eyes and laughed. But to Julie it was a disaster.

Two minutes later they were upstairs, in a spare bedroom, Julie with her back to the mirror.

'Oh! My! God!' she exclaimed as her eyes were drawn to the non-existent seat of her trousers. They had not so much split as disintegrated. Her bottom was clearly visible, both cheeks covered in nothing but fresh air and a few loose strands of black thread.

'These are my favourite trousers,' she said, with palpable sorrow in her voice. She wasn't so much embarrassed by her predicament as distraught at the loss of an old friend. 'They were Duncan's first ever present to me.' She made little attempt to hide her distress. She looked, she stared, she scrabbled with her fingertips.

Charlie slipped out to return moments later holding a well-chosen skirt on a hanger.

'Try this,' she said. 'It should go with the top you're wearing.'

'Don't be silly,' said Julie, forgetting her manners for a moment. 'Nothing of yours will fit me. We're hardly the same shape.'

'Yes, you're right. Your waist is much slimmer than mine; this might be a bit loose on you.'

Julie took the skirt and slipped it on. Charlie took the defeated, de-seated trousers and lay them neatly on the bed. 'It suits you. You look good in it.' Charlie had chosen well. The waist was a comfortable fit and the flowing style of the material slipped gracefully over Julie's rounder form. It hung well, like an £1800 *haute-couture* garment should. Julie would have died if she'd known the price. 'Take it,' said Charlie. 'It'll never replace your trousers, but it'll get you home.'

'Thank you. I will. You saved me. I will send it back to you.'

'You needn't. If you like it, you can keep it.'

'You're an angel,' she said, feeling a sudden closeness, and kissed Charlie lightly on the cheek. 'I don't know what to say.'

'Say nothing, go and join your friend. He'll be missing you.' She handed Julie her dilapidated trousers.

'No, can I leave them here, can you . . .? I can't bear to throw them away.' And she scurried off to join Foxx.

'Oh,' said Charlie, as Julie was leaving, 'I remember now. It wasn't Antelope-Beaver. It was Anderson-Bevan. He got quite agitated about it. What are men like?'

'Children,' replied Julie, knowing an answer wasn't really required. 'And thanks again.'

She skipped out of the front door and over to the car.

Under any other circumstances, Julie would have just made a new best friend.

Commander Storrington quizzed his Head of Investigations at the Sunday evening security meeting.

'Serafina Pekkala? At GCHQ-2?'

'Affirmative,' said Hoy.

'That adds a different dimension,' muttered Brekkenfield.

'Yes. She's got the highest GCHQ-2 clearance; access to everything,' confirmed Storrington. *She can read my mails, forwards my mails, trace my actions*, he thought to himself. 'She's a real danger.'

'I'm going to remove her clearance and wipe her pass key. I'll tell Security at GCHQ to detain her on sight,' said Hoy.

'No,' said the Commander. 'Don't do that. Leave it as it is. If the bird

comes back to the nest. . .' the sentence was left unfinished. 'Do nothing
and tell nobody; not for now anyway.'

'She's in on it,' added Morgan-Tenby. 'It's Bonnie and Clyde.'

Storrington shook his head and explained. 'He kicked the door open
and tied her to the bed, so no, she was not in on it - not at first. But he's a
real persuader, could talk black into white. And she left with him,
presumably willingly or she'd be dead, so my guess is . . .' Another
sentence was left un-concluded. This was out of character for the
Commander, but Hoy didn't push it. Desperate times. The silence hung
for a moment or two. 'Two birds flown,' added the Commander, thinking
out loud. 'Two birds, one Stone.' He gathered his thoughts and continued.

'The weak link: Julie Connor. She'll make a mistake and then we'll
have her.'

15

SHINE ON

Julie Connor followed Eduard Foxx through Commander Storrington's front door and closed it quietly behind her. She felt acutely aware, as she gazed around his most private of residences, that she had not only broken into his home, she had invaded his life.

Commander Storrington didn't have a house, other than the basic bothy he owned in deepest rural Scotland; he had a flat in Westminster, on the third floor. A credit card and a master key made light of gaining access. The alarm bleeped quietly indicating its intention of notifying Scotland Yard in thirty seconds of the intruder's presence. Foxx unzipped a small hand sized case, took out a pair of wires with tiny crocodile clips, an electrical screwdriver and an electronic device the size of a mobile phone. Five seconds later, the alarm stopped bleeping.

'How did you do that?' asked Julie, clearly impressed.

'Does it matter?' he asked dismissively. She shook her head. Conversation closed.

Julie took the kitchen and the bathroom, but found nothing other than evidence of an austere life, hard lived: wholefood, vegetables, fruit, salad, no sweets, crisps or indulgences. He drank Mongolian White Tea. There was a picture of his wife on the work surface next to an unopened box of Whittard's English Breakfast Special Mix. He had left his personal mobile phone bill on the side. She noted the number. On the table was a pen, which had been used to alter and edit a document that lay next to it. She picked up the document, read it and took it with her.

In the bathroom, she found cold tiles, coal-tar soap and a toothbrush. There was a hard-edged loofah, a hot tap so seldom used it had visibly seized up, and soap of a variety that had been unperfumed and unchanged for the last hundred years. She entered the barely furnished hall: no secrets, no surplus, no decoration and no frivolity, just function.

Foxx had dismissed the third bedroom. It may contain a thousand secrets, but they would take too long to find. It housed boxes, skis, scuba equipment, more boxes, unused blankets wrapped in plastic, boots, rock-climbing kit, dumbbells, old jackets, twenty empty snuff boxes, more boots and a dozen unhung wall pictures.

In contrast, the spare room had a bed and a wardrobe, nothing else. Foxx closed the door and focused on the living room. He searched through the small piles of neatly ordered papers that lay on the table. Julie wandered in after him.

'This is motive, right?' The document was a draft speech opposing the PM's Brexit Defence deal. It was erudite and well-written, but clear in its vilification of the deal and the dramatic impact it would have on the security of every UK citizen. Handwritten notes in the margins added even more venom to the invective.

'Meh.'

She dug through drawers, under cupboards and through the two piles of paper left on the floor next to the sofa, all current. And there, halfway down was the proof they needed. She read the first page. She'd seen it before. There in black and white were the detailed instructions for the assassination at the back of the hotel.

'Look proof. Storrington is our man.' She passed him the pages from the Risk Assessment.

'Really?' he said, examining it carefully. 'This is a photocopy, it's from the evidence file, not a print out from his computer. Proves nothing other than he's investigating the shooting. His gaze fell onto another sheet of paper. His eyes betrayed his interest.

'What's that?' asked Julie.

'Oh nothing. Nothing relevant.' He put the sheet on the sofa out of her reach.

She continued scanning the room, her eyes drawn to the floor-to-ceiling vinyl collection: jazz, classical, Bob Dylan, Progressive Rock from the '60s, more from the '70s and a few military bands. She walked past the sofa. A sneak glance told her that the paper that caught Foxx's eye was the latest revisions to the PM's timetable. He didn't want to share it.

She examined the turntable. It had been playing Pink Floyd's album, *Wish You Were Here* - the needle still resting on the end of the first track, *Shine on you Crazy Diamond*. Next to the turntable were the lyrics written out by hand with almost calligraphic precision.

She turned. Foxx had already gone into the bedroom and pocketed the revised timetable.

She followed. He searched the wardrobe, she searched the bedside cabinets. In the top drawer on his wife's side was a piece of A4 paper and a leather-bound notebook. It was a diary. He wrote in it every day, to his wife, to tell her about his day. It was his last remaining connection to what they once had. She carefully turned to last Thursday and read.

He pulled a large leather photograph album out from the bottom of the wardrobe. Letters and cards fell out as he pulled the ramshackle collection onto the bed. He studied them, piece by piece. This changed the game.

'What?' asked Julie. 'What have you got?'

'Colin Lewis, the innocent boy, who was with the PM and got shot in the crossfire.'

'Yes?'

'He was Storrington's boyfriend.'

'Boyfriend?'

'Yes. They were lovers: deep, sincere, heartfelt, intimate lovers. They used pet names: he called him Pookey. There are photos, cards, letters, poems - the whole declaration of undying devotion. No wonder he's rampaging like a mad bull. He wants revenge.' Foxx paused for thought. 'And he thinks it was me.'

'And me,' added Julie. She raised the leather-bound notebook. 'I've got a diary. On Thursday, he wrote pages and pages. He was devastated. Didn't mention Colin by name, but you can feel the grief in every line.' She showed Foxx and continued, 'And I found this next to it. It's a print-out of an email. This proves his innocence. It's his resignation to the PM apologising for failing in his duties to keep him safe.'

'Resigning doesn't prove he's innocent.'

'Yes it does. If it's written on his GCHQ-2 top secret email account. It's got his secret code name on it. Commander Storrington is not Dominion1431.'

Foxx should have been delighted, but he looked uneasy. Julie watched him. Was it guilt? Did he need to prove it was Storrington just to give himself an alibi? Why did he need the PM's revised schedule and why be sneaky about it? Why, yesterday evening, had he tried to get them thrown out of the Tenby's house by asking Charlie such ridiculously personal questions?

'You know the good news though,' said Foxx. 'That means the number of suspects is down to four.'

She nodded, as if she agreed; but she didn't. In her mind, the number of suspects was not four. It was one.

It was Foxx.

∼

And this is the lunchtime news.

After the furore at the weekend about the leaked Housing Benefit Document, a spokesman from the Social Services Reform Group said that the document had been taken out of context and blown out of proportion by the extreme left. There is a need to increase the efficiency and equity of housing benefit and the new graduated scales of benefit would give more to those who merited it and less to those who didn't. The system has been the subject of abuse for years and the Tory party is now getting a grip of the situation and creating a fairer system for all.

The Labour left still said that it disadvantaged recent arrivals into the country and was not based on personal need but on Tory greed.

The Labour Party had other troubles today as a team of back benchers wrote an open letter to Sturgiss, the leader of the Party saying the Party had lost its values, its balance and its way forwards. In a statement, they said Sturgiss is unelectable and is moving Labour too far to the left. A revolt in the Party would weaken Labour's Opposition still further. His defenders came out in force to say that his brand of 'honest politics' is exactly what this country needs.

∼

Bettie never looked happy. It was a waste of emotion, but this was the closest to happy the DPM had ever seen her.

'The political landscape in the UK is in a mess,' she began, drama in her voice as she fired up the PowerPoint. 'It's time for a shake-up and that's what we're going to give it.

Look at the last election. The votes were split almost down the middle: an equal and unhelpful divide between right and left. Look at Brexit: the vote to Leave won by a whisker, almost nothing in it. The Scottish Referendum was a close-run result. Even across the Atlantic, Trump and Clinton, there was only a handful of votes between them. It looks like the world is polarised and paralysed by two equal and opposing forces. Look at the UK Parliament, it's split and powerless because it's polarised on the right and the left. That's the way it looks; but it's not so.'

'I know that,' said the DPM, a little impatiently. 'There's a minority on the far right and an even smaller minority on the left. Most people are somewhere in the middle.'

'Yes, exactly. And there are a few fringe parties, like yours, for example. Your whole Liberal Party is not seen as a moderate party, just an alternative to the mainstream, like the Greens or the Welsh party.' He winced at having his party marginalised. She continued. 'Most voters are pretty centre-ist, neither socialists nor fascists; they want a tranquil, prosperous, harmonious life and fall just one side or the other of the centre, so choose to vote Tory or Labour to reflect their minimal bias. Let's be honest, so many of the Tory and Labour policies are the same – different wrapping, same content. Voters want a sane, stable, prosperous middle way.'

'So? Everyone knows that.'

'So . . . we form a new party.'

'What?' he said in an *Are you mad?* tone of voice.

'A new centralist party.'

'What are you going to call it? The Bland Party?' he said with scathing sarcasm. 'You know that centralist parties are just parties that are neither one thing nor another. Flimsy, platitudinous parties with no real policies.'

'You think I would let that happen?' Her eyes added an unspoken, *Of course I wouldn't*. The DPM was momentarily silenced. He hated it when she did that. She paused, just to make a point, then continued.

'I had a team of interns interview 92 per cent of all MPs, asking each of them for their personal top five manifesto items. Then they were presented with the notion of a party that reflected the majority of their manifesto views and a policy of strong social support based on solid economic principles that will make widespread change in key areas that really matter to people. There's a lot of party disenchantment on both sides of the House. We compiled all of their top five manifesto ideas and they are mostly the same, with very few being mutually exclusive. It's gold dust.

We've a written a manifesto that incorporates the must-have top fives of over 83 per cent of all MPs. It'll be anything but dilute. It will make radical social change and build a network of prosperity.' She slapped a thick document onto the table. 'We have a manifesto, we have over 500 MPs that will sign up to it. All we need is a leader and we have ourselves a party. This is your chance to fly!'

'It's my party and I can fly if I want to?'

'Exactly. You could shine. This is your time to shine. You would have to resign from the Liberals and start a whole new party. People want change. You would get 500 seats out of 650. Think what you could do in Europe if you had unity behind you in Britain. Think what legislation you could pass. Think about the difference you would be able to make. That has got to be worth fighting for.'

She had piqued his desire. He drilled her with a barrage of questions testing her theory. She had already started stirring up discontent in the Labour back benches. They strategised on what they would do with all that power. Slowly, step by step, she convinced him of the credibility of the idea.

'Yes,' he said. 'I like it. Let's do it.'

'Just one thing,' she added, right at the end. 'You can't.'

This was a typical Bettie power play; give and take away. She continued.

'You can't do it now. In fact, you can't do it at all, not unless the Prime Minister resigns. That is key; that's how you get your followers, by releasing them from their previous loyalties. The PM has to resign.'

'Or get shot,' said the DPM with dark humour.

'No. Definitely not. His ratings go up if he gets shot at. Though, if he actually did get shot, that could work, but we really need him to resign, we need his support and he can't give that if he's dead.'

'Well, that's the end of that plan, then.'

'Why?'

'He'll never resign. Especially not now he *has* been shot at. People will say it is cowardice and he's not going down in history as the PM that gave way to terrorism. Not to mention Brexit; the French would annihilate us if we showed the weakness of letting our PM resign mid-negotiations. They're pushing so hard, at this rate they'll want all the land claimed by William the Conqueror. He'll never resign, not until Brexit is done and dusted, which means that when I take over, I will inherit a significant majority in a broken and divided country. For this to work it needs to be done before Brexit is signed, but he won't resign until afterwards. Catch 22.'

'You're such a wimp! Make it happen. If you can't do this one simple thing, you can't be PM. Listen; whatever it takes, get Palmer out.'

16

ST JAMES PARK

'Black or Gold; do they mean anything to you?' asked Foxx, as they sat together on the wall of the Embankment, overlooking the Thames. She shook her head.

Why had Brekkenfield discharged himself from hospital for six hours, just two days before the assassination? Only two words appeared in his diary for that day: *Black* and *Gold*.

Julie was surfing Hoy's social media. His CV said he'd been missing from action for four months. Where had he been? His profiles gave nothing away. His wife's social media: nothing. Her friends: nothing; until she floundered, almost by chance, on two pictures on a seemingly random Instagram account. A picture of Hoy in full Arab garb, in the desert - it said *Iran* - and another of him and his wife making a sign of solidarity as they stood by sand-covered ruins. The timeline fitted. The caption read *The Pact*. What pact? And what had they been doing there?

No answers; only more questions.

Foxx and Connor turned their joint attention to deciphering Tenby's finances. It was a confusion of unanswerable conundrums. His money was tied up in a tortuous tangle of trusts and potentially tenuous torts that neither of them understood.

'I need coffee,' he said and hopped off the wall. 'D'you want one?'

'Yes. A flat white, please, no sugar. Can I have my phone? I'm going to call my friend in the Cabinet Office.'

'When I get back. Stay here. Don't move an inch.' He wanted to trust her. This was a first step.

'OK,' she said and he headed for the nearest coffee shop. He disappeared from sight and she didn't move an inch . . . but she did talk to a kindly passer-by.

'Excuse me,' she said, 'may I borrow your phone for a quick call? I'll give you £20.' The fourth person she asked said yes. She dialled. After two rings, the switchboard answered.

'Commander Storrington, please, I have some urgent information for him.'

'Hello, is that Commander Storrington's office? Good, please put me through to the Commander.'

'No, I need to speak to him personally.'

'No, I won't leave a message. I need to speak to him. Now. Tell him, it's about Pookey.'

She waited, the phone was on hold. There was a click then a voice, strong and male.

'Storrington here. Who are you?'

'Eduard Foxx has just broken into your flat. He saw the punch bag with the face on it, your half-written letter to the PM and your album.' She paused. 'Your Pookey album.'

'Who is this?'

'He will be in St James' Park at 15.00 this afternoon for five minutes. That's all.'

'Connor. You're Julie Connor. I know it's you. Listen to me carefully. I know what you did. I know about you and Foxx in your flat and I know how you were involved in last Thursday's assassination attempt. I can get to you and I will definitely . . .'

A cold sweat consumed her body, like a wave of death. She hung up before finding out what he would do. She feared Storrington, but knew he was on the side of good. *This is the right thing to do*, she told herself. Years of obeying rules had conditioned her. Her belief in the authorities was bigger than her belief in Foxx.

How she wanted it to be the other way round.

She saw Foxx in the distance, approaching slowly, a paper cup in each hand. She was sitting exactly where he'd left her. He gave her the phone. The firewall he'd put around it now had made it untraceable by SSS software. She hit the number of her long-lost friend in the Cabinet Office and within minutes was chatting and giggling as relaxed and animated as a schoolgirl after a first date. She explained that this was an unofficial call, she was working on increased security for the PM and, after the PM had broken protocol at Oxford to shake hands with well-wishers, she wanted to know if that was normal behaviour for him.

'I know people say he's a buffoon and intransigent,' said Julie, 'but what I need to know is, does he go off script or will he stick to a security plan? Can we trust him? I mean, he is pretty dishonest and self-centred by all accounts.'

'Off the record,' her friend began, 'politicians are not honest at the best of times; negotiators are rarely honest; Brexit is riddled with dishonest misinformation; and foreign policy is the least honest of all politics. So if you're a politician negotiating Brexit with foreigners, all hope of honesty is gone. Now the trouble with that for any PM, but especially Palmer, is that he has no choice but to pass that deceit on to the UK people, because foreigners read UK newspapers and he can't give away his negotiating position. So, Palmer comes over like a buffoon - dishonest, disorganised and unable to do a decent deal - but it's all part of the negotiating approach. He's doing brilliantly making something out of nothing, but he has so little to work with. He's doing a good job, but the British public don't get that.'

'But he's still an idiot?'

'Far from it. He's a smart, thoughtful guy. Actually he's a lovely man, doing a rotten job that no one else wanted to do. He doesn't even want to be Prime Minister. He was shafted into it. You're too young to remember, but we call it the Jim Callaghan Syndrome. Callaghan was not a spectacular politician, but he got voted into the leadership just to prevent Dennis Healey from getting it. If Palmer weren't PM, then Jacobson would be, and the world would be a much darker place.'

'But Palmer is stubborn, right? A bit of a bastard?'

'Heavens, no! Palmer's a really good guy. He has a great record behind him, but he doesn't shout about it. I'll send you some background stuff on him. I gotta go, the boss is calling.' And she clicked off the line, but Julie kept her phone to her ear and continued the conversation with an empty line.

'So I wanted to talk to you about security, do you know about the

GCHQ-2 email protocols? I don't suppose you know who Dominion 1431 is? You do? For definite? Can you tell me? Yes, of course not. Well how about a face-to-face meeting? OK, I'll see you at three o'clock, St James' Park, on the bench in the middle of the triangular lawn. Do you know it? OK, see you then. Oh, I might have a friend with me. Secret service, top guy. It's him you need to tell. Are you OK with that? Yes, I do, absolutely. He's 100 per cent trustworthy. That's great. Then I'll hang back and just let the two of you talk.' She hung up.

The trap was set. Serafina Pekkala, espionage agent in the making, set her phone to boop at 2.45. It would be the notification of a fictional conference call to be held at 3.00 with GCHQ-2 chiefs about where they were with the hunt for the assassin.

'I have to be on it,' she explained to Foxx. 'I might learn something valuable. I can't be in two places at once. You can lock me in the car and check my phone afterwards. I'll record the call if you want. Are you OK meeting my friend on your own?' Teams are built on trust. And they were a team now, weren't they? He needed to know. It was time to put it to the test.

Hoy phoned St Mary's Hospital. It had been on his list for a few days now and it was not a call he was willing to delegate. It wasn't part of his investigation, just routine. He just couldn't help himself.

'You're the second person to call today and ask exactly the same thing,' was the reply. 'I'll tell you what I told the other fella. He was in for three weeks, didn't leave his bed.'

'Didn't leave it at all at any point?'

'That's exactly what the other fella asked and I told him the same as I am telling you now, he didn't leave his bed, except for last Tuesday, when he was out for six hours. He said he had something to do, so was temporarily discharged, but was back late Tuesday and then didn't move from his bed until Friday morning. And before you ask, no, I don't know what the thing was he had to do.'

'And who was the other person who called?'

'It was his nephew.'

'Did he leave a name?'

'Yes. Edward, Edward Fox.'

Armed with a picture from LinkedIn, Foxx left Julie to meet her informant.

'Stay in the car and wait. I'm leaving your phone and I'll check it when I'm back,' he said. She smiled and nodded. A shot of remorse pricked her heart. She didn't want him to go, but she said nothing and watched him walk away.

It was sunny day. The flowers had come out of their buds in their thousands and the people had come out of their offices in their hundreds. The park wasn't packed, but it was busy. Foxx surveyed it carefully. He circled the perimeter, then circled the triangular lawn, surveyed the whole scene and approached with care.

'Target located,' whispered a park cleaner into his jacket. The hunt was on.

Were they a team? Foxx needed to know. His mind flicked back to Julie accidentally lighting up his phone and broadcasting his whereabouts in Cheltenham. He looked around for anomalies. His eyes swept past a park cleaner waving a brush in the region of some leaves. Then he turned 180 degrees, and there was another park cleaner. He headed for the bench in the middle of the grass of the large triangular lawn. It was not a lawn, it was an expanse.

As he walked, nonchalantly oblivious to the world around him, he identified two business people chatting by a tree, a man dressed in builder's clothes walking briskly and another park cleaning council operative pushing a refuse trolley . . . and a fourth. This was not right; four park cleaners. And it was a hot day. Their clothes were not loose and baggy, but big enough to conceal a bulletproof vest; the trolleys were council issue but each large enough for an arsenal of trouble.

He had his answer about Julie Connor. It was time to leave. He turned. Another trolley was heading straight for him.

Julie watched from the top of the slope on the south side of the park, concealed by the branch of a cypress tree. She watched with more than a little regret. She looked for men in uniform, she looked for people dressed as agents. Then she saw them, the bin men. She looked harder and saw a gardener, a female gardener, with a wire in her ear. She recognised them from Cheltenham.

She felt a twinge of guilt, but it was the right thing to do. Her phone buzzed with an email: she half-read it and half-watched the slow build-up of the rat-in-the-trap being taken out of circulation. She told herself again: *It was the right thing to do.*

Foxx didn't run. There were people in the park, innocent people, crossfire could cost lives. It was a game in slow motion. No one rushed, no one ran: it was vultures slowly circling their prey, getting ever closer. Foxx edged towards an exit, his route was blocked. He turned, he aimed for another path of escape and his pursuers slowly re-positioned. There was no way out.

The email was from her friend in the Cabinet Office, the background on the PM, as promised. It didn't matter for now, but she read with half an eye, as the action on the lawn ahead of her slowly moved the pieces into place. The PM was underrated. He had saved thousands of lives when working in the Health Department; cut costs and raised wages when working for Education - a quietly Christian man, a man of values.

She looked up. The vultures were in position; slowly, so slowly, closing in, but no one wanted to cause panic. She looked down and flicked through the pictures of Prime Minister Palmer as a younger man. There were newspaper articles showing him on emergency aid trips, where he'd worked alongside aid workers in the dirt and the mud. He had fostered a child, Simon. There was a picture of Simon Palmer in the article. She enlarged it with her fingers and stared.

Oh my god! She knew that face. It was Foxx. He was younger, but unmistakably handsome. It was him. Foxx was the Prime Minister's son, his adopted son.

She read more. Simon had previously been thrown out of sixteen other foster homes, had been a troubled youth, rescued from a certain life of crime by William Palmer MP, as he was then. He had settled down, taken the family name, stayed in school, passed exams and gone to university.

And now that troublesome teenager with big-hearted foster parents, was going to be taken away and no doubt executed for something he didn't do.

Julie Connor had screwed up massively. He was telling the truth. He had been saving the PM's life, not plotting to end it. He was not a terrorist; he was a protector. He was an orphan, had suffered, had found new parents and was now fighting single-handedly to save them from unbelievable horror. And she had just condemned him to death.

The six refuse men and a female gardener had surrounded maybe a hundred people, and one of them was Foxx. There was no way out. She just watched and waited and withered inside. A policeman came up behind her and spoke. She jumped.

'Move away, madam. The park is closed. Please walk quickly and quietly out of the park and out of the area.' She had no choice but to obey. There were three people-carriers behind her, each disgorging its load of policemen, all in combat gear and a serious mood. There were fourteen more vehicles surrounding the park and well in excess of a hundred officers moving rapidly and intently to the triangle lawn and their target. Foxx was finished.

The police cordon prevented her from watching and the wave of people washed her away from the area. She was helpless. There was nothing to do. She sat in the car. She waited for Foxx.

He didn't come.

Sorry Eduard, she said to herself, as she left. *I am so sorry.*

17

ON A KNIFE EDGE

Julie let the door of the hotel room click closed behind her.

The room felt like her life. Empty.

She looked at the bed they'd shared last night; the central line between left and right, the line she'd told him not to cross. Strict rules. No trespass. But only one of them had wanted him to break those rules, and the other was him. Now she was alone and life was a mess.

This was a disaster. She had sent him to his doom, and if she hadn't, she had sent herself to her doom. She didn't know what to do, but whatever it was, it wasn't here. It was time to move. She would shower, pack and go - to where she knew not. She flicked on the water and scrubbed, in the hoped it would wash away the dark stain on her soul.

She wandered out of the bathroom in a dream, clutching the towel.

The knife at her throat appeared from nowhere, the arm lock held her fast. Startled, she dropped the towel. Foxx held her tight. She had betrayed him and now he was here. The knife pressed harder. She was going to die.

One hour, fourteen minutes earlier, Foxx had been surrounded. He had assessed the six cleaners and identified the gardener. He felt no anger, only disappointment.

He had weighed up his options. Plan B was to wander blindly towards one of the bin men, grab his weapon and shoot his way out. It was not a good plan. Had he been in an enemy nation against enemy forces, he would have had so many more options, but here, next to Buckingham Palace, amidst sun-soaking Londoners on a quiet Monday afternoon, in a haven from their offices, his options were limited. This could get bloody.

So he lay in the sun and did almost nothing. That was Plan A for making his escape. He sat between two families, both with young and vulnerable children and took out his phone.

Four minutes later, he was walking away a free man.

The ballet unfolded in slow motion. He ignored their gradual circling, disregarded their choreography as they closed in like lions in the night. The quasi-council workers had guns and bullets and implements of destruction hidden from view; guns and bullets just a few hundred yards from the Palace, guns and bullets a few hundred yards from Parliament, from the Prime Minister's residence - six disguised gunman and one fanatical leader, all armed to the hilt in the epicentre of London.

'Hello? Anti-Terrorist Squad?

There's a terrorist attack about to happen in St James' Park. I am MI5. The code word is *Terrides*. There are six park cleaners pushing trolleys on the triangular lawn. Two of them have bombs and one has a gun barrel visible in his trolley. There's also a female gardener. She's with them.'

'Yes, sir. What's your name?'

'Don't be an arse. Check out *Terrides* and . . . Oh my god, It's kicking off.' He hung up.

The circle of six were now less than fifty yards away, still approaching with stealth, imagining themselves unseen. Then the world changed. Like the skyline in *Zulu*, every perimeter of the park was lined with hostile, advancing policemen. They approached with speed, guns raised. There was the essence of agitation in the park. It fluttered, then spread like a flash bomb as innocent people sensed the danger. The panic was visible. He lay face down on the grass with his hands on his head and waited for the inevitable.

A police boot stood by his head. This was it.

'Get up, sir.' He did. He looked. The six trolleys were each surrounded. The cleaners and the gardener were in handcuffs, guns at their heads. 'This is a police operation. Please leave the park as rapidly as you can. Leave in an orderly manner.' That suited him fine. He left, bought an ice cream and hailed a cab. She had been disloyal. Now it was time to pay.

~

'No,' begged Julie, feeling the knife at her throat. 'No, it was a mistake. I didn't know the PM was your dad.' She had got it wrong again. Anger kicked in, more with herself than him. 'I didn't know you were Simon Palmer. How could I? Why didn't you tell me, you idiot? Why do you make everything so difficult? Why don't you just trust me?' His grip tightened. The knife pressed harder.

'Trust you? Trust *you*? You slammed your door in my face when I asked for your help. You held me at gunpoint, pushed me out of a window, alerted the authorities by turning on my phone and set me up for a police trap.'

'Well, you kicked down my door, gave me cold water torture, tied me up, naked, held a gun at my temple and threatened to kill me; and then you threatened my relations. Fuck you, Pot! I'm just the Kettle. And you blew up my flat!'

'Well, you're so annoying. You look so small and slight, but you are so unbelievably stubborn.'

'Yeah, but you conned me and invaded my flat,' adding emphatically, 'didn't you?'

'Yes. I did. But some relationships get off to a bumpy start.' His grip loosened, she turned to face him.

'I know you didn't do it,' she said in a voice that was softer now. 'I know you're not the assassin. I know you wrote the Risk Assessment in good faith, to keep your dad safe. But I'm not guilty either. I was just the conduit of communication. It's my job. I'm not part of this. I can help. I can get information that you can't. And when we find out who did it, I can back-trace it to their computer to prove it. You need me. I want to keep the PM alive too.'

'But you set me up.'

'Yes, I did. I was wrong. I didn't know who you were then. Obviously no one does. You changed your name and shrouded yourself in secrecy. I was doing what I thought was best to keep your dad alive.' His grip released and it became more of a hug than an arm lock. She looked up at his lips and then back into his eyes. She spoke quietly. 'So, is that what it is?'

'What?'

'A relationship?' He just looked at her. 'Well, I'm naked again, in your arms, in a bedroom and you said, *some relationships get off to a bumpy start.*'

'Get dressed,' he said dismissively, like he was talking to someone who was not all there. He let go, ending the hug. She felt the release land hard in her heart, but said nothing. His instincts said kill her, but his judgement said not. His training said remove her, but his affections said *No. Not yet.* 'I'm hungry. We're going out to eat.' He beckoned her to get dressed.

There was an uncomfortable silence while she searched for clothes. The skirt fitted her well. It showed her at her best. She would wear it one more time.

'I'm taking you to dinner,' he announced. 'We'll talk about anything other than the case.'

They walked. She linked arms. He was tall by her side, but she liked that – even though she felt small. She was glad he wasn't dead, and even more glad she wasn't. She liked him - and didn't – equally. He was trouble and his existence in her life troubled her. It gave her angst. The restaurant was intimate, if not particularly good. They sat all evening, in a semi-circular lover's booth, cuddled up closer than he had intended, out of earshot of all other diners and talked about nothing . . . except the case.

In Central London today, startled on-lookers watched as hundreds of armed police stormed through St James' Park in a co-ordinated anti-terrorist operation. Seven suspects were arrested, but it turned out to be a training exercise. A Home Office Spokesperson said 'The operation was a complete success and demonstrated the speed and professionalism of all the officers involved.'

Julie had showered, again, unnecessarily. She walked across the room holding the towel carelessly, scarcely hiding her modesty. She stood in front of the handsome, controlling, innocent, noble, six foot Mr Foxx, and looked up at him. She stood so close that the towel was now held firmly between their bodies. She put her arms high up around his shoulders.

'Thank you for a lovely dinner, Mr Foxx,' she said.

'My pleasure,' the gallant replied, as he took her arms off his shoulders and placed them in a gentle, controlling, half nelson behind her back. He looked down at her, she looked up. There was a moment. He leant in and gave her a light, sensual kiss on her lips; a single kiss, three short seconds of affection, then released her arms and stepped away. The towel fell to the floor. He passed her a tee-shirt.

'Sleep well,' he said. 'We have a busy day tomorrow.'

Julie put on the tee-shirt, grabbed the towel from the floor and hid the pang of dejection that destroyed her soul. Her pride and bravado vocally reaffirmed the imaginary Mason-Dixon Line that ran up the middle of the bed. He had settled for confederacy, she wanted union.

Mr Foxx had an air of confidence even as he slipped into bed. This room was his; every room he'd ever been in was his. Her making a fuss was like an ant ranting at a mountain.

She wanted to be like him, to be liked by him; to be loved by him - so she could reject him. She told herself she didn't care. She didn't need a cuddle, and she certainly didn't need anything more. *Men! I hate you all.* She continued her long slow preparation for bed.

Her tee-shirt was too short, her knickers too small, her posture too revealing, as she bent over to brush the knots out of her hair. She looked at him with soft, submissive eyes and reiterated again how he must not cross the line or she wouldn't know what to do. He reinforced his lack of intention by falling asleep.

She slipped into bed, his bed. She lay awake, alone and unvanquished. Her heart was filled with remorse and rejection. She reflected. A panoply of emotions swirled around her brain and consumed her erratic, errant thoughts. She needed to think.

It was Monday night in London, miles from home. She was a fugitive from the law and an unwitting conspirator in an assassination. Three nights earlier, she'd had no idea how her life would change the following morning. All she'd wanted was a few things from the supermarket, and she'd come back with him. She'd been attracted to him and two minutes later had wanted to kill him. And this evening he'd wanted to kill her.

That was who he was.

He was a cold-blooded killer; she had been sure. He was the would-be assassin of the Prime Minister - that had been her only certainty, but now she had proof that he wasn't. Didn't she?

He snored gently. He couldn't have done it; unless this was not a political crime, but a domestic crime played out on a big stage. Maybe he didn't like his dad. And why didn't he like her? She thought he liked her. Charlie had said he liked her. How dare he kiss her goodnight and not follow through. This was their second night in bed together. He was an almost rapist, he had tied her to her own bedhead and now, snoring gently, he was forcing her to be alone with her emotional and physical confusion.

He was a bastard.

There was still only one certainty in her life. Men were bad. They used and rejected her.

Foxx was no different, he just did it in a different way. He was just like the rest of them. No, he was worse. She hated him. He'd tricked himself into her flat, into her emotions, into a bed in a London hotel. And the whole 'loving orphan' was a lie too. It had to be. Everything about him was a lie. And why didn't he fancy her? What more could she have done? It was her body, it must be: it was awful - fat ass and no breasts. He could have better, she was not in his league. He'd had hundreds of girls better and prettier than she was, for sure. Or maybe it was just her: her ways, her speech, her personality.

Her.

She couldn't stay in his bed.

The angst was palpable, the agitation almost volcanic, an eruption inevitable. She wanted to cry or fight or scream or kill. She picked up the knife from the desk and held it in her hand. It felt good. She looked at him sleeping; the courageous, good-looking, gentlemanly, house-breaking, home-invading, heart-pervading, degrading, neglecting, rejecting, dejecting bastard. She held the knife high in both hands, directly above the gentle, almost imperceptible, rising and falling of his sleeping, snoring, unsuspecting, unprotected chest.

She wanted to stab, to bring it down hard into his heart. Her muscles tensed. This was it. Stop!

She had to think. She had to. She had to do the right thing, the smart thing. He was the assassin. No, he wasn't. No, he was. Anger blurred her thoughts. She had no idea why she was so angry.

Why did he make her feel like this?

How dare he come into her life and screw it up so much; how dare he highlight every one of her small and feeble shortcomings, make her feel every crack in her personality, make her see everything she had tried so hard to hide from herself. How dare he be so desirably unattainable - so bad but so irresistibly magnetic? He was a killer. The evidence pointed to him. It wasn't perfect, but it never was. He'd hoodwinked her into believing in his innocence, just by using those hypnotic deep blue eyes. Gorgeous eyes, controlling eyes. But they were shut now, she was in control and she had to do the right thing.

I hate you. I hate that you came into my life, I hate the way you make me feel. No more men in my life, in my heart. Men only cause hurt and trouble, and you caused me both. You're a killer and a heartbreaker - you don't deserve to live.

And that was it.

The phone rang. It was still dark. Storrington answered with a guttural grunt. Hoy spoke with excitement and no introduction.

'We've got him. He's in hospital.'

'Who?'

'Foxx! He's in pretty bad shape. Local CID called us. Apparently, he's lost a lot blood, severe cuts and lacerations, in surgery at the moment. He'll take a while to come round, but we have to be there when he does.'

'How d'you know it's him?'

'DNA match.'

'Is he guarded?'

'They had one copper there, I said get four and make sure they're the best. I'll pick you up in an hour.'

Storrington hung up, looked at the picture of his wife through the darkness and said out loud,

'We've got him!'

And life began to feel just a little bit better.

18

INTENSIVE CARE

'Is he conscious, yet?' Hoy asked, as the nurse came out his room.

'He's just come round, still a bit groggy. Hang on here a minute.' She went back into his room. Two guards stood to attention at the door. Two more stood opposite.

'Don't underestimate him,' said Hoy, to the guards. 'He's a dangerous son of a bitch - killed a whole police force in Georgia, when he was in a coma. If he so much as moves, take his legs off.' The guards stiffened. 'He killed two of our guys in Brighton with his bare hands, when he was wearing a dress. The other's still fighting for his life in Intensive Care. Is he handcuffed to the bed?' The guard confirmed he was. 'He can probably unpick it with his teeth. Watch him.'

'Yes, sir.'

Storrington was bored of waiting, he was not a man to take instructions from a nurse.

'Come on,' he said brusquely to Hoy. They hustled past the guards. The nurse opened her mouth to defend the sanctity of her patient, but was silenced by the curt and strident tones of the tall authoritative man in his early sixties. 'This is a matter of National Security. Please leave.' She opened her mouth again to argue, but acquiesced under the pressure of his imposing presence. She picked up her tray and left.

The patient was lying with his head rolled away from them. With no regard for his well-being, Hoy grabbed a clump of hair and twisted the patient's head towards them, face to face.

'That's not Foxx.' Storrington's voice was strong, disparaging, accusatory and angry. 'Who the hell is this? And why have you brought me all the way down here to see him?' A penny dropped heavily through Hoy's brain. He confirmed his suspicions.

'What's your name, soldier?'

'Sam Stone. Who are *you* and what the fuck do you want?

'Do you own a dark blue Vauxhall Astra?' demanded Hoy, adding the registration number.

'What is this? Are you here about some unpaid parking tickets?'

'This,' said Hoy, talking to Storrington, 'is Foxx's accomplice; the guy who was in Raper's Hide with him. It was his car they used to get away. DNA told the doctors that he was on our wanted list. Brighton confirmed he was in the Raper's Hide incident, and somewhere in communication it got to us that it was Foxx, not his sidekick.' Storrington shook his head in disbelief at the incompetence of his Head of Investigations and turned to the irate patient.

'You're a man with medals, a man who has shown great bravery in protecting the liberty and values of this country, why get mixed up with someone like Foxx?'

'Who?'

'Secret agent, national traitor, assassination planner, a tactician trained in the strategic destabilisation of unwanted regimes, Eduard Foxx,' added Hoy for clarification.

'Sorry, mate. Don't know the fella.'

'Why did you go down that dark alley, Raper's Hide? What sent you down there?' Storrington's tone was urgent and incisive.

'Some tranny was gonna get a panning from three National Front anti-gay gorillas. They needed to feel some righteous justice.'

'You expect us to believe that?' said Hoy, sounding as aggressive as he could.

'Don't give a flying fuck what you believe,' he said to Hoy in tones that defined dismissive, and turned his attention from the monkey to the organ grinder.

'What's this about? I'm hurting like I just stuffed a grenade up my arse and I wanna go to sleep,' he said to Storrington. The Commander stared down at him for a silent fifteen seconds.

'The man you helped that night was not a transvestite. He was the man who planned and we believe perpetrated the assassination attempt on the Prime Minister.'

'You're fucking joking! That fucking sissy boy is a hit man? I'll fucking kill him.'

'We have that in hand,' said Storrington calmly.

'I knew I should've dropped him like an ugly tart on a Sunday morning. He was more trouble than clap on your tenth wedding anniversary.'

'Yes, quite,' said Storrington. 'Those three men were not National Front. They worked for us and were going to arrest him.'

'Oh shit! They didn't look like coppers.'

'No,' said Storrington curtly. 'That was the point.' The full impact of what he had done and what he was about to be accused of hit him like a brick falling from a fifteen storey building. 'Tell me, what happened when you went down the alley? In detail.'

Stone explained how he had pursued the supposed gay-basher, how the fight had gone down and how he got Foxx out of there. His head was ringing, he was hurting and his clarity was not helped by the drugs, but he covered all he could remember. He knew the next question.

'Did you kill them?'

'No, sir, I did not,' he replied, in a sincere and military tone. 'When I left them, they were alive.'

'How do you know?'

'I have laid enough people down in pub fights to know what kills and what doesn't. I've taken people out in hand-to-hand combat in Helmand. I know when someone is dead and when they're not; and I didn't kill them. They were breathing and squealing when I left. One of them was out, but not dead.'

'Did Foxx do it?'

'He must've done. I had my back to him when I was heading to the car, but he must be a cool fucker, because he didn't look like a man who'd just killed someone.'

'He is,' said Hoy feeling it was time he contributed again. 'He's as cool as . . .' They both ignored him as Storrington cut in,

'What happened when you left?'

Stone explained that he was going to take the transvestite to London, but changed his mind. Conscience got the better of him. He'd heard on the radio that the assassin was in Brighton and he had to go back to see if he could find him. Ironic. He was a vigilante, who wanted to play his part in trapping and capturing an assassin – and the assassin had been sat behind him all the time.

'I took him somewhere quiet, so he could change out of his girlie clothes. I was gonna drop him at Gatwick, to take the Express up to London. As I stopped the car, he twisted his stockings tight around my neck and strangled the fuck out of me. Next thing I know I'm in pitch dark at the bottom of a quarry, head hurting like a bitch and my leg gushing blood. I landed on glass, bent metal, all kinds of shit. I stemmed the bleeding the best I could, but lost so much blood I couldn't get out and lost consciousness. I was there for days. Eventually, I did climb out and lost it again when I got to the top. Next thing I know, I'm in hospital and you show up giving me grief. So where's my flowers? Did you bring me grapes, chocolates?'

'Why did you punch a traffic warden?'

'Cos he was a jumped-up jerk that needed punching. That's why.'

'And why did you hit your Commanding Officer?'

'Ditto. See above.'

'You have a problem with authority?'

'Not if the right people have it. I just don't like lions led by donkeys.'

That had resonance. Storrington smiled, almost. His voice softened.

'I have a young friend, a captain. She feels very much the same way, but she doesn't punch the donkeys. That's the difference. You, Mr Stone, are in some deep trouble. Enjoy the hospital. It's luxury compared to where you're going.'

'If it's not worse than being captured and tortured by the Taliban, I'm sure I'll be fine.' He closed his eyes, rolled his head and started to sleep.

Outside the room, Hoy spoke. 'We don't know if any of that's true.'

'I do,' said Storrington. And there was no more to be said.

~

Julie woke up, her head still snuggled deep into Foxx's shoulder, feeling intensely cared for as her naked body softly entwined his.

'Good morning,' she murmured, sleepily to his neck.

'It's afternoon,' said Foxx gently and squeezed her closer to him. She liked this Mr Foxx.

Her mind replayed the scenes of the night. She had been standing by his bed, knife in hand, anger running through her veins.

She had been wrong, very wrong about Mr Foxx. But only about his guilt; she had not been wrong about wanting to escape his allure. He was irresistible, like heroin to an addict. Trouble was her magnet. She didn't want him and definitely didn't want to care about him. Men hurt, and she knew this one would hurt more than most. That's why she was angry. She was angry with herself. The knife was a symbol, not a weapon. Her head knew what she ought to do and her heart knew what she was going to do. She lowered the knife and put it back on the dressing table.

As she did, unseen to her, Foxx lowered the gun that was pointing at her under the sheet and clicked the safety back onto lock. She stood by her side of the bed and slowly slid her tee-shirt over her head. Slipping under the sheets, right over to his side of the large two-metre bed, she laid a line of sensual kisses on the unsuspecting and unsleeping Mr Foxx. She knew if they had to work together, they needed to trust and they needed to bond; though right now, none of that mattered - lust ruled her loins. He turned to her in the silent rustling darkness, surreptitiously slipping the gun under the pillow and returned her affection. He felt her body next to his: cold, slim, smooth, wanting. He was strong, muscular, manly, but gentle. She felt him growing on her. They bonded.

And again two hours later, and an hour after that. And again, in the morning. And now, here she was, entangled in every way with this dangerous, controlling man of inevitable trouble. A slim shaft of radiant sunlight gleamed through the window and glinted on the shaft of the knife. *The penis mightier than the sword*, she thought to herself ruefully.

Foxx got up and flicked on the news channel. Julie showered away the exertions of the night.

The police have found and arrested a man in connection with the Brighton killings. A spokesman reported that he is recovering in hospital from a brutal attack from the same man who carried out the Brighton killings. But he will himself be charged later today with aiding and abetting the murder of the two off-duty policemen and with causing grievous bodily harm to a third who is still fighting for his life in Intensive Care.

It's believed that he has information about the identity and whereabouts of the man who carried out the murders. We'll give you more as we have it.

He flicked it off and started to plan his day.

Forty-five minutes later, they were sitting in the morning sun at a tiny table outside a French bakery dunking croissants and drinking flat whites and orange juice. They were the only customers and more relaxed with each other than they had ever been, but that wasn't hard. They sat and chatted, almost like lovers, a real couple, as real trust and friendship started to move from bud to blossom.

With croissants consumed, Julie slid her hand across the table to lay her fingers on his.

'He was your accomplice, wasn't he, the man in hospital who's been arrested? Did you try to kill him too?'

'He wasn't my accomplice. And I didn't try to kill him. I thought he was part of the plot to capture me, so I just choked him out.' She looked quizzical. 'I cut off the blood in his carotid artery. He would have been out for about ten minutes. I should've just left him. He would've been fine, but I chucked him down a quarry; about twenty feet. He hit his head on the way down. I was improvising.'

'So you can choke people out?' she said, as her fingers played with his. 'Maybe you can try that with me later.'

'Is everything a sex game to you? It's not the same as erotic asphyxiation, y'know.'

'Oh,' she said with evident disappointment. 'So he's not Steve, the guy who's sitting outside my mum's house? The guy who's going to . . .' It wasn't anything in Foxx's face; he gave nothing away. Maybe it was the augmented closeness that had developed after sharing intimacy or maybe it was just a slow realisation that had finally tumbled.

'There isn't a Steve, is there? You don't have an accomplice. My mum was never in any danger. You're a blagging bull-shitter.' He said nothing, just smiled the faintest smile. 'I hate you, Mr Foxx,' said her mouth, as her fingers squeezed his hands and proved she didn't. 'Next thing, I'll discover you never gutted a bear in Norway and didn't kill a thousand storm troopers in Azerbaijan or whatever it was.'

He smiled a broader smile. 'Are you questioning my manliness?'

Her look said, *Yes.*

'What,' he said in mock defensiveness, 'after my triumphs of stamina last night? No way.' *Fair point*, she thought.

'Now, focus,' he continued. 'We have work to do. I don't know if you're ready for what's coming. The next few days are going to get . . .' he paused as he looked for the right word, '*operational*. It will be dangerous. We have to find the killer and go right up against him. That's not what you're trained for. I have a place you can stay, keep your head down, until I've sorted this mess out.'

'No. We're in this together. I'm not running away. If it has to be done, I want to do it with you.'

'Be careful what you wish for.'

'No. I'm in. I want to do this.'

He leant forward and looked deep into her eyes. His whole counte-nance changed as a stony seriousness solidified the expression on his face and a menace shrouded the conversation.

'This is not a game. He's a committed killer. The danger is real. We don't know who he is or where he is. If you come with me, I can't guar-antee to protect you. Julie, he's desperate and he wouldn't think twice. He'll kill you if he gets the chance.'

'Better to die a hero, than live a coward,' she said, and then quoting Dylan Thomas, 'Anyway, *After the first death, there is no other*. I'm coming with you.'

'You're a strange one, Julie Connor.' He sat back, his tone turned from menacing to informative. 'There's something else I haven't told you. It's about Assassination Attempt Number Seven. It's brilliant and, unfortu-nately, foolproof. I can't stop it. I can tell the police, the army, the PM himself and my mum, but none of that will make any difference. Attempt Number Seven is unstoppable. We have twelve days.'

Storrington was not normally a man motivated by anger, but this whole affair had raised his blood. Foxx had invaded the sanctity of his home and stolen the privacy of his intimate, illicit memories. Connor had phoned, he had offered to help her - or would have done had she not hung up so fast. She was playing with him. He had thought her innocent. How wrong could he be!

'Hoy,' he said abruptly down the telephone, 'The Brighton autopsy, hurry it up. I want it now! And give me the status on the third man. I need to talk to him. Get the QM that signed out the gun to Foxx in my office. And find Foxx.'

His next call was to a team leader in the Planning Department, a colleague of Foxx's. His name was Merikowski. Storrington fired questions at him.

'How long have you worked with Foxx?'

'How tall is he?'

'Well, guess!'

'Would he be anywhere close to six foot four?'

'No? Are you sure?'

'And what about his belt? Did he wear a belt?'

'So who would remember?'

'Ask them. Yes, all of them. And if they think he did wear a belt, ask them what kind of buckle it had? And get back to me today.'

He hung up and reformulated his thoughts. *Julie Connor, what are you playing at? What have you got to do with all this? Do you want to help me or not? Did you signal me from the flat with his phone? Did you want him arrested in St James' Park? Or was that just a ploy?* His mind focused on Julie Connor, on Serafina Pekkala the high ranking officer in GCHQ-2, holder of secrets, and accessor of any private information she wanted. She might be listening to him now.

He didn't care if she was. He made one more call.

'Maria? I have an answer to your question. Julie Connor . . . she's foe. Shoot her on sight.'

Anderson-Bevan Report was all that was written on an otherwise blank sheet of paper. It was a puzzle. Julie had spent the morning googling. Nothing. She had made a dozen calls. Nothing. Why had Nickolas Tenby got so het up about a report that no one had heard of?

Foxx sat opposite, slowly repeating the names Tenby, Hoy and Brekkenfield.

'Agreed,' interjected Julie.

'So you don't think the DPM should be on the list?'

'No, I don't. Buchanan has motive. If he kills the PM, he inherits the kingdom, but I just don't see him being entwined enough in the world of espionage to be able to pull it off. But I don't know how to find out for sure.'

'I do,' said Foxx. 'It's simple. Ask him. I've been thinking about it. He's new to security protocols and potentially more naive than the others. So the plan is this: he gets an email from his secretary or one of his trusted assistants telling him that his GCHQ-2 account is being changed because of potential security breaches and if he wants a new one, he has to email a high security GCHQ-2 email address immediately confirming it's him by enclosing his old email address. That way he tells us if he is Dominion1431.'

'OK,' she said in acknowledgement, not agreement. 'I guess you think you can create a bogus email address with GCHQ in the name, but how do you plan to get one of his staff to send that email?'

'I don't. You do. You walk into their office, flash your high security badge and say you're doing security checks. When they go to get you the cup of tea you ask for, you write the email and send it. Sorted.' Julie said nothing. He prompted her for an answer. 'Well? What d'you think?'

'No. I think no. The only word I can find in my head when I think of that idea is "no". If we ever get stuck on a desert island together for fifty years, or more likely share a prison cell for a hundred and fifty, I still won't have quite enough time to go through all the reasons why it's a bad idea. It's a no. So what's next on the list?'

'I'm trawling Friends Reunited,' he said, his face betraying a little hurt at the vigour of her denouncement.

'Friends Reunited? It was closed down years ago.'

'Yes, but it was just too good to waste. Special Branch hacked a copy of all the files before it went. It's a gold mine.'

Julie went back to calling friends about Anderson-Bevan, while Foxx phoned half a dozen names linked to the suspects, on the pretext of arranging a birthday party for a 'mutual friend' and wanting to dig up some amusing dirt from their past for a spoof speech.

Julie ran out of people she wanted to call. Her contacts had told her a lot about many recent reports, but none of them were the Anderson-Bevan Report. She wrote down what they said - you never know.

Foxx phoned a non-entity called Greg. They chatted for half an hour, Foxx listened intently.

'Yes, of course,' he said when Greg told him things he knew already; Foxx always did that, but raised his eyebrows when a new topic emerged. He probed deeper, listened more, took notes, then hit gold. He jumped up and grabbed his coat.

'C'mon,' he said. 'We're going to meet Nickolas Tenby's wife.'

'What . . . again? We've already met her: Charlie, she's lovely.'

'No, not her. His other wife, his *real* wife - the genuine Mrs Nickolas Tenby.'

19

FARRINGDON CHURNEY

'*B* *onjour, ma Cherie!*'

Tenby spoke with letch in his voice and mobile phone in his hand. 'I'm coming to Marseille next week with the PM for the Brexit meetings. Are you ready for some fun? I'm going to push the timetable forwards. We'll come down a day early, so I'll be arriving on Friday not Saturday. The PM and I have some pre-meetings and,' he paused for dramatic effect, 'that means I will have an extra night *en France*. Will you be there, in Marseille? And your husband? *Non? Formidable!* I'm going to do to you what Wellington did to Napoleon's army at Waterloo. You'd better be *prêt à manger!* And come prepared,' he said with a dirty grin in his voice. 'You know they called me Nickolas, because that's how I like my girls.'

He chuckled. She missed the pun. He didn't care. *Au revoir ma petite, À bientôt!*'

'So who is this lady?'

'Her name is Elizabeth Tenby. She and Tenby got married in their early twenties when he was still in the RAF. Greg was in Tenby's Squadron. Two or three years into the marriage, they were driving along a country back road in Yorkshire: he was driving, fast, probably drunk, in whatever sports car he had at the time. It was getting dark. A little girl was walking her dog along the road. He almost hit her, swerved, lost control, demolished a dry-stone wall and ended up in a tree. It put his wife in a wheelchair and she has been in it ever since.'

'And what? He walked away scot-free?'

'Of course. He was charged with a whole list of driving offences, but his daddy's lawyers got him off, based principally, according to my new mate Greg, on her lying in court. But that's not the worst bit. As soon as he was free, he dumped her! She was no longer a suitable wife, so he binned her off, set her up in some chocolate-box cottage in Farringdon Churney, out of the way of his London life, and picked up with another woman.'

'Charlie?'

'No, not at first. He had a whole stream of them. By the time he joined the Foreign Office, people thought he was single and dating anyone he could get his hands on. He never spoke of his wife. Then he met Charlie and the rest is history.'

'Oh my god! Do you think she knows?'

He shrugged his shoulders.

'He shouldn't be allowed within a thousand feet of a woman. I don't know why his wife - I mean his first wife – has kept quiet about it.'

'Well, you can ask her yourself. We'll be there in ten minutes.'

Being spoken to by Storrington was like standing on the front line under a barrage of heavy shelling.

'Yes, sir,' said the nervous and diminutive Quarter Master's clerk who'd been on duty that day and was responsible for the orderly running of the gun racks in the SSS private arsenal. 'I signed it out to him. I have his signature here. It's been cross-referenced and it is his signature.'

'Did you see him sign it?'

'I checked that it had been signed.'

Storrington glowered. Heavy shelling was about to become nuclear, his tone gained more insistence and greater menace. Each word came out as a single staccato salvo.

'Did you see him sign?'

'No, sir. I didn't actually *see* him sign. But it was him and it was his gun.'

'Why didn't you see him?'

'One of the racks at the back fell over and I had to pick it up.'

'It fell over . . . by itself?' The question was unanswered. 'Has it or any other rack ever fallen over by itself before?'

The answer was so timid as to be almost inaudible. 'No, sir.'

'And while you were picking up the gun rack, Foxx left with the gun, leaving his signature, or what looked like his signature, behind him?'

The clerk nodded guiltily.

'Did you see him clearly when he arrived?'

'No, sir. He had a hoodie on, but he said his name was Foxx and he had the pass code. So I let him in.'

'Unchallenged?'

'Yes, sir.'

'Did you recognise him?'

'I'd never seen Foxx before, so I just assumed.'

'How tall was he?'

'I don't really know, he was walking with a stoop.'

'Guess. Was he nearer your height or mine?'

'He was over six foot; tall, even when stooping.'

'What else do you remember? Anything?'

'He had a black hoodie, denim jeans, big boots, or shoes, probably a biker. I think he had a scar on his face, but it could have been shadow. As I say, he was wearing a hoodie. I didn't really look at him. I mean, he was Foxx. You don't look at Foxx, not with his rep. You just do what he asks. And I did.'

'Yes, you did. You know the gun he took was used in the assassination attempt on the Prime Minister?'

'Yes, sir.' The ensuing silence was worse than the barrage: it was ten seconds that felt like a prison sentence.

'That will be all.' Storrington pressed a buzzer on his desk. The door opened and in walked two security officers. 'Take him away.'

Farringdon Churney, with its thatched roofs, cobbled corners, Norman cross in the village square and ancient bridge over the River Churt was a once-picturesque village that was being consumed on three sides by anonymous new-builds to cater for the ever-flowing London over-spill. The satnav guided them to the unspoiled edge of the village and up a narrow lane where it was quiet, quaint and rural, dotted with picture book homes overlooking rural Essex countryside. The house at the tip of the lane was their destination.

'When we come out, I must tell you about Antelope-Beaver,' said Julie, as an *aide-mémoire.*

He looked blank and said such a thing was a genetic impossibility: the required mating position would conspire against species survival.

'I've been calling round about the Anderson-Bevan Report and no one seemed to have heard of it. But there is an *Anderson* Report and a *Bevan* Report, but they are completely unrelated, other than they are both written by professors, but at different universities, following different disciplines. One is about Financial Savings in the Armed Forces and the other about Health Tourism and UK Abortion Procedures.'

'So why did you link them together?'

'I was told about them by Charlie and she linked them, or seemed to.' His look negated the need for words. 'Yes, I suppose you're right. But they are linked inasmuch as Tenby was fretting about them both and from what I've heard he's not a man that frets easily.'

Foxx pulled up and put on the handbrake. 'This is it. It's certainly pretty. Nice view too. Now, you keep quiet. I'll find out what we need to know. In fact, you can wait out here if you want to.'

'What? After the way you almost destroyed our relationship with the other Mrs Tenby, asking her intrusive nonsense questions about her sexual CV? No way. I'm coming in and may I suggest you leave all the sensitive questions to me.'

'Don't be stupid. I can do it on my own. I don't need your help.'

'You're new to this, aren't you?'

'What? Interviewing witnesses?'

'No, teamwork. I'm coming with you and staying with you. That's how it works.'

∾

Mrs Hoy had been shopping. She was tall, fit and handsome and had taken a detour to lure her husband out of the office. They sat for twenty minutes in an olde worlde traditional English tea shoppe, supping Earl Grey and Ceylon Orange Pekoe, respectively.

'Storrington is getting really ratty with me.'

'Maybe he knows.'

'No, I've been really careful, but you know him: gut feel. Maybe he just suspects something. It's a nightmare.'

'Sixth sense. He's an old blood hound. But if he doesn't know, then he doesn't know.'

'He fired someone else today. If it goes pear-shaped and I get fired, that will really cock up the plan.'

'Well then, my little man, you'd better win back his confidence.'

'How?'

She poured another cup from the quintessentially English tea pot and scooped a large serving of Devon cream onto her over-sized English scone, ignoring the decadence and indulgence that epitomised the Western world. Turning a blind eye to her increasing bulges, she peered down on her husband who, even sitting, was a good deal shorter than her.

'I don't know. That's your problem. But I know what we said in Iran. We made a pact. Nothing has changed. This is the most important thing in your whole life, the one true way for future happiness. Don't screw it up.'

'I won't. But it's Foxx that's the problem. He was the clear, undisputed perpetrator. All I had to do was catch him and prove it, but the more proof that turns up, the less proof there is to pin it on him.'

'Does Storrington still think Foxx pulled the trigger?'

'I think he's beginning to doubt it. But fortunately, he is fixated on getting Foxx, trigger man or not.'

'Good. That works for us. That's how to be golden boy again. Tell him your theory that Foxx didn't actually pull the trigger. He'll respect you for it. It's vital he trusts you. Then catch Foxx. This is your way back in. Do it. And . . .' she waited for him to finish the sentence.

'Don't screw it up.'

Hoy knew his wife was right. She was always right. But not yet, it was too soon. He knew Storrington. It was a matter of timing, and the time right now, was not right.

A wheelchair rolled its way down the corridor. Julie watched the well-dressed occupant press a button that opened the wide glass door.

'Good afternoon, are you Mrs Elizabeth Tenby?'

'Yes.'

'Wife of Nickolas Tenby?'

'Yes.'

'We're writing a piece for the in-house magazine about your husband and hoped you might spare us a few minutes to give us some background.'

'Of course. Come in.' They entered the beautiful white-walled, thatched cottage. The hall was dark, the floral wallpaper faded, the carpet had seen better days. It was tired, but homely - the outside of the house was smarter than the inside and the height of the magazine piles said she'd been there a long time. She checked their ID.

'It's lovely here,' said Julie, as they left the darkness of the corridor and looked out of the living room window across the wide expanse of fields.

'Yes, isn't it? The only way they'll get me out of here is in a box!'

She was well-dressed and finely preened. She had not known they were coming, so it was not on their account she had attended to her appearance. She was neat and prim, if a little stuffy, as was the house. It had piles of paper and a mass of books ranging from the theories of Karl Marx to the full works of William Shakespeare, but it was clean, tidy and cared for. There were fussy, frilly edged table-cloths on the numerous side tables that dotted the room; the pictures on the wall were free of dust; and the tea that arrived, after all offers of help were refused, was served in best bone china. It was all very orderly, except for the stairs, which were dusty, dark and used as a receding set of shelves. The downstairs shower room and bedroom were visible across the hall. Her living was slow, sedentary and traditional; her husband's was fast and loose. They were poles apart.

The conversation started with banal background around his school days and life in the RAF, moving on to the lavish wedding in Henley.

'You know about the honeymoon in Bali, I suppose?' asked Elizabeth Tenby.

'Yes, of course,' said Foxx. These were three words he used frequently in interviews, whether he knew or not.

Julie lent forward.

'You are separated now, I understand. That must have been upsetting?'

'For him or me?' Julie felt accused, of what she didn't know, and waited for Elizabeth to continue. 'It was after the car accident. Everything was upsetting.' A curtness crept into her voice.

'Was that when you lost the use of your legs?' interjected Foxx, with his customary tact.

'It was,' she replied.

'Greg, you know Greg from Nickolas's squadron? He said you must have been a bit bitter about that: first him driving you into a wall, then putting you through the court case, making you say what you said. Then, as soon as he was free, separating and basically disowning you. I mean we won't print any of this because we are doing a celebration of his achievements, but secretly you must be pretty upset with him.' Foxx had gone in with all barrels firing.

'Yes, except for one thing, he . . .' Elizabeth paused. Julie held her breath. Silence hung. Elizabeth faltered. Her mind changed. 'No. Nothing.'

Foxx stared into her eyes. What was she not saying? Was she still protecting her husband after all these years? He tried to read her thoughts from her expression: protecting him or protecting herself? There was selfish in her eyes. No compassion, just deceit. Realisation dawned.

'*You* were driving. It was you that nearly killed that little girl and you let Nickolas take the blame.'

'No comment.'

'Is that why he left you? You nearly wrecked his career.'

'Think what you like, but we talked at the time about him becoming Prime Minister one day and he could hardly socialise or network if he was at home looking after me, or go to glamorous balls with a wife in a wheelchair, so I left him. It was best all round.' She made it sound very simple and business-like. Her manner was soft, gentle and altruistic; a demure village lady, but with an edge. The local Woman's Institute would not want to get on the wrong side of her demeanour. Foxx pressed on regardless.

'But you didn't divorce?'

'No. My only conditions were that we remained married and he got me this house. Then he took up with a series of dreadful little airheads.

The latest is the worst. I wouldn't give her the time of day. But I'm wise enough to know that when her natural talents start to head south, he'll be off. I've seen it before.'

Julie was straining to understand how the relationship between Elizabeth and her husband worked. 'Do you have much to do with him now?'

'No, I haven't seen him for over five years. I worked for him for a while, as his secretary. He was new to SSS and needed someone he could trust, so I said I would help him out. Once he was established, I left and I haven't seen him since.'

'Does that bother you?'

'No, of course not. My life doesn't revolve around him. I don't have much of a body, but I still have a brain.'

Foxx and Connor exchanged looks. This was a chase of the wild red herring. She hadn't seen him for half a decade and knew nothing of his current life. This was a lead that would lead nowhere, so they asked enough questions about her husband's early life to keep their cover intact, Foxx did a faux loo call to check around the house, then they finished their tea, thanked her warmly and left.

'Oh, one last thing before we go,' asked journalist Foxx as an afterthought, as he stood outside on the step. 'If you had to describe Nickolas in three words what would they be?'

'Charming, devious, ruthless.'

~

The Prime Minister looked over the top of a pile of Brexit papers at Mr Nickolas Morgan-Tenby, exasperated. His secretary and gatekeeper should have known better.

'Does Commander Storrington know you're here?' asked the PM. 'I agreed with him that all my business dealings with SSS would be through him and my public appearances would be with you.'

'He asked me to come,' lied Morgan-Tenby with natural ease. 'He's so bogged down with all the extra security details needed to stop another assassination attempt that he's delegated this matter to me, and asked me to move it to the next step. I just need a quick signature of approval.'

'I want to read the full report first,' said the PM. 'I read the executive summary, but with these things the devil is in the detail.'

'I can assure you, Prime Minister, that there is no devil in this document and the detail is very boring. The full report is over 700 pages long. That's why we gave you the executive summary, especially as you have a lot on your plate at the moment,' he said, looking round at the paper piles of Alpine proportion that filled the room.

'Appreciated, but seven pages to save close on a billion pounds is too stripped-back for me. I need to see the original report by Anderson and understand how we have adapted it.'

'It's very simple,' said Morgan-Tenby, in the patronising voice he normally reserved for Charlie. 'MI5 reports to the Home Secretary, but is not part of the Home Office, but Special Branch is; MI6 reports to the Foreign Office; and the rest of the military report into the Ministry of Defence. There is colossal duplication. They all work for you, as Prime Minister and Commander-in-Chief, so it makes sense that all the security and military services report in through the same channel. It would save hundreds of millions of pounds a year. The only other aspect of note is that the head of your Special Security Service, at the moment Commander Storrington, should officially be appointed as Chief-of-Staff for all military matters. He is already the *de facto* Chief-of-Staff, this just makes it official. It's just a series of simple administrative changes. One signature and we'll take it off your hands.'

The Prime Minister was not going to be bounced into a signature. He was not new to politics, unlike his Liberal side-kick, so he knew that there was always a devil lurking in the detail. The only question was whether it was a devil that mattered, and today he didn't have time to find out.

'It needs proper consultation. Do nothing with it. Advance it no further. Talk to no one else about it. Shelve it until Brexit is signed off.' Morgan-Tenby hadn't finished, but the Prime Minister had, and the visitor was waved away.

∾

'What do you think? Waste of time, right?' asked Connor, as she drove out of Farringdon Churney.

'Meh,' grunted Foxx.

'She left him? Yeah right! You think she walked away from his family fortune to leave him clear to go on a floozy fest? I don't buy it! Lust, greed, jealousy - they're the root of all evil.'

'I can't argue with that, but I didn't see any lust, greed or jealousy. I mean, she did owe him. He saved her ass. She was driving and only has herself to blame,' said Foxx heartlessly.

'Oh, and well done for not asking her how many guys she's slept with.'

'You still don't get it do you? Standard C. A. B. technique.'

'Citizen's Advice Bureau?'

'No. Common Adversary Bonding. If you can get two parties united against a single third party, it brings them together. We do it in Regime Destabilisation all the time. If you and Charlie both think I'm a dick, you apologise for me, she's embarrassed for you and it gives you a basis for better bonding - a common adversary. In this case, me. And it worked.'

'We would have bonded like that anyway.'

'Prove it!'

'I still hate you, y'know.'

~

'Hi, Richard. This is Nick. Hope you enjoyed Charlie's company the other night. Sorry I had to bail. Bad form.' Tenby listened and made affirmative grunts, as the DPM spoke as positively and enthusiastically as he dared about spending an enthralling and enjoyable night until the early hours, with another man's wife.

Then Tenby continued.

'Good. I'm glad you enjoyed it. Look, I've just been talking to the PM about this Military and Security Rationalisation paper. Y'know, the one that Anderson drafted? The PM loved it, but said if anyone talks to him about it before Brexit is signed, he'll scream. He asked me to get you to read the synopsis and sign it off so we can move to the next step. I'll have Lesley bring it over to your office. She'll be happy to wait while you scan through it and sign it, then she can bring it back. We really need it for tomorrow's project update, I'd hate to miss a deadline because you hadn't signed it off. I know the PM is the one that should have signed it weeks ago, but he won't remember that when he's asking why we've fallen behind. Oh, and Charlie said she would love to come back over sometime. She found you fascinating. OK, cheers. I'll send that document over. Bye.'

~

'Hello Commander. This is Merikowski, Team Leader in Planning. I asked around. The consensus is that Foxx is six foot, six one at a maximum, and of the seven people I asked, six said he didn't wear a belt and one thought that he might, but only a discreet, slim, leather belt, no buckle to speak of. Oh, and he's also a local hero, revered in the Department; a role model for all the guys. I hope that helps.'

And it did.

~

Brekkenfield lived twenty miles and a short local train journey from Farringdon Churney. Foxx and Connor sat in the car in the station car park. Julie checked property records.

'She doesn't own the house. Tenby bought it and put it in her name, but it's on a lease. It was a ninety-nine year lease originally, but he bought the fag-end.'

'The what?'

'It's called a fag-end lease. If a lease has less than thirty years to run, no bank or Building Society will mortgage it and it sells a lot cheaper, but at the end of the lease you have to leave.'

'When does this lease expire?'

'In about twelve months' time. She could buy a new lease on it, but that would cost, I dunno, £600,000, maybe more in that area. It's quite a stockbroker belt. I bet that's way beyond her means.'

'Well, let's take a look.' In lieu of his trip to the loo, Foxx had snooped around and got enough banking information to hack into her account.

'He gives her nothing and I've gone back three years. She earns irregular amounts, but is pretty close to broke from what I can see.'

'Broke; and homeless next year,' added Julie. 'She has to be bitter, doesn't she?'

'Yeah, touching, but nothing to do with us. There's my train. I'll see you back at the hotel later.'

'OK, I'm going to . . .'

'Yeah, I know. Be back by ten and sober!'

The DPM read the seven pages and signed.

He felt bad signing, though he didn't know why. It had been the same with progressing the 'new fairer' Housing Bill, not to mention getting the Minimum Wage Revisions through the House and into legislation. That had been a nightmare, but he'd pushed it and he'd won - it just didn't feel like it. Something about it felt not quite right; a hollow victory. He stared down at the seven-page synopsis about Military and Security spending and felt the same deep-seated uncertainty.

But the PM supported the document, it had been worked on by the cumbersome machine of the British Civil Service and had been presented to him by his friend and ally Nick Tenby. It was fine, just an administrative readjustment that would save enough taxpayer's money to get him elected next time round. It had to be a good idea, didn't it?

He signed it and gave it back to the messenger.

Lesley smiled, perhaps a little too much, and the world became one step closer to darkness.

20

NARNIA

Foxx was in his element. He sprinted across the fields, melded into woodland, padding through the trees like a wolf. Brekkenfield lived in an old farmhouse; like him, it had seen better days. The back door creaked as Foxx eased it open. He froze, paused, listened. He heard nothing, slipped through the crack of the half-opened door into the stone-floored scullery.

Foxx moved into the kitchen. Brekkenfield was in bed. The creak of the door was barely audible upstairs, but Brekkenfield sat up, put on his dressing-gown, grabbed his pistol and made his way down. He peered cautiously into the kitchen - it was cold, bare and empty. Foxx had gone, silently slipping into the lounge.

Brekkenfield made a hot drink and shuffled uneasily into the lounge, walking within feet of Foxx and sitting in gloom and pain on the sofa. Foxx stood; a frozen statue, motionless, melting unseen and unnoticed into the bookcase, less than ten feet away from the man supping his Ovaltine. Foxx watched, then drifted like a phantom into the study.

Brekkenfield stood. He'd heard a noise again. He walked into the hall. It had come from the study; a creak of floorboards. The old house had creaked often, especially when his wife had shuffled around late at night. But now she was gone, the sounds he heard were wishful thinking. Her noises had irritated him; now he missed them. He turned, mounted the stairs and made his way back to bed.

Foxx sat back in the large leather study chair and read: employment contract, house deeds, insurance certificates dating back to the last century, MOT certificates for cars no longer owned. It was a sea of life's administration. But the answer had already floated to the surface. It was on the desk: divorce papers.

Each sheet was headed with the name of his lawyers: *Black and Gold.* Brekkenfield had come out of hospital to get divorced - to sign the papers. It all fitted. The house had evidence of an absent wife, a lack of her things, holes where there used to be completion, emptiness where it used to be whole. And Brekkenfield was broken; he was not a man on a mission. In hospital, his life had almost left him and now he was home, the life he had known had gone forever. He was tired, fragile and disengaged.

Foxx replaced the papers meticulously and, as a silent apparition, left even more quietly than he'd arrived.

Charlie had buzzed the gate. By the time she had opened the front door, Julie was pulling up at the front of the house.

'Hello,' said Charlie with genuine enthusiasm. 'This is a nice surprise.'

Julie approached, gifts in hand. 'I've brought your skirt back and these are for you.' She presented Charlie with a gorgeous bouquet of flowers.

'How kind. Thank you.' They entered the house. 'I think that makes us friends,' said the blonde teenager of thirty-two. She took Julie by the hand and scampered them both up the stairs and along the corridor and through the second door. It was a bedroom, a palatial bedroom, designed by a woman for a woman. It was a fairy world of pink and style; expensive and co-ordinated - light, bright and instantly appealing. The door closed behind them. 'This is my room,' said Charlie. 'Now, undress.'

Julie, who didn't object in principle to the proposal, was beginning to think that most people she met nowadays only wanted to see her naked. But she wasn't threatened by Charlie's teenage enthusiasm, just a little surprised.

'What kind of friends do you think we are, exactly?' she asked kindly.

'The kind that give each other things: you brought my skirt back, which you needn't have done, and I have a present for you.' She handed

Julie an elegant be-ribboned box about eighteen inches square and four inches deep. 'This is for you.'

Julie was taken aback. She hadn't really expected to be invited in, let alone be given a gift. She pulled the ribbon. It fell away. Charlie was holding the box on her two upraised palms. Julie carefully opened the lid. As she prised it up, her eyes opened with wide amazement.

'I don't believe it. Is this . . . are they . . .? Oh my god, my trousers! Risen from the dead!'

'Not so much a repair, more of a rebuild,' chipped in Charlie. 'I had them remade to the exact same pattern. They are your original trousers, except for the seat and the legs and the side panel. But the waistband and the zip are original, and they're the bits you touch when you put them on, so I kept them the same.'

The material was pure luxury, the cut was perfect. These were her trousers, but better; handmade and beautifully finished.

Julie couldn't curtail her smile, wider than she had smiled for years.

She took off her dress and slipped on the trousers. The fit was perfect, just like it had always been. Her trousers were back. She admired herself, looked at the front, turned, looked at the back and felt Duncan returned all around her, tight, snug and safe. A tiny tear tickled the corner of her eye. 'And I also got you this,' Charlie produced a top; a highly tailored, exclusively designed, white silk blouse to go with the trousers. Julie put it on.

'I love it. It's gorgeous, but I really can't accept it. I mean, it's not right. How could I ever repay you?'

'Well, that's the point of presents,' said Charlie, like a ten year old explaining how life works. 'You don't have to repay them. Did you repay your boyfriend when he bought them for you?' Their eyes met, their minds worked in unison and they both burst out laughing.

'Yes, I probably did, now you mention it.'

'Yeah, me too, with my husband,' chirped Charlie, between her giggles. 'And have you seen how many dresses I've got? Exhausting!' The laughter continued. It was good being with Charlie. She made Julie feel young again. It'd been too long. The laughter continued, the conversation became easy and relaxed. Being with Charlie was natural and her offer was easy to accept.

'Will you stay and chat for a while? I've got champagne.'

Two minutes later they were both sitting on the bed, a glass of champagne in hand and reassuringly gentle companionship by their side.

They talked clothes, fashion and bottoms that were too big for one's trousers. Charlie assured Julie that her form was perfect and she would trade figures any day of the week. And Charlie never lies. They talked about hair styles. Charlie had only dyed half her hair blonde, the rest was honey brown. When she let it hang lose and forwards she was blonde; when she swept it back and clipped it down she was honey. They played with Julie's hair, she looked instantly cuter. They talked about the champagne, the bedroom and chocolate, before covering a hundred other topics. Then they stopped, took a drink and let a moment's silence take hold.

Charlie picked her moment.

'I know,' she said, 'that you opened up to me last time you were here, so that I'd open up to you. I felt bad, because I had nothing to open up about. Nicki's a good husband for me and I have a nice life. What's to say?'

'Is he actually legally your husband?' asked Julie, diving in.

'He's my husband in every way, except legally. We got married on a beach in Thailand. It was beautiful. He made vows and we shared commitment, but no, in this country we're not legally married. He's already married. Her name's Elizabeth. She's a right Miss Marple, all genteel and kind, then bites you in the ass when you're not looking.'

'So you know her then?'

'Oh yes. I see her every couple of months. Nicki won't see her anymore, not since she worked for him, so meeting me is the only way she can get any information about him. She's so nosey. I tell her a lot of nothing and give her my beauty-queen speech about everyone in the world working together in peace. Then she patronises me and I pay for tea.'

'Why do you do it?'

'Misplaced sympathy.'

'No, I mean let people patronise you. I think you're very astute, cleverer than you let on.'

'Thank you, but Nicki likes me being dumb. About six weeks into our relationship, I had an intelligent conversation with him. Well, I thought it was intelligent . . . y'know about politics and the way of the world. It turned him cold, like I had just grown a beard and my tits had fallen off. It was like a cold shower. I'd lost my sex appeal - in fact *all* my appeal - so I said something dumb, he laughed and we were all good again.' Julie smiled, but didn't feel she had fully made her point.

'Are you reading this?' she asked, picking up a first edition copy of *To Kill a Mockingbird* from the bedside table.

'Kind of. I like the main man in it. He always tries to help people and see the good in them. That's me; I like to do that. Except, he's a smart lawyer.' They both took a synchronised sip of champagne.

'Anyway I don't mind people thinking I'm dumb. They expect less of me. The only one who winds me up is Lesley, Nicki's PA. I don't mind her talking down to me. I know her personality needs to do that to make herself feel good; but she is so rude. And selfish. But I always try to be nice to her. I bought her some jazz records, original vinyls from the fifties and sixties, one of them was signed by Charlie Parker. It cost me a fortune and took me ages to find. She didn't even say thank you.'

'You should call her out on it next time you see her,' said Julie. Charlie just laughed. 'What's funny?' asked Julie, feeling that she'd been the one to say something stupid.

'You said *call her out*. That's such a northern expression. It's funny to hear you say it. It took me back to my childhood days. But I will. I will say something next time I see her.' They talked a while about what a super bitch Lesley was and Julie slowly moved the conversation back to Nickolas.

'What's he like? Is he into his job or is it just an amusement to pass the time?'

'No, he's very ambitious. I mean *really* ambitious. He would sell his own mother to get ahead. I think he's trying to pimp me out to the DPM at the moment! I like to help, but I do draw the line at that.' She laughed.

'But he is clever. People don't realise that. You know the coup in Zalekistan? Well I shouldn't tell you this, but that was Nicki. He planned it. He got others to do it, of course; he always does. That's what makes him so clever. Apparently, it was a great success. He was so happy after it. He gave me a Porsche and bought himself a boat; it's enormous. He likes it, but we hardly ever use it.' She prattled on about the boat and the parties they had had on it when he first got it and spoke lavishly about her husband's cleverness.

Julie sat enjoying the champagne, as Charlie enjoyed talking about her husband's prowess.

'He's a real negotiator. You know Field Marshall Grafton?' Julie felt like the ignorant one, as a blank expression crossed her face. 'Well, he heads up the whole of the army now, since two months ago. And Admiral Stubbings, he runs the whole Navy, but he's only been doing it for six months. Nicki bet me a . . . well it doesn't matter what he bet me, but he said they would get those jobs; like, he could see the future. That was over a year ago, when they came to dinner. They hopscotched up three layers to get the job. Is it hopscotched?'

'Leapfrogged?'

'Yes that's it. You see, my Nicki can spot a winner a mile off. That's why he's so keen on making friends with the DPM before he becomes Prime Minister. The DPM is nice, but no match for Nicki. Nicki will wrap him round his little finger in no time. I guess in a way I'm part of that. Should I feel a bit bad about it?'

It was a question Julie declined to answer. Instead, she asked,

'Who else came to dinner?'

'Dozens of people. An RAF buddy of Nicki's came, but he doesn't run the RAF, he's only Second-in-Command, but he is real handsome. He said he'd take me up in a helicopter and a fast jet and he did. I nearly came in my pants!' She laughed in recollection of the excitement. 'It's funny how Nicki mixes with military people: the most action he ever saw was when he had tonsillitis and was off work for six weeks. I had to hand-feed him with ice cream. He's such a baby. He also invites people from erect committees.'

Julie spluttered on her champagne and couldn't help laughing. 'I think you mean select committees.'

'Yes, I know. But when I first heard it, I thought Nicki said *erect* committees and I couldn't wait!' She laughed at her own stupidity. 'But they certainly were a group of stiffs; so boring. But apparently me smiling at them helps them pass the right laws. I don't get it myself, but if it helps Nicki, then I do it.'

'But he doesn't get involved in politics, does he? He's just in security,' remarked Julie, trying to pitch another interrogatory question in a light-hearted voice.

'He never used to, but now he's into everything: housing benefit, the Census, National Health, everything. I think his main job is too easy, so he finds other things to get involved with. Sometimes I think he works so hard and is away so often, he'll work himself to death.'

'And then his wife, his first wife, would get all his money,' said Julie, using tact levels she had learned from Foxx.

'She can have it. I don't care about that. I don't need his money. But I would lose my little Michael O'Velly.' Julie resisted the temptation to correct her to *Machiavelli*. 'Then what would I do?'

Somehow, as it does with girls and champagne, the answer to that last question involved batteries, sex, men and personal preferences.

Julie was careful not to drink more than a glass or two because she was driving - or maybe three - and didn't want to give away any more than she had already. A second bottle appeared. Charlie confided about Nicki's macho tendencies in the bedroom, which prompted Julie to ask,

'Do you have separate bedrooms? This surely isn't his bedroom?' she asked, looking round the pink and feminine room.

'Gosh no, not when he's here. His bedroom is the first door at the top of the stairs. That's where you'll find me when he's home, but when he's away, I like my own space. I once tiptoed back here when he was asleep. He gave me such a spanking! He's the lightest sleeper ever. If I flutter my eyelashes too loudly, he wakes up!'

Julie looked at her watch. Hours had rushed by. She wasn't going to be back by ten o'clock or sober.

'Oh my god, look at the time. I have to go. I have to meet Eduard.'

'He is lovely,' said Charlie, 'but a bit odd. Did you . . .? ' She looked at Julie's face. 'Oh my god! You did, you little minx.' It took another ten minutes to talk about stamina, testosterone and tantalising. Julie had to leave. She folded her dress back into the ribboned box and they wandered downstairs, still talking.

When they were finally heading for the front door, Charlie picked up a book off the table, 'This is for Eduard. I'll be honest with you, I'm not really into puzzle books, but I know he is. So will you give him this?' She handed Julie an advanced level *Join the Dots* puzzle book. 'I bet he can't do the Million Dollar puzzle on page sixty-four. It's for true professionals,' continued Charlie.

Julie didn't voice her concern that there might not be a profession of dot joiners, but instead said she was sure Eduard would love it and gave Charlie a big kiss.

'Goodbye,' said Charlie. 'Goodbye.'

It felt inexplicably final. A little jolt inside Julie said it would be the last time they would meet. She ignored her irrationality, kissed her again and left. As she walked to the car, she asked over her shoulder,

'Does my arse really look good in this?'

Charlie smiled, blew a kiss and shouted, 'Perfect.'

And Charlie never lies.

Julie walked just a little wobbly into their hotel room. Foxx got off the bed and answered her question her with a long hug. 'Did you miss me?' she had said, with big eyes looking up at him.

'No,' he said, as he gave her another kiss that betrayed his real affection.

'Me neither,' she replied, as she kissed him back. 'Now, what about Brekkenfield?'

'He's innocent. He was out of hospital to get divorce papers signed. *Black and Gold* is not code, it's the name of his lawyer. What about Tenby?'

'Guilty. I don't know what of yet, but I'm sure he is. Charlie blurted out all kinds of stuff. I just have to make sense of it all.' Her speech was as blurred as her thoughts.

'Yes, but is he guilty of assassinating the Prime Minister?'

'Probably not. But I know he's guilty of something.'

'Yes, you said. You clearly don't like him. Don't let personal feelings get in the way. Are you drunk?' She smiled at him. 'How did you get here? Did you drive?'

'Of course,' she said, bleary eyed. 'I'm in no condition to walk.' She kissed him again, then paraded herself up and down wiggling like an overzealous catwalk model. 'Look what Charlie got me. It's my trousers, reborn. I love 'em. Oh yes, and she got you a present too: revenge for your silly puzzle book gift.' She handed him the *Join the Dots* book. 'She said you're a professional and should be able to do it. Me, I doubt it. I doubt you could join anything, especially a team. Did I tell you that you're a rubbish team player?'

Foxx placed the book on the bedside table and picked up his jacket.

'Are you going somewhere?'

'Yes.'

Can I come?'

'No,' he said without any real feeling. She followed him out of the door and into the car.

As they drove, she asked,

'Have you ever heard of the Zalekistani coup?' Her brain was coming back on line as the champagne befuddlement faded.

'Yes.' He spoke with feeling. 'It was bloody and it was a mess; a completely butched job.' She googled and gave edited highlights as she skimmed Wikipedia.

'Four hundred civilians died, the Government regained control, then there was a counter-coup and over three thousand civilians were killed over a five-week period, five hundred and sixty-two people were arrested, three hundred were executed, the Prime Minister was hung in public.'

'Jesus!' she said. 'And this was only a few years ago. I thought coups were a thing of the past and mostly in Africa.'

'There have been over sixty coups in the last fifteen years. I know: I caused three of them. There have been recent coups or attempted coups in Turkey, Italy, Spain and Greece, all in the last fifty or sixty years. And Thailand has them regularly, like moon festivals, normally in a very civilised manner. But Zalekistan - that was a filthy bloodbath. It was fuelled by corruption and greed, and oil money; it had nothing to do with politics. It was shameful that the international community didn't intervene, but they were probably behind it!'

'I was right, then. He was guilty of something. The charming, smiling Mr Morgan-Tenby organised it and then bought a luxury yacht.'

The anticipated outburst of condemnation from Mr Foxx didn't come. He drove in silence, thoughts internalised. He was definitely not built to be a team player.

They parked by a Tube station and walked five streets to his flat. As they entered his block, a man across the road sitting in a car surrounded by empty coffee mugs, doughnut boxes and takeaway wrappers, picked up the phone and made a call. As Foxx and Julie entered his front door, the SWAT team was already on its way.

'Nice place you've got here,' said Julie with deep sarcasm. 'It's an art nouveau installation, right?' She surveyed the mayhem. Every drawer had been opened and emptied on the floor, every cupboard stripped out, every piece of furniture searched and left in disarray.

'Thank you. But I am thinking about changing my cleaner.' He deftly removed the top of his hi-fi amplifier and took out a small device. 'It's a damp meter,' he said, as he started searching for bugs, video feeds and recording devices. He found seven and disabled them.

The flat had been stylish and modern before its invasion. He had taste, some of it expensive. Julie restructured the scene in her mind and imagined it before heavy boots had torn it apart. Foxx scrabbled through the dishevelment, throwing things into his bag as he went.

'I approve,' said Julie, as five packs of new pants hit the inside of the holdall. He peered out of the window.

'Time to go,' he said, as if packing up a picnic. Julie looked out of the window. A dozen heavily armed officers were running into the building. Adrenaline struck her heart. She was not used to this level of excitement. Champagne bravado had long since evaporated; all she felt was fear.

'Are they going to catch us?'

'I didn't come here to get caught.'

She allowed herself to feel better.

'So what's the plan, then?'

'Sit in there.' He pointed into a wardrobe with a few suits and shirts still left hanging in it. All of a sudden, she felt worse again. There was a knock at the door. There were voices, boots and no doubt a battering ram at the ready.

'That's your plan? Hiding in a wardrobe, hoping an army of armed men don't find us?'

'Pretty much. Now get in.' She obeyed seconds before the front door flew off its hinges and the flat was stormed by a team intent on their destruction. Her heart beat so loudly, she was sure they would hear it. She counted the seconds waiting for the inevitable disaster to strike.

Foxx closed the wardrobe door until it clicked shut, then reached above his head in the darkness and rotated the clothes rail. A door opened on the other side of the wardrobe. They tumbled out and into safety. He silently closed the secret wardrobe door, turned to her and said,

'Welcome to Narnia.'

She smiled. She was alive. She was in a flat of calm and quiet, a flat hidden by a façade, a flat unseen by the outside world. She stood in a flat that was a metaphor for the man.

He grabbed a thick wad of bank notes and a few other necessities and stashed them in his now bulging bag. They left by the Narnia front door, skipped down the grand staircase right down to the basement, as they had done in Berkeley Heights. Exiting through the bin door, they hurried along an alley and into the back door of a large building, went up the lino-covered steps, through a door and into the carpeted splendour of a five-star hotel lobby.

Across the lobby was a large revolving front door, but just before they reached it they descended a wide staircase to the left, pushed open a glass door and found themselves in the familiar walkways of the London Underground. Passing the ticket office on the right and the barriers to the left, they exited the station on the other side. As they re-emerged at street level, they took ten steps and arrived at the car, five streets away from Foxx's front door. They got in and drove away.

'A quick dinner and then early to bed,' announced Foxx.

'Oh good,' she said, enjoying her lust and celebrating the fact that she was neither dead nor arrested.

'Maybe I'd better lock you in the bathroom again!' He smiled at her and spoke softly. 'We're on an op tomorrow. The PM will be there, alone, at 6.oo a.m. We have to be there before him. He will be an easy hit, an assassin's dream and we have to stop it. We're not calling the police, because this is the PM's personal secret, but if we get it wrong, it will be the last thing he ever does.'

Two hours later, Julie was sleeping in his arms, sated. He lay awake, as he so often did. He felt the pressure.

If I get this wrong Julie dies, my dad dies, the country loses a leader and the trail will go cold.

He hugged her warm, naked body and felt cold rush through his veins.

He cursed himself for writing such a comprehensive document. He had to beat his own best planning. He had to beat the assassin at their own game.

He had to win.

He had no choice.

21

GRAVE DANGER

The Prime Minister kissed his wife. This morning, he didn't feel like a Prime Minister, he just felt like a dad; any dad who'd lost a child. He never said where he was going. He didn't have to. She knew. He wouldn't let his only daughter down on her birthday.

'Give her a kiss for me. Tell her I still miss her.'

'I will. I always do.'

He stepped lightly down the stairs, leaving the lights off. They were in their own home, their cosy house in the country. He slipped out of the side door, down the side of the garage, round the back of the coal shed, under the fence and into next door's garden. Borrowed keys in hand, he slipped into the driving seat of his neighbour's old Mitsubishi estate car. He was two miles down the road, before he doffed the cap from his head.

He drove slowly and carefully, his head full of memories and empty of thoughts. But it was not sad, not totally. He felt a smile when he thought of her face and how she'd gripped his fingers so tightly. He remembered the happy days like they were yesterday. She'd only been three when they'd lost her and the decades had slipped by. She would be a doctor now or a lawyer or working for the United Nations. She could be anything he wanted, in his mind, in his memories, in his aspirations.

It was a clear, blue-sky morning. The birds would be singing when he arrived, the dew would still be moist on the ground and tranquillity would be all around.

It made him feel alive.

He just had to stay that way for the next hour.

Foxx and Connor were at the Garden of Rest long before the Prime Minister's alarm clock woke him. It was dark, as black as a bible and so quiet you could hear the moon set. Foxx was alive and alert. Julie was in the passenger seat, still coming to terms with the morning. He'd given her the gun, bullets and instructions. She'd clicked open the cartridge and lodged in the bullets with her thumb, then clicked it shut - her fingerprints left on every part.

She resisted her thoughts. *He's setting me up. He's come here to kill his father and lay the blame on me.*

'Tell me something about you, Mr Foxx,' she said, still sleepy in her voice. They had a long drive and she didn't want to think about what would be there when they arrived.

'Like what?'

'Your most and least favourite pastimes, out of bed and outside work?'

'Most favourite; being on the southern plateau of Mount Kei in the Denali National Park, Alaska. It's a fifteen mile hike through unspoilt temperate rainforest, a clamber over lose rocks for a couple of miles, then a glorious free climb up a 2,000 foot cliff onto the plateau shelf. It's like you're in heaven, totally alone. Unbelievable, life-affirming, ensconced in nature; wonderful.

Least favourite . . . bridge; a game that's mind-numbingly boring, for those in their late-nineties waiting to die. It's the only way these people can make three friends - futile, desolate and inexplicable.'

'Not keen on card games, then?'

'If I were playing bridge, whilst sitting on a bridge, I would jump off. '

'Not keen on bridge players either, then?'

'NQOK darling!'

'What?'

'Not Quite Our Kind!' he said in his most superior and mock condescending voice. 'What about you? Favourite thing to do, money no object?'

'Tonga. There's a private island there. It costs £10,000 a week, maybe more, but you get a house with total privacy, your own pool, chef, clean-

ers, power boat. You could see no-one for a month or you could go to the
mainland and enjoy local life. I'd stay there for as long as funds lasted,
doing pottery, learning the viola and making love, day and night, to
Duncan, if he were still here.'

'And who would you take now, if not him – a new boyfriend?'

'Not you for a start! No,' she thought for a moment. 'No boyfriends.
I'd take a girlfriend – twice the fun and none of the trouble.'

They chatted, Julie hiding her fear, Foxx hiding his frustration with
the triviality of the conversation; both doing what they had to do to
prepare for whatever was to come.

They arrived in deep lush agricultural farmland and parked on an
area of wasteland overshadowed by a hedge.

Foxx locked the car and they stepped through a gap in the hedge to a
footpath that circled a small hill that rose ahead of them. The path to the
left led to the back of the hill. They went right and followed it for half a
mile, through a small woodland, then along a hedgerow, no doubt
unchanged for centuries. The hillock rose up to their left. The Garden
of Rest appeared before them in the distance, dark and down to the
right. They approached, found their vantage point and sat in silence.
Waiting.

'Over there,' he whispered. Her heart jumped, frightened for the first
time by the reality of meeting the assassin. 'That's where he'll be.' He
pointed up the hill at the perfect sniper's vantage point. It was a clear
unimpeded sight line between hide and graveside. The trees around the
Garden of Rest broke at that point. The target would be in the open,
unprotected, unmissable. There would be a single crack in the countryside silence, then the father would fall, spilling blood on the resting place
of his child. It was the only spot where a shot would work - unless the
assassin entered the cemetery, walked past the gravestones and took out
the Prime Minister by hand or by sidearm. They waited on the side of the
hill, facing each other, Foxx watching the empty nest above, Julie
watching the empty graveyard below.

'Ahead of us,' he whispered, familiarising her with military jargon, 'is
twelve o-clock. The entrance to the cemetery is at two o'clock.' He pointed
about sixty degrees to the right. 'The path we came down is at four o'clock
and the sniper will be behind you at six o'clock.' He turned and pointed.
'Keep your eyes on everything from nine o'clock to three o'clock and I'll

take the rest.' Silence fell again and she gazed through the morning twilight, waiting.

Gravel crunched under slowly turning tyres. The car stopped, the engine turned off. The door closed almost too quietly to hear, the footsteps over gravel dying away in the breeze. And there, alone, but observed, was Foxx's adopted father. He was alone in his thoughts, alone in the morning, alone with his lost love. He knelt, talked, prayed, lay flowers, then sat on the edge of her marble graveside, like it was her bed at home; in a world that was hers and his alone.

Julie felt her heart beat faster. Foxx felt the grip on his gun tighten. A second was a lifetime; a minute was forever. The man was open, vulnerable. One shot and he was dead.

Julie watched the graveyard. She dared not blink, scanning for movement, watching every rustle of branch, every sway of twig. She watched, on edge, on guard.

Then movement.

Imagined at first.

Julie tensed and tapped his knee. He swung round to see a shadow behind the leaves at the entrance of the Garden of Rest. He took aim with his pistol. The shadow moved slowly - moved closer. There was no clear shot. Should he shout, should he run, should he shoot?

He held his nerve. The shadow became a person, the person had been kneeling. She stood, she walked towards the PM. Foxx had her in his sights. She was the killer. This was it. If Foxx had a rifle, she would be a dead shot; with a pistol, success was not so certain. He raised the gun to his eye, ready to take the shot. He had her, he could take her down. The figure knelt again, not taking position to shoot, she knelt in prayer. She removed her Laura Ashley headscarf: she was old, she was praying, she was not the threat. He relaxed his stance, but kept the pistol high.

'Watch her,' he whispered almost silently, as he took vigil on the sniper's nest. Two minutes. Five minutes. Twelve minutes, both on high alert, adrenaline pumping, heart thumping a relentless beat in Julie's ears. The old lady stood. Julie nudged her companion and she took vigil on the non-existent sniper. Foxx followed the old lady with the barrel of his gun. She walked slowly, she walked solemnly, but she walked away. The PM was alone once more.

Minutes ticked. Twenty minutes, twenty-five, twenty-eight, twenty-nine. Foxx wanted an enemy he could see. If he could see him, he could kill him. Invisible, he was an incalculable and uncontrollable danger. Twenty-nine and a half minutes. Foxx pointed the gun hard at the nest, waiting to see the rifle barrel appear. Thirty minutes. Julie jumped. A bird flew from the branches, wings flapping. The PM stood up and slowly – so slowly – walked away.

Foxx waited for the crack to split the silence, the gunshot to end the mission; but the PM left unharmed through the ornate arches and headed for his car. Foxx sprinted across the hillside to get a view of the car park, to see if the killer had improvised, changed plan, switched tactics.

The Mitsubishi engaged drive, the PM swept gracefully out of the car park and was gone.

Foxx returned to Julie, who was still watching the empty graveyard, dutifully intent. They looked at each other. Anti-climax or relief? They walked together down the long, straight, bumpy path, along the hedgerow, back to the car.

'No show,' she said. No reply.

'Again,' she said. Again no reply.

'There have been three possible attempts,' she continued. 'The one when you weren't with me did happen; the two when you were with me didn't happen. Is that a coincidence?'

'Well, it wasn't me, so if it was one of us, it was . . .'

She kicked him hard in the back of the knee. He buckled. She pushed him down. The gun fell from his belt. She scrabbled and grabbed it. The shot missed as it whistled past Foxx's ear.

Foxx had not seen it. He couldn't have done. As he answered Julie's last question, a red laser dot appeared on the back of his head. Julie didn't think, she reacted. She kicked him down. The rifle cracked a shot, the bullet scarcely missed his head. He raised his head to look. Another shot cracked the air.

'What's happening?' she asked.

'Someone's shooting at us,' he replied deadpan.

'Take this,' she handed him the gun. 'Shoot back.'

'What if it's the Secret Service? D'you want me to shoot the good guys?'

'Yes, if they're shooting at me! And stop putting your head up or it'll get shot off.'

'Number one: shut up and do as I say. Number two: I needed to put my head up to see where he was shooting from. Number three: follow me and keep down.' He crawled through a tiny gap in the hedge. 'This will give us cover. Now keep low and run.'

They ran hunched and fast along the length of the hedge, until woodland obscured them from their hunter. They were within sight of the car. She caught her breath. He was as fit as a whippet, but she kept him in range. He ignored the car, turned right down the other path and kept running.

'Where are you going? The car's over there!' she panted.

'We're not going home. We need to find out if it's the assassin, and if it is, we need to take him out.' Julie's head went into a whirl. He'd said it would get dangerous. She had heard about Operations, about the blood and bullets, but she'd only ever sat at a desk. 'I need you with me. Can you keep up?'

'I'm with you Foxx. Just don't get me killed!'

'No promises,' he said and ran down the path at the back of the hill. She guessed he wanted to get behind the assassin. She put more effort into running and kept him in sight for the full length of the hill. He stopped fifty yards ahead of her. 'Come on! Over here!' he shouted, unnecessarily loudly.

She caught him up, spent ten seconds catching her breath and stood straight to show she was ready. A bullet flew through the bushes and missed her by inches. Foxx took a single return shot, then silence.

He signalled his intentions to her and they both ran further along the path, crouching below hedge height until Foxx stuck his head past the end of the hedge. Rapid fire broke out. Julie collapsed face down onto the path. Bullets bounced and ricocheted, leaves were ripped off their branches. She wanted to let fear rule her body, but her mind said no. Bursts of adrenaline turned into blind exhilaration. Her heart beat faster, her lungs dug deep for breath. She was frightened, but that just kept her sharper. She didn't believe she would die. Not today, not yet.

Foxx indicated to retreat. They slid twenty paces back up the track. On one side of the track, looking up the hill, was the hedge, on the other, a steep wooded slope downwards. Julie had wanted to crawl higher up the hill from the path to gain the advantage of height, but her experienced operational tactician indicated to slide off the path and down the slope.

The trees and the incline gave them cover. They ran along the edge of the tree line, until Foxx indicated to stop. There, fifty yards across an open field, was a tall Victorian mill, being used as a barn. Two centuries ago, grain had been fed into hoppers high up in the roof line and ground by stones driven by a now defunct waterwheel. The faded brick had mellowed into the countryside, the weathered oak of the loading doors, thirty feet above the ground, matched the peeling eves of the sharply angled roof. The chain and pulley hung still from above the high loading door down to the ground, like it had for over a hundred years, still catching glinting reflections of sunlight. It had no windows.

'Run directly at this angle,' said Foxx, pointing. 'You'll be under the cover of trees until the last fifteen yards. Then run like hell, get round the corner of the building and you'll be out of the firing line. There's a door one the other side. It's not locked.

'How d'you know?'

'I've been here before.'

'Where will you be?'

'Right behind you, so don't slow me down. Now go!'

She ran, gently at first, keeping low. Twenty paces out, she heard him behind her and she sprinted, dived round the corner, flung open the door and ran inside. Foxx was with her. He shut the door. There was no gunfire, but had they been detected?

'Now what?' she asked.

'Up that ladder,' he said. It was the height of a house and led to a large platform, a mezzanine floor larger than her whole flat. They scaled the ladder and stepped onto the platform. She could see the sunlight through the crack between the old oak loading doors. There was a tarpaulin hanging up against the wall, hay bales at either end of the floor, a few farm implements leaning against the wall and a rope dangling down from the roof.

'Hide here,' said Foxx, holding the rope. 'I'm going up there to get a better vantage point. As soon as he's through the door, he's a dead man. Here take this, just in case.' He handed her a small pistol. She had not seen it before. *Scarcely bigger than a Derringer*, she thought. She examined it closely and read the word *Derringer* across the handle.

Her unformed questions were left unanswered. He shinned up the rope at speed and out of sight. Once in the rafters, he pulled the rope up after him. She felt suddenly alone. She stood, clicked off the safety and felt the pistol in her hand. She had never even held a gun before she met Foxx, let alone fire one. She thought, she planned, she hid.

She held her breath and listened to the silence. The breeze clinked through the chains that hung outside the loading doors. The wooden beam that supported the pulley creaked gently. The chains clinked louder. They clinked in rhythm. The clink got closer. It wasn't the wind, it was a man; a man climbing the chains to avoid walking through a door - a door he knew would lead to his death. The assassin was here, now, outside the loading door, five feet from where Julie was hiding.

He pushed the doors gently with kid gloves. They swung slowly open flooding the platform with morning sun. He took two steps in. He knew she was there and it was time for her to die. She gripped hold of her breath, froze her every muscle, silenced her heart. She did all she could to save herself.

He looked, saw the tarpaulin. It seemed to billow. He lowered his eyes to the floor. One tiny tell-tale tip of a small lady's shoe ruffled the rugged folds of the hanging canvas. He said nothing. He raised his gun to her chest height and released three bullets in rapid succession. It took no more than two seconds. He waited for her body to fall.

Foxx peered down from his bolt hole in the roof. Had his plan succeeded or failed? He couldn't see. He held the rope firmly in both hands.

Julie's dead and mutilated body did not fall out from behind the tarpaulin. Instead, she stepped out from behind the hay bales, pointed the pistol at his head and felt her fingers fumble the trigger. He was tall, six foot four, with a large metal buckle on his belt. The steel toecaps on his shoes had clinked against the metal chains as he had climbed. He was dressed in black and no more than ten feet away from her. She pulled the trigger, the gun waved like a dandelion in a wind storm. She was so close, too close to miss - but she did.

She had pulled the trigger, missed the man, fumbled and dropped the gun. He smiled and slowly raised his pistol with intent to kill. Foxx flew into combat, swinging on the rope like a trapeze artist, smashing directly into the assassin. The man in black flew back onto the other set of hay bales. His pistol dropped from his hand, skidded along the hay-strewn floor, teetered on the edge of the platform and fell thirty feet onto the barn floor.

Foxx gained position. The man stood and faced him, standing a good four inches taller. Foxx looked at the him, stared at the long lurid scar that ran right across his face and said in surprise,

'Dirk? Dirk, what the fuck are you doing here?'

'Killing you!'

Foxx was off guard. Dirk punched hard. Foxx flew backwards, losing his gun. Dirk took a knife from a sheath on his belt, Julie ran towards him, broom in hand. The head of the broom resting square against her body, the pointed end of the handle was thrust like a lance into his abdomen. He fell backwards. She kept on pushing. He stumbled and made a grab for the bales. She kept on pushing. He lost his balance, he missed his grip, she kept on pushing. He fell backwards off the edge of the platform, thirty feet, taking the ladder with him. He landed harshly, smashing down on bales, pig troughs and an old chain that lay on the floor below. Foxx stood, lightly dazed. He had to shoot Julie threw him his gun. He stood by the edge of the platform and fired at the assassin below.

The man in black with the steel-toe shoes and the heavy metal belt buckle was hobbling at speed out of the door and out of sight. The shot had just clipped him. Moments later, the sound of a motorbike starting, revving and disappearing into the distance said that the threat had gone and their target had escaped. It was a failsafe situation. They were safe, but they had failed. The assassin was free.

Foxx and Julie sat on the hay bales at opposite ends of the platform.

'Sorry,' they said in unison.

'I missed him,' said Julie in deep regret. 'I won't miss next time.'

'I shouldn't have put you in that situation,' said Foxx. 'I hope there won't be a next time.' Julie wasn't listening.

'Now what?' she asked, as she looked down thirty feet at the ladder lying on the barn floor. 'Jump?'

'Hang on a minute,' said Foxx. 'I've got an idea.'

∼

Twenty minutes later they were in the car. Forty minutes later they were in a random rural hotel dunking a second-rate croissant into their morning beverage of choice. Foxx had coffee, Julie chose whisky. Then another whisky.

'Are you OK?' asked Foxx, 'because you look like shit, to be honest.'

'I feel better than if I'd been behind that tarpaulin.' She was not in the mood for accepting sympathy and probably wouldn't get any, so she leant forward and talked business. 'I don't get it. Why didn't he shoot the PM? He was there, he had a gun, he had ample opportunity?'

'Because we prevented it. We kept him from perching in his sniper's nest.'

'No, baby, no.' she said softly, but firmly. 'I'm no expert, but it was a deserted country spot. He could've shot from the end of the graveyard, in the graveyard, by the front door or over-looking the car park. I want to think we saved the PM, but you know we didn't. We just stood there and watched. So why didn't he shoot?' It was a question that was not going to be answered, so she asked another. 'Who was he?'

'His name is Dirk Swengen, South African. Calls himself Blackheart. Worked in Operations, is freelance now, Black Ops, anything dirty. He's a friend of mine.'

'A friend?'

'Kind of. I think he's a bit sore with me. You saw that scar?' She nodded. 'He blames me.'

'You did that?'

'Not exactly. It was in Azerbaijan, in that prison. He's the guy that killed all those prison guards.'

'So it wasn't you?'

'No, but I couldn't tell people that, because officially he doesn't exist, so people thought it was me, and I never disabused them of the idea. And my reputation built from there. It's useful: intimidation through reputation. If people think you can gut a live bear, they leave you alone. When we went to my flat, the copper on stake-out could have arrested us, but he didn't. He called SWAT because of my reputation. Roosevelt said, *It is better to negotiate with soft words and a big stick than negotiate with soft words alone.* My reputation is my big stick.'

'So you're not a hero, then?'

'I just saved your life,' he retorted indignantly.

'Well I just saved yours and I'm no hero. Did you gut that bear in Norway?'

'Never been to Norway.' Julie shook her head and said quietly to herself,

'Just when you think you know someone!'

In Julie's head, a little bit of her hero died. 'I had you down as a mean-minded, indestructible, fast-fighting bad ass. But you're just a knob jockey.'

'Don't you mean desk jockey?'

'Whichever! Were you even in Azerbaijan?'

'Yes. I had to get arrested to speak to a source who was in prison and then kill him. Dirk came in to wreak black death on everyone else and get us out.'

'And?'

'I got the information, saw a chance to get out, so I did.'

'And left Dirk?'

'This is espionage, not the US Marines. You get the information and you get the hell out. He would've done the same. He knew the risks, he knew the rules. And anyway, he got out . . . with a scar to prove it. And for some reason, he blames me.'

'Is that what this is about?'

'Hell no. This is about killing the PM. Killing me is just a bonus.'

'So why didn't he finish us off?'

'He was injured. I saw him limping as he left the barn. No point in him taking unnecessary risks.'

'So why didn't he kill the PM?'

'If we find that out, Ms Connor, we will have cracked this case. Maybe it's about theatre. The PM is making a speech later today in Basingstoke. It was going to be in Barrow-in-Furness, but was changed to somewhere easier to protect.' Julie cast her mind back to the revised schedule that Foxx had found in Storrington's flat. 'That was scheduled to be the next hit. There'll be an audience, journalists from around the world, TV cameras: a much better arena for his theatre of blood. If the PM is going to die today, he will die in front of the Press.'

CALL OUT

'I've got a lead on Julie Connor's present location,' called out Hoy, his voice laced with excitement.

'Have you found her car?' asked Storrington.

'Yes.'

'Where is it?'

'In her garage.'

'So, what's the lead?'

'She was in a motorbike accident.'

'And she's in hospital?'

'No, it was two years ago.' Storrington's face showed mounting frustration. Patience was not his strong suit. 'She had cuts and bruises, but her boyfriend was killed.'

'So?'

'So, his car is still registered in his name. She never sold it. It came up on an ANPR camera entering London on Sunday, just after we raided her flat. I've circulated the plate and set up an alert on all ANPRs. If it comes up on any Automatic Number Plate Recognition, we'll know about it within thirty seconds.'

'Well done, Hoy. Good work.'

Hoy tried not to smile, but praise was his life blood. His boss continued. 'The PM is speaking today in Barrow-in-Furness . . .'

'I thought it was Basingstoke.'

'No. That was a red herring. We circulated a phoney updated schedule just to confuse any terrorists, moles or assassins. He'll be in Barrow. Do we have ANPR cameras on the M1 and M40?'

'Yes, but they're notoriously unreliable.'

'OK. Is that all?' Hoy nodded and left. Storrington picked up his mobile and made a call.

'Maria, get the boys up to Barrow-in-Furness. Foxx might be there or he might be in London, but your first priority is to keep the PM safe.'

'On it, Commander. We'll be wheels-up in five.'

He hung up and allowed himself ten seconds staring out of the window, thinking about her, Captain Maria de la Casa. She was good at her job. He liked that.

He liked her.

Nickolas Morgan-Tenby stood by his PA's desk. There were half a dozen administrators and assistants within earshot.

'Lesley, call a meeting of the Joint Chiefs. I want to re-evaluate contingency plans for civil unrest. We've seen it get out of hand in France and Germany; we need to be ready for it here.'

'Yes, right away. Do you want all of them there?' She knew the answer before she asked.

'Of course I'd like them all there, but I know that the Air Chief Marshall is travelling a lot at present. If he's not available, you could ask his Second-in-Command to attend.'

'Understood,' she said, covert message received.

'Also, ask them each to nominate four senior officers to bring with them,' he added.

'Shall I pick them off this list?' she said knowingly, pulling out a sheet of names from her top drawer.

'Yes, good idea. Make it for as soon as I get back from France. Keep it confidential. Oh yes, and Charlie will call in later.' Lesley rolled her eyes. Her boss lent forward and mouthed, 'Be nice.'

'Really?' she mouthed back.

'Nah, not really,' he said with a humourless smile, walked back into his office and closed the door.

It was a sunny Wednesday afternoon. The remnants of an early alcoholic al fresco lunch lay on the wooden topped table in front of them, but it was not the wine that had numbed Julie's feelings, nor the whiskey breakfast. She didn't know how she felt about anything. She'd been scared, very scared, but unable to believe that she might die. She had almost been shot and had saved Foxx's life through instinct, not intelligence. She had tried to shoot another human being and to her regret she'd missed. She had wanted to kill a man. That was bad. And then there was Foxx - she had not wanted to be attracted to Foxx, and was; but now wasn't and wanted to be.

The morning in the hotel room had involved a few disguised and unwanted tears, a shower and then anticipated intimacy . . . but when it came to it, she didn't fancy it. It had been awkward and she'd declined. She sat drinking the last of her wine and pictured the scenes of the morning. None of it made sense, none of it felt real.

But it was.

'Why didn't he shoot the PM?' she asked again. 'Why be there if he wasn't going to take the shot. And why did he try to kill us?'

'You've answered your own question. He was there to kill *us*. He's not working for Storrington, I'm sure of that. He is the hit man; and we were the target. The PM was the bait.' Julie waited for fear to settle in her heart at the thought of being pursued by a ruthless assassin, but it didn't come.

'How good is he, this Dirk Blackheart?'

'The best. Bond times ten.'

'Then why did he miss? On the first attempt at the back of the hotel, why did he miss?'

The waiter came over, cleared the plates and asked if they wanted anything else. They asked for the bill.

'We have to get to Basingstoke,' said Foxx, looking at his watch. I doubt Dirk will be there, because I didn't know it would be Basingstoke when I wrote the plan - unless he's improvising. But I want to be sure.'

She wondered about the wisdom of being in an area of high police population, but said nothing.

'D'you think there was a video of it, the hotel shooting?' asked Foxx, thinking aloud.

'D'you want me to find out?'

'No. I'm on it.' He wandered off and made a call.

Julie made one too. She knew it was bad idea, but a better alternative eluded her. She phoned the mother of her four-year-old godson. They chatted, laughed and then came to the crux of the call. 'I want you to do something for me, but if it goes wrong it will land you in so much trouble you probably won't see Rupert until he celebrates his 21st birthday.'

'Sounds exciting. What do you want me to do?' replied Selina, the DPM's Assistant Private Secretary. Julie told her in detail, step by step, but didn't tell her why. 'Got it,' said the DPM's APS. 'This is going to cost you an evening of alcoholism, Miss Julie Connor.'

'Sure. That's a definite. So what's it like working for the Prime Minster-in-waiting?'

'OMG! It's mental here! He's all over the place. A lovely guy, but never held high office before, or any office really. We'll beat him into shape, but he moves the goalposts every day.'

'I thought he was a Steady Eddie.'

'He is, but he has a political advisor, Bettie Slaker and she's a head-case. Manic, gets him running around in all directions. We call her Marion.'

'What like Maid Marion, because he's her Robin Hood?'

'No, we call her Marion because he's her little marionette. If you want to know what he'll be thinking tomorrow, you just need to know what she's thinking today.'

'So she's the power behind the throne?'

'Seems to be. I gotta go. Two o'clock to three o'clock, right?'

'Exactly.'

'OK. Be good, little Connor. Bye.'

Foxx wandered back and announced, 'I have a guy that'll be sending over a copy of the CCTV of the shooting. They've made it highly classi-fied, but he owes me. You got anything?'

'No, not yet, but I do need to be in an internet café between two and three.' She pulled out cash to settle the bill. 'Oh yes, there's someone else we need to check out. Probably a dead end, but you never know with puppet masters.'

≈

The DPM sat in his office. It was 2.24 in the afternoon. His email pinged, it was marked urgent. He read it and phoned Selina, the APS who sent it. She wasn't answering her phone, so he walked round to her desk. No sign of her.

'Where's Selina?'

'At a Home Office meeting until three.'

He returned to his office and responded to his high security, top priority email without delay. Then, as instructed to maintain security protocols, he deleted his reply. He had more pressing matters to worry about.

The PM could be stubborn. How could he persuade him to resign? He would have the conversation next week after the Brexit talks in Marseille; but he wasn't hopeful. The last time he'd brought up the subject, the PM had just looked at him and said,

'Me? Resign? Over my dead body.'

It had just gone 3.00 when Selina, popped her head round the door.

'Were you looking for me, sir?' she asked the DPM, keen to help.

'Yes. Just to say I dealt with that security matter you sent me.'

'What security matter? I didn't send you anything.'

'Look, here. It was at 2.24 today.'

'I was in the Home Office meeting with the Home Secretary and twenty-three of his people, no laptop, phone or iPad. I didn't send you anything. May I see?' She looked at the email. It was sent from her account. 'I didn't send you that. You've been hacked. I hope you didn't reply?'

He sheepishly admitted he had.

'Can I see the reply?'

He confessed to deleting it. She looked at him amazed. 'Sir, may I say that this is serious. There's been a breach. I need to make the call – to Security. They'll be able to confirm where the email was sent from, but if it wasn't from within this building then you've just given a highly classified secret to an unknown hacker.' His face fell. He knew he was in trouble.

She could see he needed support. She put a reassuring hand on his

forearm and their professional relationship took an instant and immeasur-
able step forwards.

'Richard,' she said more softly, 'I really should call Security, but let me
call a friend in the IT Department first. Maybe we can keep this under
the radar'

She dialled knowing that the trace would lead to an internet café
many miles away, where someone had gained remote access and somehow
hacked her passcode.

'How could that happen?' he asked rhetorically. She shook her head
and muttered,

'One of life's little mysteries.'

≈

'Yay!' said Julie under her breath.

'What've you got?' They were sat together in her boyfriend's sporty
hatchback.

'The DPM. You told me to ask him, so I did. He's just blindly sent me
his top secret email address. And. . . . t'dah . . . he is *not* Dominion1431.
He is *not* our man. He has given me a different email address.' She deleted
the email and closed the account.

'Good call,' said Foxx. 'We're now down to two. It's Hoy or Tenby.'

≈

Charlie sat demurely outside her husband's office, quietly absorbed in her
laptop. There was no one around except for Lesley who had not said a
word, but malice got the better of her.

'What are you doing?' Lesley asked her, conversationally.

'Online trading,' replied Charlie, unaware of how odd that sounded
coming out of her mouth. Lesley couldn't resist the hint of a bitter
smile.

'Do you spend a lot of time doing that?'

'Yes, I do.'

'Most of us call it e-Baying, dear. Is it e-Bay you use or do you prefer
that other one, what's it called now . . . ah yes, HisCash.com?'

Charlie didn't answer the question, nor did she miss the slur it contained. She thought about what Julie had told her. *You should call her out on it next time you see her.*

'Lesley, I want to say something to you, is that OK?'

'Yes dear, anything you like,' replied Lesley, eager for more ammunition.

'It's this,' continued Charlie gracefully. 'I bought you those concert tickets. They were very hard to come by. I got them for you because I know you enjoy jazz and Sanborn in particular. I gave you a set of old jazz records. You and I know they're worth thousands of pounds and I just gave them to you as a present. And . . .' she paused just slightly, 'and I regularly give you my husband four nights a week for your pleasure and his. The least you could do would be to say *thank you*, or at a minimum, be polite to me. I don't expect you to like me and of course, I don't expect you to respect me, but manners cost nothing.'

'What do you mean, me and your husband! How dare you?'

'Lesley,' she said calmly, 'I copied the pictures and the videos from Nicki's phone.' She flicked through her pictures. 'It was Saturday, when he was supposed to be having dinner with me and the DPM. I'm sure you remember: it was the first time you wore the spreader-bars. To be honest, they suit you. I refused to wear them, a bit slutty for my taste, but you seemed very happy in them. Here, look.' Charlie showed Lesley the picture on her phone. 'And I see you also enjoyed the new whip.' She showed her a video clip. 'Actually, it's mine. I mean, I bought it. It's my whip. Stings like a bitch, doesn't it? I bought it with you in mind. He's never used it on me - he respects me too much for that. I just left it in the toy drawer. He thinks I never go in there and wouldn't miss it. But next time he uses it on you, just remember; it's mine and I bought it specially for you.'

'So does he know that you know?' asked Lesley, seething deeply.

'No, he doesn't know and he doesn't need to know.'

'Well, he does, because I'll tell him when I dump him. You can have your husband back!'

'Oh dear,' said Charlie with soft, sincere sympathy. 'If only it were that simple, but unfortunately Nicki is not a simple man. He really doesn't take rejection well. You would need to find another job, outside the Civil Service. He can be terribly mean. The last person who left him ended up with a false criminal record. I'm so sorry, but I'm afraid you're stuck with him, and me, until he's finished with you. So, all I'm saying is if you could just be polite, I would really appreciate it.' She packed up her laptop and put it in her bag. 'Tell Nicki, I'll see him later, at home.'

'Enjoy it while you can,' said Lesley in a voice laden with threat. 'Nickolas is throwing you out and I'm moving in. He's been planning it for weeks.'

'Oh, I see,' replied Charlie. 'He told you that?'

Lesley smiled meanly and said nothing.

Charlie sat down again, close to Lesley and looked sorrowful. Their eyes met. 'Lesley,' she said calmly, 'd'you think you're the first woman he's said that to? If he wanted me out, he would've done it years ago. But there's one reason why that's never going to happen.'

'What's that then?'

'It's my house.'

The shock on Lesley's face was a picture. Charlie continued.

'Mr Taylor did it. Nicki asked me to get Mr Taylor to arrange his Inheritance Tax Planning and he put the house in my name. Nicki signed the papers, but to be honest, I don't think he really read them. So it's my house.'

'But you'll never be able to run it without Nicki's money,' said Lesley, desperate for any point-scoring she could salvage.

'Thank you for your concern, but I'll be OK. Lesley, I didn't mean to upset you. Nicki is difficult. It's hard for us both, so we might as well be nice to each other.'

There was nothing else to say, so she stood up to leave.

'Charlie,' said Lesley.

'Yes?'

Lesley squinted her eyes as evil consumed her face. She hissed quietly, 'No one beats me. Least of all you. Mrs Morgan-Tenby; you're dead. You are a dead woman walking. Goodbye.'

With an unwanted half-tear in her moistened eye and with all the dignity she could muster, Charlie left. It would be the last time she would ever enter the building.

And all because Julie had said the words: *You should call her out.*

ANTELOPE-BEAVER

F oxx idly scanned the MSN news briefs on his phone.

PM to talk today about employment after Brexit.

Defence Industry prepares for cuts. 'We are being neutered' said a Senior Defence Official.

Housing Bill passed with a majority of one. Benefits are on a sliding scale. 'We can now help more people more fully,' said the Social Services Secretary last night.

Minimum wage higher after Brexit, but Labour says loopholes need to be closed.

Home for troubled teenagers is to close through lack of Government funding - Foxdale Children's Home is to close its doors for the last time at the end of the year.

'Census statistics will show a more comfortable and untied Britain,' said a Gallup spokesperson.

Interesting typo, thought Foxx, but his mind was not really on the screen.

'D'you think Mr and Mrs Hoy use Alexa?' he asked.

'I've no idea. Why do you ask?'

'Alexa is a marvellous invention. It's like bugging your own home. You connect a microphone in your own house to the outside world of the Internet.'

Foxx tapped into the Hoy's IP address and then hacked into their private computer. 'Deep joy! They do! It's not Alexa, but something similar. Mr Hoy, Head of Investigations for the Special Security Services, has bugged his own home. It's a long shot that he'll say anything incriminating, but I'll record it all anyway. I tried to do the same with the Tenby's after our visit, but the firewall was too high. Let's see what it brings.' He hit a series of keys on his laptop and it was done. He continued, 'What about you? What have you got?'

'I've been working on the Bevan Report. It was important to Tenby, so I thought it might be important to us. Bevan is an apparently altruistic, do-gooder, university professor and Chair of the Faculty of Social Economics, but behind his fallacious façade of fairness, he's a really pernicious and devious racist. The paper purports to be about the administrative requirements of making UK abortion services available to foreign nationals, but really it's a review of how we charge non-residents to use our National Health Service.

He doesn't define the term "non-resident", but in one of the fourteen appendices he's done some serious calculations on how much the NHS would save if it only treated people whose families were here when the NHS was started on 5th July 1948, and at each ten-year point after that. In the 2000s he's worked it out year by year. For example, if you had to be in the UK for five years before being entitled to use the NHS, then it would save the government over £6 billion, and if it were ten years, the amount saved would be three times as much, which out of a £102 billion budget is significant. The proposal is that, like abortions, the whole Health Service should not be used free by new immigrants who have not yet entered the UK. But the paper goes on to recommend that they should not have any rights to free health care for the first twelve months of working here full-time. In a post-Brexit Britain, that would be quite palatable to Parliament and to the voters.'

'So?'

'To be sure of getting it voted through, they removed the twelve-month limitation clause, initially. But get this: a new clause that slipped in on page 89 of the green paper says that the timescale can be altered by the

Minster of Health, at any time, *according to need*! And there's no clause to say he can't apply it retrospectively to people already in the country.

The Bill was pushed through with a majority of one and it's now law. If the Health Minister wanted, he could make everyone who entered the country after, say 2001, pay for all their health-care costs and nothing under the Law could stop him. That's the thin end of an enormous wedge of money.

Now the really interesting bit: the research was sponsored by a private donation to the university from a certain Mr Nickolas Morgan-Tenby.'

'What's that got to do with us?'

'I don't know, but it's the same with Anderson: different university, but Tenby financed the research in the same way. It's about saving money in the military by combining command structures at the top. I don't fully understand it, but it looks like it would make Storrington, Commander of the Joint Chief Staff Committee and that would somehow save hundreds of millions of pounds. It's not law yet, but my APS friend says that the DPM signed a memo this week to recommend it should become law. It seems a hurried and slightly suspect piece of legislation, so they'll no doubt bounce it through the House and into law while your dad's busy sorting out Europe.

I checked deeper and found five more pieces of legislation that Tenby has been involved with through select committees. It doesn't make sense. What's Tenby up to? He's not even a politician. What's his plan?'

Foxx shook his head. His mind was elsewhere.

'Take a look at this,' he said, decrypting as he talked. 'I have a theory about the hotel shooting and I'm hoping this will bear it out.'

He showed her CCTV footage from another hotel's loading bay that showed in the background the exit that the PM had used. The picture wasn't good. Tenby and the PM came out together followed by Colin Lewis who stood behind the PM. Moments later, the shot caused panic and devastation. The Prime Minister had moved at the last second and both bullets penetrated the heart of his innocent aid behind him.

'He missed,' said Julie, stating what was already known.

'No,' said Foxx emphatically, 'he didn't. He didn't miss. It was a dead shot. Colin Lewis was the target.'

She rewound the last ten seconds.

'See? A double tap straight to the heart; a perfect aim. Look at it again from the beginning.' They watched.

Tenby had stepped out next to the PM, but not in the sniper's line of fire. Tenby dropped the file he was holding; deliberately or not it was hard to tell. The PM, true to character but not like a statesman, knelt to pick up the papers before they were spoiled by the rain-soaked ground. Four seconds after he knelt, Colin Lewis was hit by two shots to the heart and died instantly.

'The distance was 1,247 metres. At about 1,700 mph, that's 770 metres a second, so it would take a shade over one and a half seconds for the bullet to hit the target. The sniper pulled the trigger a full two seconds after the PM knelt. That's a lifetime in the mental clock of a sniper good enough to make that shot. He didn't miss his target. The target was Colin Lewis, Head of Resources, the man who hired the sniper for the job - even though I doubt he knew what the job was. Dirk was covering his tracks.

Think about it,' continued Foxx, getting more excited. 'Who knew about his plan? Me, because I wrote it, you because you forwarded it, Tenby or Hoy whichever it was who asked for it, and Lewis, the person who hired Dirk. Dirk tried to kill us to keep us quiet. He succeeded in killing Lewis for the same reason. He wants us out of the way before he assassinates his prime target.'

'Why?'

'I've no idea. It makes no real sense to me. Come on, we're going to Basingstoke to look for a man with a scar, a limp and a very bad attitude.'

'Nickolas, Charlie was here.' Lesley spoke with concern in her voice. 'She was blabbing about the list. She knows something's up. Somehow, she's worked out what we're planning. She was asking too many questions about select committees.'

'What? *Charlie*? You're kidding? She's as dumb as a dog with dementia. She doesn't even know what a select committee does. She thinks they're called *erect* committees!'

'I know she doesn't, but I'm afraid she'll ask someone to explain and she'll shoot her mouth off. She said she was going to talk to some people about it, but she didn't say who. Someone in the police, I think she said.'

'Jesus. Are you sure?' His tone changed. 'This is serious.'

'Yes, Nickolas, it is. She's a danger. We have no choice now. You know what you have to do, don't you?'

There was a long, prolonged, protracted silence on the end of the phone. 'Don't you?' repeated Lesley.

'Yes. I do. I'll get it done when I'm back from Barrow. I've got to see this through up here first. It's all prepared. Today should go,' he paused for a second, '. . . very smoothly. Then I'll deal with Charlie.'

It was almost like driving with Duncan. It had a good feel to it.

'What music do you want on?' It was a question she'd always asked Duncan before a long journey. But Foxx was distracted, his eyes were on the rear-view mirror.

'Leave the radio on for a moment.'

A statement from the Office of the Deputy Prime Minister said that the proposed reforms on military spending, based on the Bevan Report, would have no impact on defence capability. It is merely a streamlining of executive functions - using administrative efficiencies to save taxpayers' money.

Meanwhile, the Prime Minister is talking to a group of industrialists today in Barrow-in-Furness about his plans for economic prosperity after Brexit. This is his last speech before his final talks on Trade Deals and the European Defence Strategy in Marseille. He expects some tough questions from his northern audience as there are extensive Defence contracts held by companies in Barrow. The speech had been moved to Basingstoke amidst security concerns, but the Opposition said he was speaking to a softer southern audience and ducking the bullet. In response, the Prime Minister has announced this morning that the speech would go ahead, as originally planned, in Barrow-in-Furness, where unemployment is amongst the highest in the country and fears of lost defence contracts would make it even worse.

At the Old Bailey today . . .'

'Oh my god, Foxx! How are we going to make it to Barrow in time?'

'We've a bigger problem right now.' She looked behind her. A police car was tailing them. 'He was parked up, saw us pass and has been following us ever since.' Foxx turned left. The police car followed him, then a moment later, a second one. He took a right. The police convoy stayed in pursuit. 'Buckle up. This could get messy.' He took another right. At the end of the street, there was a blue light and a police car parked right across the road. The two police cars in the rear-view mirror closed in behind them.

Storrington picked up the phone. It was Hoy.

'We've found them, Foxx and Connor, in London, heading west. SWAT are on their way.'

'Good work. At least he's not in Barrow. That means the PM is out of immediate danger. Keep me informed.'

He phoned Maria.

'Foxx is in London. Stay there, but stand down. The PM's safe today. Just do a sweep of the area and wait for my further orders.'

Dirk 'Blackheart' Swengen smiled.

He lay with his rifle - his eyes firmly on the cross hairs - high up in a disused office block in Barrow. He had a perfect view of the Prime Minister's platform and a clear and easy getaway. He quietly thanked Foxx for such a foolproof plan, relaxed and made himself comfortable. Today would be a good day.

Foxx drove sedately towards the police road block then, with no warning, he took a sharp left down a narrow cobbled mews, slammed the throttle, squeezed at speed between a builder's van and a wall, slid round a ninety-degree bend and emerged on a one-way road. He shot down it the wrong way, dodging cars and increasing speed. He took the next turning and floored the throttle. The hot hatch sped to 80 miles an hour; two more turns and speeds of almost 100 miles an hour for the length of a long straight street. He slammed on the brakes and approached a junction. He ignored traffic lights, barged cars out of the way and sped down the trunk road like a bat released from Hades. He entered the Euston Tunnel. Once in, he slowed sharply, applied the hand brake, spun round 180 degrees and joined the traffic in the other direction, adopting their speed of 38 miles an hour. He drove inconspicuously, if a little closely, to the big truck in front of him. Police cars hurtled down the other side of the road.

'Are we safe now?' she asked.

'No. They know the car. Every copper in London will be looking for it and as soon as the helicopters spot us, we're finished.'

'Would it be so bad, getting caught by the police? I mean, they *are* supposed to be the good guys. We could tell them what we know. We need some help. There's a chance they would see it our way.'

'Yes. A one per cent chance! There's a ninety-nine per cent chance we'll get banged up for life, the Prime Minister will be executed and Blackheart will walk free. But worse than that: if we're in a cell, Blackheart would find us. We'd be dead. It would be like shooting a fish in a barrel. Not a good plan.' He turned off, heading north. 'We need to ditch the car and grab a cab. Can't take the Tube - CCTV.' He was heading out of the centre of town. So far so good.

A police car passed in the opposite direction. Four seconds later, it swung round, hit the siren and gave chase, but Foxx was round a corner, out of sight, and had taken a left before the police had caught up. They'd lost him for now. The road led to an industrial estate. A dead end. When there was no more road, they stared in front of them. Fifteen wide steps headed down to a canal. They had no choice. The car bumped unhappily down to the tow path. Two minutes later, driving down the canal, they found a foot bridge. It claimed the wing mirrors, but got them safely to the other side. London is a criss-cross of canals and railway lines, passable by a few road bridges, each of which would have police checkpoints. But for now, the police would be looking for them on the wrong side of the canal.

'We'll never get a cab here,' said Julie. 'Dump the car and we'll get a bus.'

'Or a motorbike. I have an idea.'

'A motorbike? Really?'

He said nothing and drove briskly north. The road ahead was blocked. He took a back route. Sirens filled the air. It was only a matter of time. He approached a low bridge under a railway line, took a sharp left before it and flew past a litter of businesses that occupied the arches under the rail tracks.

'Come on, come one,' he said to himself. 'There's got to be one somewhere.' He drove another fifty yards. 'Yes, that'll do.' He swung into a mechanic's workshop under one of the railway arches and parked as deep into their garage as he could go.

'Yes, mate, can I help you?'

'I need you to look at my car. It needs a service, oh, and some new wing mirrors. Keep it indoors. I don't want it left outdoors.' Foxx pulled out a wad of bank notes from his pocket. 'This is for looking after it and I'll pay for the service and repairs on top.' They left hurriedly on foot and found themselves in a local market. Foxx bought a leather jacket and Connor bought a headscarf.

At the far end of the market, they crossed the road and made their way up a narrow alley that led to a street of rundown shops. They crossed the next road and hurried along a walkway that ran behind the shops and then walked another half-mile along a scruffy residential street, doing their best to look natural and nonchalant. The street ended in a T-junction. They looked left - flashing blue lights in the distance. They looked to the right - a dozen police motorbikes 200 yards away, awaiting instruction. Julie took a quick look behind her. A police van was heading slowly up the road towards them. Trapped.

Ahead of them loomed a housing estate, built badly forty-eight years ago and now renowned throughout London as a no-go area. It was gangland and no unknowns were allowed in, not without fear of their life. Police avoided it - the last three times they'd crossed the red line, it had led to riots. Julie held Foxx's hand as they trotted across the road up the broken tarmac and across the red line that ran the width of the path with the spray painted words: *No Fucking Entry*.

The upside was they were safe from the police. The downside was that they were white, English and probably going to die.

It was dismal, derelict, detritus: wood, old newspapers, rusted car parts, cans, bottles, mattresses, takeaway wrappers strewn across the walkway. The design of the building was dark, it overhung their path - a mugger's paradise. It was not a happy place. Illegals, drug addicts and criminals squatted in the half light of the condemned buildings that the council were too scared to destroy. Paint peeled, plaster cracked, graffiti sprawled the walls. They felt eyes on them, they felt the threat in the air.

'You have friends here, right? People you know? People who'll look after us?'

'No, 'fraid not.' The path opened up into a wider space which, in any other setting, would have been a courtyard. They heard people aggressing behind them and saw hostiles in front of them. They were trespassing and knew it. More unfriendly inhabitants appeared. The jeers started. The moral darkness was closing in. Foxx ignored them and, with Julie in hand, kept walking. They were in the middle of the estate now. There was a row of houses ahead of them, small and incongruous between the tall, tatty tower blocks. The houses had been painted, but badly. A motorbike, parked by the middle house, gleamed like a tropical fish caught in a mud puddle. It was expensive, fast and new.

Their path was blocked. There was no going forwards, no going back. They had encroached upon the cockroach's kingdom and now they would pay the price. It was London, but it was lawless, an estate where Police, regulation, legislation and civilisation meant nothing. It was as rough as it was feral and run by the gangs. A melee of agitated inhabitants showed disapproval at the dismissive, disrespecting attitude of their invaders. Knives appeared. They began to close in; closer and closer, more and more numerous. The threat was more real than even Foxx could have anticipated.

'Foxx, I'm frightened,' whispered Julie.

'Why?' he asked obtusely.

'There are twenty of them and only two of us. And one of us is you,' she said pointedly. He looked at her indignantly. 'The only fight I've ever seen you in was this morning, and you went down like a rag-doll, first punch.'

'It's OK. I'll talk us out of this.'

But it was the other side that spoke first.

'Wass you doin' here? Ain't your place, man. Back out. Leave your wallet and leave the girl.'

'Fine. No problem. Take the girl. She likes being kidnapped. Look, I'll trade her for that motorbike over there.' Julie just looked at him.

'You funny guy. You get this knife in youse face, motherfucker. The girl stays, your wallet stays, you go. Or you die.'

'Ok, that's fair. Have the girl and have my wallet.' He walked towards them hands in the air. 'But I do need the motorbike.' He approached a group of five heavily tattooed, muscular, aggressive gang members, lowered his hands, took a breath, took the stance and took them out - all five of them. His fists took out the first two, his Thai boxing feet flattened the third, he parried the knife of the fourth and threw him to the ground to the sound of breaking bones; and a straight set of karate chops saw the fifth buckle, kneel and fall. It took no more than seven seconds. He was fast and unrelenting.

He advanced on the next group like a rampant tree-shredder, felling all who came close and tossing them to the sides. Arms were broken, knives flew free and were kicked over to Julie. He ploughed a furrow of carnage through the unsuspecting crowd, leaving blood, battering and bruises behind him.

'Gun. Ten o'clock,' shouted Julie. Krav Maga was a fighting system developed by the Israeli Secret Service and perfected by Eduard Foxx. A random body was judo-hurled towards the shooter, as cover for Fox's lightning advance. The shooter raised the weapon, but too late. His neck broke and Foxx slid the weapon across the concrete to Julie's feet. It was a cartridge-fed shotgun. The scene had cleared. Broken assailants groaned, or crawled away or started to regroup at a distance. A door to the house opened. Out walked Rafiq. It was his estate, his gang and his motorbike. He and his brother ruled this world.

'You back off man and you get out alive. You fuck with us anymore and you die badly.'

Foxx walked over to him, and said, 'I need to explain something.'

Rafiq drew a knife and flicked it open. Someone died every time he did that. Today it wasn't Foxx. Two kicks and Rafiq was crippled: a punch and he was disarmed. Foxx spun him around, stood behind him, looked straight at Julie's eyes, held Rafiq's chin and twisted sharply. His neck broke. Rafiq fell dead to the floor. No explanation necessary.

The door banged open. Out walked three men. One was the boss's boss, Rafiq's big brother. The two men behind him had guns at the ready. Rafiq's brother was a mountain, the muscle that won them respect. He saw Rafiq on the floor, growled and hurled himself at Foxx. Foxx punched; no effect. Foxx kicked; no effect. Foxx stumbled, the mountain grabbed him.

'You die!' he growled, as he held Foxx's head at arm's length, ready to remove it from his body.

The bang was deafening and the pain felt by Foxx was intense. Julie had released one of the barrels of the sawn-off shotgun - 200 tiny balls of red-hot lead leapt at 1,000 miles an hour from the muzzle and disintegrated the head of Rafiq's brother, peppering Fox with stray lead.

Another decisive bang and the two armed men standing together lost their faces. Foxx hobbled up, mounted the bike and clicked the engine into life.

'Get on!' he yelled.

She mounted and held as tightly as she knew how. They sped through scattering bodies to the far exit of the estate, her head scarf lost to the wind. When the exit was less than fifty yards away, when they were less than four seconds from freedom, Foxx swerved hard, left the pathway, crossed the remnants of grass that was once a lawn, descended a dozen steps and sped down into the sculptured world of the skate-boarder's concrete. He aimed at the steepest slope, hit it at sixty miles an hour and flew skyward, out of the park, over a fence and onto the public highway. Head down and they were away.

He passed her one of the helmets that was hanging from the handle bars. She put it on his head. The other she placed on her own. They were free from the gang and in disguise from the police. He rode carefully and legally back to their hotel.

'We have to warn Storrington.'

There was no way they could get to Barrow in time. This was out of their hands. Foxx emailed Storrington the two Barrow pages of the Risk Assessment. It gave details of the office block that was being renovated with direct sight line to the PM, and the large, fully foliaged oak tree that obscured the view. He sent details of the plan to have a tree surgeon fell the tree that morning. He sent everything that was going to happen in Barrow on that day, with warnings and cautions for Storrington's team to follow. *He will make Armageddon look like an afternoon in Disneyland. Be very, very careful*, wrote Foxx. He warned of booby traps, bluffs and explosives. He did all he could. It was up to Storrington now.

Then he phoned an unlisted mobile number, a number he'd been tapping in his office before all this kicked off. It was the Caribbean gang boss, who ran the estate next to Rafiq's. Foxx answered none of his questions, but just told him:

'Rafiq and his brother are dead. His top six soldiers are dead or in hospital and another twenty are in bad shape. If you invade now with all the muscle you've got, you can claim that estate as your own. Be merciless. Babylon won't bother you. They're too busy looking for an escaped terrorist. It's yours. Kick the Rafiquies out, sell as many drugs as you want.

I just want one thing: he has under-aged hookers and human slaves locked up in there. Feed them, clothe them, keep them safe. I want them. I will arrange for their collection. Everything else is yours.' Foxx clicked off. It was a tick on his to-do list. The Rafiqs were no longer a problem and their illegal slaves would be freed. He lay back on the bed, felt the pain in his shoulder and waited for Julie.

She returned from the local chemist and administered the best First Aid she could. Foxx had come out a victor, but not unscathed. One minor knife wound, a worthy collection of bruises from his adversaries and a back full of lead shot from his partner. But he would live.

She had said, *I won't miss next time* and she hadn't. She looked at his peppered back and looked at the book by the bedside, *Join the Dots*, and smiled. She patched him up, a little more firmly than she strictly had to, enjoying it every time he winced like a girl. She teased him, but tended him with love, patiently, carefully, until it was done. She sat on the edge of the bed and stared at him. This was the first opportunity they had had to talk.

She started.

'You killed someone. I saw you.'

'Right back at you, Pekkala.'

'Explain what just happened, please.'

'They're the Rafiq brothers . . . or were. They're the most heartless of low lifes: kidnapping, child prostitution, sexual slavery, fearsome extortion, drugs, murder, rape, torture - human abominations. The police can't get them, even though they know they're behind it all, but without willing witnesses, they can't make it stick. The Rafiqs ruled through absolute fear and no one will ever give evidence against them. I've been working on how to deal with them, but I guess I've solved that now. I knew he had a motorbike. I know everything about him. And I knew the keys would be in it, because no one would ever dare steal Rafiq's bike. Except us.'

She looked at him, bruised, bleeding, patched-up. She relived him twist a man to death and take a dozen others down with his bare hands. She tried her hardest to ignore the feelings it gave her. It was animal, it was base, it was inexcusably exciting. There is nothing as charming as a dangerous man. She wanted to be above that - but knew she wasn't. She needed to chastise him, put him in his place.

'And the fighting? Was that just to impress me? And all that riding down the steps and jumping over the fence when there was a perfectly good road ahead of us. That was just showing off, wasn't it?'

He said nothing and felt no need to talk about the guns he'd seen in the mirror, pointing straight at her back.

'Are you so keen to impress me,' she continued, 'so keen to get back into my bed that you'll do motorbike stunts? Do you really think I'm that shallow? It's not going to work, y'know,' she said, quite untruthfully, as she lowered him back on the bed and helped him take his mind off the pain.

25

REAL BARROW

ews Flash: In Barrow today, a further assassination attempt on the Prime Minister was foiled by the bravery of our security forces, but has claimed the lives of two security officers. A lone gunman took position in a disused office block overlooking the Prime Minister's party, but advance forces prevented the attempt. It is believed that explosives were used to enter the building and unconfirmed reports suggest that the gunman was shot dead at the scene, but as yet, this is unconfirmed.

The names of the two officers who were killed in the line of duty have not yet been released.

～

'Captain Maria de la Casa's phone. Number One speaking.'

'This is Commander Storrington. What the hell happened? And where's Maria?'

'He got the drop on us. Two dead, sir. The rest of us did the best we could, but he was clean away before we even got close.'

'Where's Ma . . . Where's Captain de la Casa?'

'The explosion messed her up, sir.'

'Messed her up?'

'Yes, sir. She's with the medics right next to me, but her hearing hasn't come back yet, not fully.'

'Put her on.'

'Hello, sir.'

'What happened . . . I said: What happened?'

'It was a colossal fuck up, sir. Cosmic cluster-fuck. I told them not to break formation and they did. Two was a maverick. I told him *hold*, but he thought he had a shot, leant out to take it and the shooter took his head off. Six entered the building, looking to be a hero. The doors on the second floor were booby-trapped - still picking up the pieces. By the time we got to the top floor, the shooter was gone: some kind of aerial glide, out of the back and away. But at least the PM's safe.'

'Are you OK Maria? Are you hurt?'

'No sir. Not hurt and not OK. I'm more pissed off than ever. Ears ringing like St Paul's. I want this son of a bitch and I want him dead.'

'Captain,' said Storrington reverting to Military, 'you are a professional, you will get him, but no emotion - emotion clouds the mind, emotions get you killed. Get you and the team back to base. Deal with it.'

～

Tonight, police raided the house of Al Akbar J'zeer, a known terrorist, who is believed to be behind the recent failed assassination attempts. J'zeer was killed in the raid. His brother and three other men and a woman were arrested under the Anti-Terrorist Act. More news is expected later.

～

It was evening on Blackfriars Bridge. Lights glistened on the Thames. Julie Connor and Eduard Foxx sat on the parapet of the bridge, dangling their legs sixty feet above the cold, turbulent water.

'D'you think they killed Blackheart?' she asked.

'Meh.'

'That is annoying, y'know. You need to know that. Can you stretch your answer to at least two syllables?'

'No . . . They would trumpet it for sure if they'd got Blackheart. Killing J'zeer was a publicity stunt; had to happen sooner or later. The public now think the PM is safe, but he's not.'

They lost themselves in contemplation, staring at the dark slow River Thames far below them. Minds drifted. Foxx broke the silence,

'If I was forced to be a bridge player and mix with bridge players and actually play bridge, this is the sort of bridge I would throw myself off!' He looked at his partner and the gun she was holding. 'Now you. Are you going to throw it?'

'Nah. I thought I'd keep it.'

'Keeping a double-barrelled murder weapon with your fingerprints and no doubt your DNA all over it is not a smart move. We came here to chuck it in the Thames. I want to see it hit the water.'

'I killed him. I shot him. I shot *them*. I'm a mass murderer. I should feel remorse, or anguish or at least sick to the pit of my stomach. I don't feel any of those things. And . . .' she paused at the horror of herself, 'I enjoyed it. I liked it. That's why I am going to chuck it. It's my evil and it has to go.' She tossed it far out from the bridge. They watched it arc through the air and splash as it hit the water.

'Well done,' he said encouragingly.

'Willy bugger shit fuck!' she said. He looked at her confused. 'Dick bastard flap wank!'

'What are you doing?'

'Swearing.'

'I'm not sure that *flap* is actually a swear word.'

'What happened to my old life? I was miserable, but I was happy being miserable; a quiet, self-deprecating, man-hating, semi-reclusive civil servant. Now look. I drink whisky for breakfast, ride motorbikes, run from the police, get wrapped up in a terrorist conspiracy, get my flat blown up, have random casual sex with you, break into houses, get shot at and kill a man without remorse. I might as well take up swearing as well. It's tragic. This is not my life, y'know. When this is all over, assuming we're not dead or in jail, I want my old life back. I want to be me again, not some homicidal Lara Croft megalomaniac. It's so like heroin or cocaine: tempting, seductive, but will kill you. I don't want it. I want to run and hide and leave it all behind me. All of it.'

'All of it? Even me?' asked Foxx, sounding not as casual as he meant to.

'Well, I'm not asking you back to my place – look what happened last time I did that!'

'OK, you can come to mine.'

'Really? As I recall, you needed a new cleaner and I ended up in Narnia. I don't know, Eduard. You're very appealing . . . but you're a man and you are trouble. I'm not sure I need either of those things.' She paused, then moved the conversation on. 'Have you got the broadcasts from the Hoy household?' He tuned into the cloud.

They sat and listened.

They learned.

The Hoys had affection for each other, though only one of them wore the trousers. They were religious and prayed together, but there was agitation in the household. They had made a pact in Iran – a pact with each other - and he needed to act on it. She was angry with him. He was not living up to his sacred promise. *Iran*, she said over and over. *Iran, don't forget Iran.* Storrington was the problem; Storrington and the Prime Minister's assassination.

'Oh my god! It's him,' Julie said to Foxx. 'He's in with Islamist extremists, in with J'zeer. That's what he means about the pact in Iran.'

They listened for five more minutes.

Mrs Hoy, his wife, was pregnant. Mrs Hoy senior, his mother, had died a few months before. He had been away for most of her illness, so had taken four months off work to care for her in her final months. He was the diligent, caring, Christian son. He'd taken her to places she dreamed of visiting: Bethlehem, Lourdes, China and Iran. In Iran, Mr and Mrs Hoy had decided to start a family and she had made him promise that he would work less, be home and make time for them. That was the pact: the sacred promise in Iran.

Since he'd been back at work, the hours had started to mount up. Then came the assassination attempt on the PM. Hoy went back to working until midnight. He loved his wife. She understood the pressures of his work, but he had promised her that he would ask Commander Storrington for a month off, as paternity leave. He hadn't asked. He said he couldn't find the right moment. She was annoyed.

There was no hint of terrorism or anarchy. It was domestic. He had to man-up and that was all there was to it. They left the broadcast with their Alexa equivalent playing romantic music and the kitchen table being romantically mis-used.

Foxx turned it off and Julie spoke first.

'I didn't think he did it,' she said, changing her stance faster than a U-turning politician.

'Agreed. It's not him. I wasn't so sure, but I am now,' said Foxx. 'So you know what that means?'

'Yes,' said Julie, 'we're down to one. But did he do it?' She took out her phone.

'Who are you calling?'

'Neil, one of our IT guys - fancies me. My pet geek - everyone should have one. I'm asking him if that email came from Tenby's computer at home.'

'Duh, if he can tell you that, why didn't we ask him right at the outset?'

'I told you. He can't trace the email back blindly to see where it came from. It can't be done and it would raise alarms, but if I tell him a specific computer, with a specific email address at a specific time, he can trace it from the IP without going through official channels.'

He picked up.

She asked.

He refused.

She asked again. They debated, negotiated, bartered, bribed. A deal was done. She hung up.

'Add prostitution to the list.'

Seconds later the phone rang. 'Neil?' She listened and nodded.

'And can you check the satnav in his car? Was he home? Great. And his phone?' She waited. 'Wow, that's perfect. You're a star. Yes. Yes I will - a promise is a promise. No, no photography! Now go away.' She hung up.

'Well?' asked Foxx after a long silence. 'Was it him?'

'Meh,' she said.

He stared at her. The silence was long and golden.

She cracked.

'Yes, it's him. Tenby is Dominion 1431.'

26

TWO INTO ONE

His anger was like a fireball hurtling down the corridor. The closer it got, the more ferocious it felt. Morgan-Tenby stormed past Lesley's desk, into his office and slammed the door. She took a deep breath; stood, picked up her notepad, straightened her skirt, knocked on the heavy wooden door and entered.

He turned and stared.

She said nothing. His face was red as he spat out words like venom.

'Barrow was a debacle. Storrington completely fucked it. We had a plan and he put his no-good, not secret, ninja team in and bollocksed it all up. Cock-fucker! We had it right – all planned - until Storrington screwed it up for us.'

'But we can use it to our advantage.'

'Two dead soldiers? You bet we fucking can. We can get him out. I'm going to have that sanctimonious bastard once and for all. He's finished. History.'

'Can I help with that?' she asked, notebook poised.

'No. I'll deal with it.' She was snubbed.

'What about Charlie? Have you dealt with that?' she asked in not so subtle counter-snub.

'Don't push,' he growled. 'I said I would and I will.' She pressed home her point.

'I think you should. She has a very loose mouth and . . .'

'Enough! Charlie will be dealt with. Now leave.' She reached the door. 'Get me Hoy.'

The large oak door of her boss's office was firmly shut, but she could hear the lambasting from within. She smiled. *Poor Mr Hoy*, she thought to herself with no sympathy at all.

'What are you? An amateur? This is the top league now. If you're not good enough, just say so. How could you not know that the sniper was going to make another attempt? You personally put the PM's life in danger, you should have . . .'

'With respect,' interrupted Hoy - but he never had the chance to speak.

'Listen, you snivelling little schoolboy, you never interrupt me.' Tenby pulled himself up to his full height and geared up to full force. 'I'm Second-in-Command and you're nothing.' Hoy felt himself shrink into his own shoes. 'It's not even a real job, it's just a secondment. We've borrowed you, like a cup of sugar, and we can throw you back any time we please. Don't you ever interrupt me again and don't ever disagree with me, ever - especially in a meeting. Your job is to say *yes*. Got it?'

'No,' said Hoy, feeling shorter than he'd ever felt before. 'Counter-views stimulate discussion which helps Storrington formulate the right answer. It's my job to argue.'

'Not with me, it isn't. Not if it's a job you want to keep. And you need to be careful whose shirt tails you hang on to. Don't back the wrong horse. Screw up here and your fast-track opportunities are finished. No-one will care what you did at the FBI or Anti-Terrorist. Screw up here and you'll find yourself as a plod on the beat. D'you understand me?'

'Yes, sir,' mumbled Hoy, stunned by the ferocity and realising this was not a battle he was going to win. This was a side of Tenby he'd never seen before.

'We're changing the PM's flight to Marseille,' continued Morgan-Tenby. 'We're not flying from Northolt. We'll fly from Biggin Hill - just me, the PM and two security guards. I'm taking his security into my own hands. Arrange a decoy Range Rover convoy and outriders to go from Number 10 to Northolt, then find me an old low-key car and a couple of plain clothes officers. Keep this quiet. Tell only those who need to know . . . which is *nobody*.'

'Yes, sir.'

'And we're leaving a day early.'

'On Friday?'

'Yes, tomorrow. So we need to be ready.'

Hoy knew Northolt well. It was a secure RAF base in West London where Royalty and Prime Ministers always flew. Biggin Hill was a little local airstrip in Kent used by day-trippers and enthusiastic amateurs. Hoy stood and thought about the security implications.

'That's all. You're dismissed.'

The schoolboy left the room.

Lesley buzzed through. 'The Air Chief Marshall is here to see you.'

Morgan-Tenby, portly and sociable opened his door and welcomed the visitor with a big beaming convivial smile. 'Air Chief Marshall, what a joy and a pleasure.' He gave the reluctant visitor a two-handed hand shake. 'I'm so pleased you were able to come over. Come in, come in. May I offer you some tea or coffee? We have five varieties of tea and three of coffee, and some particularly fine Scotch, if it's not too early for you?'

His smarm hung in the air like a heavy evening perfume as he slid back into his office - a slug on a slime-trail of his own oiliness. The door closed. Lesley fetched a sparkling water for the visitor, which she poured into a cut crystal glass and took in on a small silver tray.

'Yes, Air Chief Marshall. The Prime Minister's safety is our prime concern. As you know, he's flying from Northolt. I need you to make sure Northolt doubles the guards, that the PM's plane is checked today and then have it closely guarded until we fly. When he's in the air, he is under your jurisdiction. We need to keep him safe.'

'Yes, we both do.'

'And Air Chief Marshall, it would reflect very badly on you if anything happened to him when he was airborne.'

'It won't. But I can see you're clearly governed by self-interest, as you'll be on board as well.'

'I will, I have a date with a very pretty woman. I wouldn't want to be late or arrive in anything other than one piece.' Lesley winced.

The men, who clearly didn't like each other, shook hands and pretended, at that moment, that they did. The Air Chief Marshall could not wait to leave, get outside and breathe the clean, fresh god-given air.

Lesley looked at Morgan-Tenby, scathingly. He looked at her with oblivious irritation.

'We have to get this done,' he said. 'It's taking too long. We need to make the world a better place.'

～

'Foxx!'

He grunted.

'Foxx!' said Julie. 'Wake up and listen to this.' He half-opened one eye, the buckshot in his back reminded him why he wanted to be unconscious. 'Guess where Bettie Slaker lives.'

He didn't.

He didn't even try.

'Get up. We're going for a drive.'

'Where?'

'You'll see.'

Foxx drove. The car, though his, was registered in a false name. Julie sat with her feet on the dashboard, much to his evident disapproval. But today, Julie was definitely Serafina. She had the bit between her teeth and he had buckshot in his back.

'Where are we going?' he asked again.

'Farringdon Churney.'

'Really? That's a hell of a coincidence. That's the same village as . . .'

'No,' she said stopping him, 'Not just the same village - the same house! Betty Slaker house-shares with . . .'

'Mrs Elizabeth Tenby.'

'*Exactement!* The very same. They know each other.'

'Are you sure?'

Julie sent a text to the Assistant Private Secretary of the DPM.

What does Bettie Slaker look like? The reply was almost instant.

Miss Marple in a wheelchair.

'Correction. She doesn't know her, nor even house-share with her. She *is* her! Bettie Slaker is Mrs Elizabeth Tenby. She's two people. How is that possible?'

They arrived at the house in Farringdon Churney. They parked discreetly behind the hedge. Four minutes later they were driving away.

'That was a waste of time,' said Julie.

They had knocked. She had answered. They were not invited in. She held her panic button in her hand.

'Good morning. May we come in?'

'No. What do you want?' Her voice was curt. She pulled up the phone. It was lightly chained to the armrest of her wheel chair, like a pair of spectacles round the neck of a geriatric.

'Mrs Tenby, are you also Bettie Slaker?'

'Yes.'

'Why do you have two names?'

'That's rich, coming from you two. Bettie is what people have called me since I was a child if Elizabeth is too formal, and Slaker is my maiden name. Not that it's any of your business, Mr Foxx, or whatever your real name is.'

'Why didn't you tell us who you were and that you work for the Deputy Prime Minister?' Her face alone said it was a stupid question.

'Why should I? You didn't ask. You came here to tell me how pretty the fields were and to snoop around trying to find some dirt on my husband. The conversation was not about me or my job. Why would I suddenly say: I am a political speech writer? And if we're on the topic of career choices; why are you an assassin?'

Foxx ignored the question.

'How are you going to stay living in this house when the lease expires?'

'My personal finances are none of your business. And nor is it any of your business if my husband is a mean, selfish, uncaring bastard. Now go. You're trespassing and I'm calling the police.' She clicked a button and the door closed, she picked up her phone and started dialling. The unwelcome visitors left.

'That was a waste of time,' said Julie.

'Not entirely. We know that she knows who we are. She's getting her updates from the inside and not from the media, and she's sensitive about the lease.'

'D'you think she's behind it all to get her lost love on the throne?'

'What? In return for a lease extension? Nah. I don't see it. I don't think she's working with Tenby. It seems unlikely. I mean, she loathes him. Why would she be working with him?'

'She must be. It is a pincer movement on the DPM. He's just the pawn in all this. The Tenbys are in cahoots for sure.'

'Proof?'

'Gut feel.'

'Not convinced. We need to find a glass of wine and somewhere quiet. We have a puzzle to solve.'

27

JOINING THE DOTS

oy knocked firmly on the door. His heart was in his mouth, as if the door belonged to the headmaster and he was about to be expelled. He loved his job. He loved puzzles, investigations and solving crimes, but he was a backroom boy and proud of it. He hated confrontation. That's why his wife won every argument. He never argued, he just agreed. He thought she liked it. She thought of it as his one failing.

And now, still bruised from the Morgan-Tenby lambasting, he was knocking on the door of the most powerful man in the country to tell him he was wrong. This was not going to go well.

'Come in.' Storrington was standing. He indicated to Hoy to sit.

'Sir, I want to talk to you.' Storrington took a pinch of fresh snuff from a tin that must have dated back to Victorian times and sniffed. 'Foxx is our number one most-wanted. We have Operations out looking for him, we have the police tracking him down for the Brighton killings, you have your own team on high alert to take him down and I have all my investigators scouring a world of evidence to prove it's him. Well, the thing is, you see, I . . .' He stalled.

'You what?'

'Well, sir, I . . .'

'For god's sake, just say it, man.'

'I don't think he did it.'

Storrington just stared. The need for justification had come. Hoy held up the report, but put it down again. This was not a reading exercise. He shuffled uneasily on the chair and prepared to speak. Storrington, bored of the silence, filled the gap.

'Foxx is six foot tall. The shooter was my height, which is six foot four. Foxx is not a belt wearer, certainly not one with a large metal buckle, like the one that would have caused the scratching on the concrete. He's never been seen to wear steel toe-cap shoes and we found none in his flat, but the sniper does. Foxx is a good and competent agent with a fearsome reputation, but he's not a sniper, never has been. It was a tricky shot. And as far as I can find out, he had no motive. Is that what you were going to say?'

'No, sir. I mean, yes, sir. I was going to say, he didn't have time between leaving the office and getting home to get in place and take the shot. Also, he left too many clues: the hat, the instructions with his name on it and, of course, his gun.'

'And,' continued Storrington, 'the Quarter-Master never saw him sign the gun out. I had the signature checked by a graphologist, who said it wasn't him.'

'I don't think he's a killer,' continued Hoy. 'Well, I mean apart from those incidents in Azerbaijan and Georgia. I mean he *is* a killer, but not indiscriminate. He didn't kill Sam Stone, he only choked him out. And he did warn us about Barrow, and the booby traps, which makes him either very arrogant or on our side.'

'Yes, I agree. He left a bomb in Connor's flat. He could have killed my men, but he didn't. It was a flash bomb, just a lot of smoke and a big bang. It was a message.'

'A message? Why didn't he leave a note?'

'But he is involved, deeply involved, I just don't know how. Is he really on our side or bluffing? Is he in this on his own or in league with someone else, a sniper who is six foot four? And what about Julie Connor? Why is she involved? Is this to do with her position in GCHQ-2? She handles our top team's email. I suspected that this might be an inside job, not Foxx, but someone else, someone senior, but I dismissed it as outside the range of credible possibility. Is it you?'

'No, sir,' said Hoy, taken aback. 'Certainly not, sir.

'No, I didn't think it was, but I've been waiting for you to come and have this conversation with me first, before I was sure. For the record, it wasn't me either.'

'And it wasn't Brekkenfield,' added Hoy. 'I checked.' Storrington looked at him either surprised or impressed. 'And Foxx checked him out too. I think Foxx suspects the senior team, but I can't believe it. I have a different theory, but I am not convinced of it yet.'

'What, that Connor is behind it all - she's the mastermind?'

'Kind of. What if Foxx didn't kidnap her, but she kidnapped Foxx?' he pondered. 'What if she is using him, blackmailing him, or is his seductress? She lost the love of her life two years ago and has been quiet since then. This could be her revenge on a cruel world.' Storrington didn't entirely buy it.

'I don't envy you this investigation work, Hoy. He paused in a moment's reflection. 'Let's take Foxx off the shoot-on-sight list, but we'll keep Connor on it for now.'

'OK, Chief, and I'll change the direction of our investigations. There's something here we don't understand. We're looking at jigsaw pieces, but can't see the whole picture.

'Well if anyone can sort it out, it's you. You're a strong asset to this Department. Just have more faith in yourself.'

Yes, sir. Thank you, sir.'

'And your wife? Suzi, isn't it?'

'Yes, sir.'

'I hear she's pregnant. Is that so?'

'Yes, how did you know that?'

'You're not the only one with sources and investigative ability. She'll need you at home. Will you be taking paternity leave?'

'Yes, sir, if I may.'

'I insist on it. Solve this, keep the PM alive and you can have three months paid leave when she pops.'

'Thank you, sir. I won't let you down.'

'No. Don't. That's the deal.'

Julie sat on the bed, knees up, wine in hand, leaning against the head-board. Foxx sat on the chair, his feet on the mattress next to hers, pad on his lap. He stared at the pad, it was blank. He stared at Julie, she was silent. He stared at the puzzle book that lay unopened beside the bed. It spoke to him.

'Join the Dots,' he said. 'We have to join the dots.'

'What dots?'

'There's Tenby. He's Dominion 1431.' He put a dot in the middle of the sheet, with initials next to it. 'And he hired Dirk "Blackheart" Swengen.'

'No.' intercepted Julie, 'those dots don't join. Put Colin Lewis in the middle of them, then join Tenby to Lewis and Lewis to Blackheart. Remember? Tenby invited Lewis to a party at their house, Charlie mentioned it. Tenby then asked Lewis unofficially to put him in touch with someone in Black Ops, then Blackheart killed Lewis to cover his tracks.'

'OK,' said Foxx. 'Then there's you,' he placed another dot. 'And here is me. He asked you to get the plan, you asked me. So these dots can join.'

'And you can join me to Blackheart, because Dominion 1431 asked me to make contact and give Blackheart a coded instruction, just once. After that, any dialogue must have gone on between them with burner phones or through some social media channel.'

'Then there's the Prime Minister. Where does his dot join?' Silence. He showed her the pad with the dots.

'That's all the *how*, it's not the *why*. That is *how* he did it, which we knew already. What we don't know is *why*. We need more dots.'

'Like what?'

'Bettie Slaker? She used to work for the PM as a speech writer, for Tenby as a secretary and for the DPM as an advisor; and she is Tenby's wife, who is about to lose her house,' suggested Connor.

'OK. I'll add the DPM too.' They both stalled again. They were just saying names with no idea how or why they connected to the assassination.

'So,' added Julie, 'what about Anderson and Bevan: abortion regulations and military spending cuts? Two unrelated issues that Tenby got aerated about.' Foxx put two dots in the far corners at the bottom of the page.

'What other select committees has he been on?' asked Foxx.

'Just a lot of political nonsense and posturing, nothing earth-shattering. There was one on Minimum Wage only applying to UK residents.'

Foxx placed another dot, 'and that Housing Reform Bill and something about Student Voting Rights. That's about it. Nothing sinister. Oh, and some Social Services Review and the Banking Bill, which was more about freezing and seizing assets of up-risers and terrorists. It's all very random.'

'What else do we know about him?'

'He's a nepotist. He's getting his friends into top jobs in the Military, but I suppose that's how it's always worked.' He scribbled some more dots, and flicked on his phone to the list of names he'd seen at Tenby's house.

'OK, Bettie Slaker, friend and advisor to the DPM. What's she been up to?' asked Foxx.

'Well, she was fired by the PM after getting him into power, but latched on to the DPM, who everyone says will be PM anyway when Brexit is all done and dusted - without the need to shoot the current PM first.' He poised his pen. That gave him no more dots to add, but he did connect a line from Bettie to the DPM. 'I can't think of anything else. What else is going on?'

'Brexit,' said Foxx decisively. 'They say that the PM is doing a terrible job in Europe: poor trade deals, bad relationships and about to sign up to a Defence Strategy that weakens the country, shares our secrets and kills our Defence Industry.'

'And Tenby has major shares in the Defence Industry,' chipped in Julie. Foxx added a dot for the whole defence industry.

'But the PM has no wriggle room. He has a minimal majority. That's why he can't get a decent deal done, so he has to settle for the most middling mediocrity he can.'

'There's unrest in the back benches,' said Julie, adding what seemed like a political non-sequitur.

'So?'

'So, my mate Selina says there are rumours of a new party: a strong, decisive, centralist party that's already gaining popularity. What if Bettie is working behind the scenes to build support for this party and plans to put the DPM in control of it?'

Foxx dotted down a new party, then stared at the myriad of disconnected dots.

'What else is there? This makes no sense, no sense to us. No sense to us at all.'

'Census?' added Julie.

'Ha, ha,' he said, showing no humour. 'I said: sense *to* us, not Census.' The room collapsed into silence, as they stared at the dots. They stared. They thought. They said nothing. There was nothing more to say. The silence was complete and long and heavy.

'Hoe. Lee. Fuck!' exclaimed Foxx, as he scribbled lines between the dots like Van Gogh on cocaine, Matisse on amphetamines or Seurat on speed. 'I don't believe it! Cunning little bastard.'

'What? What is it?'

'It's a coup! It's a fucking coup. Tenby is planning a military coup to take over the country. He doesn't want Storrington's job, he wants the whole country. Oh my god. Brilliant. He's a maniac!' Foxx spun the paper around.

'Look. Dirk shoots the PM, the DPM takes over pre-Brexit and appoints his best mate and buddy Tenby to head up SSS. Meanwhile, the Anderson legislation goes through. It looks innocent, but it makes Tenby all round Chief-of-Staff of the whole Military and also reinforces the civil unrest provisions already in statute, posing as anti-terrorist legislation, which no one will oppose. Then, with a thumping great majority behind him, because of the new populist, centralist party, the new PM takes a firm line with Europe and gets the deal we want. OK, that's a bit of a leap, but he could at least get a better deal than the one that's on the table at the moment, even just by starting all the negotiations again. Then, he's a hero as we go into the post-Brexit implementation. That's where the Census comes in.'

'How?'

'For the first time, the Census has recorded how long everyone's family has been in the UK. That's the one thing in common in all the pieces of legislation that Tenby has been involved with. Anderson's abortion paper covers the wider implications of paying for health care in this country if you're a foreigner. The Census allows a sliding definition of what a foreigner is. It could be a non-resident or - and this is the crucial bit - it could be someone who is a full resident, but has only been here for a year, or five years, or fifteen years. So with ease they could demand that anyone who's moved here in the last ten years has to pay for their healthcare.'

'And Housing Benefit and Social Services,' added Julie. 'They could all be matched to Census results and only long-term Brits qualify.

'Yes' said Foxx getting more exited as he spoke. 'And the minimum wage, and voting rights. It's a barrage of legislation that disenfranchises anyone who moved here potentially since 1948. So once in power, out of Brexit and with a majority, they deprive recent immigrants of houses, health, jobs and the right to vote.

'They'd go ballistic. There would be uprisings, rioting in the street.' It slowly dawned on her. 'Oh my god, he's laid down all the pieces in advance.'

'Exactly! As soon as there's any trouble, which he would no doubt help to inflame, the civil unrest modifications take over and he declares martial law, seizes their assets, removes the PM and takes control. This list,' he said, showing his phone screen, 'are his key, high-ranking allies already signed up to the plan. Goodness knows how many more there are in the lower ranks. They're all ready to enforce control. And that, my dear Connor, is a coup.'

'We're looking at a wholesale military takeover of the country?'

'Yes.'

'Hoe. Lee. Fuck.'

28

SNUFF

The evening wore on. Lunchtime alcohol had worn off, but two further bottles of red kept their blood alcohol levels suitably high. Foxx and Connor were sitting together on the bed, clothed but entwined.

'Shouldn't we tell someone about the coup?'

'Yes, Storrington. But that's a conversation that'll go better face to face and only when we're no longer on his wanted list. We need to find Dirk,' said Foxx, stating the obvious. 'If you want to feed your new trigger-happy blood lust, he's the one to aim it at. Then we can close in on Tenby and find out how much Slaker is part of this. But nothing will happen until after the Marseille trip. Blackheart will be in hiding and Tenby will be acting like the big shot Brexit negotiator.'

'When's the PM flying out?'

'The day after tomorrow - Saturday.'

'Is he flying from Heathrow or Gatwick?'

'Northolt.'

'And the next attempt is on the plane, right?'

'Hardly! Blackheart is working for Tenby, and Tenby will be on the plane, so I don't think they're going to blow it up! No, we can stand down for a while.'

'I think we should get down there just to make sure that Tenby does get on the plane.'

'Tenby will be on the plane. He's not going to miss his Billy Big

Bollocks Brexit negotiations. Anyway, it's Northolt, the airport equivalent of Fort Knox.'

'So he couldn't put a bomb on the plane anyway. So much for your plan!'

'Except the crux of the plan is a plane switch.'

'What's that?'

'Doesn't matter now, because it's not going to happen.' He topped up her wine, put her laptop out of reach and cuddled up close.

Dirk Blackheart sat in a darkened basement bedroom of a cheap seaside hotel, staring at a computer screen. A lace bomb lay next to him, ready to be fitted along the wings and in the fuselage of an innocent plane flying into Biggin Hill from Torquay tomorrow. He would fit it tonight under cover of darkness, but for now he had other issues on his mind.

The Prime Minister snuggled up to his wife. They'd been together since he was fourteen. Life without her was unimaginable.

'I love being with you,' he said quietly and gently. 'I've enjoyed every one of our years together - every moment.'

'Don't make it sound so final! You're only going to France tomorrow, not the moon.'

'No, I didn't mean that. I mean you're the best wife anyone could ever want. I'm glad you got to be married to a Prime Minister, but I'm sorry he's the one that will go down in history as *the worst PM ever*. That's what people call me.' She turned her head to look up at him.

'No, that place has already been taken by your predecessor. It was he who got us into this mess. And Chamberlain, not to mention Eden or Alec Douglas-Hulme. You're not even in the top ten worst Prime Ministers. You've kept the Party together, stopped the negotiations going pear-shaped and won billions back for Britain. And you're definitely the best PM I've ever been married to.' She kissed him lightly on the cheek.

'Yes, I've been successful in not making a bad agreement, but that's just stalling. I was wedged into an impossible situation. I wish we could go back and start again.' Silence hung idly in the room. 'I'll resign after Brexit is done, not because it's what the country wants but because it's what I want. And I won't be a non-exec at a bank or a large pharma company. I want to retire and spend time with you - all the years of too many hours, all the nights away and weekends going through red boxes; I just want time with you.'

'I'm here when you're ready. I'll always be here.' She kissed him on the lips. 'Just come back safe.'

～

Dirk enjoyed making people unsafe.

He enjoyed the planning and the stalking, but the ultimate high was righteous murder. *A man needs a hobby*, he told himself. *And it's not murder, if they deserved to die. It's just capital punishment - another day in the office for an SSS field agent.* Someone had to make the world a better place.

Strictly speaking, Dirk Swengen no longer worked for the SSS or any of the UK Security Services. He had failed his last Psych Eval; or so they said. He knew he hadn't, they just wanted an excuse to get him out. They said he needed a period of normalisation - whatever *normal* meant. He'd been killing since he was fourteen, and been paid for it since he was eighteen.

That was his normal.

Helena, his shrink had said that he'd lost '*socially normalised restraint*' - fancy words for *psychopath*. Inaccurate: he was just *results focused*. She had said he could no longer differentiate between his reality and the true reality – *perceptual distortions* she'd called them. He didn't agree; she didn't know what the true reality was. It was up to him to keep the world safe. His boss had said he'd *lost his moral compass*, which was a joke coming from a government that had orchestrated the coup in Zalekistan.

He had been one of the best SSS agents, but his licence had been rescinded and his contract terminated. They'd thrown him away. Except, nothing in government was quite that simple. There were always jobs, dirty jobs that needed to be done. A highly trained operative, who's happy to live off the grid and work off the books, had his uses; however unstable. So he charged highly and worked occasionally. The rest of the time was his own. He lived in one of his many basic homes, finding ways to pass the days. And nights.

Helena was a typical shrink - she had warned him that he had *excessive, intense, impulsive relationships* – and she hadn't even known the half of it. How he'd smiled.

But she talked nonsense about self-harm and warned him about a fear of losing people – as if it were a bad thing! Absurd. That was the joy. There was no self-harm - he gave the harm to the people he loved. They all left, they had no choice, but he watched them hold on for as long as they could, fight to stay with him . . . until life seeped away. It was not his loss, it was his love. Helena knew nothing.

It was true he had urges, so strong sometimes, but all men did. It was true that he believed in his own power, but that was just self-confidence. It was true that if he wanted things, or people or gratification, he just took them; but didn't he deserve it? He'd served the State and got almost nothing back. His wealth, such as it was, had been stolen from people who didn't deserve to keep it. He'd been a loyal foot soldier for fifteen years – for what?

So of course he lived by his own reality and for his own reward. Why wouldn't he? That was sanity epitomised. He had time, money and the best job in the world. The killing was fun, the money was nice, but the reward was the power. He loved the power - seeing it in their eyes before they died. Beautiful.

And when he wasn't working, he needed to keep his power alive - and how better than with beautiful, admiring, helpless, captivated ladies. He had had many and loved them all, until they couldn't hang on any longer and he saw the hope in their eyes fade and die. That could be a week, a month or a day. That was the fun of it.

But he wasn't having fun tonight. He was rankled.

It was late, it was dark. The hotel room had a faint odour of desperation. The lace bomb was set. The outcome was inevitable. The job was done. Idle minds do the devil's work, he needed to be busy. His thoughts jerked and turned. Focus was hard, especially when irritation set in. He needed calm; concentration. But the irritation was eating away at him. It had to be dealt with. He sat back in his chair, closed his eyes and traced his thoughts back, just like the shrink had taught him. Back to the source of the irritation, back to the root cause; back to Julie Connor.

She had fooled him. She'd not been behind the tarpaulin and had made him look stupid. And for that, she was going to die - preferably intimately and slowly. He promoted her from Housekeeping to Amusement. Should he just shoot her or subdue her for his later pleasure? The pain would be mean, very mean. One way or another her hours were numbered.

But first he had to find her.

He tapped his screen into life. He navigated, hacked, waited. The screen paused; then gave him a list of all the calls she'd made in the last month. He flicked to her billing address, credit details and long-term call history. A few more clicks, and yes . . . he had her signal . . . but no location. That's odd. He tapped again, still no location. Foxx had fire-walled her phone. SSS tracking couldn't get past it. The word *Untraceable* stretched across the screen.

He couldn't kill her if he couldn't find her.

Blackheart was calm. He liked a puzzle to solve. He dived deeply into the dark web, lurked and skulked amongst low life and illegality until he had what he wanted. A program. He ran it and fed in Julie's number. It gave him a pulsating feeling and a pulsating dot in a hotel room on a street on a map of North London.

Julie Connor, you're mine.

She would be easy to kill at any time he chose. He allowed his mind to drift, to dream about the capture and the imprisonment, the torture and the sexual perversion: the straps, the leather, the joy, the pain. He fantasised about how she would die and the climax at the moment of her death. *It will be a seminal moment*, he thought to himself, and smiled.

His work was done, he wanted to sleep. It was time. He was tired but his leg hurt. It hurt where the bullet had grazed him. Anger hit him. He hated his anger, it blurred his thinking, but he hated Foxx more. Foxx had to die. Foxx knew about the plan and Foxx was smart. Blackheart had been careless. Foxx should already be dead.

Frustration struck Blackheart's fist squarely against the hard, immobile wall. His anger was always self-destructive. He needed harmony, a dream, a target, a safe place to hide in his brain. He found it. It wasn't Eduard Foxx, nor Julie Connor; it was pure recreation, a perfect pleasure.

She was so beautiful. He wanted her. His mind soothed the angst away. He needed her, she would be his harmony. It would be slow, sexual and inextricably enjoyable. This was his reward. He deserved it, it was so right – his power, her compliance, his brutality, her beauty; she would give him everything. He would give her love for the rest of her short life. He clicked to her picture and smiled.

Charlie was so pretty.

Charlie was a joy.

Such a shame that the frailty of her body would let her die too soon. He would collect her tonight after Biggin Hill. It would be too easy. He would hold her, hurt her, hug her, humiliate her, pamper her, play with her; then let her blood flow slowly across her all too pretty face - watch her gasp, see the hurt in her eyes, let the spasms in her body excite his, feel her fade, let her be his girlfriend for as long as she held together, and then, when the time was right: snuff her out like an unwanted candle in the wind.

Snuff and she would be gone.

29

LONDON TO NEWBURY

I t was Friday morning. The Prime Minister packed the final items into his bag to fly from London to Marseille. An unknown plane prepared to fly from Torquay to Biggin Hill Tenby kissed his wife goodbye and Blackheart sat on a motorbike in a North London street waiting for the phone of Miss Julie Connor to move out of the safety of her hotel room and into the Kill Zone. The pieces had all moved into place and the day had hardly begun.

A nearly naked Julie Connor sat upright in bed next to a nearly sated Mr Foxx and clinked glasses. They smiled at each other and felt the warmth of the bed and the warmth of mutual affection. They had time and they had each other. Nothing was going to happen until tomorrow.

'Life's improving,' said Foxx.

'How d'you work that out?' she asked, laying her hand on his and drawing small circles with her fingertips.

'Well, your breakfasts have graduated from whisky to champagne. That's surely a step forwards.' He leant over and gave her a quick morning kiss. 'Do you want some orange juice in that?'

'Certainly not! Why spoil perfectly good champagne? Anyway, I never mix my drinks.' Her eyes were big, coy and moisty, as she looked at him in soft focus through the morning light. She drank, cuddled in closer and let lightness wash over her.

'It's a relief, y'know, knowing who the enemy is. I know we have to catch him and we have to stop Blackheart, but I agree, it feels like life is beginning to make sense again. Maybe we can get Storrington to go after Blackheart.'

'We can't risk giving ourselves up yet. He might believe us, but he might just have us arrested. Then we're not only out of play and can't stop Blackheart, but we're sitting targets, in some cell somewhere. He would find us, and . . .'

'Fish in a barrel,' said Julie. There was a pause, then she spoke again, needing confirmation of what she already knew, 'It is him, isn't it?'

'Who, Blackheart?'

'No. Tenby. Tenby is our man, right?'

'The evidence is good.'

'Yes, but not perfect.'

'Look, he's planning a coup, he's been involved in a lot of very dodgy political manoeuvres, he's an ambitious, conniving, self-seeking, ruthless, two-faced dictator-in-waiting; and don't forget, he ordered the Risk Assessment and the hit. We have him banged to rights.'

'Yeah. I know.' She kissed him and drank another sip of her exotic grape juice.

'And Dirk, your mate that wants to kill you, he's good, right? Like Rambo Max.'

'Yep. He is a one-man, mean, clean, killing machine,' he replied, with his brain in neutral. His thoughts had moved back to his libido and getting the champagne glass somewhere out of harm's way.

'But he missed. At the hotel. He didn't get the prime target,' persisted Julie.

'No,' said Foxx, frustrated. 'Colin Lewis was the target. It was a dead shot.'

'Yes, I know that. But if the bullet took almost two seconds to arrive, then he could have shot Lewis and still got another couple of shots off at the PM before Lewis went down. If he's that good, he could have got both of them.'

'I guess, but it was a tough shot,' said Foxx. 'The PM was crouching by then, moving around gathering papers. He wanted to be sure that he had the kill shot or no shot at all.'

'So what about at the Garden of Rest? You know we didn't stop him from doing anything. He chose not to take what was the easiest ever shot and the simplest possible get away. And don't tell me it was because he wanted to do it in front of the TV cameras and the world's Press, because that doesn't hold true at the back of the hotel. The PM was avoiding the Press-trap that Blackheart had created.'

'Which is why he didn't take the shot. He shot Lewis, but waited for the PM to be in front of the cameras.' Serafina was on full form and not convinced; it didn't sit right. She thought slowly and spoke even more slowly, working it out as she talked.

'You know we thought he'd missed the PM and hit Lewis by accident? Well, I've been thinking; Mr *James Bond times ten* has had four opportunities to kill the PM and the PM is still alive.' She stalled.

'So?' prompted Foxx.

'Well . . . if he's that good, then anyone he targets, dies. The PM is still alive.'

'So?'

'So, the Prime Minister's not the target.'

'So who is?'

'No idea, not yet,' she conceded.

'OK, let's think it through. There've been four opportunities: he took two and left two. He shot at the hotel and at Barrow. He didn't shoot at the graveside nor offer the poison at the dinner.'

'So who was with the Prime Minister at the hotel and at Barrow, but not at the dinner and obviously not at the graveside?'

Foxx ran names through his mind. The answer didn't work, so he computed again. Again, it didn't make sense. He ran the algorithm in his head a third time. Confusion consumed his face.

'It's not possible. It can't be.'

'What? Who is it?'

'There's only one person it can be: only one possible target.'

'Who?'

'Tenby.'

～

Julie got off the bed, sat on a chair and stared at him.

'That doesn't make sense. Why would he order his own killing? And why were you asked for a Risk Assessment on the Prime Minister, not on him?'

'Because,' said Foxx, 'it would be too obvious to ask me to plan a hit on my boss. But to plan a hit on the PM when my boss is often with him, especially in public, is foolproof. He gets the perfect plan for assassinating Tenby, whilst making it look like a stray bullet from the PM.'

'So why did he order his own killing? I mean he didn't, so who was it that *did* ask for the Risk Assessment? If not Tenby, it would have to be someone inside the Service who knew the systems and had access to his email account. You would have to hate him a lot to go to all that trouble.'

'Somebody does,' replied Foxx, as it all fitted into place. 'He broke her legs, he broke her back and he broke her heart, then he ran off with a floozy and is now going to let her lose her home.'

'Bettie Slaker!'

'She used to work for SSS, used to be his secretary. I bet you she still has access.'

'So, I was right. This is about lust, greed and jealousy. So what about the coup? Has that been cancelled now?'

'No, that's very much on. But I did think he wasn't clever enough to plan a thing like that. Slaker is behind it. She probably has a pet general tucked away to take over, or maybe it's not a military coup, but a political coup, setting the stage for some nasty, fascist, nationalist extremism. It worked in Germany, it could work here.'

'So, is the DPM part of this?'

'I doubt it. He's just a puppet, the marionette.'

'And Slaker is Maid Marion. I mean Slaker is behind the whole thing.'

'Jesus!' Fox stared his accomplice in the eye. 'That means the next hit is on. We have just over twenty-four hours before the PM and Tenby fly to France. If Tenby is the target, then it's the perfect hit. It will go down in history as an airborne explosion to assassinate the PM, but the truth is my dad will be nothing more than collateral damage. I'll pull him off the plane before they take off, but let's get some evidence first. We need to know if Bettie could have accessed Tenby's PC.'

Julie was already on the phone.

~

Blackheart sat on his motorbike and looked at his watch. If she didn't move soon, he would have to head down to Biggin Hill. The plan was set, the plane was wired, he could leave it to unwind towards its inevitable consequences, but there was a twist, and for that he had to be there. It was a twist, and he was the knife.

But to kill Serafina Pekkala before he went would make the day complete.

'Hi, Julie,' Selina was speaking on her private mobile, not the office number. 'How are you doing? No, I'm still here. Not fired, not dragged away by the Secret Police. Oh, and I've got the funniest ever picture of Rupert with his head in a box. I'll send it to you. So what can I do for you today? Steal the DPM's credit card, hide his passport, kidnap his grandma?' The DPM's APS spoke with affectionate sarcasm to the best friend she hardly ever saw.

'No, nothing so bad.'

'Just a bit bad then?'

'Meh.'

'Meh? What the hell is *meh*? Are you mixing with fourteen year olds?'

'Yeah, pretty much. Look, can you get into the Triple S HR system?'

'Never tried. Hang on, let me see.' Julie waited to the sound of computer keys being tapped. 'No, I don't have access rights.'

'What about SSS administration assignments or even the appraisal system?'

'No, 'fraid not. I can't get into anything Triple S. Anyway, why are you asking me? You're the Triple S shining star around here. Just log in and find out yourself.'

'Yes, but I can't do that unless I'm in the office.'

'Oh sorry, I didn't know you'd retired! Why can't you go to the office?'

'Long story. D'you know anyone else who might be able to help? I really need to get an answer before the PM flies to France tomorrow.'

'I'll see what I can do. And you absolutely totally definitely have got to tell me what this is all about. Is there a man involved?'

'Could be. I mean, yes. Or no. He might be. I mean, yes, he is involved, I'm just not sure if I'm involved with him.' Foxx, who was sitting next to her in the softness of their post-coital duvet, threw a glance in her direction, then back to his laptop. 'I really appreciate your help. Just get back to me if you find anything. And I promise you full disclosure when we meet. Love to Rupert.'

'OK, sweetie. Speak soon. *Ciao!*' The DPM's APS hung up and smiled. Her mousey librarian friend was having way more fun in life than she was, for once. She was pleased and intrigued. She clicked onto her privileged access to the PM's diary and looked at his schedule. It had been revised; he was flying today. Julie had got it wrong, she had said it was tomorrow. Probably didn't matter. She picked up her phone to call Julie back, but her boss, the next PM of the UK needed her help. She picked up her notepad and scurried into his office.

She could always call Julie later.

∾

Dirk looked at his watch, annoyed. He had to go. Time was up. He started the bike. It was big and black and powerful; a reflection of him. He revved. He turned it off again. For once, he let his heart rule his head. Five more minutes, just five, then he definitely had to go.

∾

'I have to go to the office,' announced Julie abruptly. 'I've got no choice.' Foxx looked at her like she was mad. 'Newbury, not Cheltenham. My access has probably been barred, but I can bluff my way in and borrow someone else's terminal.'

'Why? What can you do there that you can't do here?'

'Almost everything. In the office, I have access to an infinite amount of information. Like when did Bettie work for Tenby? Did she ever work for Ops?'

She stopped, made a connection and continued. 'Tenby had tonsillitis for six weeks.' Foxx looked disbelieving. 'Yeah, I know. Six weeks! Wimp! Anyway, if she was working for him at that time, would she have been redeployed anywhere else while he was away?'

'Like with Blackheart, for example?' added Foxx.

'Exactly. I can also find out if she still has access to Tenby's emails and when she last accessed his PC. But I have to be in the office to do that.'

'OK, take the car. I've got the bike, if I need it. Go, be safe, and do – not – get – arrested!' They kissed. 'And get dressed first!'

She stepped out of the hotel, crossed the crowded street and clicked open the car door.

Dirk lowered the dark visor across his face, clicked the bike into life and clunked it into gear. Sometimes the heart, however black, knows best.

~

The Assistant Private Secretary left the DPM's office and picked up her phone to call Julie again.

'And I need it now,' boomed the voice of her boss unseen from behind her desk. She put down the phone and made a mental note to call Julie later. What the boss wanted, the boss needed to have.

~

Julie headed across North London, aiming diagonally through the metropolis towards the M4 that shot westward from London and in four-teen junctions would take her to Newbury. She saw a motorbike in her rear-view mirror. She slowed, so it would catch up and she could see if it was like Duncan's. Old habits die hard.

He was four cars back. She dropped motorbikes from her mind and took a left. Two cars followed; and the bike. It was a large bike, maybe it was like Duncan's. One of the cars behind her took a right.

She pulled up at a set of red lights. The car behind her pulled up to her left, then filtered off as Julie's lights remained red. The large black pulsating motorbike pulled up next to her. She despised motorbikes, but could never stop herself from looking. It was the Duncan in her. It was a Honda, a big black, powerful, noisy Honda. Duncan would have approved.

The rider notched it into neutral and sat back. She glanced up. He was looking at her, she knew it, even though she couldn't see through the visor. She smiled curtly and dropped her eyes. He was tall. Her eyes rested for a second on his belt. The buckle hit her subconscious like an Exocet. It was him - Blackheart. He'd found her.

He slipped his far hand into the rear pannier, pulled out a gun and pointed it at her head. She slammed the throttle, jumped the red lights. He had to belt his gun and click into gear. He roared up behind her. It took but seconds. He was beside her, gun being drawn once more. She braked sharply, he braked. She powered forwards, he did the same. There was no left turn and no right. And there was no one around. She was trapped - like a fish in a barrel.

He raised the gun and pointed it at her head.

She flicked the steering wheel to the right, smashed into his bike. He wobbled, careered out of control, regained his balance and pulled back the throttle in chase. She flicked the steering wheel again and knocked the bike sideways. It fell, it slid. He flew. He was down. She floored the throttle. The last she saw in her rear-view mirror were man and bike sprawled across the floor.

'Eduard. Eduard,' she screamed down the phone. 'Blackheart. Gun. Oh my god!'

She explained. He told her to take a route that was not so obviously heading south west. She did. She drove for ten minutes, hardly taking her eyes off the mirror. She took lefts and rights, and headed back into town before heading back out, losing herself in the maze of London, hiding in a city of ten million people. She pulled up at a junction, waiting to cross, but the morning sun was low and dazzling. She lowered the sun visor to see more clearly, and there on the other side of the junction was a man, a tall man. Blackheart. It was impossible. He waited for a car to pass, then raised the gun. Julie flung open the door, reflecting the sunlight back into his eyes, as he pulled the trigger. The light momentarily blinded him. The shot missed and she headed her car straight for him. He shot twice more. Her head was down. She mounted the kerb. He ran. She hit him. He rolled off to the side, very undead. She left the kerb and sped down the road away from him.

What would Foxx do? She was driving too fast to phone. With no original thought, she did exactly what Foxx had done. She was just north of Paddington. She sped down the fastest road she could find, took a myriad of illogical turnings, found a railway line, took a screaming left, flew past the businesses under the arches until she found a garage. She swerved in and braked hard.

'Service it. I'll pick it up tomorrow,' she shouted behind her as she left the car, radiator steaming, scarred by collision and punctured by gunshot.

She ran hard, along the railway line past the arches, across roads like she was a blind person playing 'Chicken', down alleys, past the back of shops, exactly as Foxx had done, until she came to a canal. One hundred yards to the right was a footbridge. Moments later, she was on the other side of the canal, out of puff. She hopped on a bus, hopped off and dived into the Tube. She darted down to the platform, took a train, changed train, headed back on herself two stops, got off and left the station. She was safe. She looked for a cab. None to be found. She rounded the corner, saw a minicab office, grabbed a car and ordered him to take her to Newbury. She lay low on the backseat and counted her blessings.

This spy malarkey was not for her.

The bang smashed out the windscreen. The blood splatter covered the back of her legs and his brains coated the back window. The driver slumped in his seat, shot, with half a head and no life. The car charged forwards, out of control. She waited. It took only seconds before it smashed into parked cars, spun over and slid on its roof before ramming harshly into the motionless brick wall of a suburban garden. Julie was thrown and hurled like a rag-doll in a spin drier. Her body flexed and bent, her bones collided with metal and the sudden inertia took the wind from her lungs. She waited for the next shot.

It didn't come. There were police sirens. They were almost upon her. She ignored the pain. Within moments, she slid snake-like out of the window, along the pavement and into the small garden of a private terraced house. The police sirens were only feet away. As she slid down the side of the house and into the back garden, the police had arrived at the scene. She was out of view. She stood and ran, over the back wall and hobbled down the grassy driveway that ran along the backs of the houses. She grabbed her phone.

'Eduard. He's fucking psychic. I can't lose him. I dumped the car, ran, took buses, switched tubes, doubled back on myself and still he found me.'

'It's your phone. Dump your phone. He's following the phone.'

'OK. OK. Got it. Dump the phone,' repeated her panic.

'And now I have to dump this one. If he's on to you, he'll be on to me.

Go. Dump it.' She ran. He sprang into action. The hotel was no longer a safe haven. It was time to go.

Julie ran to the end of the alley, tempted just to toss her phone over a wall into a garden, but didn't. As the road emerged ahead, the traffic was slow. Lorries passed at no more than ten or fifteen miles an hour. She readied to toss the phone onto one of them. It rang. It might be Eduard. She looked. It was her best friend, Selina, the APS of the DPM. No time to take the call. She had to dump the phone.

~

'Come on Connor, pick up the phone. I am not leaving this stuff on your voicemail.' It rang out and stopped. Selina dialled again.

'Pick up, you witch,' she said to herself with benign affection. It rang and it rang.

Julie stood there frozen. *Answer or run. Answer or run.* Good sense said run.

She clicked answer.

'Yes, yes, quick, I have to run.'

'Oh. Right,' said her friend taken aback. 'It's nothing. It can wait. Are you OK?'

'What is it?' asked Julie urgently.

'It's just that you said the PM was flying tomorrow. He's not. It's been changed. He's flying today. In about two hours.'

'Shit! From Northolt?' she asked knowing that every extra second on this call was a second closer to her death. *Ditch the phone, ditch the phone.*

'No, Biggin Hill. It's a big secret. The DPM is only one of less than half a dozen people that know. Tenby's the pilot. Fancies himself. Used to be RAF.'

'You're perfect. A star. Love you. Gotta go.' She hung up and dialled Foxx. It just rang. Oh god. He's dumped his phone.

She clicked off the call, tossed her phone onto a passing skip lorry and ran like hell in the other direction. She defied the obvious. She took a left and a left and a right and used alleys when she could. She came out on a small parade. There was a bike shop, a motorbike shop, full of bikers. She walked into the middle of the shop and shouted.

'I need help. I need to get to Newbury in forty-five minutes. I'll pay you £200 if you can get me there. Who'll help me?'

This was England. Everyone looked away or looked at their feet. No one spoke.

'C'mon!' she disparaged. 'Can you ride fast or not? Who'll help?'

'I will, lady,' said a strong voice behind her. 'You know you got blood over the back of your legs?'

'Yes, my boyfriend did that. He beats me up. Now, get me the fuck out of here.'

Duncan would have loved it. How she would have loved it, if it had been Duncan. He rode fast and smooth. Google said one hour, nineteen minutes; the bike said thirty-seven minutes as they arrived at her now favourite and familiar Hilton hotel, just off Junction 14. She cleaned up, did her hair the best she could and got back on the metal stallion. He took her to the door of an office block on the other side of Newbury.

'Can I borrow your phone for a quick call?' she asked giving him no real choice. He handed her his phone. She tried Foxx one more time. He answered.

'I told you to dump the phone. He'll kill you. Dump it!' he yelled down the line at her. The biker looked. He couldn't hear the words but he could hear the shouting. Julie moved further away and spoke quietly and rapidly.

'It's not my phone. The PM; he's flying today. From Biggin Hill. Last-minute switch. Tenby is the pilot. Takes off in about an hour. The DPM knows, therefore Bettie knows, therefore Blackheart knows. Foxx, it's all on you.'

'Got it!' he said sharply. 'Go. Get Slaker. See you on the other side.' And he was gone.

'Thank you,' she said to the man in dirty leathers, as she deleted the last number called and handed back his phone.

'Dump him,' he said. 'Don't call him, just dump him. He's trouble.'

'You're right there. Maybe I will. You've been a hero. Thank you.' She gave him £200, as promised, and a kiss on the cheek for good measure.

She stared at the anonymous nameless office block that was the GCHQ-2, HQ. She glanced through the glass doors before running the gauntlet of the GCHQ-2 security guards that protected the building.

She knew the danger.

She took a deep breath and headed in.

30

FLIGHT TRACKER

Foxx was frantic.

When he woke up that morning, his father had been safe. The pilot, who was the perpetrator, would have kept the flight on track. But now the perpetrator was the victim, they were flying from Biggin Hill and they were flying today. His world was upside down.

He called his dad. The phone was off. He called his dad's office. They were cagey and useless. He called Biggin Hill and demanded to leave a message for the Prime Minister.

'Yes, sir, very funny. So far this week, we've had bookings from two Obamas and a Trump; last week we had M. Theresa, Mr W. Anchor and an H. Potter with his girlfriend Val de Mort,' said the pedestrian old man on the phone; he was clearly going to be of no help.

Biggin Hill was well over an hour from Foxx's current location; he made it in twenty-two minutes. The Rafiqs knew how to tune a motorbike.

~

Julie approached the security desk with a swagger.

'Hi, Frankie. Long time, no see. How're you doing?'

'Doing fine, Miss Connor. My Janice has had a baby girl since I last saw you.'

'So, you're a grandfather?'

'Yes, and loving it.'

'I haven't got my pass on me. Can I get a temporary? I'm only going to be a minute.'

'Sure,' he said. 'You're hardly likely to blow us up, are you?'

He handed her a pass and in she went. She waited for alarms to ring or for armed fighters to rush out, but everything was normal, disturbingly, boringly normal. She logged on as her assistant and started searching. The HR system was unfamiliar, so it took longer than she wanted. All she had to do was prove beyond a reasonable doubt that Bettie Slaker could have done it. She had motive, but did she have means and opportunity?

She got into the HR system: *Search,* click; *Employees,* click; *Bettie Slaker,* click; *Service History,* click. Employment Record: Three years and seven months. She had a pension, a health record which confirmed her disabilities, appraisals for every year – all blank. She worked as Executive Assistant to Nickolas Tenby and for a period of five weeks, at the time her husband had tonsillitis, she had worked on a temporary re-assignment.

Where? Click: *Operations.*

'Yes!'

Connection number one.

When she was in Ops, Bettie had attended a conference for under-cover operatives. Mr Foxx was not there, but Mr Swengen was. Bettie knew, or had at least met, the black-hearted Dirk Swengen.

Connection number two.

But had she invaded Tenby's computer? Had she got her husband's passcode? Did she log in as him? How the hell could Julie find that out?' She wandered to where the geeks lived and homed in on her chosen socially inept, infatuated favourite.

'Hi, Neil,' she said, knowing she already owed him. 'I need you to do something else for me.' She sat next to him, with her hand carelessly on his leg. 'I need you to go back into Nickolas Tenby's home computer and find out if it was accessed by his secretary of old, Bettie Slaker. Can you do that?' She slipped her hand a little higher up his leg. His fear of authority wanted to say *no*; his fear of losing the lustful attention of a good-looking woman said *yes*. Lust won.

'Are you using me?'

'Yes. Do you have a problem with that?'

'No. I was just asking. I'll get on it right now,' he said obediently.

Julie sighed with relief. They were winning. Foxx would stop Blackheart from blowing up the PM and from finding her. She would prove it was Bettie and get the Anti-Terrorist Squad on to her; and together they would stop the coup. Success was so close she could almost touch it.

Not even with a gun to his head, did the man at the Biggin Hill reception desk talk. He knew nothing. Foxx wished him no harm, but he had to stop him calling the police. He dealt with him as gently as he could, then darted up the stairs to the control tower. There was one lone man on duty.

'Where's the Prime Minister?' Foxx asked as he pulled out a gun and explained, 'I'm trying to save his life. The more you delay the greater risk his life is in. Now help me. Which is his plane?'

'That one,' said the man, pointing at a sleek business jet, motionless on the ground, just off the end of the runway.

'So he hasn't taken off yet. Thank god.'

'Thank god indeed. It was a narrow escape. At the last minute, they discovered that the plane was faulty, but luckily another plane had just flown in, let's see, from Torquay. They hired that at the last minute.'

'Where is it? Where is it now? Show me.'

'Just there.' he said, pointing. 'At about 2,000 feet and rising sharply. The Head of the Secret Service is flying it.'

'Get them on the radio.'

'No can do,' said the controller, who was clearly getting much too used to having a gun at his head. 'We lost radio contact as soon as the wheels left the ground. At first, I thought it was a fault, but then realised it's all hush-hush Secret Service stuff and they will have their own comms with the pilot and the PM.'

'So, we can't contact them?'

'Not unless you're in the Secret Service and you know all their mumbo-jumbo.'

Fox grabbed his phone again and dialled his father's number. It didn't even ring, it was dead.

'What's their call sign?' asked Foxx. He clicked into his plane tracker app and watched his father flash his way across the Kent countryside climbing ever higher.

'Get me the Air Force!' demanded Foxx. The controller looked quizzical.

'What, all of them?' He didn't have the number.

'How long until he hits the coast?'

'About six minutes.'

'Of France?'

'About ten minutes.' Foxx did a mental calculation. It couldn't be done in time. He couldn't get an RAF plane off the ground in that time, let alone intercept. And anyway what would they do? He needed to think.

'Where did they board the new plane?' he asked.

'Down there by Hangar Number Two.'

Foxx sprinted down and ran into the hangar, a phone was ringing. He followed the sound to a cupboard. He opened the door and out fell the PM's two personal bodyguards, tied, gagged and undignified.

'Who did this?' asked Foxx. 'Was it a tall guy about six, four, scar on his face?' They nodded.

'Is the PM on the plane?' They nodded.

'Is Tenby flying?' They nodded again. 'Anyone else on the flight?' They shook their heads.

'Arseholes! You just killed your Principal. You'll never work again.' He kicked them sharply and looked back at the flight tracker. They were over the channel. Their light was still flashing. Flashing was good. He willed it: *Keep flashing, keep flashing.*

'Yes!' said the geek, clapping his hands like they had magic in them. 'Bettie Slaker had access to his computer and his emails.'

'When?'

'Five years ago, when she was his secretary, but it was never terminated. Theoretically she never left, she just stopped getting paid. And when she was here, he really trusted her. She accessed all his files, emails, even the GCHQ mails. She had complete rights to everything and still does, no matter how confidential. That's so against the rules,' he exclaimed, oblivious to his own activities.

'So when did she last access his computer? Either at work or at home? When?'

'Woah. That'll take a bit longer. Slow down.'

'I can't slow down.'

'Why? What's the mad hurry?'

'She's about to murder the Prime Minster and her ex-husband.'

'Seriously?' he said grinning , not through humour, but nerves.

'Yes. Please hurry.' His grin faded. His mind couldn't compute. He was now in the front line. She was depending on him. He blushed.

Foxx needed to think. He needed a plan. It was too late to stop the flight. His only hope was stopping the explosion. The plane was over France, their radio was down. There had to be answer. Fox needed to think.

Julie 'Serafina Pekkala' waited. She waited for what seemed like forever.

Neil nodded and moved his chair an inch or two further from the screen. He had finished.

'So? Did she send that email?'

Neil thought for a while and gave the best answer he could.

'I don't know.'

'So, what do you know?'

'I know that she has accessed his computer recently, mostly just nosing around, usually at two or three in the morning – kind of electronic stalking. She didn't leave much trace, but she did go through his files and get into his emails. So she could have sent it, or she could have just been nosey.'

'But she definitely accessed it, recently and often?'

'Yes.'

'And she could read his emails and all his files?'

'Yes.'

'And he wouldn't have known?'

'Correct.'

'I love you,' she said as she kissed his forehead.

'So,' he whispered in her ear, 'do I really get, a y'know . . . what you promised?'

'What – here?' she said loudly. He blushed. She smiled and looked at a nearby meeting room. 'I'm going in there,' she said, leaving Neil uncertain if that was information or invitation.

She stood, turned and her world changed.

'Julie Connor? I am arresting you in connection with the assassination of the Prime Minister under the Prevention of Terrorism Act 2005. You do not need to say anything, but anything you do say may and will be used in evidence against you.' She looked to see where she could run, how she could hide. She was cornered in an open-plan office by the Head of Security, two armed guards and Frankie, the grandfather to his Janice's newborn child.

'I suggest you come quietly, my dear,' said Frankie shakily. 'There's a shoot-to-kill order out on you and they won't hesitate to use it.'

She complied. They walked her down to the Security Office on the ground floor and awaited the arrival of the Military Police. She had no way out. She was caught, stuck, trapped - like a fish.

Foxx sat on the ground, leaning on his bike, still in the airport, too agitated to move; too preoccupied to leave. He wrestled with impossibility. Dirk had gone, free to continue his killing spree. The bomb was on the plane. His father was going to die. The coup was ever closer and there was nothing he could do about it. He remembered the words of his first boss in Operations: *You can't stop a coup*. But for now, he didn't care about the coup; all he wanted to do was to stop a plane from being violently ripped apart at 35,000 feet. He wanted to save the man who had saved him. He sat. He thought. He did all he could to cast emotion to one side and focus.

The explosion had not happened on the way up, so wasn't triggered by increasing altitude. It was his guess it would be decreasing altitude that would trigger the explosion, but it could be a phone signal.

Foxx was a tactician. It was his job to achieve the impossible. But how?

How do you get someone out of an aeroplane, that you cannot contact, that's doing 500 miles an hour, at 35,000 feet, at a temperature of minus 70 degrees, over foreign soil? Even if he could jump out, he hasn't got a parachute and would be hit by a 500 mile an hour wind then sucked into the turbine, which wouldn't matter because he would have frozen to death anyway. If he signalled them to land, the bomb would be triggered by decreasing altitude. It was impossible.

Foxx needed help. He stared at his SSS phone. To turn it on could be the end of him; not to turn it on could be the end of his father. It lit up, as did someone's screen in GCHQ. He scrolled through his directories of numbers and selected *France*. The list of French Connections was short.

'*Jean-Paul, Bonjour! C'est Eduard le Renard ici.*'

'Ello, Monsieur Foxx. 'Ow are you?'

It would be a stretch to say they were friends. Jean-Paul was French Secret Service. They had worked together in Syria and South America, but they weren't close.

Foxx asked for help. He gave the call signal of the plane and its present location, then demanded that two fighter jets be sent up to observe it. The answer was short.

'*Non.*'

Request denied. He added that the Prime Minister was on board and that there was an emergency, but not exactly what it was.

The request was reluctantly accepted.

Seven minutes later, two fast jets took to the sky, heading for the PM's plane at a cruising speed of over 1,500 miles an hour.

Jean-Paul hung up and wondered if he'd just been a hero or had just lost his job. The pilots enjoyed a hunt and seek mission and envisaged flicking some rigid digits at *Le Rosbif* Premier.

Foxx sat with his eyes shut, letting his internal on-board computer work through every possible scenario. How to save the life of the Prime Minister?

'Got it!' shouted Foxx. He called his friend back.

'Patch me through to the pilots.'

'*Bonjour,*' said Foxx. '*Nous avons un problème catastrophique, mais j'ai une idée.'* Foxx was fluent in Kazakh, Russian and five other languages. French wasn't one of them.

'I speke Ingleesh,' said the pilot. 'I zee ze plane now. Is normal, no *problème catastrophique.* Iz good.'

'I need you to do something. Can you . . .'

'*Putain de merde,*' cursed the pilot with shock and consternation, as he banked at 90 degrees to avoid the debris.

'Is blow up. Ze plane is blow up! *Bordel! Une boule de feu. Finit!*'

As the two jets had approached from behind, gaining rapidly, flying towards the red sunset, a short mile or two out, the Prime Minister's private jet exploded, erupted into flame, was engulfed by a ferocious fire-ball and burst into a million pieces.

Three thousand feet above them, a jumbo jet heading for Heathrow saw it all.

Foxx had been watching on the screen of his flight tracker. The light had flashed and flashed and stopped. He had lost. It was over.

31

GOING HOME

The pilot of the British Airways jumbo jet heading to Heathrow from Central Africa saw it all. The flight check mechanic, the co-pilot and the purser, they all saw the executive jet flying a few thousand feet below them. They saw the French fighter planes. They saw and misinterpreted the reflection of the sunset as a flash of red on the wing of the French jets, and less than a second later they saw the executive jet burst into flames, then explode into a catastrophic supernova of shock waves, fire and debris. It was fierce, ferocious and final.

'Holy Mother! Did you see that? They just shot it down!'

'Yeah,' said the co-pilot breathlessly, scarcely believing what he'd seen. 'Did you see the flash of red on the wing? That was the missile being launched. They shot him down. Jesus! There gotta be some bad people in that plane!'

The gasps started in First Class: seven separate people had seen it happen and ten more had seen the fighters bank sharply away - almost a hundred saw the fireball cross the sky. The news spread rapidly through the cabin. By the time they landed, 400 people on a jumbo jet arriving from Africa knew that the French Air Force had just shot down a plane over French soil, but not one of them knew who had been on board.

Foxx sat on the ground motionless. He tried to make it real, tried to focus. The police sirens got closer. He was numb. Dumbfounded. The wailing of the approaching police convoy seeped slowly into his consciousness. The police: they were coming. For him. He turned off his phone. He stood. He had to go home. He had to tell his mum. He had to be with her.

He mounted the bike, and with no real recollection of starting it, nor of the roads he travelled, he found himself a mile away, his mind a blur, as he headed instinctively for home.

Debris rained down on French fields, like confetti at a funeral. It covered gardens, houses and villages: scraps of burnt-out wreckage, a wing tip, tiny pieces of charred black flesh and a suitcase - the Prime Minister's suitcase. A farmer and a hundred other people called it in, but the gendarmes already knew. The Armée de l'Air Française had told them before the brutality even hit the ground.

'Mum. It's me.'

'Hello darling, how nice to hear from you.'

He was in a call box five minutes from home. On any other day, he would just have walked straight in, but today was not a straightforward day.

'I'm coming home.'

'That's lovely, dear.'

'I have something to tell you,' he said, in sombre tones.

'Then tell me now, dear,' said his mum, ever practical. He didn't know how to put it, how to say it, how to warn her; but she had to know before she learned it from the news.

'It's about Dad.'

'What about him?'

'It's bad, very, very bad.' He was having difficulty focusing his thoughts, let alone expressing them.

'Just tell me,' said his mother in her most matter-of-fact, pragmatic voice.

'He was in a plane, flying over France and the plane . . . it blew up. There's nothing left. I'm afraid he is . . .' he couldn't bring himself to say it. 'They blew it up and there were no survivors.' There was a long silence on the end of the phone. His mother chose denial as the best reaction.

'Don't be so silly, dear. You can be so melodramatic sometimes. He's fine. We were only talking about his retirement this morning and he intends to live it long and hard.'

'I'm not being silly, Mum, nor melodramatic. He's dead.'

'No, he's not. He's alive and has just passed Waitrose. I just spoke to him about ten minutes ago. He asked if I wanted anything because he was passing the supermarket. I said no. He'll be here in five minutes.'

Foxx hung up. He chose denial as the most suitable reaction. He simply didn't believe it.

The Prime Minister sat in the back of the black Jaguar, as it drove gently past his local Waitrose. He hardly believed what had just happened. As if it weren't hard enough being a Prime Minister, particularly one that was trying to negotiate an impossible exit from Europe with a minimal majority drawn from a flimsy coalition of uncomfortable bed partners, all this extra security was getting him down.

He understood the threat was real. Colin Lewis had died right next to him; Barrow had been highly emotional, with the loss of two military lives scarcely two hours before he made his speech. He knew it was real, but he tried to shut it from his mind. It was not callous, nor cavalier; it was the only way he could concentrate. So, the shenanigans of today were just plain and simply discombobulating.

He was not happy with pretending to be in Number Ten. He was unhappy about abandoning the military precision of Northolt for the enthusiastic civilian approach of Biggin Hill. But if his security advisers told him it was safer to have only two bodyguards rather than an army and fly from a field, rather than a world class military base, who was he to argue?

He wrote notes in the back of the car that he would transcribe into his memoirs.

. . .

Biggin Hill. Waited fifteen minutes for the plane. So much for being a world leader. Boarded - me, Tenby and the security officers, but plane was marked as unsafe. Waited around. A sniper's dream. Then we all boarded another aircraft.

Dirk Someone turns up, one of Brekkenfield's agents, tall guy with a long scar, tells me my wife has been reported ill and is in hospital. I call but none of our phones work. Bloody Biggin Hill.

Dirk says he arranged for me to visit her and I will fly tomorrow. Tenby was keen to get there early, he had some meeting with someone, a woman no doubt. It was agreed that the two security officers would stay with me, but after a meeting between them in one of the hangars, it turns out that Dirk is my minder for the night and the other two guys caught the plane.

Went to Bromley General. I waited in the car. Dirk goes in to find out which ward Sally is in and it turns out that it's some ninety year old woman of the same name and someone had got their wires crossed. Relieved and delighted it was not Sally - pissed off someone got it wrong. An extra night at home – good for me! I'll fly from Northolt tomorrow – back to original plan. But this never happened to Obama!

'I've got a signal, if you want to call your wife, but best be quick, the whole network is playing up tonight,' said the driver, as he switched off the phone jammer under his seat.

The Prime Minister phoned, said he was coming home and handed the phone back to his new protector.

'Why are we going this way?' asked the PM, as the car turned off to arrive at the back of the house. The real answer was to avoid the policeman at the front of the house, but the answer given was, 'New security procedures.'

It was a quiet rural location. There were neighbours to either side, fields and woodlands behind the house and a back gate. The Jaguar pulled up at the gate. The driver kept the doors locked and turned to face the VIP passenger.

'Just thought you'd like to know, the plane you were on has just exploded over France. All dead.'

'How do you know?' asked the PM, surprised.

'Because I blew it up.'

'Really?' asked the PM in disbelief. 'So why did I escape death a second time?'

'Who said you did?' The driver produced a pistol and pointed it at him. 'Prime Minister, prepare to die. I'm going to shoot you here, so your wife can see your dying body and hear the last gasps leave your lungs. And as you're dying, in no state to protect her, I will shoot her in front of you. And the dog too.' He paused. He held the gun tight and prepared to shoot. The PM was rigid and stalwart. He didn't move a muscle. If he was going to die, he would die a hero. He closed his eyes. He heard the click as the gun was cocked. The PM opened his eyes, stared at the gunman right in the eye and saw his finger curl round the trigger. He heard no bang.

The gunman slowly pressed the end of the barrel right against the cold stolid forehead of the Premier.

'You're dead and your wife is dead too, unless you agree to stand down.'

'I will not subject myself to terrorism,' he said, with his loving wife filling his every thought. 'I will not resign as Prime Minister, just because you're holding a gun at my head. It is not going to happen. So shoot me.'

'You're not reading this right,' clarified Blackheart. 'You are already not the Prime Minister, either because you step down or because everyone thinks you're on a plane above France. Everyone, except your wife, thinks you were on board. That's why I have to kill her too. So stand down. Announce it tonight. And don't get smart with me. If you say you will step down and then you don't, I'll kill your wife, your brother, your sister and all their children, then cripple you, so you live to feel the pain. Get it in your head: one way or another, you are no longer Prime Minister.'

The man who was still Prime Minister said nothing.

'On your way now,' said his captor, as he unlocked the doors. 'Resign tonight. Or everyone you care about dies. And I mean *everyone*.'

The Prime Minister opened the door and closed it firmly behind him. Danger turned to anger, but he had no weapon, no skills of karate; he was a politician, all he had was words. He leant in though the open front window, standing on a pedestal of moral high ground, and had the last word. It wasn't much, it was churlish and inconsequential, but at least it wasn't nothing. Blackheart engaged 'Drive' and drove off into the night.

∽

Julie's eyes flicked around the concrete room with its one small high oblong window, a table and four chairs, all occupied. She sat, in silence, thinking, waiting to be collected, to be at the mercy of the Military Police. Military Prison, in some basement of a top-secret military base: no lawyer, no rights, no record. They could do what they liked. *I could just be disappeared or a sitting duck for Blackheart.* In a civilian police cell, it would be harder for a military man to get in and take her out. She was in danger of death or a life condemned to a dank dark prison cell.

But none of that seemed to matter. She was on a mission. Her mind whirled. She had to get it right in her head.

Bettie Slaker had needed Tenby's money; they were still married, she would inherit. It was simple: need and greed. Or was it anger? Bettie was in danger of losing her house, not to mention the clumsily concealed jealousy of all the young floozies; or revenge – maybe Tenby really had been driving when the accident happened. Or was it political? Had she used her husband to help create the platform and now she needed to dispose of him? That would leave the way clear for her reign of terror through the marionette man who would soon be leading the country - the automatic accession to PM from DPM . . . that was Bettie's work for sure.

Julie looked around the room, at Frankie and the other guards. If she was going to act, she needed to act now.

The Prime Minister stood in his front room, his wife on one side and his adopted son on the other. The Scotch was in a glass, in a hand that was still shaking. He recounted the story.

'And then he drove off?' asked Foxx at the end.

'Yes. I got out. I had to have the last word. He was tapping in the satnav, so I stuck my head through the window and said: "You can tell your boss, whoever he is, that I am not resigning." And he said: "I think you'll find that you are. And he's a she, anyway." Then he drove off.'

'So you didn't have the last word.'

'I did. I had a whole stream of them, but they were rather vulgar and not worthy of repeating here.' His wife looked reproachful.

His son looked quizzical. 'You didn't see the address he was entering in, did you?'

'No. not exactly. It was some place in Essex definitely. Two words, maybe Farlington Churchtown.'

'Faringdon Churney?'

~

'Storrington? It's Eduard Foxx here. I need your help. I don't have time to explain, but Dirk Swengen is your man, a Black Ops freelancer who calls himself Blackheart. He's the assassin and is heading for Farringdon Churney right now. I'll send you the address. He's meeting his accomplice. She's behind all the attacks. There's more you should know. Meet me here tonight, just you. It was Swengen who killed your men in Barrow. And Lewis. He needs to be put down.'

Storrington had only one question.

Foxx answered.

'Six foot four.'

Storrington hung up. The hunt was on.

~

'Hello, Anti-Terrorist Squad? This is Julie Connor at GCHQ in Cheltenham. I have information about a current terrorist attack. Please note this down.'

Julie was in the ladies toilet. Frankie had escorted her there. He had said that she would leave the cubicle door open and he would keep an eye on her, but when he got to the ladies, he waited outside. He had no desire to enter a female toilet. He knew there were no windows and assessed that she was not a suicide risk. He knew Julie, he liked her, she was a good sort - apart from being a terrorist. She gave him big huggy kiss in gratitude and slipped his phone out of his inside pocket and went into the privacy of the ladies to do her business.

'There is an on-going terror attack. The Prime Minister's life is in jeopardy. We have significant and convincing evidence that the plot to assassinate the Prime Minister has been planned and run by a cell in Farringdon Churney, led by a woman.' She gave the postcode. 'We believe the occupants are engaged in an assassination attempt right now. The trigger for the bomb might be her telephone. Do not let her use it. She has engaged the services of a number of top rogue operatives. They are the ones that killed the officers in Barrow. They are very dangerous. Do not let the locals near the place. You need to plan the assault with care. I have to go now. We're tracking activities. Thank you.'

She gave her Frankie a big phone-replacing hug and hoped to god that Foxx had got Blackheart before Blackheart gets her.

32

BLACKHEART'S TRIUMPH

B lackheart was king of his world. He had total freedom, living by his own rules, outside society and without fear of the law. It was a life without restraint or restriction. He drove his black car towards Farringdon Churney through the black night with no lights, at great speed, because he could.

It had been a good day. He had deposed a Prime Minister, assassinated a would-be military leader and changed the balance of power in one of the world's most significant countries – and, as always, had done it from the shadows. He loved his job.

But a job isn't finished until the clearing up is done; and that meant a trip to Farringdon Churney and to Mrs Tenby aka Bettie Slaker. She was treacherous, manipulative and self-centred – all qualities he admired. More than that, she was ambitious – a character trait which could generate more work for him in the future. He had studied her, stalked her and researched her carefully as a potential partner in business. He approved - her wheelchair made her no threat and her lack of sexuality made her no temptation. They'd spoken only once to agree the terms and define the task, but emails and burner phones don't allow you to look someone in the whites of their eyes nor to read darkness in their soul. This was his mission tonight.

She was expecting him to make contact, but not in person. He was deliberately off-plan to catch her off-guard – that's how to get the real measure of a person. The visit would be as much a surprise as it would be brief. Blackheart didn't want to risk being seen with her – just a quick in-and-out to get paid, to lay some unseen incriminating evidence on his employer as insurance in case he should ever need it; and to decide if he could trust her.

He had left an angry, deposed Prime Minister behind him, had pointed the car towards Essex and flicked through his Communications Tracker. He searched on Julie Connor.

Yes! Arrested - Borden Army Base - Military prison. *Easy target.*

His fake ID would get him access to the cell, then all he needed was a well-practised 3-2-1: three seconds, two moves, one broken neck.

Job done.

'Maria,' he said, forcefully down the phone.

'Captain de la Casa here, sir.'

'Captain, we finish it tonight. This is where it ends. It's not Foxx. It's Dirk Swengen and some woman. She's the brains, he's the trigger. We need to take them both out. No court case, no trial by jury. We conclude it tonight.'

'Yes, sir.'

'Co-ordinates coming over now. Arrive with stealth. Be very careful.'

'Yes, sir.'

'Maria, I mean it. Be careful on this one. It could be booby-trapped. He's dangerous and he has nothing to lose. Don't let him, or her, near anything that could be a detonator. Don't take any risks.'

'It's Captain de la Casa, sir, and I will take him down, whatever the cost. Sir!'

Four minutes later she was airborne making a beeline for a little commuter village in Essex. Tonight would change the course of history. She had to get it right. She had to earn the respect of the only man it was worth receiving it from. She would not let him down.

Storrington stood on the roof of his office building in Whitehall, by a large letter H, losing patience and building frustration. How long did it take to fly a chopper from Battersea to Westminster? Urgency was everything.

He called Brekkenfield.

'Stay tuned into the frequency,' he said. 'It's going down tonight.'

He called Hoy.

'Get in the office. I need you on point. You're in charge until I get back. And get a car to meet me at Biggin Hill.'

'Is that where it's going down?' asked Hoy.

'No, I have a house call to make.' He hung up and pinched a sniff of snuff from his pocket.

At last, he heard the throbbing familiarity of rotating wings echoing up the Thames and pulsating along the large white walls of Whitehall. It touched down for thirty seconds, the Commander stepped aboard. He gave the time-honoured sign of an upward pointed finger swirling once and the wheels left the ground.

Blackheart didn't drive to the front of the house - Blackheart never drove to the front of a house. He took a back road, saw a wide verge and tucked the car right up against the thick dark hedge. He jogged effortlessly across a small field, up a short footpath to join the track that led to the back of her house. He leapt, cat-like, onto a low flat roof and crossed it as silent as the night itself. There were no windows opening directly onto the flat roof, but at the very front edge, if he leant forwards far enough, he could reach, touch and prise open a badly sealed upstairs window. As quiet as air, he breezed through the window and into what, under previous owners, had been a young child's bedroom.

He set to work. In his business, incrimination was insurance. He left a copy of the Barrow letter, the one that had instructed the tree surgeon to remove the old oak that had obscured a direct shot at the PM. He left a tee-shirt with Foxx's DNA sweated into it, straight from Foxx's wash-bin. He left parts of an unfinished lace bomb, like the one that had just downed the plane, lying next to Foxx's plan for the attack. Then he took out a small Samsung tablet and a USB drive. He hooked into her Wi-Fi and began the download onto her computer. He was simply attending to unfinished business.

He heard a noise, not with his ears, but with his intuition. He pulled out his hand cannon and watched the download bar on the laptop spin and loiter. The download stuttered before regaining pace. He picked up the gun and removed the safety catch. Someone was going to die tonight and it wasn't going to be him.

Keeping a chopper quiet is not easy; arriving by stealth, almost impossible. The hill behind the house would shield some of the noise, and the wind direction was on their side. The pilot set the chopper to silent running, which was a misnomer, but landed far enough away not to alert suspicion.

'Formation. Stay in formation. No exceptions,' briefed Captain Maria as they landed. 'Beware booby-traps. Assume every door is rigged. Go in through the windows. Look for trip wires. He's a tricky son of a bitch. When you see him, no questions, talk with your gun. Then find her. If we can take her alive, we will. We want her to talk. He likes explosives. Any sign of a detonator, shoot first, think later. This is not about revenge. We're here to kill him. One more thing: none of you are to die. That's an order. Got it?'

'Yes, sir. Captain, sir.'

They touched down and ran in formation to the cottage. The clouds obscured the moon, the world was shades of black. Silently, they slid open the front gate and took position. The plan was simple: hide in the blanket of night, reconnoitre through the windows, then enter, two to check the downstairs and two upstairs, shooting anything that moved. This time the captain would be leading from the back. She was the third pair, following them in to reinforce where needed.

She signalled the two pairs to move in. They slid out of sight, to the side of the house, to where the large lounge window overlooked the fields. Maria knew her role - stay put and watch until they were inside.

But she didn't. She broke formation.

Her eye was caught by a window on the dark side of the house, it was upstairs and it was open. She needed to know what was inside. The plan said *stay*, instinct said *go*.

She went.

Her team crept like ninjas to the window of the lounge.

Maria leapt onto the flat roof, almost as silent as the night. But not quite.

Intuition inside the darkened upstairs room told Blackheart to pick up the gun.

She tiptoed across the roof towards the window.

Her men tiptoed round the other side of the house to peer into the front room. Bettie Slaker was sitting by a casual table, reading papers. They exchanged glances. She was the one.

Maria drew closer and closer to the window.

Blackheart unplugged the fully downloaded USB drive, slipped it in his pocket and took two steps across the room, knelt and raised his hand cannon towards the open window. The floor creaked as he moved.

Bettie heard it. There was someone upstairs, someone in her house. She picked up her phone.

Maria eased herself gently off the roof and into the window.

Blackheart took aim.

The team saw the phone, saw the lady pick it up, saw her go to press the buttons: Detonator! Four automatic weapons opened up in synchronicity, and in four short seconds they pumped two hundred bullets into the would-be assassin.

Blackheart blasted twice at the silhouette in the window. She was a fish in a barrel, she flew backwards, blasted out of the window frame and landed slumped and motionless on the ground, twelve feet below.

He grabbed his tablet and left through the same window that Maria de la Casa had just flown out of.

The team stared through the lounge window.

'She's not making a call now!' said Number Four, looking at the mincemeat that was once a person.

'Did you hear something?' said Number Three

'Like what?'

'Gunfire.'

'I think the whole county did.'

'No, not us. A pistol shot. Round the back of the house. C'mon, let's take a look.'

'No mate. Formation. We're not to break formation. Everyone ready?

OK. In we go!' All four of them piled in through the large shattered hole that had once been a window.

Blackheart jumped off the roof and walked rapidly down the back track, retracing his steps, away from the house, away from the body of Captain de la Casa and into the darkness.

33

THUMBS

'Clear,' shouted the team downstairs.

'Clear,' shouted the team upstairs. Number Three approached the bedroom window cautiously, gun at the ready and peered out. It was pitch black. The clouds cleared and the moon turned the opaque shape on the ground into a body - the body of their captain.

'He shot Casa!' he yelled. His eye fell on the open garden gate. Assumption drove his command. 'He left through the gate. Get him.' Eight boots charged out of the house.

Number Three headed for the captain.

'Leave her. She's done. We gotta get Swengen.' He left. They ran fifty yards, two to the right, two to the left. They stopped, looked, listened. Nothing.

~

Storrington had landed. He made his way deftly to the track that led to the back of the house, there was a gap in the clouds, the moon lit his way.

He strained his eyes, there was a figure coming towards him. A tall, slim figure shrouded in shadow.

'I'm police. Are you Storrington?' said the figure, as he walked at a pace towards him.

'Yes,' said Storrington. 'Give me an update.'

The figure became clearer. He was the same height as Storrington: six foot four, his belt buckle just visible, a gun already in his hand.

'I just shot your captain.' The gun was fully raised, his finger ready. But Storrington flicked his wrist.

A knife with a four-inch blade flew like a silent missile through the cold night air and stuck deep into Blackheart's bicep. His grip on the gun weakened. Storrington leapt forwards.

Blackheart punched with his left. Storrington should have gone down, but he stood like a statue repelling rain. He raised his thumb and jabbed it hard into Blackheart's neck and then into two vital pressure points. The gun dropped.

A ferocious upper-cut flew at the Commander's face. Storrington grabbed Blackheart's arm and threw him. The toes of his boots sparked as they scuffed the stones. Blackheart was down. Storrington turned to pick up the gun, but it had vanished into the darkness. Blackheart pulled a second gun from his ankle and aimed it at Storrington's head.

The team heard the shot. They turned and ran back.

Blackheart had drawn his gun, Storrington had been a target too big to miss. He had aimed, but too slow. The gunshot flew out of Maria's pistol as she sprinted in agony along the path. Blackheart went down, but he wasn't dead. She aimed to shoot again.

'No!' said Storrington. 'Give me your gun.' She passed her sidearm. He held it firmly. Blackheart opened his eyes and looked up at him. 'For Pookey,' he whispered and put a bullet through the left temple of his lover's killer. The body fell. Vengeance assuaged.

'Are you OK,' they said in unison. Storrington assessed the blood, the shell shot damage to her bulletproof vest and the pain with which she moved.

'What the hell happened to you?'

'I'd rather not say, sir, not now. Not if I don't have to.'

They hurried together towards the house to meet the four heading in the other direction.

'Status?' demanded the Commander, as they marched in a team back to the house. They each reported and led him to the front window. All six of them stared in. The scene was carnage.

Then, through the silence of the night, there was the metallic sound of rifle behind them. They turned. A dozen barrels pointed straight at them.

'Police. Identify yourself.'

'Special Security Service, Commander Storrington. Who the hell are you?'

'Anti-Terrorist Squad.'

'Who called you here?'

'Julie Connor.'

'Figures.'

'What's happening here? Looks like it's all over and done.'

'Yes. But we need some delicacy. National Security. My team have been in. The house is clear. A woman is dead in the front room and the would-be assassin is lying on the track up that way. I want him removed pronto. We can do it or you can do it, but he needs to be bagged up and disappeared.' He led the DI in charge round the corner of the house to the lounge window.

'Jesus H Christ,' said the DI, as he looked at the blood-sodden wheelchair and its scarcely recognisable contents. 'You know whose house this is, don't you? That's Bettie Slaker, friend and advisor of the DPM. What the fuck happened?'

'I'll tell you exactly what happened,' said Storrington, considering the destabilising impact of having the DPM's personal advisor being linked to an assassination, especially one that would have put her boss in the PM's seat. He thought slowly, looked at the gory theatre of blood, took a deep breath and spoke clearly.

'Yes. I will tell you exactly. She was murdered by a dangerous terrorist cell, all of whom were killed by the brave actions of your Anti-Terrorist Squad, with a loss of one officer's life. The bodies have been removed by the PM's SSS and identities will be revealed in due course. Can you and your team work with that?'

'Yes, sir. That works for us.'

'This is a matter of the greatest sensitivity. It is a moment in time that could change history; for the worse. I need to depend on you. It has to be handled like this. If you have any doubts, leave now and we will deal with it.'

'No, sir. My team is discreet. We'll handle it.'

'Good. My team will pull out. Call me when it's sorted. I'll arrange for you and your team to meet the PM, so he can thank you personally.'

After exchanging respectful valedictions, Storrington, flanked by

Captain de la Casa and followed by the team, marched with purpose down the track behind the house.

'This is where he fell,' announced the captain to the team, as they passed the spot. 'We put a bullet through his head.'

The team had switched off all outside communication to maintain Operational Radio Silence. Storrington clicked *Comms* back on.

'Sir,' crackled the shaken voice of Hoy. 'The Prime Minister is dead. His plane was shot down over France. We have a whole jumbo jet of witnesses that say they saw it. It's already all over the news. There's even a clip of the fireball aftermath on YouTube. It was the French. The French Air Force shot him down.' Storrington cursed under his breath. He had failed in his prime duty as leader of the SSS.

Maria heard the transmission. She felt her failure hard. They had killed two assassins, but not saved the life of the Prime Minister. She would be cast out, back into the Syrian desert, by the only man she wanted to be close to.

Storrington seethed within. He wanted revenge, he wanted retribution. The episode at the cottage was too little, too late. What would Captain de la Casa think of him now?

'One more thing,' added Hoy. 'We have Connor in custody, in Borden. How do you want her dealt with?'

'Decisively! I'll handle it.'

They approached the choppers. The team boarded. Storrington took off his headset and beckoned de la Casa to join him at a confidential distance from the team.

'I have one more job for you. Drop the boys at the base and give them beer and whisky. Tell them they did good. There will be no repercussions. Then get back on the chopper. I need you in Borden. I need you to deal with Connor. Alone.'

She nodded. He gave her precise instructions. She boarded the chopper and was gone. Storrington made his way to his helicopter. Ten paces out, his phone rang, his personal phone. He stared at it. It never rang, not since Lewis died.

'Storrington! It's Julie Connor.' His shock was palpable. 'I'm in Borden. Get me out.' She had asserted her right for her one phone call and had chosen Storrington. The transformation was complete. The self-effacing civil servant from Cheltenham had gone from invisible to invincible as she told the country's most powerful man what to do. 'You don't want me talking to the people here. You need me there. Get me out.'

Storrington's thoughts raced. *How did she know they'd just been talking about her? How had she got his personal number? Who the hell did she think she was?* His reply was curt.

'First, you're on the hit list; shoot-on-sight. Second, I don't take orders from you.'

He hung up.

Two minutes later, the cell door clanked shut. Julie stared at the dark gloomy, windowless wall and realised that it might be the last room she would ever see.

∾

The DI was on the ball. He cordoned off the house and kept his team on guard. As requested, he called Hoy, who agreed to handle the investigations. He cleared the scene before SOCO got there and asked two of his team to bag the body of the assassin, if SSS had not already done it. He knew Storrington was a powerful man, he had influence; the DI was determined to get a long overdue promotion out of this.

∾

Foxx listened to the Prime Minister, his father, and watched the reaction of the PM's chief and respected advisor, his mother. It was late and the whisky in his father's hand was not his first.

'I won't stand down. I won't give way to terrorists.'

'Do you want to be Prime Minster?' asked Foxx.

'Hell no. Who would right now? I'd give it up tomorrow, if I could. But if I resign, it weakens our hand in the Brexit negotiations. It shows we're in disarray. It would be even worse . . . if that's possible.'

'Actually, not really possible, to be honest.' The PM's Chief Advisor looked at him with deep maternal disapproval. 'Sorry, I thought this was a family honesty session.'

'But,' continued the Prime Minister, 'I don't want to put you and the family at risk. And that scar-faced driver threatened everyone I know. Nor do I want to be remembered as the cowardly PM who ran away. There are times when duty supersedes desire.' He was talking himself in circles.

'If there was no Brexit and no terrorists and you had a free choice, what would you do?' asked Foxx.

'Retire.'

'So you want to strengthen our Brexit negotiations, not give way to terrorists, keep the family safe, be a hero and retire.'

'Yes. Impossible. I know.'

'Not necessarily.' A plan was forming the mind of the tactician whose parents thought he still called himself Simon and worked as an innocent administrator deep in the heart of the Civil Service. 'What if we see it differently? What if the news is right? What if the French Air Force did shoot your plane down? How would that strengthen negotiations?'

'That's not what happened!'

'It didn't have to. We just need enough people to believe it did. There were French fighter planes right behind the jet when it blew up. And there's a jumbo jet full of witnesses. And in the current jingoistic climate, we only need people to think it might be possible. Look at JFK.

'True. People love a conspiracy theory. It would be an embarrassment that would put the French on the back foot. It would mean that the French killed two of my close protection guys and slaughtered Tenby, poor guy.'

'And you, nearly. Embarrassing? It would be colossal. We would have them over a barrel. We could threaten war! We could bring a new negotiator in without a loss of face and they could start at the beginning again, on a totally different footing. It would reposition the defence negotiations completely. We could bring in a real tough ball. I have someone in mind who would do that very well.'

'But that means the terrorists would still have won, and we'd have let the French take the blame.'

'Don't worry about them. The terrorists are finished.' Foxx looked at his watch. 'They'll be dead or behind bars by now.'

'You're very well informed for a Foreign Officer researcher?'

'Meh.'

'Oh, do speak properly, dear,' said his mother.

'You want to be a hero?' continued Foxx. 'The plane was shot out of the air at 35,000 feet and everyone knows that you were on it. Let me tell you what happens next: you survived! Now that is a hero! And an honourable reason for retiring.'

'Don't be stupid, son. No one will believe that. It's not possible.'

'Really? What about, oh . . . what's her name? That woman on the Yugoslavian DC9 that got blown out of the sky by a terrorist bomb in 1972, Vesna Vulović. She fell 33,000 feet and survived with two broken legs; and to stir up political enmity, the Croatians blamed the Czech Air Force. Or that Lancaster tail gunner in 1944, Nicholas Alkemade. He jumped at 18,000 feet with no parachute. True, he landed in fir trees, but when they found him, he was sitting in the snow completely unharmed, having a smoke, giving them the thumbs-up. You'll be a hero; injured, but not dead. All you have to do is keep out of the way for six months, recovering. So off you go. Upstairs and pack.'

'Where are we going?'

'Tonga.'

'Tonga!'

'Yes. It's heaven.' He thumbed through his screen and showed them pictures of paradise on earth. 'And you'll be completely incognito. You need a rest and you can catch up on all the things you always wanted to do. Come home when you've recovered, get knighted or lorded or something and live your life in peace and harmony. It's the perfect solution.'

The footsteps echoed up the long dark stone-floored corridor that led to the dark and dismal cell in a basement in Borden. The door to her prison opened. Julie waited for the figure of man, six foot four, with a gun in his hand. She turned, she looked up. It was a woman.

'Are you Julie Connor?

'Yes. Am I on your shoot-to-kill list?'

'Yes . . .'

Julie nodded stoically.

'. . . terday, but apparently not today. My name is Maria. Will you come with me, please?'

'Do I have a choice?'

'Yes,' said Maria looking round the hell hole she was holed up in. 'You can stay here if you want.'

They marched together out of the building and strode across the concrete pad to the waiting helicopter. Thirty seconds later they were airborne and heading for Westminster.

Storrington's chopper flew straight to Biggin Hill. The car took him to the door of the house of the Prime Minister's widow. He knocked. She answered.

'I'm so sorry for your loss. It's a sad day.'

'Not so much. The country's loss is my gain,' she said breezily. For the second time in an hour Storrington was taken aback. He'd never imagined that the Prime Minister's gracious and beneficent wife was a lady so callous. But he pressed on. This was the address that Foxx had called him from and it was Foxx he'd been expecting to open the door.

'Is Eduard Foxx here?' he asked, as he stepped into the hall. The Prime Minister's widow led him through to the drawing room.

'No. I'm afraid I don't know an Eduard Foxx, but please come through.' And standing six foot tall by the fireplace was Eduard Foxx. 'You don't know my son, Simon, do you? He works for the Foreign Office.'

'He's your son?'

'Yes, I am. Simon Palmer, pleased to meet you,' said Foxx. They shook hands as Storrington's brain raced to catch up.

'I'm very sorry for what happened to your father,' said Storrington.

'Me too. Bloody liberty,' came a familiar voice from the kitchen. The Prime Minister walked in with a fresh bottle. 'Whisky, Commander?'

Foxx looked at the shock on the Commander's face and added,

'Best make it a double.'

34

THE END

J ulie Connor sat at a table in the middle of a large room, in the heart of a large building, in the epicentre of Westminster. There were no guards, she was not handcuffed, she could have attempted escape, but was disinclined. She sat, elbows on the table, head in hands, not dispirited just disinterested; not depressed just tired and hungry. She had done all she could do.

The door opened behind her. She couldn't even be bothered to look up.

'Hi. How are you doing?'

She knew that voice. She raised her head to see Eduard Foxx smiling right at her.

'Did we win?' she asked.

'Yes.'

'Blackheart?'

'Dead. Storrington thumbed him to death and just to make sure, the lovely lady who brought you here put a bullet through his head.'

'Am I under arrest?'

'No. You're a hero. You cracked the case.'

'Then I want to see Storrington. After that I want a pizza and a bath.'

'He's waiting for you in his office. I'll take you there.'

'Are you joining me?'

'Later. I have to see a man about a job.'

~

Foxx entered an interview room on the third floor. The occupant looked at him with no recognition.

'These are yours, I believe,' said Foxx, laying a set of Astra keys on the table.

Realisation dawned.

'You cock-nosed, dress-wearing, pansy-boy terrorist! I am gonna punch your face so hard, you'll need an enema to clean your teeth,' shouted Sam Stone.

'Before you do,' said Foxx calmly, 'd'you want a job? This is an interview room and I'm interviewing you for the position of Senior Field Agent in our Operations Department. You have talents and we could use them to protect the nation, destroy real terrorists and do some good. It's top class, top secret stuff. It pays ten times what you earned last year and is right up your street - you can punch people and get paid for it.'

A flow of profanity involving donkey's mating habits, nun's anatomy and unlawfully intimate acts ensued. But Foxx remained un-punched.

'So, is that a yes?'

Stone nodded, all charges were dropped and the deal was done.

~

As Foxx re-joined Julie, she was explaining the plot, the coup and the list.

Storrington sat in silence, pulled a tin from his top drawer and took a pinch of snuff.

'I need a copy of that list. It's the garrison of our new open-air Antarctic Military Base.'

'I didn't know we had a base there.'

'We don't, but for these traitors, I'll build one. Now, Connor, I will need you for the next week to unravel this mess. Then I have a temporary secondment for you, a special assignment supporting the ex PM over the next six months. I hope you don't mind travelling'

'Travelling? Where?'

'Tonga.' Julie approved. 'Foxx, I have a vacancy in my senior team. My Head of Planning and Strategy has just been assassinated. I want you to consider taking his post. Start by going to France tomorrow, as a special liaison to - how can I say - *guide* the investigations appropriately. You'll be back next Friday.

Connor, we've reserved a room for you in the Marriot Hotel across the bridge. Foxx will show you how to get out of here. There's a car downstairs waiting for you and a pizza on its way to your room. And . . . Thank you.'

Foxx led her to the front door.

'I'll see you on Friday evening, OK?' said Foxx, as she left. 'At 7.00, in the lobby of the hotel. D'you think we can spend some time together?'

She looked at him, thought, shrugged her shoulders and replied, 'Meh!'

~

Hoy lay in bed with his wife.

'We got him, case closed! That means I get my three months' maternity leave. And Storrington asked me if I wanted to make the job permanent.'

'That's wonderful. I'm very proud of you my little Clouseau. But I think you mean *paternity* leave. No . . . thinking about it, maybe you're right!'

Hoy's thoughts were still at work. 'I visited the third man, today. He's out of Intensive Care. He was the only one from Raper's Hide to survive. He was poisoned, poor guy, but he'll live. It wasn't Stone or Foxx, it was Blackheart. He came out of the alley, jabbed him with a syringe and he passed out. It was Foxx he was after.' Hoy rolled over and kissed his wife. His hearing caught up with his brain. 'What d'you mean, maternity not paternity?'

'I think you'll take very well to motherhood.'

'Yeah. Me too.'

~

She stood to attention in her boss's office.

'Captain de la Casa. I'm not disbanding the team. Not yet. Give them two weeks' leave. And take it yourself.' He gave a dismissive wave of his hand and continued with his paperwork. He looked up again, she was still standing there.

'That's all. Dismissed.'

'Permission to speak freely, sir.' Storrington put down the papers and reluctantly looked up.

'Granted.'

'Sir, my name is Captain de la Casa, not Maria, when I'm at work.'

'Noted,' he said, in his most disinterested voice. 'Is that it?'

'No sir, not quite sir, there's one more thing.' She took a deep breath as her stance become more commanding. 'When we were in Cheltenham, you invited me to tea. I would like to decline the offer.'

'As you please.'

'I don't want any different treatment.'

'You won't get any.'

'Really?' she said, as her posture reflected the hardening of words. 'I had a very hard time becoming a Captain, harder than any of the boys, like the Army was against me, and then when I am a Captain, I get all the toughest assignments.'

'Are you complaining?'

'No, sir. I like the tough ones, but I want to know if you were behind it – pushing me, testing me?'

'No. The Army did that.'

'But you chose me for this gig – that was favouritism, right?'

'Wrong again. You're fearless and I needed someone I could rely on, I didn't know who else I could trust. My choice was dictated by the needs of the mission.' The tension in her stance visibly reduced. She stood at ease and smiled.

'Good. I only want what I earn.' She paused. 'My papers came through,' her voice lighter now. 'I'm going to be a Major – did you know that?' Surprise crept across his face, followed by an evident delight.

'No, I didn't. Congratulations.'

'So instead of tea, would you like to celebrate with me - dinner at my house, in the Peak District, next Thursday. And also breakfast the following Tuesday. It's a long way from London, so it would be more convenient for you to stay over between Thursday and Tuesday. In my house. With me. For the weekend.'

'In *your* house?'

'Yes, sir. And I would need you to . . . do your duty.'

'My duty?'

'What with being away behind enemy lines, well my needs on the home front have not been met - and even when I was home, I had to rely on my own . . . er, handiwork - what you might call 'do-it-yourself' and that never has quite the right result.'

'Are you saying what I think you're saying?

Yes, I am. I need you to get down and dirty, and take a few days off from being *Commander* Storrington and come and sort me out.'

'Really? And why would I do that?'

'Because you love me. Don't you?' He looked surprised and answered almost indignantly.

'Of course I love you. I've always loved you.'

'I know,' she said. 'And what was the last thing my father said to you?'

'If I don't come back, look after my baby girl.'

'Exactly!' she said as she sat side-saddle on the corner of his desk. 'The first twenty years you did well, best second dad ever, but I've hardly seen you for the last five. You've been very neglectful.' She was almost chastising him. 'Have you seen my house? Have you seen the state it's in?'

'Yes I have! And that's my worry!'

'It's upside down! Half-built, half-decorated, half-habitable. I'm no good at that kind of thing, but you're the most practical man I've ever met. Come on Pops! Spend next weekend with me - long walks. I've got whisky. You can cook. We can do the house together. What d'you say?'

'Can I call you Maria?' he said with mocking sarcasm.

'Of course!'

'Then pick me up at five.'

'Permission to hug, sir.'

'Denied. Get out!'

≈

Foxx had a busy week offending the French. He was a natural and set back the *Entente Cordiale* many decades.

Julie liaised with the Prime Minister and his wife and saw them safely on the plane. She would visit them in Tonga. She colluded with Hoy and sifted through evidence, helping him make the case and close it. As Storrington's trusted advisor, she spent time with him going through 'the list' and deciding on the best course of action to dissolve the caucus of conspirators that surrounded the coup.

She spent Tuesday in her flat in Cheltenham, collecting clothes, assessing the damage, planning redecoration and collecting some valuables. The flat was only lightly damaged, but she wasn't sure she could return.

Life had changed so much in a week, to move back into the flat would be to move backwards in her life. That chapter was closed. She loved Duncan, she always would, but she had a life and she had to move forwards. She sat and talked to him. He stood in his picture, smiling.

'I love you Dunk, but I want to move on. I'll keep you in my heart, always, but I want your blessing. Is that OK? Speak now, or forever hold your peace.'

Duncan said nothing. He just smiled through the glass.

She smiled back and confided in him.

'I didn't think I would ever want to be in a relationship again, but I do. I really do. I miss it. It's a risk, but I'm going to do it. I've been alone for long enough.. I need to turn this erotic, erratic friendship into . . . into something more. I don't know how Foxx will feel about it, probably just make that stupid noise, but it feels right to me, and that's what I'll tell him.'

She looked at Duncan's photo. She looked at Lisa's next to it. She leant forward and kissed them both.

'I love you.' she said to them, then stared into Duncan's eyes. 'I loved you more than anyone and, because your life ended, I thought and felt in every sinew that mine had to end as well, but it doesn't. When you left, so too did my strength. I gave it away.'

She cast her mind back to Tess and the whole mess of the D'Ubervilles.

A strong woman who recklessly throws away her strength, she is worse than a weak woman who has never had any strength to throw away.

'I will never be as strong as you or as good as you, but I need to be the best me I can be. I know it's weird, but I need to do it. It feels right. Bless me, Dunkie, the phoenix is reborn.'

∾

It was Friday evening. The lobby of the Marriot Hotel bustled: people arrived for the weekend, couples arrived for dinner, friends arrived for drinks. Julie 'the Phoenix' Connor waited for Foxx. She was nervous. He had often made her nervous, but not like this. This was different. She had words to say; and just saying them seemed so much harder than chasing terrorists, fighting assassins or shooting gangsters. She looked at her watch. He was not here yet.

She looked hot, not flustered hot, but sexy hot. Her hair was coiffed, her face was alive and her life had returned. She was wearing those trousers and it felt good. The clock above the reception desk clicked onto seven. She kept her eyes on the front door, but sign of Foxx there was none.

At that moment, a hand laid itself gently upon her shoulder. She turned. *Blackheart!* she thought. But it wasn't. It was Foxx.

She didn't mean to, but she fell momentarily into his arms. She had missed him more than she thought. She stepped back and looked at the man who'd been her life for a week, in a week that had changed her life. She knew she needed to tell him, but within moments they were talking work, swapping stories of the past few days and sharing the lightly honed highlights of wrapping up the case. She had to tell him how she felt, but heard her mouth say,

'The evidence is good, but . . .'

'Shush, don't you dare!' he said. 'The evidence is very nearly perfect.'

'Yes, but how did she get the souvenirs upstairs? And if she wanted your dad dead, why did Blackheart take him off the plane? And why didn't anyone check the date that the Risk Assessment was uploaded onto her computer? And how could she afford to pay him? And why did . . .'

'Really shush!' he said more emphatically. 'The evidence is good.'

'But it's not perfect.'

'And we know it never is. We won. They did it. Case closed. End of story.' He placed his finger gently on her lips to forestall any riposte she might have had. 'I have something much more exciting to occupy us with.'

Foxx was carrying a bag, which he unzipped slowly.

'I was wondering, Miss Connor, if you would like to spend a playful weekend with me?' She peered into the bag. It was full of handcuffs, latex, leather and other accoutrements of sensual domination. She smiled, eyes incredulous.

'Are you mad?' she said, looking at him like he was a fool. 'None of that is going on me!'

'I thought you liked that sort of thing. You had all kinds of equipment in your flat. The handcuffs you slipped out of?'

'Yes. Lisa and I went to a fancy dress party. Once. It was just fancy dress. I looked hot. But no, none of that stuff is going anywhere near me, especially when you're in the room!'

'OK,' he said, as he dropped the bag on a passing bell boy's trolley, telling him, 'Room 227'.

'Who's in room 227?' asked Julie.

'No idea. So let's spend the weekend together, anyway.'

'Foxx, I would love to.' This was it, this was the chance to tell him about her love. 'But I can't. I'm spending the weekend with someone else, with my ... with someone special.'

'What? You told me you didn't have a boyfriend or a fiancé or a husband.'

'True, I don't. We're more like ... partners.'

'Since when? I thought you hated men!'

'Since Wednesday. Meet Selina.' The new PM's new Personal and Private Secretary walked up and gave Julie a big affectionate lip kiss and stood hand in hand like lovers are supposed to.

Foxx smiled a disbelieving smile. He thought about how he and Julie had been together, it made no sense. Then slowly the many times that she'd said she didn't want a man in her life seeped into his memory; and about how she'd been adamant that on her dream holiday in Tonga she would take a girlfriend not a boyfriend and about the two pictures on her mantel piece – one boy, one girl.

He looked at Selina. It all started to make sense. She was a fine looking woman and very relaxed being so close to Julie. He looked at Sera-fina Pekkala and saw strength and confidence, with happiness on her lips and a glint in her eye. He had to admit to himself, they did make a good couple.

Disbelief turned to approval.

'So, what are you two doing this weekend?'

'Oh,' said Selina, 'we're going to a big event, we wouldn't miss it for anything. We're there every year. D'you want to come?'

'Depends on what it is.'

'It's the world tournament. I've got front row tickets.'

'OK. What's the sport, cricket, football, rugby, darts?'

'No, silly! Bridge!'

Foxx stood and stared. The girls smiled at each other, like a pair of perfectly attuned teenagers. Foxx shook his head, walked away and muttered to himself,

'Just when you think you know someone!'

THE END . . . (nearly)

EPILOGUE

Weeks had passed. Foxx closed the door on his redecorated, refurnished flat and skipped lightly down the wide circular staircase that led to the lobby and the road. He had shaved, buffed, polished and beautified. He was not one to preen, but had made an exception for today. He was heading out to find Charlie. He told himself he had made an effort not because he was drawn to her, nor because he was going to see her at work, where the possibility of her being surrounded by an array of attractive models was significant, but because it was the right thing to do when paying respects to a widow in mourning. He stood on the pavement and spoke.

'Google. Take me to Triple A Portfolio.'

Half an hour later, outside a modern sleek office block, he was doubting the veracity of his electronic Tonto. It was a much too prestigious part of the City. A nameplate on the marble pillars said, *Triple A Portfolio, Third Floor*. He took the lift, but as soon as the doors opened, he knew for sure he had it wrong. The modern sculpted reception desk had walnut in-lays saying *Triple A Portfolio,* the glass screen at her back that shielded her from the open-plan office had *Triple A Portfolio* emblazoned across it, even the carpet had the name woven into it. This was not a cosy, 'young wives who lunch' amateur modelling agency, this was a high powered City firm. This was the wrong Triple A.

But he was in now. He approached the receptionist and asked, 'Is this Triple A Portfolio?'

Rather than look with sarcasm at any of the many indications that it was, she just smiled politely and said, 'Yes, sir. How can I help you?'

'Is this, er . . . it's not a modelling agency, is it?'

'No, sir, it's not.' Then realising it might have been an obscure compliment, she added a slightly awkward, 'Thank you.'

'And is there a Charlie Tenby working here?' he asked, knowing the answer before the question was finished.

'No, sir, I'm afraid there isn't.'

'Thank you. Sorry. Wrong place.' He turned to walk back towards the lift. As he did, his eye was caught by a woman walking across the open-plan office towards reception. He thought nothing of it. There was a trace of familiar, but no connection made. He pressed the lift button.

'Eduard.' He didn't register the voice behind him. 'Eduard Foxx.' He turned and there was Charlie's sister.

He didn't even know she had a sister, but the family resemblance was striking. She was shorter, had darker hair clipped back in the austere style of a successful business woman, she wore glasses and had not been blessed with the apparent curves and instant allure of her younger baby sister, but she was definitely family.

'Hello,' he said, with a disarming smile. 'I'm looking for Charlie, Charlie Tenby. Does she work here?'

'Eduard. You are an idiot.' She removed her glasses, shook down her hair and Charlie appeared in front of him. The transition left him wrong-footed. 'Come in. I've been expecting you.' He followed her as she walked across the office in sensible flats. His brain was playing catch-up.

She was a secretary! Charlie Tenby had a proper job. She must know people. Her business suit was elegant and stylish, the movement beneath muted and disguised. This was a different Charlie. She headed for an office with CEO written on it, walked in and closed the door.

'Welcome. This is my office. Please take a seat. I'll get my cheque book. That's why you are here, I suppose?'

'Yes, of course,' he said, like he always did.

He sat, intrigued by his surroundings. The cards on top of her desk said *Penelope Clarke, CEO.* Charlotte Penelope Clarke was the posh name her mum had given her, as a leg-up in life. It had worked.

'I thought you did modelling.'

'Yes, I do,' she said with that familiar soft-faced Charlie look. 'Financial modelling. I'm very good at it.'

He stood and looked at the certificates on the wall. She had a first-class honours degree from Cambridge. *That was why she'd moved to St Ives from Guildford for three years; it's only ten miles from Cambridge,* thought Foxx. And an MBA from Harvard. 'I spent a year in Boston', she had told Julie.

'Why didn't you tell us you were smart?'

'You never asked. I always answer whatever question I'm asked as honestly and truthfully as I can. The first question the DPM asked me was which university I went to, so I told him. The first question you asked me was how many guys I'd slept with. You get what you ask for. Drink?'

'Yes. Thanks. G&T. Oh, no. Maybe not. I've heard about your Gin and Tonic. It's infamous office gossip,' he said, with a smile.

'I make a very good G&T,' she replied in mock indignation, 'when I want to.'

His eye was caught by her Ph D certificate from the London School of Economics on a subject that contained a lot of words, none of which made any sense to him other than financial and modelling, and he didn't even really know what that was.

'So what do you do here?'

'Basically, it's an investment house. People give us money, we invest it and on a good day we give them more back. I started with £10 million of Nicki's money in the fund. I have to admit that was very useful in getting us started. Now, eight years later, we have £5 billion under management.'

'And this is your company?'

'Yes.'

'So, Nicki knew you did this?' he asked, as she continued mixing his drink.

'No way! He would have dumped me in an instant. He liked me, how did he say, *'dumber than a dead dingo's donger.'* I was just his *bird* with a bird brain. He hated it if I ever showed I had more than one brain cell, but he did ask me to get an Inheritance Planner, Mr Taylor, which I did. He helped me draw up all the documents to move Nicki's money around. Nicki never really took an interest in it. I moved everything where I wanted it. I even ran his bank accounts online. Nicki could be so smart, so trusting, yet so dim. I was only his bird but I mocked him with my stupidity. I enjoyed mocking him, but I did double his money, so he came out on top. As he always did.'

'Are you also a computer hacker?' asked Foxx.

'No.'

'So, you can't hack into your husband's computer?'

'No. But I didn't have to. He logged on when he got home from work and when he went to fix his dreadful G&Ts, I had full access. If I needed longer, I would call his mistress and sit him in the conservatory to talk to her. From his desk, I could see the back of his head in the conservatory, so he couldn't creep up on me. When he came back in the room, I was sitting like his dim, angelic, fairy cherub in my seat in the corner.'

'Did you often go into his computer, then?'

'No, not much. Only when I needed to get the job done.' She sat behind her desk and picked up a sleek DuPont pen. 'Would you like me to make the cheque out to Mr E. Foxx?'

'Best leave the name blank,' said Foxx. He watched her write a cheque for one million pounds, as they had agreed. 'You're not going to tell me your real name then?' she asked. His silence confirmed he wasn't. She sat back in thought. 'If I was going to be a secret agent, I'd call myself *Tequila.*'

'You need two names,' he said, pushing her in his mind to say the word *Sunrise* and restore his belief in the predictability of women. 'You know, like Black Heart, or Serafina Pekkala. You can't just have one name.'

'Prince did.'

'Yes, but Prince wasn't a spy.'

'How do you know?' Foxx had no comment.

She filled in the cheque stub. This was quaint. Everything she did was electronic. This was the first cheque she had written for as long as she could remember.

'Why me?' he asked. She paused from writing.

'Nicki kept talking about you. He said you were the smartest agent in the whole service. He loved your work and laughed at the brilliance of your plans. He told me you were a genius, but when I asked what you had done, he would just tap his nose and say 'Top Secret'. Annoying or what? So I gave him his first dubious G&T and when he went to fix it, I had a quick look at what he was laughing at. It was just innocent curiosity.'

'Innocent? I don't think so!' said Foxx, as he pieced it all together. 'This is all you, this whole thing. You did it! It was you who used his login on Dominion1431 to ask for the Risk Assessment.'

'Yes, of course. I asked you what it would take to assassinate the PM, and you said, *all it takes is a million pounds and a bit of imagination*. I wasn't sure then if you were negotiatinging your fee or defining how much it would cost a terrorist organisation to set it up, but I went for it anyway. And then to confirm, when you came to the house with Julie, I said: *It's our little secret* and that *I owe you a million thanks*. And you said: *My pleasure*. So I guessed you must've known all along it was me.

And because you're so smart, you knew that the PM was never the target. Nicki was often with the PM, so all I had to do was pick the right opportunity.' She stood up, looking as sweet as ever. 'You'll have to wait for the ink to dry.'

She handed him the cheque, written beautifully for one million pounds.

'So, you just wanted to murder your husband? Lust, jealousy and greed.'

'What are you talking about?' She looked at him, slightly hurt. 'I loved him. He was an arrogant prima donna, but no-one's perfect. Lust, jealousy? Nah. I didn't mind him playing away. On the contrary, it gave me a night off and more time to get my Ph.D. and set this place up.'

'So it was greed? It was about the inheritance? But what you hadn't counted on was that he was still married to Bettie, so it all went to her.' She looked at him affectionately, like he was a child trying to work out why spoons are shiny.

'Not really. His will was made out to me in its entirety – estate planning. But to be honest, his estate is worth something less than a million. Everything else, I had put in a trust years ago, so I get the lot anyway.' She smiled like a teenager who had just won a local dancing contest. 'But you're missing the point. I don't need his money. I have the fastest rising investment management company in the City. I'm already richer than he ever was. It's not about the money.'

'But you still killed your husband.'

'No, I didn't.'

'OK, you got someone else to kill your husband.'

'No, that's not really what happened.'

'Your common-law non-husband then.'

'Sort of, but not really. It had nothing to do with him being my husband. It's more complicated than that.

When you first arrived at my house, I thought you had got it and understood what was going on, but then I was worried you were not seeing the bigger picture.' She sat next to him and put her delicate fingers affectionately on his forearm. 'That's why I sent you the *Join the Dots* book, as a clue,' she said softly, with her wide Charlie-eyes. 'I wrote you a note on page 64 in invisible ink, except I used onion juice. I thought that's what spies did. I thought you would have got it by then, especially after I left the list of names on his desk for you to find. You remember, when you visited the house and I went to get you both your tea, I left the list for you in plain sight. I thought that would be enough to point you in the right direction.'

'Yes, of course,' said Foxx, 'I got that,' simultaneously realising how much he'd missed and lying to the person who never told a lie.

'So, you see, it wasn't really a husband I had killed. You know the horrors he was planning. Thousands would have died or suffered because of his arrogance. He was out of control. I had to save the country. I had to stop him. I didn't kill a husband, I removed a dangerous enemy of the State. The fact that he happened to be my unlawfully wedded husband was irrelevant – it just made it harder, emotionally. At first I had no idea what he was up to, but the more I watched, the more worried I got. It took a while for me to work it out, and even longer to believe it, but it became obvious - he was planning a military coup and he had to be stopped.'

'So he was in cahoots with Bettie?'

'No, not at all.' She slipped her long blonde hair back out of her face. 'He was inadvertently working in parallel with Bettie. It was ironic, because he loathed her and had nothing to do with her. But between them, in their own separate ways, they would have caused a lot of trouble.'

'Elizabeth was a fascist, racist xenophobe that had control of the DPM. Nicki was a power-hungry moral vacuum that had control over the military. Given the chance, they would have changed history. It would have been apocalyptic. Expulsion orders for whole families who had settled here since 1945 would have been followed by a substantial immigrant tax, terrible deprivation of human and social rights and the creation of a disenfranchised under-class, not to mention terrible fighting and civil unrest.' There was genuine horror in her voice. 'It would have finished the country and been the literal death of thousands and the financial death of millions. What could I do about it, a dizzy-headed blonde?' I knew what was going to happen, but I couldn't do anything to stop it. I was a nobody. No-one would even have listened to me. I didn't know what to do. So when Nicki told me you were the cleverest agent in the Service, I called you in to sort it out, despite your ridiculous fee. I liked Nicki, I liked him a lot, but he was too dangerous. It was the hardest thing I ever did.'

'Did you ever meet Blackheart?'

'No. I spoke to him once on the phone just after Serrafina Pekkala sent him your plans. Even his voice scared me. I wanted to be anonymous, but he wouldn't take the job until I told him I was Nikki's wife, so I was half expecting a blackmail demand after it was all over!'

'Do you know who Serrafina is?'

'No, no idea. I never met her. Do you know who she is?'

'I thought I did.'

'Anyway Blackheart texted me to say that he was coming over to pick up the other half of the money in person. I nearly died of fright at the thought of it. And then the next thing I hear is that he got on the wrong side of Storrington at the back of Elizabeth's house. Storrington said she was part of the plot. She wasn't of course, so I don't know what he was doing there.'

'I do,' said Foxx, at last one step ahead of Charlie. 'He got the wrong Mrs Tenby. You told him you were Nikki's wife, so he thought you were his real wife.'

'Poor Elizabeth. I didn't like her, but I never wanted that to happen to her. It was fortuitous, though, because I did need to stop her.'

'Why? Because she looked down on you?'

'No, because of the influence she held over the DPM. And I felt guilty. You know the Centralist Party that would have given them all the power and the majority they needed to do what they wanted? Well, that wasn't her idea, it was mine. I wasn't thinking. At one of our teas, I did my 'Why don't we all work together' beauty-queen speech and gave her my idea. She repackaged it and drove it ahead. When I realised what I'd done and the damage it would cause, it was too late to unravel it.

'And what about Colin Lewis?' Her whole face changed. Tears moistened her eyes.

'I was mortified. I was so sorry. Shocked. I had never expected that. That was not in my plan at all. But it was my fault. I had chatted to him at the garden party. I had played stupid with him and asked him the code name of his wildest, baddest, most ruthless hit man and he told me. He thought a code name could never do any harm, but he didn't know I could get into Nicki's email and ask Serafina Pekkala to put us in touch. As soon as I heard that he'd killed Colin, I knew he was covering his tracks. And it was my fault. For that, I will go to hell. I am so sorry.

I went to his graveside again yesterday to lay flowers. Someone has put a footstone on it. It's beautiful. It just says, *Shine on you Crazy Diamond*. I don't know who did that.'

'Someone who loved him very much, for sure,' said Foxx.

'The PM's OK, isn't he? I mean he wasn't in the plane, was he? He's OK?'

'Yes, he's fine. But you've been a real nuisance and you need to make amends. He's staying incognito in Tonga at a cost of more than £10,000 a week. I need you to pay for it.'

'No problem. Is there anything else I can do?' Foxx thought. They talked a while more, then it was time to go. As he was leaving, he threw out a casual suggestion.

'I don't suppose you fancy dinner?' he asked.

'Very sweet, Eduard, but I'm pursuing different avenues. Maybe you should ask Julie. You might have more luck there.'

They walked to the lift. He got in and turned. He could at least have the final victory by getting her to be predictable; he knew she would say *Sunrise*.

'Tequila what?' he asked as the doors shut.

'That's obvious,' she replied. 'Mockingbird.'

THE LATE NEWS

After his miraculous survival from the dramatic aircraft explosion six weeks ago, Palmer gave a brief press conference from his clinic at a secret location in Switzerland. His assistant, Julie Connor, read a statement.

"My recollection was being knocked unconscious by the blast and coming to, falling through the air, tangled in some of the cargo bound for Marseille. It was the sail-sheeting for a luxury yacht, which acted as a parachute, allowing me to drop into the Lac de Marsin, where I was saved by a fisherman for which I am eternally grateful.

I accept and support Richard Buchanan's accession to Prime Minister and I resign from politics for the foreseeable future. I thank you all for your kind wishes and support."

Sitting next to his assistant, in a wheelchair, was ex-Prime Minister Palmer, bandaged almost head to foot having suffered severe burns and significant physical trauma.

President de Guesclin of France still strongly denies that the French Air Force had anything to do with shooting down the Prime Minister's plane.

R M Jacobson, the new leader of the Tory Right said, 'This is grounds for declaring war on our old enemy across the Channel. All British patriots should boycott patisseries, Pret a Manger, French polishing and French kissing. The comedy stars, French and Saunders, asked Mr R M Jacobson if *a 50% boycott would apply to them. As far as we know, there's been no response.*

Another seven MPs have joined the new centralist Democratic Capitalist party, giving Prime Minister Buchanan 520 out of a total of 650 seats and the biggest majority in the last 100 years, beating Labour's 418 seat landslide in 1998.

The Brexit Secretary, William Williamson, confirmed a set of highly successful talks on Defence. His new negotiating partner, the reappointed head of PM-SSS, Commander Storrington, said that Europe has to comply with our terms or we will demand the immediate expulsion of France from the Defence Union.

The Housing Bill that was only passed in the last few months will be scrapped.

The Census results are expected out at the end of the week. 'The contentious 1945 Clause, containing questions about how long a family has been resident, has been removed and all information on the topic destroyed,' said a Home Office Statement today.

Twenty-seven victims of human trafficking held captive for fourteen months in a North London Estate have been granted the opportunity to return home or to take British citizenship. They found freedom some weeks ago after the Rafiq brothers, a pair of notorious local gangsters, fought a duel over the leadership of the gang. Both men died in the incident.

Mohammed Akbar J'zeer, the brother of Al Akboar J'zeer, who was arrested and charged with terrorism crimes and the Brighton Triple Murder, died in his cell today of heart failure.

Lesley O'Halloran, the assistant to Mr Morgan-Tenby, is still at large. She is believed to be implicated in what police called 'professional malpractice'.

In the biggest reshuffle for over fifty years, the Army, Navy and Air Force are changing many of their most senior officers. "We aim to be the most progressive, efficient and up-to-date Military in the world," said a Defence Department Spokesperson.

The new Prime Minister spoke at the Lord Mayor's dinner tonight. As a confirmed bachelor, the Press were surprised to see that he turned up with an attractive female companion, whom he referred to as his friend, Penelope. She is Dr Penelope Clarke, his new adviser on fiscal policy and monetary issues. They were holding hands, so the Press are speculating that she may be more than just a friend. The Press have dubbed her 'Pretty Penny' and say that, although she is unlikely to change history, she is a welcome addition to the PM's rather grey entourage.

And finally Foxdale Children's Home has been saved from closure. A mystery donor gave a cheque for one million pounds, saying he wanted to put the Fox back into Foxdale. The following day, a further anonymous donor, believed to be from the City, offered to finance the home for the next twenty years if they changed the name to The Colin Lewis Home for Crazy Shining Diamonds. The owner was only too pleased to agree.'

'There's a happy note to end the evening on.'

'My name is Peter Jones.'

'And my name is Amanda May Hewitt.'

'Thank you for watching and goodnight.'

THE END

Dear Reader,

I would love to get your feedback. I am working on three more books and reader comments are invaluable.

If you liked You Think You Know Someone, may I ask you to post a quick review on:

Join the online community by signing up to the mailing list at www.jbholman.co.uk where you can expect book giveaways, excerpts of future books, and even (if you wish) a chance to be put on our opinion shaping panel.

Be one step ahead, register now and follow us on social media!

THANK YOU!

But please **NO SPOILERS!** This book twists and turns, especially towards the end. Please do not give away any of the plots or the 'whodunit'. It is only fair to let other readers enjoy it without spoilers.

That's the fun of a thriller!

Thanks for your review,
J. B. Holman

For more information please contact the author at
contact@JBHolman.co.uk

ABOUT THE AUTHOR

'Sensational, stunning, world class'

'A master story teller who subverts your every expectation'

J.B. Holman is a writer who has specialised in mastering the English language since the age of two. After humble beginnings as an administrator, the author has been a freelance advisor gaining privileged insight into the workings of arms manufacturers, consulting on confidential matters with HM Government, operating in war zones and helping develop the efficiency of the Police force. This is the fifth book J B Holman has written to date, with the author's only regret being burning the previous four.

Hobbies include macramé, stilt walking, refereeing lacrosse, oriental cookery, making things up and dancing like a demon at hen parties.

facebook.com/jbholmanbooks

twitter.com/jbholmanbooks

instagram.com/jbholmanbooks

goodreads.com/jbholman

ACKNOWLEDGEMENT

I would like to thank the wonderful and entirely ethereal *Helena Ashakura* for her support, friendship, intense inside knowledge and for leaking intimate information faster than a sieve full of politicians. Without her this work would have been entirely possible.

HELENA ASHAKURA

Ms Ashakura, psychologist and specialist in the workings of the secret service worked for ████████████ having spent █ years as a ████████████████ for ██████████ and ████. She conducted psychological evaluations on ████████████████ and ██████████ during the ████████ affair. She believes in open government and complete freedom of information.

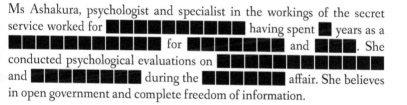

FUTURE BOOKS

Title Unknown

A prank call, twelve missing container ships, some refined uranium and an ever more complicated relationship. Foxx and Connor race to unravel the smoke and mirrors of an international mystery to prevent a container ship being parked in Southampton High Street. Based on a real life event that nearly happened.

Chimera Syndrome

Amanda is an innocent, charming, popular actor enjoying increasing success. She is best known for playing an assassin – the antithesis of her real self - until she wanders blindly into a manipulative plot and can't get out.
Her only choices - be an assassin or die.

Darkness

There is a landlord who lives downstairs, the guy who rented the flat upstairs and his girlfriend. One is victim, one is saviour and one the perpetrator – the question is, which is which? A tense psychological thriller entwining three dysfunctional lives . . . and two dead girls.